consumption

Also by Kevin Patterson

The Water in Between

Country of Cold

consumption

a novel

Kevin Patterson

Nan A. Talese

Doubleday

New York   London   Toronto   Sydney   Auckland

PUBLISHED BY NAN A. TALESE
AN IMPRINT OF DOUBLEDAY

Published in the United States by Nan A. Talese,
an imprint of The Doubleday Broadway Publishing Group,
a division of Random House, Inc., New York.
www.nanatalese.com

Originally published in Canada by Random House Canada,
Toronto, in 2006. This edition has been altered and
published by arrangement with Random House Canada.

DOUBLEDAY is a registered trademark of
Random House, Inc.

Book design by Donna Sinisgalli

Library of Congress Cataloging-in-Publication Data
Patterson, Kevin, 1964–
Consumption : a novel / Kevin Patterson.—1st U.S. ed.
p. cm.
(alk. paper)
1. Inuit women—Fiction. 2. Conduct of life—Fiction.
I. Title.
PR9199.4.P38C66 2007
813'.6—dc22
2006036573

ISBN: 978-0-385-52074-4

PRINTED IN THE UNITED STATES OF AMERICA

1 3 5 7 9 10 8 6 4 2

First U.S. Edition

Dedicated to the memory of

Thomas Arthur Patterson

1964–2005

For the sick, the poor, and the ashamed

Sign above an alms box in
Aix-en-Provence,
described by M.F.K. Fisher in 1953

consumption

part one

eskimo poetry

Here I stand,
Humble, with outstretched arms.
For the spirit of the air
Lets glorious food sink down to me.
Here I stand
Surrounded with great joy.
And this time it was an old dog seal
Starting to blow through his blowing hole.
I, little man,
Stood upright above it,
And with excitement became
Quite long of body,
Until I drove my harpoon in the beast
And tethered it to
My harpoon line!

Recorded and translated from the Inuktitut by the
Danish ethnographer and explorer Knud Rasmussen
in *Report of the Fifth Thule Expedition, 1921–24*

chapter one

Storms are sex. They exist alongside and are indifferent to words and description and dissection. It had been blizzarding for five days and Victoria had no words to describe her restlessness. Motion everywhere, even the floors vibrated, and such motion was impossible to ignore, just as it was impossible not to notice the squeaking walls, the relentless shuddering of the wind. Robertson was in Yellowknife, and she and the kids had been stuck in this rattling house for almost a week, the tundra trying to get inside, snow drifting higher than the windows, and everyone inside the house longing to be out.

It was morning, again, and she was awake and so were the kids, but they had all stayed in bed and listened to the walls shake. Nine, or something like that, and still perfectly black. She had been dreaming that she was having sex with Robertson. She was glad she had woken up. Even the unreal picture of it had left her feeling alarmed—though that eased as the image of the two of them, entwined, had faded. In another conscious moment she was able to blink the topic away and out of her thoughts. As it had been.

She could hear her girls, Marie and Justine, whispering to each other in their bedroom. She couldn't tell what they were saying. She heard the word "potato." Pauloosie, her son, her oldest child, was silent. She listened carefully and thought she could hear him turning in his bed. And then the wind wound up and just howled.

As a girl she had not been this restless, waiting out storms with her parents on the land in a little iglu, drinking sweet tea and lying on caribou skins. It had been more dangerous then but less frightening. Storms make an iglu feel more substantial somehow. This house, on the other hand, felt as if it were about to become airborne, and it would have if not for the bolts tethering it to its pilings. It had been made in Montreal, of particleboard and aluminum siding, before being shipped by barge to Hudson Bay, sagging from square with each surge of the sea. Where the door frame gapped away from the kitchen door, snow sprayed through in parabolas. These wee drifts persisted as long as the door stayed closed. After five days they seemed as permanent as furniture. The wind whistling under the house kept the kitchen floor nearly as cold as the stone beneath it.

That stone slid, in its turn, through the town, to the shore, and then under the ice of Hudson Bay, angling shallowly out into the sea basin like a knife slipping between skin and meat. And on top of that water was ice, a quarter million square miles of it, arid and flat and sucking in the frigid air from the High Arctic like a bellows— blowing it down through Rankin Inlet and into the rest of the unmindful continent. Chicago would be Rome but for this frozen ocean, not that its significance is known to anyone who doesn't live alongside it.

Rankin Inlet, Repulse Bay, Baker Lake, Coral Harbour, Whale Cove: variations on the theme of shelter from the sea, each of these hamlets lies on the west coast of Hudson Bay, named by nineteenth-century whalers seeking safety. The smallest is a couple hundred people and the largest of these, Rankin Inlet, is two thousand, almost all Inuit, with a handful of southerners, Kablunauks, among them.

The people exist along this coast against a backdrop of a half million square miles of tundra, gently rolling treeless plains. In the summer, this land is boggy and moss-bound; in the winter, frozen and blasted lowlands, eskers of rock protruding through shallow snow. The Inuit lived here for ten thousand years, pulling their living from this meager forage until the 1960s, when they accreted in the little government towns built along the coast and left the tundra empty of human inhabitants for the first time since the glacial ice had melted.

Victoria and Robertson had been married a year when Robertson paid to have this house shipped here for his new family to live in. It was twice the size of the housing department shacks offered to the rest of the community; this benefit of marrying a Kablunauk had been re-marked upon in Victoria's presence since the house had floated its way to the bay at the edge of the town. The other young families were crowded into the back rooms of their relatives' cramped houses, and privacy such as Victoria knew was considered an uncommon luxury.

Robertson was not from here, and so no toothless and snuff-spitting aunts had been assigned to their family. The drawbacks of mar-rying a Hudson's Bay Company man had been explored by dozens of women in the town, but this single advantage held. She lay in her bed now and listened to her daughters squealing and whispering and calling out to each other. This was an intimacy, she thought, that could never be available to a family who shared their house with another. She was lucky, at least on that score. But then, she thought, there might be a dif-ferent kind of intimacy available to the cousins and brothers who had grown up unencumbered by the rind of privacy.

She was thinking about that when the banging at the kitchen door began. Victoria thought the door had become unfastened, and she leapt out of bed to close it before it was torn from its hinges. When she got to the kitchen she turned on the lights and saw her father standing just inside the door. Drifted snow stretched out alongside him on the kitchen floor. His eyebrows and eyelashes were coated in ice, and his caribou parka shed granules of snow steadily as he stood there.

"*Qanuipiit?*" he asked.

"*Qanawingietunga,*" she replied. As good as could be expected, any-way. They were all bored, certainly, but the furnace was working and there was food. Which was rather a lot to express with a shrug and a single word, but sufficiently severe terrain makes for a pronounced economy of expression. Consequently, Inuktitut is the very language of economy.

"*Ublumi anarahkto.*"

A little windy? Her father's understatement made her smile. Justine and Marie appeared in the kitchen, drawn by the sound of conversation, and when they saw their grandfather in his sealskin kamiks they paused behind their mother. Twelve and fourteen years old, they were nearly as tall as the old man and were not prepared to greet him while dressed in their pajamas. Pauloosie loomed up behind his younger sisters in a flannel shirt and jeans. The old man reached inside his jacket and pulled out a plastic grocery bag. He held it out to the boy. "*Tuktu,*" he said.

Pauloosie took the bag of caribou meat. "*Koyenamee.*"

"*Igvalu.*"

The steaks were frozen into pink and cartilaginous bricks. Pauloosie took the bag to the kitchen sink and peeled away the plastic. He began rinsing the meat off with cold water, picking away the bits of hair and tendon that stuck to it. Victoria and her father watched him. "How is Robertson?" Emo asked.

"He's in Yellowknife again. Gets home next week."

"*Ee-mah.*"

"He's bidding on a contract."

"He works so much." The old man looked around the kitchen as he said this, as if scanning the house for evidence of the man's absence.

"He does." Victoria followed her father's eyes around her kitchen defensively.

"Do you need anything here?"

"Not really." Which was to say: nothing at all.

"I didn't see the lights on."

"There's ice over the windows."

"You should tell the girls to put some clothes on. It's ten in the morning."

"They will."

Justine and Marie were down the hall and out of range before Victoria's backward glance even came close to them.

"Your mother wanted me to see how you were."

"Why didn't she phone?"

"It's not working again."

"Do you need money?"

"No. We just forgot."

"I'm going to the bank when the storm lets up. I could take care of it."

"If you want."

"I will."

"Do you need some fish?"

"We still have char left over from the fall."

"Tagak shot a *nanuq* last week."

"A good one?"

"Eleven feet."

"That will get him two thousand dollars, anyway."

Emo stood there a moment, studying his daughter. If Emo had been the man his own father-in-law was, he would have pushed Robertson off the floe edge and into the sea by now. He turned to the door and opened it.

"*Ublukatiarak, attatatiak,*" Pauloosie said.

"*Igvalu, irnuktuq,*" Emo answered.

After her father was gone, Victoria cut up a pound of bacon and began frying it. Justine leaned over the kitchen table, opening her math book to do her long division. Marie sat closest to the stove with her Nancy Drew mystery: *The Secret of the Old Clock.* On the cover, a blond and dauntless Nancy peeked worriedly from behind a tree larger than anyone in the room had ever seen. Pauloosie laid the caribou meat on the counter and began cutting thin strips off it with his hunting knife and stuffing them into his mouth. After a few minutes of this, the bacon was finished and Victoria put a plate of it down in front of the girls.

The wind surged again and rose a half tone in register. Victoria looked out the window at the blowing snow. Pauloosie retreated to his room wordlessly. Her daughters read silently beside her. Storms like this make you appreciate a house. All you had to do was keep from losing your mind.

chapter two

■

When Victoria was ten years old, in the summer of 1962, she was brought on board the government ship *C.D. Howe*, a red steel supply vessel that traveled along the west coast of Hudson Bay each summer. Her family had noticed how she spent her days squinting into the sky for birds she could hear but not see and peering at stone cairns, Inukshuk, she thought were people. The *C.D. Howe* conducted tuberculosis screenings and ran a vaccination program together with general minor medical care and eyeglass dispensing. In the late 1950s, the people remained for the most part on the land, coming to the coast in the summer to trade the furs they had accumulated over the winter, and to catch char and *arviaat,* beluga whales. While they camped there, steel freighters plied the coast, dropping off crates of fox traps and rifle cartridges and flour and tinned meat at the Hudson's Bay posts, or, in the instance of the government ships, inserting medical appliances into ears and pushing naked chests against X-ray plates and collecting sputa in metal cups.

Emo and Winnie rowed their children, Victoria and Tagak, out to the ship a few minutes after it anchored in the inlet. It was August and there were twelve families camped, waiting for the trading ships. It was getting colder but was not yet cold enough to travel easily on the land. And the rain had come. The walrus hunting was finished until the ice froze again, the deer were far inland, and char were no longer running, so the people were bored and had spent the previous several weeks playing cribbage and arguing. When the government ship appeared, it was greeted as a break in the boredom, and everyone climbed into the boats to visit with the iqswaksayee.

The lab on board the ship processed their sputum samples on the spot and the doctor dispensed antibiotics for the ear infections and provided spectacles to the squinting children. Victoria had wire-framed glasses strapped to her head and gasped at the sudden clarity of the world. All the children were weighed and measured. With the doctor were two nurses who were not nuns but another kind of nurse, whose devotion to their profession was less absolute and more understandable: "nungurayak" was the name for these women, which meant "false nun." The nurses who spoke enough Inuktitut to understand the etymology of their title were constantly amused by it.

One of these women steered Victoria into a waiting room with her mother and father. Her mother teased Victoria about her glasses, but all she felt was a suffused contentment. Even at a distance, she could see the world now, found it many times as rich and detailed and complex as she had previously understood. One image burned itself into her memory: her father standing in the companionway of the ship in his spring boots, kamiks, and caribou parka, brown and lined in a way that had surprised her. Beside him: her mother, her marriage tattoos almost obscured by her tan, which stopped just where her father's did, at the throat. There, their skin became as pale as a char's belly, and remained so right out to their wrists.

She studied the lines on the backs of her father's hands, and the fineness of the stitching on his waterproof sealskin boots. She noticed the skepticism in the eyes of her mother, which she had not appreciated before, and the unease in her face as she stood in the Kablunauk ship. A moment earlier, the iqswaksayee had finished explaining to her, through the interpreter, how to care for Tagak's ear infections. He turned then and walked crisply away, the scent of perfumed soap and shaving cream wafting to her wrinkling nose. Behind her parents, Victoria could see the drip marks in the paint on the ship's bulkheads; she could see the gray in her parents' hair and how much skinnier their faces were than she had realized.

In the cramped waiting room were squeezed Victoria, her parents, Tagak on his mother's knee, the iqswaksayee, Caroline Kapak, the woman hired to interpret the local dialect, and Siruqsuk. Siruqsuk was one of the oldest of the Inuit elders in the area, though she was not accorded the deference usually paid to the very aged because of the low stature of her family and because of a whispered-about scandal to do with a long-dead husband and her sister.

Siruqsuk had lived on the margins of several encampments and was discreetly and grudgingly given food by her nephews when there was enough to share. Victoria had been aware of her for as long as she could remember, though they had not talked often. The iqswaksayee spoke in his flat and guttural Kablunuktitut language, and Caroline Kapak translated. "He says he's sorry but the X-rays show *puvaluq*. You're both going to have to go with the ship to the sanatorium." Victoria wondered if she was going to have to live with Siruqsuk while her parents were away when she realized Caroline was looking at her and the old woman.

The ship made for the Hudson Strait, and then for the open Atlantic and around to the Gulf of St. Lawrence and, eventually, Montreal. Siruqsuk and Victoria watched from the stern as the ribbon of shore disappeared behind them. Victoria kept a firm grip on her heavy skirts in the wind and the old woman put her stringy arm around the girl's shoulders. Victoria asked what she knew about where they were going. Siruqsuk told her there would be plenty to eat when they got there and that the other Inuit in the hospital would take care of them. They could both feel the ship's engines throbbing through the deck. Then the fog closed in and they went inside.

When Victoria descended the gangway in Montreal, she was met by Père Raymond, an Oblate who had lived for twenty years in Lake Harbour on Baffin Island and spoke a dialect of Inuktitut that the girl had not heard before. He was kind and attentive, if barely comprehensible. He guided her into a black and unfathomably fast taxicab, which scattered tall men and women in black clothes like an amauk among tuktu. L'Hôpital Saint-Paul was built of gray granite and run by nuns, likewise constructed, who spoke only French. Victoria had not realized that anyone but Père Bernard and the nuns from Chesterfield Inlet spoke this language. After he ushered her in, Père Raymond said goodbye self-consciously in Inuktitut and asked her to be patient with the nuns. She looked at him with puzzlement as he left.

That night, the nuns supervised her prayers and then closed the heavy wooden door to the room she was to sleep in. She lay down in a small, hard bed with a window over it, at eye level if one stood on the mattress. Beyond was the fleuve, as they called their big river. The next morning the nuns woke her and brought her once again to Père Raymond, who would accompany her to the train station. She had seen photographs of France in Père Bernard's church and had listened to him speak of his own home, and she had formed the impression of a confluent geography dotted with enormous stone churches and emitting a different variety of cheese from every hollow.

It was the variation in this land rattling past her window that surprised her most. Each time she fell asleep and woke again, she found herself looking at an entirely different sort of tree, and then there were the cities and the fields of rye and corn in Ontario and the preposterously large "lake," the Superior one, that sat on their left for most of a day. The Oblate priest maintained unwaveringly that this was fresh water—Victoria gave up on challenging him on the point and concluded that the difference in their dialects was more important than she had thought.

The priest was mute on the subject of why he had left Lake Harbour. He told Victoria that the sanatorium they were traveling to was a place she would love more in retrospect, after she was home again and healthy, than during her stay. He told her she was lucky to be alive now,

when the infection in her lungs was curable with antibiotics and surgery—only a few years before it had not been so. Many friends of his
had died of this sickness in Normandy when he had been a boy; the cattle and the farmers exchanged tuberculosis infection with one another
in a constant cycle of blood-streaked coughing and fever. She had spent
enough time with Breton priests by this point to think to herself how
odd it was that this Frenchman was suggesting that she was lucky not to
be more like him.

After the Superior ocean came more miles of forest, taiga similar
to that she had glimpsed on the tree line south of Arviat, but more vigorous, and studded with poles holding wires, and occasionally with
roads. Then the land gave way to flatness that reminded her of the barrenlands, marked into squares like the quilts the nuns made in Chesterfield Inlet. She saw men working the land, and the priest told her they
were cutting grain, gathering the plant that they turned into the flour
with which they made bannock. They stopped for a day in a place called
Winnipeg, which she had seen pictures of, more than she had of the Superior ocean, anyway. Or of land as level and brown and dry as tightly
stretched and scraped caribou skin.

The priest took her for a walk around the railway station, across
Main Street to Broadway Avenue and into the lobby of the Hotel Fort
Garry, which looked like a brighter version of the granite convent of
the nuns in Montreal. The desk clerk clicked his tongue at the priest and
so he took Victoria outside again and they walked up another street to
the Eaton's store, where the priest bought her a pen and notebook of
her own, and a coat and some boots and a sweater and a skirt and leg-
gings. Around them streamed crowds of people on every side. Victoria
had lived her life traveling with her family of four, and her uncle's family of six; counting the summertime congregations on the coast, and the
nuns and priests and patients in Chesterfield Inlet, she had seen perhaps
one hundred other human beings in her life. There were this many
within her field of sight at any moment in the Eaton's store. When the

priest spoke to her in Inuktitut, people looked at them and did not smile. They spent the rest of that day walking silently around the loud streets, and even as it was becoming dusk Victoria did not stop staring at everything around her.

That evening, they got back onto their train. It launched into motion as she was climbing into her bunk after saying her prayers—at the priest's insistence. She fell asleep to the swaying motion of the train, and all that night she inhabited dreams that were louder and more rapidly moving than anything she had known. She thought to herself, in her sleep, that this was odd, then she settled back and enjoyed them, less worried that she was going mad.

The following day passed in a green and auburn blur of Jack pine and black spruce and tamarack trees as the train headed north. The farms began to thin out and the grain fields gave way to pasture and then to bush. After the evening meal, the priest told Victoria that the next day they would reach the hospital, where she would remain until she was cured.

Would there be other people there who spoke her language? she asked.

There would be.

Victoria said good night to Père Raymond and crawled into her berth. Behind the black felt curtain she removed her dress and changed into the coarse woolen nightgown the nuns had pressed upon her in Montreal. As she fell asleep she listened to the priest whispering his own prayers, over and over again, the click of his rosary beads in counterpoint to the rattling of the train.

After the vigor of Montreal and Winnipeg, The Pas was a forlorn-looking place. By the time the train had come to a stop in the station, Victoria had seen enough to be disappointed by the bush town's muddy streets and its drab hardware store and bars. Père Raymond and Victoria were met at the station by a female orderly, a Cree woman who introduced herself as Donelda Pierce. The priest stood by the train and did not move when Donelda motioned for Victoria to follow her. He was continuing north, to Churchill on Hudson Bay. Victoria wanted to stay with him. When he got off the train at his final destination he would be only three hundred miles from her family. He had lived on Baffin Island and would have known how to handle dogs—two weeks' travel, once the ice was hard. The priest stepped back onto the train and waved goodbye as it began to pull away.

In the hospital, the children slept in white-painted steel frame beds in great open wards. Every night the lights were turned off abruptly at nine and no further reading or speaking was allowed. The lights were switched back on at six in the morning. Breakfast was at seven and the ward rounds at eight. The children were expected to be standing beside their beds when the phthisiologist visited them to listen to their chests and examine their fever charts. Every week they were weighed and had their sputa collected; every two weeks their blood was drawn, in a wincing and whimpering morning.

They took their medicines—their weekly injections of strepto-mycin, and every other day the pills: isoniazid, pyrazinamide, and ethambutol. One of the boys turned bright yellow from these pills; the whites of his eyes looked more like yolks, and his urine, he claimed, was the color of tea.

The children became, for the most part, healthier. They gained weight, and they became more active, but their homesickness was profound. At night, among the boys especially, the sound of weeping was nearly as steady as that of coughing. Altogether there were twenty-five other children and a dozen adults—in another ward—brought down from the Keewatin Territory, a term she had not heard used to describe her home before. Donelda, who appeared every morning to help feed and dress the youngest children, told her that *Keewatin* was from the Cree—Donelda's language—and meant "north wind." Donelda's people considered Victoria's home country to be uninhabitable by men. When Victoria first walked with the other children on the grounds, she met adults from areas north and south of where her father hunted along

Hudson Bay. Walking among the unfamiliar trees, an older man and a woman knelt to speak their language to her, but their dialect was different and she understood little of what they said. It was tantalizing to be among people almost like her family, whose language was almost the one she spoke. When they gave up and walked away, Victoria began sobbing and ran inside.

The other Inuit at the sanatorium were mostly Padleimiut, from the inland areas near Churchill, to the south of the land Victoria's father hunted. Their dialect was nearly as difficult as the priest's had been. For *thank you,* they said "mutna" rather than "koyenamee" and the differences went from there. It sounded like they were speaking with gravel in their mouths.

For Victoria, and two other children, the pills did not work. Even after six months she had not put on weight, and Donelda asked her, in her halting Inuktitut, if she was homesick. Victoria said she was, but she was eating as much as she could fit in her belly every mealtime.

She and the two other "nonresponders" were examined at particular length every week. Their pills were changed—escalating doses of different antibiotics—and they were X-rayed more often than the others. Her companions in illness were a brother and sister from Salluit, on Southampton Island, where Victoria's family had gone to hunt walrus two winters previously. The boy was named Abraham and the girl Faith; they were Nakoolaks, and their dialect was closer to Victoria's than anyone else's in the sanatorium. Faith was sixteen and her brother seven. They had younger twin sisters named Hope and Charity, which Faith had learned to relate to the adults in the sanatorium to elicit a smile. When Victoria learned the names of Faith's sisters, she only nodded gravely and inquired after their health.

After his daughter had been taken away on the *C.D. Howe*, Emo decided to bring his family back to Chesterfield Inlet until the ice froze. They struck camp two days after the government ship had disappeared over the horizon and began walking south along the coast. Winnie was angry with Emo for having allowed the doctors to take Victoria away, and did not speak to him for the first seventy miles of walking. In the rough clumps of tundra grass and eskers, this had amounted to several days. Tagak and his father had had to content themselves with each other's conversation.

It was getting late in summer and the rain was beginning. At night it turned into sleet. But it hadn't snowed yet and so they stayed in their canvas tent, purchased several years earlier with the earnings of a good winter's fox trapping. The tent was patched in many places and looked like clothing as much as it did shelter. It leaked anywhere the cloth was not absolutely taut.

When l'Hôpital Sainte-Thérèse came into view, Tagak pointed to it and his mother and father looked up from the sleet-sodden tundra grass immediately in front of their feet. The three-story wooden building stood out like a navigational marker, as high as it was wide, visible for ten miles in any direction. That evening they ran out of daylight and had to camp on the tundra in the rain, within sight of the twinkling lights of the hospital.

Emo's dogs were in Chesterfield Inlet and his winter gear was cached on the edge of the community near where the dogs were tied up. He had asked his brother to feed them fish he had dried for this purpose. Fish is poor food for fattening dogs, but it was not yet winter and the dogs were not working, and anyway, the caribou hunting was bad. Emo sat at the tent entrance and looked toward town as the last of the sun's glow disappeared to the southwest. He heard dogs baying and thought he could recognize his own. He missed them. A hunter without his dogs is hardly a man at all.

In the tent behind him, Tagak was trying to lash a leather trace onto a steel harpoon head. The harpoon was for seal and, perhaps, if the season wasn't too late, for arviaat, beluga whale. They had caught a whale early in the summer and had shared out the muqtuq with the entire hungry community. The food had gone quickly. No more whales came down the coast that summer. But the biggest problem was that there were so few tuktu that year, as there had been for the last two years. Emo thought that the mosquitoes, which were even more than routinely ferocious that summer, had killed them. He had advanced this theory to the other hunters and they had dismissed him. But it was still what he thought.

It was not a disaster to have sent Victoria away. There was food on that ship, and the girl had not looked right for months, all that sweating every night. He didn't know if they would send her back, however, and he didn't know how long she would be away. For ten years the Kablunauks had been coming north in the summer in their ships to find people with puvaluq and take them away. He had heard of a few who reappeared, a year or two or three later, fat and with strange clothes. But there had been many, many who had not, and no one knew whether they had died or decided to stay in the south. He had also heard that sometimes the children—God help them—were raised by the Cree. Those children were thought to never come back to their parents. This was why Winnie was so angry at him.

It wasn't the only reason. Emo had decided that after he collected his gear he would take the family to Rankin Inlet, where the nickel mine had opened. The mine owners were providing wooden homes to Inuit men who were prepared to work there, to live in one place and eat bannock and tinned meat. After the last years of dismal hunting, it seemed to Emo a fair exchange. Winnie thought otherwise. She believed that their dignity would not be preserved, living in the shacks the mining company had built, tucked close to one another like dog pens. Emo thought it was better than starving. Winnie said it wasn't. It was therefore a difficult dispute to resolve. But the decision was, in the end, his.

She did not understand how hard he had hunted for the meager amounts of food he had brought home these last two years. She did not realize that he didn't see as well, and couldn't run as fast as when the deer first began disappearing. If he could just explain to her how hard it was out there, she might see why living in the Kablunauk town made sense. But he was unable to tell her these things. He imagined she would find such words embarrassing. He imagined she hadn't known all along how hard he had been hunting.

Nuns taught the children mathematics and reading and the catechism. These women were mostly young, their minds still supple enough to conceive of the yawning immateriality these lessons would hold for anyone trying to eke out a living on the barrenlands. Victoria ate up the lessons like the vanilla pudding they were fed, a concoction so sweet and smooth it was almost implausible. Victoria and the Nakoolak children in particular were told to eat as much of it as they wanted. But still they did not gain weight and they did not stop sweating at night. By midnight every night, they had to rise to change their sheets, and again at four, the nurses having wearied of getting up to do this for them. Victoria and Faith helped with Abraham's bedclothes and then they all went back to bed and woke in the morning hardly rested, still damp, febrile, and flushed.

The classes distracted Victoria from the stubborn course of her illness. She found herself entranced by maps, for instance, her eyes wandering all over the atlases and globes, following the coast line of the Arctic Ocean around the pole to Greenland and Spitzbergen and the long swath of Siberia, reaching around almost to touch Alaska. The nuns taught them English and French; the aids taught them Cree, less formally. Together they learned that, as different as this world they lived in was from what they had known, there was a larger one all around, infinitely more varied and strange. It was this realization that changed the way they thought about the sanatorium, made them see even it as a kind of sanctuary too.

Within this strange comfort, little Abraham affected a gravity so complete, he was comic. Every time the three nonresponders gathered for their after-supper walk around the hospital buildings, he opined that the weather was going to get colder. Faith was the natural leader of the group, and when it was time to come inside she led them into the kitchen, where extra helpings of pudding awaited them. Every night they ate until they felt as if they would burst, and then they went to sleep feeling full and happy and healthy—until the night sweats woke them.

For many months the three children existed in a stalemate with their infections. They did not gain weight, but neither did they lose it. The iqswaksayee told them every week that things were starting to look up. All of them wondered whether this was good news or bad. Faith joked to Victoria that he was referring to heaven, but not in earshot of Abraham.

The stalemate was broken in February of their first winter. Abraham awoke one night coughing paroxysmally and over the course of fifteen minutes woke all the other children on the ward. One of the older girls went to get the night nurse. When she appeared on the floor, hair askew and halitotic, she turned on the overhead light and revealed his bedclothes to be covered in clots of blood, hanging from his sheets with tentacular adherence. The nurse picked the pallid little boy up in her arms and swept down the hall, blood leaking off them in a steady trickle. He blinked over the woman's shoulder at his sister until he disappeared.

Emo, Winnie, and Tagak had been traveling by sled for two days and when they finally pulled up at the foot of Rankin Inlet, they were all very tired and cold. Tagak, five, slept in his mother's arms, who was napping herself and woke up only when she heard Emo call to the dogs to stop. Emo walked away a few paces, taking in the bay as it stretched around him in the darkness. He could see the wooden mine head in the half light. Against the stars and the moon he saw the enormous pile of crushed nickel ore awaiting shipment the following spring, and he could hear the creaking of machinery. He had not been here since the mine had opened; the hunting in the area had been poor since then—a consequence, Emo thought, of so many men living so closely with one another, a state good for neither them nor the animals.

Winnie stood up and stepped off the sled, waking Tagak in the process. In the dim light the three of them watched the mine head and listened to the noise emanating from it. Emo's father had never had to make such a decision. Emo began testing the snow around them with his panna, seeing if it was hard enough for blocks. It was. Winnie started unpacking the gear.

In the morning, Emo dressed and stepped out of the iglu. Winnie lit the stove and put snow in the tea billy. Emo walked over to the mine site.

The mine office was in a low wooden building painted red, with snow drifted around it as high as the windows. Emo walked in through the front door. There was a man inside drinking coffee, who was enormously fat, suspenders stretching over his belly. He was talking on the telephone and ignored Emo for fifteen minutes while he spoke.

When he hung up he asked, "Are you looking for work?"

Emo lifted his eyebrows.

"You can start today. Come with me. My name is Mr. Johnson."

Emo followed him to the storeroom in the back. Mr. Johnson took his name, making up his own English spelling and shortening it. He gave him an employee number and entered him on the company rolls. He handed Emo a pile of gloves, socks, woolen underwear, canvas overalls, leather boots, and a headlamp. "From now on, you'll come to work in work clothes. These'll come off your pay, so take care of them." He showed Emo where the showers were and told him to wash up. Emo stood under the water, which could be colder or less cold depending on how you turned the tap but was mostly quite cold.

Then Mr. Johnson showed him how to put the clothes on, even the underwear. And when Emo was bundled up, feeling nearly immobile, he led him over to the mine shaft. As they walked, he told him, "You'll be wanting someplace to live. We have some rooms empty and I'll show you where they are tomorrow. Are you still living on the land?"

Emo nodded yes, his whole head and neck moving in a single awkward motion.

"Do you have family in town?"

Emo lifted his eyebrows again and then he nodded for good measure.

"Well, all the more important that we get you into a house then. Kids?"

Head pitching forward and backward. "One. Two."

"Not sure?"

"One's in the south."

"Coming back?"

"Don't know."

"Sick?"

"Yes."

"With what?"

"Teeth problems," he said, recalling the reaction other people had had to learning there was TB in his family.

"They took her south and you don't know if she's coming back because of teeth troubles?"

"Yep."

"Now there's an argument for regular brushing."

After Abraham's death, Faith stopped rising at night to change her bedsheets; Victoria studied her motionless shape as she changed hers, and for a while envied her the rest she was getting. But then she heard her sneeze and understood that Faith was entirely awake but did not care to rise long enough to make herself more comfortable. And when, one morning a month later, Faith did not rise when the lights were turned on, but lay there, cold, and pale and thin, as beautiful as a creek willow in blossom, she was not surprised.

Victoria's operation was performed the week Faith died. Afterward, the pills finally started to work. She slowly stopped perspiring and her hair stopped falling out. After three months, it was decided she no longer had to sleep in the hospital, and so she went to stay at Donelda's house, where she improved her Cree and helped to raise

Donelda's infant girl, Beatrice. Donelda had another child, a boy of thirteen, who seemed as pleased as Donelda to have someone new to speak with. His name was Alexander.

Donelda's invitation to Victoria to stay with her was like summer breaking in an afternoon. She had packed her little bag and was waiting for Alexander to meet her at the entrance hours before he was scheduled to come.

The house that Mr. Johnson gave Emo was twenty-two feet square and heated with a coal stove that glowed red when it was stoked, the boards around the chimney smoking softly and the potential for house fire high. There were three small windows and linoleum on the floor, two tiny bedrooms and a kitchen that melded into a living room. The rent cost Emo two thirds of what he made in the mine. Between rent and buying his work clothes, a clock, flour, and oil, he did not receive a paycheck for the first three months he was employed.

But Tagak, now six years old, had grown quickly, putting on weight every month: bannock in the morning, and tea; in the afternoons, frozen char and more tea; and when his father came home at night, tuktu, or nautsiaq, depending on what Emo had been able to catch on the weekends.

They ate more Kablunauk food than they ever had, because of the same problem as in Chesterfield but worse: too many men in one place scouring the land all around for food. The caribou simply stayed away, although increasingly they were staying away from every place now. There were stories about families coming into Baker Lake: children with ribs jutting through their clothes, eyes sunken into their heads, hair reduced to brittle white fuzz.

But there were still seals to be caught, and when the spring came there was char. Winnie erected a drying rack outside the house and hung the split fish in the wind alongside the other women, who were doing likewise, chattering and gossiping.

The mine was unlike anything Emo had experienced. The first day, when he had been taken to the tunnel with the rest of his shift, the man walking behind him, speaking with a thick Repulse Bay accent, had said, "It's okay, it's dark and noisy, but everything is fine once you get used to how dark it is."

They lined up as those in front stepped into a small car that descended into the mine shaft, Emo watching as it returned for another five men and descended again. When it was his turn he balked, his eyes widening. "What's going on there?" a voice shouted out of the darkness, and the foreman walked forward, a huge bearded Kablunauk. "Step on!" he shouted at Emo. Emo looked at him, unable to speak, unable to move. The man shoved him bodily into the car, and Emo shut his eyes.

The man with the Repulse Bay accent whispered, "It will be okay— we will go down now and there will be more light." The car lurched and they descended. Emo kept his eyes closed and gripped the side of the car more tightly than he had ever held any harpoon trace stuck even in a thrashing and pulling arviaat. He would have preferred to be in a qayak attached to any number of whales intent on doing him injury than to be where he was. The car descended in a jerking fashion for many minutes, and then it stopped.

The mine, he discovered to his surprise, was warm, warmer than anything he had ever known on the surface. "The deeper you go, the warmer it gets," Eric, the man from Repulse Bay, said.

"Why?"

"I don't know," Eric answered. "You get used to it." He helped Emo turn on his headlamp and then walked into the mine shaft, Emo following tentatively, bowing his head and squinting.

The work was very hard, gathering up the ore and placing it on the little cars. Kablunauks and some of the Inuit miners who had been there awhile operated machinery to move the big rocks. The smaller rocks, however, were gathered up by hand and lifted into the ore carriers. This was Emo's job, together with Eric. The two worked alongside each other, sweating in the improbable heat and pausing often to rest and drink the tepid, oily water that was provided to them. When the bearded foreman saw them pausing, he shouted at them to resume. His name was Johanson, and he had come from Norway to work here. Eric said that he lived in the town with an Inuk wife, the daughter of a miner from Coral Harbour, and it was thought that he did not treat her well. Not that it was any of their business. But he could certainly yell loud.

Emo and Eric worked all that day, filling up an ore car and sliding it back along the tunnel into the darkness and then filling the next one, until a whistle sounded. Then they climbed back into the car and ascended into the night. It had been dark when they had descended and it was dark when they reemerged. And this is how Emo's life as a miner proceeded.

During this time, Victoria's absence was not much discussed, but it was at all times felt. Winnie grew sad whenever the subject of daughters arose and, although she did not speak of it to her husband, she periodically approached the priest to see if he had any news of Victoria. It was her impression that contact between families and children in the south was discouraged; it would only worsen the homesickness that afflicted them. Winnie asked Père Bernard to write a letter to her daughter for her, but he always found an excuse. He would have to find out for certain where she was staying, and would she be able to read it anyway?

After many such visits, Bernard told her that he had heard from the sanatorium and that Victoria was doing well. He did not know how much longer she would have to stay, but the medicines were working now. There had been an operation, which had been successful, and he would let Winnie know if he heard more.

The following five years unfolded like a fever dream. Victoria's Cree was soon unaccented, Donelda told her. The three of them laughed on into the night after supper was over, in that melodic language that seemed to begin always on the sides of the tongue and behind the molars, so full of aspirated vowels that it was not so much spoken as it was exhaled. Beatrice grew to standing and then walking and Victoria spent so many hours with her, shepherding the little girl along the wide muddy streets of The Pas, that the first word Beatrice ever said was in Inuktitut—aka, no, wrinkling her nose and refusing a piece of bannock.

Within a few months of moving in with Donelda, Victoria had begun to look more like the other girls her age and less like Alexander. It was also as if she had been forgotten by the doctors at the sanatorium. She attended classes run by the nuns, who understood that her illness had been slow to respond and who enjoyed her presence in their classes. She was a pleasure to have around and so no one asked why she was there so long. Victoria became Donelda's confidante, and together they gossiped in Cree about the complex personalities and motivations of the nuns, about the uneven competencies of the doctors. Within all this tenderness, the memory of that other, more difficult place she had lived faded until the tundra was almost an abstraction, the place on the map above the dashes marking the tree line. The first year she often had asked if there was news from her parents, but as even the idea of a home other than this place receded in her memory, she stopped asking about her parents and her little brother. She learned to read and do arithmetic in English. She went weeks without thinking in Inuktitut. The nuns discouraged conversation in that language in the classes, and she no longer walked the grounds with the other children but scampered home to Donelda, Alexander, and Beatrice to help with supper and to chatter merrily about the books she had read that day.

In the evenings, Victoria sat up after Donelda had laid Beatrice down and listened to the radio: to the local news, and then to the BBC World Service and Voice of America. She kept a globe in the kitchen. Donelda told her the only way to get smart was to stay interested in the world. She asked Victoria if she ever thought she would see any of these places, and Victoria shrugged. She wasn't completely convinced that Algeria, Malaysia, and Vietnam actually existed as physical locations. It didn't matter. Even as word-pictures, they entranced her.

Alexander was two years older than Victoria. After she came to stay, they became almost like siblings, fighting with and shrieking at each other at violations of privacy and manners. Donelda dispatched them both to their rooms with swats of her broom often enough that it became inevitable that a kind of complicity grew between them.

For four years the freighters ran up the coast to Rankin Inlet to collect the nickel ore and transport it to foundries in Quebec. The cold war was on and the American military was placing large orders for stainless steel with every steel maker on the continent.

The *Ithaca,* a ten-thousand-ton ore carrier out of Trois Rivières, shipped the last load of ore of the season in 1965. The ice was late coming in and the mine's owners had tried to get one more load out before freeze-up. The *Ithaca* was making for the Davis Strait when an Arctic low exploded over Hudson Bay, eighty-knot winds throwing freezing rain and the tops of waves off in spumes of spindrift, forcing it to run off south; initially it had sea room, with four hundred miles to the southern coast, but the storm did not ease and, heavily laden, every time it tried to turn she threatened to roll right over on her beam ends. The carrier was driven high up onto the rocks east of the Churchill River mouth and became a familiar site to travelers flying north who refueled in Churchill, its iron hulk rusting slowly on the rocks, the nickel ore within it spilling out steadily and scattering over the beach in the course of subsequent years. When the storm finally abated, that portion of the ship above the surf line was nearly intact. The bottom was shredded into a thousand evil-looking steel shards, however, and there was no discussion of refloating it. Given the expense of working in the Arctic, the ship wasn't even cut up for salvage, but simply left there, becoming an orange-red landmark, jutting out of the sea ice five hundred yards from the beach. In the winter, polar bears slept inside it during the bad weather.

The enterprise lost the last of its luck with the death of that ship. Nickel was found in northern Manitoba and Ontario, as well as in Utah, Mexico, and Brazil—all on rail routes and adjacent to towns where trained miners and mechanics could be induced to live. The cold war warmed a little too, and the demand for nickel-alloy steel diminished. As the price of ore began a slow descent, the workings of the mine became at the same time steadily more expensive and the investors in the south steadily more agitated.

The closing of the mine was announced to the miners on a fall day in 1966. They had been aware of the dour moods of the foremen and the office personnel, but they had long assumed these to be their natural resting states. That so much effort could have been put into moving the heavy equipment here, building the houses for the miners, sinking the mine itself into hundreds of feet of igneous rock, so deep below the surface that the mine shafts themselves were always warm even in the winter—this seemed miraculous to Emo and was one of the things he remembered most clearly afterward. The idea that all that stupendous effort could simply be abandoned seemed preposterous to them.

And so when they were told to return their work clothes, that they could go on living in the houses for now, but that they should make some arrangements to move on in the near future, this all came as an astonishment. As strange as the idea of crawling into the depths of the earth to chip out rocks for the Kablunauks to put on boats and take away was, the idea of stopping this now and putting back on their hunting furs and taking their families back onto the land seemed even more laughable. After they were told to go home, Emo walked away from the mine site down to the sea edge, where his dogs were tied up on the ice. He looked up at the sky and at his own neglected dogs and finally at the canvas clothes he was wearing. And then he walked home to make the same bewildered explanation to Winnie that all the men were making to their wives that night.

On the Oiseau River, just north of The Pas, the sun shines through the poplar stands oblique and glowing orange on spring afternoons. The bond that had grown between Victoria and Alexander eventually moved them to walk out there, without ever much discussing why. It was Victoria's sixth year in the south, and her sixteenth in the world. They sat down on one of the granite rock faces that lined the river, and the sunshine was almost hot on their faces even though patches of snow still shone through the pickets of tamarack and black spruce. The slow-to-dissipate winter cold radiated up and off the rocks and the soil, and the heat fell down upon them from the sky. Their feet were wet from crossing the river and so they untied their shoelaces and lined their shoes and socks together alongside them, warming in the sun, their pale glistening feet freed after a winter's confinement.

She had stretched her hands behind her as she tossed back her hair, her long neck arching, and when her fingers had touched his against the rock, she did not pull them away. They sat like that, eyes shut, sunning themselves like tortoises, until she felt his lips sliding along the side of her neck. Then his teeth ran along her collarbone and she bit her own lip, her fingers curling into the granite extrusion. His warm breath flowed over her shoulder and neck and the soft spot at their juncture. Though it was only his lips that touched her, she raised her hips against nothing but the weight of her own clothes, so frustratingly light and unresisting. Her hands gave way to her elbows, and her neck bent back so far her scalp touched stone. He lifted her glasses from her face.

Alexander was strong, in the manner of certain boys raised without fathers who adopted that position early and intuitively. He cut wood for the stove every morning before going to school while his mother made breakfast—this had been his responsibility since he was eight. Even when it was very cold he did not complain. In school, however, he was not inspired. He talked of getting a job with the Hudson's Bay Company and working in the network of stores that supplied two hundred towns in the boreal forest and the Arctic with food and hardware. He imagined himself alone a lot, traveling in the bush and fending for himself. It was the first time Victoria had encountered the romanticized idea of self-sufficiency. Her father, the most self-sufficient man she knew, would never have sought isolation, loneliness. She watched Alexander that afternoon, as he ran his fingers over her abdomen, and thought to herself that this was a dangerous idea.

She saw clearly the prospects he would face, approaching the Hudson's Bay Company for work. The Bay Boys, above and below the tree line, were English. Her foreknowledge saddened her, and that sadness compounded her affection for him. When they walked out to the Oiseau River that spring, they held hands and listened for others. They spoke about trivialities, about the immediacies of the day, and she deflected discussion of anything with implications beyond a week. He was older, and inclined to plan. She wouldn't have it.

When school let out, Victoria and Alexander disappeared into the bush. Every morning, they woke and rose together, picking up fishing rods and—in Victoria's instance—a bag of books, and headed out to the river. Because the fishing was known to be so poor there, they were almost always alone. And there was rarely any difficulty carrying their catch home. Donelda teased her son about his lack of fishing prowess, asked him if he needed her to show him how it was done. Victoria spoke up then. "He's getting better. Pretty soon I'll have him up to speed." She reminded them both how she had caught char in the Arctic with just a kavitok, a fish spear. Both Alexander and his mother suspected she was misremembering a little—that she probably had not fed the whole family, as she suggested. The truth was that Victoria no longer knew which of her memories of the north were accurate and which she had distorted.

Most days she and Alexander lay together on the rock along the Oiseau River in the summer sun, Victoria reading *The Lord of the Rings*, Alexander resting his head on her bare belly. Propped up among the stones at the water's edge was his fishing rod, the line hanging slackly and running into the current.

The town was left reeling by the closure of the mine. Johanson and Johnson and all the other Kablunauks boarded an airplane and just disappeared, their wives left adrift. They were not the first to start fami-

lies in the Arctic and then abandon them, but what was unprecedented
was the sense of dislocation the hunters who had become miners knew.
They had come off the land and made the disorienting transition from
that way of life to the one that involved houses and paychecks, and they
had negotiated that transition with skill. But now the paychecks had
abruptly stopped and it was clear to no one what was to be done. Some
of the men simply dug their komatiks out of the snow and headed out
on the land with their bewildered families. But for most of them the
prospect of resuming that way of life was too much. The set of skills
necessary to make one's way on the tundra was extensive and particular. Once they moved into houses, those skills atrophied. Faced with
reacquiring them, most simply demurred.

Winnie, who had resisted moving here, now had no enthusiasm for
living on the land. Emo thought they could do it again. But for now,
he reasoned, they could live in the house and he could hunt. It was
self-deception and he knew it even at the time. Nomads move because
they must. Land like this does not tolerate stationary populations of
hunters—even in small numbers. The tuktu continued to avoid Rankin
Inlet. For a year, Emo made long forays out on the land, trying to reach
them. But when he found them, rather than camp nearby and follow
them, he had to shoot only one and return to Rankin Inlet. He and the
dogs usually ate a sizable portion of the meat coming home. The
arrangement was a losing proposition from the outset.

The mining company did not make good on its threat to evict the
miners from the houses. It simply evaporated. The government anticipated the difficulties of the miners and to some degree it stepped in
to help them. Food relief arrived on ships the following summer, with
a bureaucrat to administer it, and that was it: they were all changed utterly.

Victoria sat in a straight-backed chair at a table in the treatment
room off the children's ward—occupied now by children she had never
met. They all stared at her through the window between the ward and

the little white room lined with cupboards full of bandages and stainless-steel appliances. She seemed to them a hybrid version of themselves, an Inuit woman in a long, stiff-collared cotton dress, strong and healthy-looking. The phthisiologist had finished examining her and now washed his hands in the sink in the treatment room. He and Donelda nodded to each other.

"Miscarriages are common in TB patients. We see it all the time in the older girls and young women, especially if they're not responding well to the drugs. But she"—he nodded at Victoria—"has done very well, was cured a long time ago, actually. I'm not sure why this happened, but she should be okay."

Donelda nodded at this, anticipating and dreading the next question.

"Which raises the matter of why she is still here. She finished the medications long ago. And she's sixteen, after all. Time to go back to her parents." He pushed his glasses back up his nose. "I'll ask the matron to write to the priest in Chesterfield Inlet. Why didn't you initiate this a long time ago?"

Donelda did not, could not, answer.

"I suppose it was our responsibility. Poor thing. As if anyone there will still remember her. As if she would even remember what living there in the winter was like." And then the doctor walked out of the room.

That night, at the kitchen table, Alexander sat rigidly and told his mother, "I'm going to marry her." Victoria looked at him wordlessly, alarmed and also moved by the display of loyalty.

Donelda replied, "That is not going to happen," and passed the peas.

"Look, I love her, I'm going to take care of her here. This is where she lives now."

Donelda would not look at Victoria. "I've made up my mind. Victoria is practically your sister. What was I doing, letting you two spend so much time together, anyway?"

With that, Victoria stood up, cutlery clattering, and ran for the kitchen door.

Donelda watched her run out into the night. She hung her head for a moment and then lifted it. She dished potatoes onto Beatrice's plate.

When the Norseman landed and sent up a great shower of snow from its skis, two families approached the airplane. Victoria recognized her mother and father on the edge of the airstrip, waiting.

For Siruqsuk, the old woman she had left with six years ago, none of the transforming effects of the sanatorium applied. She had not become beautiful and tall and she had not learned excellent Cree and adequate English and French. In the Strait of Belle Isle, with Newfoundland on the port and the equally blasted coast of Labrador to starboard, the old woman had pitched herself into the sea. Victoria had watched her floating in the water, growing smaller and dimmer in the fading light. That night Victoria had not gone for supper. In the morning they had asked her if the old woman was feeling all right and Victoria said she hadn't seen her.

Peter Irnuk, Siruqsuk's son, came over to welcome Victoria back to the Arctic and to ask her what she knew of his mother. In the windy airport, as the Norseman taxied loudly back to the end of the runway to take off again, she explained what had happened, and he turned from her. His son, Simionie, two years younger than Victoria, had come with his father. Simionie did not turn from Victoria but stared at her, and kept staring, as she picked up her suitcase and walked over to her own parents to begin her reacquaintance with her family.

After they picked her up at the airstrip, Victoria's parents led her to their little house in Rankin Inlet. Victoria looked around wordlessly as they walked into town. She had visited this place as a six-year-old, she remembered, but she did not recall so many buildings here. Even the idea of her parents living in a wooden house surprised her. But, she thought, it would be easier to get used to than what she had expected.

The house, when they reached it, was nearly identical to the one Donelda had lived in, made from the same plans distributed by the Department of Indian and Northern Affairs: spruce two-by-fours and plywood, easy to put up and suitable for building on rock and permanently frozen soil. The mine, the church, the government, all used the same blueprints, and all across the north were the same handful of building types, painted off-white on the inside and, for some reason, always teal green on the outside, the paint peeling quickly in the face of blowing granular snow, as if from a pressure washer.

Tagak was bigger than she had been prepared for: on track to reach six feet and growing steadily on the reliable diet of tinned meat and bannock. Their parents were no longer young, and Victoria could barely talk to them. Her Inuktitut was clumsy and imprecise; even Tagak sounded smarter than she did. She was four inches taller than her father, and gagged when she tried to eat igunak, and ran outside crying after looking up and seeing the horrified expressions of her mother and father. They did not follow. Victoria recovered her composure and went back inside, still shuddering at the taste of the half-rotted walrus meat. No one commented on her display.

There was no school here yet. Some of the children had been sent to the residential school the church ran in Chesterfield Inlet, fifty miles to the northeast, but Victoria's parents refused to consider that idea—she had been gone so long already. She took to spending afternoons in the church, visiting with Père Bernard, who had moved here from Chesterfield and whose familiar face comforted Victoria as much as her parents' did. He loaned her books: *The Lion, the Witch and the Wardrobe;* Knud Rasmussen's *Report of the Fifth Thule Expedition; The Power and the Glory.* When she wasn't visiting the priest, she hung around the Hudson's Bay store. There were men there who were amused by her comfort with English idiom, and who gave her candies, and trinkets to pass along to her parents. They sometimes made lewd jokes with her, insinuating that a few sticks of licorice merited some recompense, didn't she think?

One day, she met a new man there, John Robertson—quieter, more serious, and more attentive than the rest. He was the only one of the Bay Boys—the only person in her life now, apart from the priest— who spoke to her as Donelda had, as if she had opinions worth hearing.

She asked him if he had any news from down south—had the Soviets invaded Prague after all? He wasn't exactly sure, but such a question caused him to dismiss with one mental shrug everything he had been told about Inuit nature by the other Bay Boys.

The morning after, he told her, "It's as bad as you guessed. There's a tank division in Prague, and the border is closed."

"And Dubček? Has he been arrested?"

"He is in Moscow now. 'For consultations,' the Soviets say."

She shook her head.

"I listened to the BBC World Service on the shortwave last night. You can come listen sometime, if you like."

"Victoria," Père Bernard began, "*je te vois visiter les hommes qui travaillent au magasin, tu dois comprendre que tu es devenue très belle, et ils l's'en apperçoivent. Je ne crois pas qu'ils aient les meilleures intentions á ton égard.*"

She nodded as she sat in his kitchen. He left the door to his cabin open when she dropped by, for reasons she didn't fully understand. Even in the summer, the wind here was cold. People walking by on the road looked in and saw them drinking tea, and waved, and wondered why the priest was leaving his door open and wearing his parka as he sat at his table.

"*Je ne suis plus un enfant, Père.*"

"*Tu n'as que dix-sept ans, ma fille.*"

"*À mon âge, ma mère etait déjà mariée depuis un an.*"

"*Tu n'es pas ta mère, Victoria.*"

"*Evidemment.*"

"*C'est difficile, n'est-ce pas?*"

She nodded.

"I understand that you're lonely, and the men at the Hudson's Bay store are friendly, and can talk to you about where you've been. But you must be cautious with them. None of them will marry you; they want wives from where they come from themselves. And when they've made enough money here, they will leave. Even if they have children here. Even if they're needed."

Sitting on the rocks by the ocean flats at the head of the inlet, Victoria wondered what Alexander was doing at that moment. (He was setting a net in the North Basin of Lake Winnipeg, rain just starting to fall in the late afternoon and the wind rising ominously, clouds darkening in the west. Even in his first year of what would be a lifetime as a commercial fisherman, he could tell it was time to get to shore.) She missed him. She had sent him a half dozen letters, written on paper Père Bernard gave her, which he had not answered. She hadn't been surprised. Her letters probably only served to make him feel guilty, embarrassed that he wouldn't be replying. She thought he probably missed her most when her letters arrived, and that without any prospect of seeing her again he wished she wouldn't write him. She was mostly right.

Victoria missed him hard. She missed having sex with him, she

missed lying in the sun with him, and she missed smelling him on herself. She imagined kissing him hungrily. She felt her throat tickle and
she coughed. She coughed again, holding her hand to her lips. Nothing.
Not even a fleck. She breathed deeply, feeling for any sensation of infection, unwellness. She felt as if she could run twenty miles. Her
shoulders sagged with disappointment. The priest could mind his own
business. Her mother could mind her own business too. A week earlier
she had brought home a month-old copy of the *Winnipeg Free Press,*
which she had read by oil lamp light that night, in their kitchen. In the
morning she had arisen to her mother lighting the stove with it, point-
edly using the whole newspaper when she normally used only a handful of dried moss. Afterward, Victoria tried to remember the stories she
had read the night before, about the Beatles, the war in Vietnam,
Trudeaumania. She couldn't, really. She asked her father if he would
buy a radio, and he just stared at her.

"Hello," the voice said. She turned around and it was Robertson,
standing diffidently, twenty feet from the rock she sat on. She stood as
she nodded to him.

"Hello."

"It's a nice day," he said, gesturing at the gray, streaked sky, clouds
like steel wool scudding low overhead and, in this wind, about as abra-
sive. The sea behind her was white-capped and purple, the waves building in the rising wind.

"It's not that nice."

"No, it isn't." He grinned. "But in this climate, you take what you
can get."

"I suppose it might be called an adequate day."

"You're the only person in town who speaks the way you do."

She shrugged. "It's the nuns. Do you have any news for me?"

He blinked. "The war in Vietnam is going badly for the Americans.
The Viet Cong has never been as bold as this before."

"How will it end?"

He pursed his lips. "It's hard to see the Americans losing."

"Sit down and tell me more."

"There are student riots in Paris. It seems they are angry about Vietnam too, but I don't really know why. People are frightened there. They think there could be an insurrection."

"What's that?"

"A rebellion. Like in Prague. Except the students seem to want a Communist government." The wind lifted his thinning hair off his scalp and stood it on end.

She was enjoying the sight of his head, outlined by his hair like a pussy willow.

"It looks like the American president might not run for reelection. Because of the war in Vietnam."

"People are pretty upset about it, huh?"

"It appears."

"And what else?"

"I forget."

"No, you don't. You're embarrassed, all of a sudden."

"Not really."

"Okay."

They both looked at the bay.

By the time they had met three times on the flat rock at the head of the bay, the whole town had noticed. Winnie and Emo had not mentioned it. Victoria introduced a tone of uneasiness into their home, and they reasoned to themselves that maybe she was better suited to be a Kablunauk's wife now than an Inuk's. This was too painful an idea for either of them to utter aloud.

One day Victoria was walking back from church when she met Simionie, Peter Irnuk's son, the one who had accompanied him to the airport the day she returned with the dreadful news. He waved at her. Unaccustomed to being greeted, she assumed he was gesturing to someone else and she ignored him. He waved again and then walked quickly up to her.

"Qanuipiit?"

"Uh . . . okay," she said, switching to Kablunuktitut.

"I mean, you're back, after being away for a long time."

"Yes."

"Is it hard?"

"Not really," she said, shifting from one foot to the other, her kamiks transmitting every aspect of the ground beneath her feet—after six years in leather-soled shoes and boots, it was like removing earwax and suddenly hearing.

"Good," he said.

"I have to get home now," she said.

"Okay," he replied.

Despite herself, she found herself smiling a little.

Robertson bought his hunting cabin from the longtime store manager, whose drinking habit no longer allowed him to undertake protracted trips on the tundra, restricting him to the store and to his house across the road from it. The old Scotsman lurched back and forth over the course of the day, the week, and steadily he grew more wobbly. The people had grown familiar with the life cycle of the Hudson's Bay men, and they recognized this terminal phase. The only question was whether he would grow yellow and die here, or survive long enough to get on the freighter the next summer and die in the south someplace, unknown, the subject of neither sympathy nor gossip.

But in the store manager's dissolution, Robertson blossomed. He did the work of his superior without comment or complaint, and he did not allow the other Bay Boys to express the disdain that would otherwise have come so easily to their lips. In this, the store continued to work well, and the town observed that too. Robertson was considered one of the fairest and most competent store managers they had seen, even though he wasn't experienced. The priest considered his involvement with Victoria to be inappropriate, but this criticism was not widely felt. Robertson did not beat her, and he was only a few years older than her himself. The townspeople told him they wanted him to stay and, increasingly, they mentioned this to Victoria. She just shrugged when people referred to her friendship with Robertson. He had a radio. And let her listen to it.

"There was no hope there and that was why I left. The northern cities, Birmingham, Manchester, they just looked to me like they were collapsing. Every month there was another mill closing, a thousand more men out of work with no expectation of finding another job. The coal miners, the steel workers, all in the same situation. It sounds hysterical to say out loud, but over there you could get the idea that the world was coming to an end. Every year worse than the one before it." Robertson paused to take a sip of his whiskey. There was a storm blowing off the bay, and the windows rattled. She listened to him, unable to fully imagine the place he was describing, but now better able to imagine this man before her.

"The pubs were where you saw it the clearest. There was this place down the street from my parents' house. The Flagging Stallion. Used to be it was busy at lunch and then not again until suppertime, and then all night it was packed. By the time I left, it was jammed by eleven in the morning and stayed that way until eight or nine, when everyone was just too tired to keep drinking. More fights too. Fights all the time, and women, drunk as sailors, vomiting outside. Nobody had anything better to do."

The flat light to the southwest slipped in under the clouds and lit the cabin briefly. She watched him in the orange light. He looked puzzled and almost angry.

"I'm not saying that it was anyone's fault. The world changes and people have to too. But all that change, in such a short period of time. It was so hard on those people.

"My sister Ethel got pregnant. The guy was an out-of-work millwright. They moved to Australia. Then my brother Harold, he had been a machinist, moved to London, and got a job delivering sandwiches. I hadn't really considered leaving until then, but suddenly it was clear to me: it was time to go. I heard it was easy to get a visa to Canada. I landed and started moving, asking around for jobs as I went, and never stopped until I ended up here. It seems kind of like a dream to me. It's still a little hard to believe."

"Simionie Irnuk came to talk to me today," Robertson said, watching the sun set through his cabin door one night in June, nearly midnight and the sky riotously purple and orange. She turned the radio off and straightened her clothes. It was almost time to go home.

"What did he say?"

"He asked me if I loved you."

"What did you say?"

"That that sounded like a good idea."

"You didn't." She laughed.

"I did."

"You shouldn't play with him."

"I wasn't."

Victoria looked at him again, and she saw the face of her new lover soften. She breathed in deeply then, and felt her chest catch. She touched his ear, and he caught her hand in his and kissed it.

"Good night," she said.

All he could do was nod.

When she became pregnant, she recognized the sensations. She told Robertson one night when they were sitting on the step of his cabin, watching the aurora borealis. In the darkness, she could not see his expression. He nodded and did not speak. Subsequently both of them avoided mentioning her pregnancy, though they continued to spend evenings together whenever he got away from the post.

Neither were Emo and Winnie eager to discuss their daughter's condition. Their connection with her felt too tenuous, and if what they assumed was true, that the Kablunauk was the father, then it seemed inevitable that their affiliation with her would diminish further. And she, their only daughter. Winnie wept quietly to herself about the matter. Emo felt panicked whenever he thought about it, whenever Winnie alluded to it, so he simply refused to discuss the subject. When Victoria returned home from her spells out at the Kablunauk's cabin, she worried for the sanity of her parents, who were so much jumpier than she remembered from her childhood.

Even when Victoria was eight months along, her belly hugely swollen on her long, thin consumptive's frame, she refused to participate with Robertson or anyone in any conversation that had to do with reproduction. She attended Père Bernard's masses with her mother and father on Sunday mornings and she smiled and waved at the people who greeted her. She did not mention Robertson, and neither did she bring him to church with her, and she did not discuss her having to leave to urinate twice during the service, or her wide-gaited and comic waddle. Eventually she became too large for her parka and had to buy a zippered nylon coat from the Hudson's Bay store. Then she was unable to close the zipper, and so she had her mother sew a panel she could zip to the front of her coat to afford her otherwise exposed belly some shelter. Her coat was navy blue, and for reasons known only to Winnie the zippered panel was crimson. By the end, Victoria looked like a drake mallard waddling the slippery paths through the hamlet and still refusing to discuss her circumstances. When Elizabeth Makpah, who sat across the aisle from Victoria's family at church, accosted her in the Hudson's Bay store and bluntly asked what her plans were, Victoria replied that they would have potatoes tonight, with a caribou roast. Maybe a can of corn.

When Dr. Balthazar appeared in town, it took weeks before there was a general consensus about what he was doing there. With his heavy-footed step and bearded face, he was more like a prospector than the wire-framed and crewcut federal government doctors they were used to. He was American and clearly young. The assumption among the Bay Boys was that he was a draft dodger. There was sufficient residual diffidence lingering from the influences of both the old Inuit culture and the old British one that no one interrogated him on the point.

Previously, the closest doctor worked at the church-run hospital in Chesterfield Inlet. The position had been filled by a succession of odd-tempered men drawn by the isolation and potential for ego indulgence. Joseph Moody, the last such man, had left Chesterfield Inlet in 1969. He had performed general surgery, including cesarean sections and major abdominal operations, and had strutted through his tenure like Douglas MacArthur wading ashore at Inchon. Inevitably, there had been a book, *Arctic Doctor,* detailing his triumphs.

Balthazar was a different sort of man, deferential and malleable. The nurses at the clinic in Rankin Inlet accepted him quickly and the storied conflicts from Moody's day were not reenacted here. The nurses were grateful for that, which is not the same thing as being confident in his ability.

Victoria lay in the treatment room, gasping and terrified, as an Irish nurse, with glinting hair and sardonic manner, examined her. This was a business nobody had prepared Victoria for. The Irish woman's lips pursed as she appreciated the width and thinness of Victoria's dilated cervix. When she was finished, she sat down on a stool at the head of Victoria's bed and addressed her chin. "My dear, you are going to have your baby in the next hour or two. We will deliver you here. There isn't time to ship you out—you'd likely have your baby in the airplane if we did that." Then she picked up the telephone to inform the new doctor of her decision.

Balthazar was only just in the door, toque and beard covered in snowflakes, when Victoria felt the urge to push, and she did, and within twenty minutes—Balthazar matching her pant for breathless pant, exhorting her until he was hoarse—her little irnuq had crept into the world. What a bushy-haired little wonder he was, his bright black eyes wide open, more serene even than Victoria, who felt exhaustion and pleasure ripple over her like a summer line squall. Twelve hours after

that, the nurse sent Victoria and Pauloosie home and they fell asleep together in her parents' aromatic chipboard house.

Balthazar had confided to Victoria afterward that he hadn't much
experience in obstetrics. The laconic Irish nurse reckoned that it would
have been more worrying if he had delivered many babies and still had
become so agitated at what had been a pretty effortless affair. "Effortless," Victoria repeated to herself, and wondered what room the Irishwoman had been in. A kind of half-guilty affection bloomed between
her and the young doctor.

But Victoria was grateful that neither the Irishwoman nor Balthazar
had made her feel ashamed of herself that evening in the nurses' station,
the way she had felt throughout the pregnancy, especially after telling
Robertson. When her mother and father were presented with the fact
of their grandson, they softened as well, and her mother did not again
mention Père Bernard and having to meet his eyes.

A baby changes everything. The moment Pauloosie was in the
world, wearing Robertson's surname, his father became a part of the
community. Robertson was the father of an Inuk boy now and possessed
a stake in the place that he had not before. And in his doting on the
child, the way he walked through town wearing an amoutie, his son's
wee head poking up from the back of his hood, it was clear he was also
making a claim on the place. None of the white men who had left had
acted like this.

Three years after Pauloosie was born, Victoria delivered Justine.
Two years after that came Marie. These were happy times. Robertson
had officially become the new Hudson's Bay store manager, though he
had functioned in that capacity for some time already. He went on long
hunting trips with his father-in-law and with the younger hunters, and
was regarded as reasonably competent, at least for a Kablunauk who
hadn't ever fired a rifle when he arrived. Oddly, it was Robertson who
guided Victoria back into the community. As they did their rounds after
a hunt, sharing whatever meat he brought in off the land, he was the

butt of gentle teasing about his strange-shaped iglus and white man's ways, which was a welcome that extended also to her.

It was later that things started going wrong in their marriage. There was a fourth child, a boy. His fate was never subsequently discussed by Robertson and Victoria, but he lay always between them, nonetheless.

The pregnancy had been the easiest of them all. When Victoria began laboring at home she had called her mother to come over to stay with the kids, and then she picked up her things and walked to the nursing station.

When the nurse called Dr. Balthazar—who by this time had delivered his share of babies—he wanted to know if he could arrange a medevac. No, the nurse informed him, there wasn't time. Ten minutes later he arrived, with the wild-eyed, unfocused look he commonly wore when called unexpectedly from his apartment. He washed his hands and put on a gown and Victoria joked with him that one of these days he was going to realize that she had easy babies and that he didn't need to get so worked up. They both looked up as they heard Robertson arriving at the nurses' station, bantering with the clerks, at ease.

The first stage was done in an hour, and she felt the baby moving through her with vigor and strength. She loved him already, knew he was a boy. When she had told this to her mother after the ultrasound, Winnie had named him Anguilik, after her own father, who, with this name, would now be reborn. She had touched her head respectfully to her daughter's belly and whispered, "Welcome back, Father." The story of how Emo and Anguilik had met, one spring evening on the ice outside Repulse Bay, when Emo had come north looking for a wife, was part of the family's mythology. The idea of Anguilik's return to them delighted everyone except Robertson. But he knew better than to mock these ideas aloud.

When Victoria had left her mother to waddle over to the nursing station, Winnie had been weeping already, and Victoria had hugged her for a long time—until the strength of the contractions grew to the point that they could not be ignored. Winnie's father, dead twenty years, had been the informal leader of his little band; the young people no longer spoke of him, but everyone over forty remembered his name. Victoria's son was eagerly awaited. At the grocery store the week before, she received more congratulations and inquiries into her health than she had with the other three put together. She was uncomfortable with this for two reasons: she had grown accustomed to her near invisibility in the town; also, she was old enough to remember the presumption that babies generally do not survive, that they haven't even begun to decide whether they'll stick around until their fontanelles have closed up together with the easy exit skyward.

And then the baby crowned, and his head emerged and Balthazar grinned at her. The nurse inhaled sharply. Robertson spun his head to where the nurse pointed, as did Balthazar. The baby's head had retracted back inside Victoria to his ears. "Turtle sign," Balthazar and the nurse whispered at the same moment. The nurse pulled Victoria down to the very edge of the bed and, lifting her knees back to her chest, pushed on her abdomen as Balthazar gripped the baby's head and heaved. Robertson blanched. The nurse called for help then and, when the second nurse arrived, hissed, "Shoulder dystocia" to her. The new nurse gripped Victoria's other leg and pressed likewise upon her as Balthazar desperately fumbled.

When a baby's shoulders are too large to clear the mother's pelvis, there are ten minutes to act and only ten minutes. The umbilical cord is squeezed closed in the birth canal and the child cannot expand his chest enough to breathe, and grows steadily bluer until he is delivered, whole and in time—or in parts. Bringing the knees to the chest is the first move, hanging the buttocks off the end of the bed is the next— these change the relevant angles favorably. When this does not work, the physician can twist the baby around in the birth canal, in the aptly named "corkscrew" maneuver. When this does not work, sometimes fracturing the child's collarbones will allow the shoulders to roll in enough to be delivered. By this stage, all measures are desperate. In a city hospital, with an anesthetist standing in the next room, and a surgeon right there, a cesarean section can be life-saving. But ten minutes goes fast.

Blood ran from Victoria in a steady stream; she grew paler and paler, and the child, the grapefruit-size ball of his head just poking from her, grew bluer and bluer until he was almost the color of an aubergine. No operation was possible there, and when the sequence of relevant steps pursued methodically did not work, Balthazar became frozen with grief, moving more slowly, not less, and what happened was: the baby died.

When her son had finally been pulled from her, Victoria held out her arms and Balthazar, weeping, placed the dead baby in them. She put the baby to her breast, shuddering and whispering, "Eat, baby. Please eat . . ." Tears ran steadily down her cheeks and off her chin and onto the baby's head. Robertson stroked her hair, whispering, "Shhhh, Victoria, you're going to be okay. Everything's going to be okay." His relief that she had survived, to continue to tend to him and his other children, struck her at that moment as inconceivably self-absorbed. With her last bit of strength she hissed at him, "Get out of here!"

His head flew back with a snap.

When he did not immediately move, she shrieked, "Get him out of here!" And he rose from his position hunched on the father's stool and left the room, under the gaze of the horrified nurses and the doctor, himself paralyzed with grief and shame.

When Balthazar visited her a few hours later, Robertson had not returned. "Victoria," the doctor began. "I did not act as quickly as I ought to have . . ." But she did not have enough energy to assuage his guilt and turned away from him on her stretcher. "It's no one's fault," she said. And until much later, when she knew him better, she believed that.

Victoria's parents and the priest and the other mothers in the hamlet attributed the death of her son to, variously, God's will or Victoria's excessive pride. But it wasn't fated that her boy should die. Her boy was meant to grow up strong and handsome. He was supposed to have married Faith Nakoolak's oldest daughter, who was not born either, as a consequence of the frayed strands of fortune. Faith was meant to have survived, and so was Victoria's boy. They were supposed to live, and be happy. He was to have been Victoria's favorite child, and this would have been apparent, though she would have denied it. He was also supposed to have been Robertson's son in a way that Pauloosie could never be. He was supposed to have been the child that held them all together.

In dying, he ruptured Victoria from Robertson, flaked her away from him like a leaf of shale. Robertson was attentive enough when Victoria returned home the next day. He had sent the kids to neighbors', and had cooked a meal. But the truth was Victoria's intuition had been right—he was relieved that his wife was safe, had not much wanted another child. Alongside Victoria's grief, he was outrageously unperturbed. He would not grieve for the little boy, his own son, her own grandfather. And each time he assured her stupidly that "everything is going to be okay," he made it more certain that they never would be. Made it more clear that he really was as foreign, and as selfish, as he seemed.

Everything changed in a moment for them. Like a summer frontal system crossing the sun.

eyes

They are how the world is taken in and so we should not be surprised that the world marks them tellingly. Arcus senilis, *the old physicians called the opaque gray rings around the pupils that appear in men in their fifties, women in their sixties. Those with high cholesterol are said to develop such rings sooner and more prominently, but this may just fall into that portion of medical "knowledge" that sees diagonal creases in the earlobes as a sign of incipient heart disease: if it's true, it is only slightly so.*

We understand better what to make of brown rings in the corneas of young people with failing livers and psychoses: they are awash in copper—Wilson's disease. Copper salts accumulate in their eyes, and in their livers and their brains. When the problem is identified, the copper can be leeched out with noxious drugs, but only if someone takes the time to spot the brown ring in the first place and then wonder what it is.

The cornea is the clear covering over the iris in which the copper deposits collect and in which the senile arcs of age first show themselves. A healthy cornea is perfectly transparent. The particular hue of an iris has given rise to any number of songs and epic ballads, but the much more important cornea is without poetic interest. It is an oddity—uniquely sequestered from the rest of the body, almost inaccessible to the immune system. Tissue typing is not required prior to corneal transplant, and the cornea is the only part of the body in which cancer never arises. Think about the aloof Swiss, insulated from centuries of carnage all around them simply because they chose not to participate.

But when the cornea becomes diseased, the loss of function is a catastrophe. Corneal opacification is one of the commonest causes of blindness among

children, especially where medical care is unavailable; it is usually caused by
Chlamydia trachomatis infection, acquired in the headlong slide through the
birth canal. The swollen, milky eyes that result are called trachoma, found
anywhere chlamydia infection is—that is, anywhere men and women make love
to each other. When the nurse dabs erythromycin ointment in your daughter's
wee folded eyes as you catch your breath after she is born, the nurse is
impugning your virtue and she is doing the thing that reduces childhood
blindness by 90 percent. A single squirt of eye ointment and the child sees.

Between the cornea and the iris lies the aqueous humor: transparent, watery,
the substrate against which the fibrils and interwoven multicolored tendrils
of irises dazzle. Iridologists believe that the complex patterns woven into the
brightest parts of our eyes possess meaning in proportion to their complexity. They
may be right; the lingering question is whether we can interpret that meaning
usefully. Snowflakes are infinitely and fractally varied too, and their variations
reflect the atomic structure of water and the van der Waals forces acting on the
hydrogen molecules. Great lessons about the structure of matter, or, at least, of
water, can be taught using the range of variation within snowflakes, but—though
it would make a good story—it wasn't simply by peering at mittens in snowstorms
that molecular theory was sorted out.

Behind the iris, the lens bulges forward, another transparent sac surrounding
clear jelly. Within this translucent gel form crystals and scars from hundreds of
thousands of hours of work focusing light and gathering insight. These scars cause
opacities called cataracts, which possess the same potential for catastrophe as
their homonyms. The repair of these is the best work doctors do. The Inuit became
old when they could no longer see well enough to sew or shoot—sight was lost
long before will, or knowledge. The Arctic, when men move upon it, is awash in
light; all that the black dirt absorbs in the south the snow sends back skyward
here. The air is lit from below and above and the light simply dazzles. Within the
squinting eye, taking it in, the lens is cooked incrementally.

A cataract may be cured with surgery that lasts fifteen minutes and
requires no expensive regimen of pills and intensive care. Old men and women
blind ten years go walking on the land a week after the operation, stepping

lightly and certainly on the moss and rocks. By comparison, every other therapy offered for every other problem is immeasurably crude.

The crudest of all of these are eyeglasses, of course—condemning the myopes to a lifetime of dependence on the fragile appliances we ask them to strap to their heads. For accountants, perhaps, this is not a difficulty, but for men and women who run and hunt and go to sea, eyeglasses are as incapacitating as a dependence on any other crutch. And consider how common myopia is now among southern children and young Inuit. A generation or two ago it was so rare as to be worth reporting; when Victoria needed such strong lenses, the doctor on the C.D. Howe checked her refractive error three times.

Consider the debility that such a condition poses for anyone who does not have access to an optometrist. It would be not much less troublesome than a missing leg. Maybe even more—with a missing leg you could still hobble to a ridgeline and shoot straight.

And yet we have no idea what causes this most common of all the diseases of affluence. If it was near work, then more women should have had myopia than men, and yet they did not. And now that ophthalmologists buy themselves large houses with the proceeds of refractive surgery, one wonders how acute the interest in understanding and interrupting the pathogenesis of myopia can really be.

I *enjoy the journals I receive here for their own sake.* The Journal of the American Medical Association, *the* New England Journal of Medicine, Lancet, *the* British Medical Journal, *the* Annals of Internal Medicine: *these are like jewels, with writing about all corporal aspects of humanity rigorously prepared, as precise as a gamma knife. There is a kind of poetry in that precision. Any expectation that the writing within them is dry and unemotional is defeated upon contemplating the case histories—anecdotes of children and adults with malignancies and plagues defeating initial diagnosis: lymphomas and tropical fevers, inapparent self-injury, and malabsorption disorders. In the accounts as they are printed, the uncommonly clever and usually Bostonian doctor plucks the answer out of the clues in the data and the patient is saved. How can one not applaud?*

I am moved by these accounts, but the truth is that they do not much help me. I pore over the journals, trying to learn, but when things happen quickly, as bad things generally do in medicine, all that knowledge seems to retreat from me. I delivered Victoria's son, and both her daughters—the older, eccentric one, Justine, and the intense skinny one, Marie—and in each instance all I did was gape as her babies fell into my hands. And still she remained patient with me. She was even patient with me when her last baby died as I tried to deliver him.

If I had been as clever as those Bostonians, I would have become an ophthalmologist. I wanted to, applied to all the residencies I could find, in America. But as the replies came to me, thin and perfunctory, I realized that among the men I had approached to be references, one at least had seen me clearly. I finished a general internship at a community hospital in Yonkers and then I looked for a job. There was an advertisement by the Canadian government, looking for doctors in the Arctic, where the turnover was rapid. I came up here.

Behind the lens, and the vitreous humor—yet another transparent and particular gel—is the retina, the film of the eye's camera. Here are the only blood vessels that may be directly witnessed in an unincised body; they sit in a transparent mesh at the back of the eye. All the illnesses of rich people may be glimpsed here. The poor develop river blindness and trachoma and congenital cataracts: all at the front of the eye, and while they are young. Age and rich living seep into the back of the eye. It is here the wealthy grow blind. The banker's high blood pressure tightens the retinal arteries in stiff wires now coppery, now silvery in appearance. Diabetes prompts new vessels to sprout here and grow across the retina, shading it from the light slowly and then abruptly as the new and ill-formed vessels burst and bleed across the field of vision.

The optic disk is at the back of the eye as well, a visible outpouching of the brain itself. When tumors grow inside the skull the evidence of the pressure they exert may be seen here, in the bulging of the optic disk. It is a bad day when an unremarkable-sounding headache is being assessed and the optic disks turn out to be swollen and distorted: this is called papilledema and it is usually terrible news. The patient, at that moment, may hear her physician *inhale sharply and lean abruptly forward, turning the clicking wheel of his ophthalmoscope—taking in the portent of trouble full in the eye.*

The poets talk in their excessive way about eyes as the windows of the soul. And perhaps sometimes they are that. But they reveal things this side of the soul as well. The desperation of the poor marks the fronts of them and the indulgence of the rich marks their backs. The eyes have it, the essence of us and our lives, marked all over them, awaiting the perceptive observer. Shining corneas and reddened sclerae, engorged eyelids and oedematous periorbital tissue: none of us is as placid, or opaque, as we try so hard to seem.

chapter four

Victoria revved her snow machine as she rounded the broad curves of the Little Meliadine River. The storm that had confined them all to the house for that endless week had been over for five days and, ever since, a high-pressure system had hung over the tundra with air as clear and incisive as cut glass. The snow machine sounded like an electric kitchen appliance grinding rocks. It whined and howled and chattered and flung her along over the snow so fast, her tears froze.

Beside her, along the bank, the tops of creek willows poked out of the snow, looking like a dusting of pepper. Here and there the drifts had been pawed away by the tuktu, and the willows were chewed down to the frozen sphagnum moss that otherwise covered the ground. As the sound of her machine rang out down the river, the tuktu grazing there rose up on the shallow embankment like packs of large dogs and trotted slowly to the crests of nearby ridges to watch her pass. She was twenty miles and an hour north of town. Their cabin was almost at Twin Lakes, and was one of the farthest out of any of the hunting cabins. Robertson was proud of that fact.

He had phoned that morning to tell her he would be another week in Yellowknife. His business was taking longer than he had expected. He didn't bother to apologize. She thanked him for letting her know. The trip before, she had gone to the airport to pick him up on three successive days before he remembered to call her to say he was delayed. She had been a little irritated. Nobody likes to waste time. But it wasn't as if she was disappointed, then or now. And, though she wouldn't have put it so directly, even in her own mind, it gave her ammunition for their next argument. If they could overcome their postures of mutual indifference to have one.

Her machine swerved and slid over the stretches of bare river ice, but Victoria did not slow until she could see her cabin in the distance, three miles downstream. Then she let up on the accelerator and crept at walking speed, looking carefully all around. She knelt on the seat and lifted her head high, so she could see. There was smoke curling out of the cabin chimney.

When she reached the bend in the river in front of the cabin, she slowed the machine until it had just enough momentum to crawl up the bank, and then stall. She watched the cabin for a moment. She could not see movement within it. But a fire had been lit. She swung her leg off the snow machine and stood.

When she opened the door to the cabin, she felt warm air flowing over her, and as her eyes accommodated themselves to the dark she saw the glow of the woodstove, and the man crouched over it, feeding it bits of scrap wood. She sloughed off her parka and went to him, pushing him backwards onto the single bed that lay along one wall.

"How long have you been here?" she asked as she kissed him.

"Ten minutes," Simionie answered.

"You got the cabin nice and warm."

"Maybe it was more like half an hour."

"Or an hour." She pressed against him, and felt as if she were waking from some numb place.

"Or an hour," he admitted.

Emo wrapped his rifle in stiff, spotted canvas and tied the bundle onto the komatik. The dogs were yelping and dancing on their lines, tethered on the sea ice in the inlet abutting the town. The dogs of the other hunters sat watching, just beyond lunging distance. In the west there was open sky. The dogs were hungry and eager to move.

He whistled to the lead dog, a bitch named Kanyak, for whom he felt an affection that rivaled any other in his life. She threw herself against her lead and the sled flew forward. The other dogs, jerked into alignment by the tautened leads, began panting into the wind. The old man ran alongside for fifty feet and then knelt on the komatik, one hand on a walrus-skin whip, the other holding a line tied to the cross struts. The dogs knew the way.

They passed the wooden Peterhead motorboats, pulled up on shore the autumn before. Snowdrifts concealed their length, revealing only ten of their twenty-five feet. The oldest of them had been built in the 1950s and had been kept going through a succession of engine replacements and shorings-up. The cedar planking had been repaired with spruce two-by-fours, carved to fit, to the point where they had become like the Bay Boys, creations as much of this place as they were of their origins, although still made of wood and hence foreign. Snow was piled even in the wheelhouses, swept in from between dried planking and ill-fitting windows. For twelve weeks every summer these boats charged across Hudson Bay, down to Churchill for goods brought there on the rail line, or north to Coral Harbour for iviaq, bloody and bellowing, tusks stabbing the air as they died.

Emo's own father had traveled to Newfoundland in 1925 to ferry such boats back to the trappers grown briefly—disorientingly—rich from arctic fox. In the summer when the foxes were mangy and shedding, the men hunted arviaat from these boats too, and filled caches along the coast with dried meat and lamp oil and ammunition, for the long winter hunting trips. To find the caribou, the hunters had to move fast, and if they carried food for the dogs with them this was difficult. Coming home, they were laden with meat, and the problem was less acute but, of course, neither was it necessary to move at any speed.

Snow machines had come to the Arctic in the late 1960s and early 1970s, just as the last of the people had come in off the land. The sequence of decisions—to move into a house, and to kill the dogs—had been constant in each of the hamlets along the coast until no one lived on the land. Whale Cove, Repulse Bay, Chesterfield Inlet, and Coral

Harbour had all grown inexorably, accreting like crystals in a supersat-
urated solution, the barrenlands emptying as the towns swelled. Twelve
people and two families to a house, and tuberculosis running through
each of these hamlets like a rumor. Life in the settlements was as difficult in many ways as life on the land had been. An iglu, or even a small
river valley, would only ever have held one family, after all.

The death of the dogs had been hard. The sled dogs had lineages as
carefully remembered as those of the hunters who depended on them.
They could smell approaching bears at night and find their way home in
blizzards so blindingly dense that all that could be done was to trust
them. In the course of half a dozen years they had nearly all been shot—
if you lived in a house, a snow machine was an altogether less cumber-
some thing to take care of. You could leave it for two weeks or three,
and it would still be waiting for you and ready to run. If you still lived
on the land, the business of keeping the dogs active was simply part of
the day, and anyway it was lonely out there and the companionship of
the creatures, surly and unpredictable beasts though they were, was val-
ued. If you lived on the land, the business of carrying gasoline and oil
was difficult—but not if you lived beside the Hudson's Bay Company
depot in town. This thing that made it so much easier to travel quickly
on the land made it impossible to remain on it.

Following the move into towns, some put their dogs on islands in
the bay in the summers, with seal carcasses. The old men shook their
heads over this; it wasn't how they had been raised to treat dogs. A few
hung on to their teams, as Emo had, but the status of dogs changed
from essential to ornamental in about five years.

When Emo's dogs got to the floe edge, ten miles offshore, he called
to them to stop and threw out the snow hook. The wind was settling
and it was abruptly quieter. He stood on the sled and studied the ice.
He could see nautsiaq, ringed seals, upwind—tiny black dots to the
north. Emo stood on the snow hook, driving it into the thin, packed
snow to ensure its purchase. He unwrapped his rifle and slung it over
his shoulder. The tide held ice pans against the floe edge like crackers

spilled casually on a plate. Between them lay the open, purple, and viscous water, with whitecaps scudding across it leaving streaks of foam and slivers of ice broken free and running.

Emo walked toward the seals, watching them carefully. They were sleeping, but awoke in turns every few minutes to smell the air, for bears and for men. From this distance the movement was subtle, and difficult to see—the outline of the black dot against the ice seemed to shimmer for a moment. When Emo saw that, he stopped moving. The dogs behind him were silent and watched him attentively.

That same Saturday afternoon, Dr. Balthazar sat in his office at the nursing station, surrounded by medical charts. He was alone in the place; no one needed tending to. Earlier, the on-call nurse had been there, seeing some kids with ear infections. Balthazar had told her that he had to stay to catch up on his charting and she had nodded "whatever" to him and gone home. For most of the day he had done just that, writing carefully in his almost feminine script chart summaries of patients he knew well, and referral letters to specialists in the south. But then he began daydreaming. In the empty clinic, it was easy to push aside the charts and imagine a different life. Around him were the records of two thousand acquaintances. By this point he had been coming north for three-month stints for seventeen years and he knew almost everyone, except a few of the very healthy men. But the kids, and all the women, and anyone old—over sixty, that is—he knew those people well. Walking through the chart room and sliding his eyes at random over the various names summoned up for him almost two decades' worth of maulings and depressions and complicated childbirths: the Katoongie clan and the terrible asthma they had as kids, the fire that had burned the Panigoniaks so badly. And then the Robertsons. He brought Victoria's chart back to his office and flipped through the earliest records in it, pages that were brittle and crumbling. Soon, the chart would be split into two, with volume one relegated to the basement, where the records going back more than twenty-five years dwelled. But in the meantime, within the spare and data-laden language of the chart—such agony here. He turned the pages over, one after the other, rapt, imagining the girl.

What she probably remembered most strongly from her operation was the overwhelming smell of the ether the instant they turned it on—the olfactory equivalent of having a flashbulb go off in front of one's widely opened eyes. She would have thought, *What a strong smell,* and then stopped counting backwards.

The anesthetist had passed a twin-lumened endotracheal tube into her throat, one branch of the tube riding in her right main bronchus and lung and the other in her left. The tuberculous cavity was in her right lung and so the air in it was sucked out through this tube and the lung collapsed upon itself, like a balloon hooked to suction. Ventilation was maintained in the other lung—the anesthetist hooked that half of the tube up to a ventilator, which wheezed and sighed over the following two hours as the surgeon made a deep incision between Victoria's ribs, high up on the right side. The intercostal muscles connecting the ribs were exposed, and the surgeon pushed a blunt-tipped clamp through this muscle and into the chest cavity. The air rushing into the chest as the pleural space was opened sounded like a gasp. He inserted the rib spreaders and squeezed them apart, revealing the glistening chest cavity gaping open beneath. At the Clearwater Sanatorium where Victoria had been sent, the chest surgeon did little other than operate on tuberculous lungs, and was adept at these procedures, having done them by the thousand for the previous twenty years. Excising a lung was considered routine, almost vulgar in its simplicity—nothing like the complex anatomy of the abdomen, say, or, especially, the neck.

The right lung lay within this child's cavity-ridden chest like a wilted flower, collapsed and unbuoyant. The surgeon felt the upper lobe between his fingers and identified the scarred and rotten abscess within it, feeling like a piece of cookie sewed inside a sponge. He clamped the right upper lobe bronchus and prepared to divide it. The accompanying pulmonary veins and arteries were clamped in turn and ligated on both sides of the clamp. When he had cut and sealed the tubes supplying and receiving blood and air from that lobe of the lung, the surgeon directed his attention to the ligaments supporting it, and cut each of these in turn. Then he lifted the lobe through the rib spreaders like a child from the womb, cupping it in his hands, clamps and ligatures dangling like amnion and umbilical vessels.

He next picked up a tool that looked like a stubby-jawed stainless-steel wire cutter. With a dull click he snapped the little girl's ribs, removing the middle third of each rib that had overlain the cavity.

When the ribs had been excised, he began sewing the strips of intercostal muscles to one another with long-running silk sutures. When he was finished, Victoria's chest wall looked as if it had been tattooed with long stripes of black ink that ran in zigzag patterns from her breastbone around to her back. He closed the skin overlying this work and placed two chest tubes into the space between the lung and the chest wall. Then the anesthetist began pumping air into and out of the right lung. It reinflated quickly and forced air in a bubbling crimson froth out of the chest tubes. As the lung began to rise and fall within the chest wall, the deribbed skin overlying what had been the lung cavity bulged out and sucked in with each breath from the ventilator.

Soon Victoria was breathing on her own and the anesthetist pulled the tube out of her throat. She began coughing and then vomited over and over again.

The surgeon's name was C. W. Henderson, and he wrote a description of the thoracoplasty he had just performed on the hospital chart by hand with a fountain pen. A copy was sent to the Fort Churchill hospital, and had remained on her medical chart ever after, in steadily more tattered and yellowing form. Decades later, these brittle pages would be read like ritual in the clinic in Rankin Inlet, the reader's chest feel-

ing tight and full of ache for that little girl, splayed open like a char and
so alone.

Simionie looked at the hollow in the right side of Victoria's chest,
which bulged out and sucked in with her quietening breath. Her long,
black perspiration-laden hair lay over their bodies like wet kelp. At last
he moved, to reach out, to run his hands over her collarbone and then
into the pocket in her chest wall, lighter in color and coarser in texture
than the skin around it. Her eyes remained shut and her head on her
pillow.

He thought that he might be embarrassing her by touching her scar,
which she never referred to but never covered. He watched her face
more carefully and, at that moment, in that intimacy, it seemed to him
that his touch was purely evidence of the tenderness between them. In
just a few minutes, after the glow between them faded, it would not be
possible again.

The cabin was cold; the stove had only been lit for an hour and their
breath smoked in the dim light from the window beside them. The
early-afternoon sun was just off the horizon, thin and diffused by the
dirt on the cabin window, not potent enough to create a proper sun-
beam but enough to draw a weak shine from the walls—in the same
way moonlight makes snow seem just a little brighter than it is.

Simionie knew the provenance of her scar and her complicated history with Robertson, how she had practically been driven to him. He
had not intervened then or subsequently, at least not overtly, but he had
always watched her. As he watched her now.

When she had come back to Rankin Inlet, she had seemed as much
a stranger as any of the Kablunauks who came north to work. She was
tentative while walking on the ice in kamiks, and fell often. She ate seal
cautiously and was seen often at the Hudson's Bay post, trying to buy
candy. She was also often at the priest's house, borrowing books and
magazines. When the ship arrived in the spring she stood on the shore

eagerly and spoke to the sailors comfortably and received gifts from them that the community inspected carefully, albeit from a distance. But although a stranger, she remembered some of their secrets and understood their whisperings. Some thought it would have been better for everyone if she had not come back at all.

When she had climbed down from the airplane he had been struck by how tall she was, and how straight she stood as she looked around for her parents or anyone else she might know. She wore wire-framed glasses too small for her face and her clothes smelled of harsh laundry soap and lye; the high-collared dress she was in could only have been provided to her by a church or a hospital, and no one in the north who is that skinny is healthy. But she spoke their language.

She still stood a head taller than any of the women around her, a full foot taller than her mother. She was at all times visible in any group—she was so beautiful, she would have been visible enough in any event—and she did not pursue the favor or friendship of the other women, who considered her arrogant and affected. Her loneliness became more evident with passing time rather than less. She was not like her own people.

He had seen this at first glance. The Norseman's propeller had stirred up dust and flying gravel and everyone standing there turned away as the prop wash settled, everyone but Simionie, who had just gaped. And now his mouth fell forward upon her chest, and he ran his lips over her ribs, his tongue finding the corrugations of her surgical scar. And she lifted her chest into and against his mouth.

It was a bull Emo shot, two hundred pounds, fat from a winter's worth of feeding on mollusks and capelin sifted out of the seabed muck. The bull had kept his head up as Emo approached and was about to conclude that something was amiss when the bullet hit him. When Emo was younger he lay as still as he could at moments like that, his face pushed into the snow, eyes shut, hoping the stalk had not been ruined, hoping and not breathing. And when he lifted his head again, often, he would be looking at outwardly propelled rings in the crack of water—solidifying slush washing up on its edges.

He had learned not ever to stop looking and not to waste any time hoping but rather to wait motionlessly for the instant he was sensed, and then to take whatever shot was afforded him. Sometimes he could hear the bullet slap into the seal's hide just as it entered the water. The seal was often lost when this happened, bleeding to death beneath the ice, but this time the bullet had caught the bull in the neck and had spun it sideways, away from the ice hole it had been heading toward with velocity. It had died a few feet from its refuge—a steady stream of arterial blood pumping out onto the snow. A small rivulet ran from the seal's neck into the hole, fanning out in the sea like a tiny red estuary.

He rolled the animal over and put the tip of his knife beneath the skin at the base of the animal's pelvis. He cut away the hide around the seal's anus and genitals and then extended the cut on either side to the flippers. He rolled the hide off, cutting gently where required, but mostly simply pulling the skin like a sweater up and over its head. The seal, released from its skin, emerged as a pink and steaming tube of muscle, head, and fins.

He ran the knife up the animal's centerline and its intestines spilled out onto the snow. He split its sternum and opened its chest without pausing. He ran the knife around the edge of the diaphragm and cut away the heart from the pulmonary arteries and veins. He laid it on the snow. The trachea and lungs followed, and then the stomach, intestines, liver, and kidneys. The dogs could smell this now and yowled with impatience.

He removed the fat surrounding the intestines and carefully laid it out on the snow: this was the favored part of the seal and was given to babies and to the fragile elderly. Emo wrapped this, as well as the liver, the kidneys, the heart, and the stomach, in waxed brown paper and put them in his pocket. He cut steaks off the animal then, and the brisket, and the rump roasts. Within a few minutes he had reduced the seal to a dozen carefully chosen cuts of meat, ribs, and a spinal column. He wiped his knife in the snow and then on the seal hide and put it back into its sheath. He wrapped everything but the spine in a plastic bag he had brought and put the bag over his shoulder. He picked up his rifle and began walking back to the sled to pull the ice anchor free and let the team eat the remains of the seal.

chapter five

The morning began with Pauloosie beating on the kitchen door with a frozen char in an effort to knock the ice off the fish. He had declared that he would no longer eat Cheerios for breakfast. The banging awoke Victoria and the girls and together they all listened to him go at it and they all rolled their eyes. Eventually, Victoria got up and headed for the kitchen, flipping on light switches as she went. Running a hand through her exuberant early-morning hair, she opened the refrigerator and got out the milk, shutting the door with her hip as she scooped bowls out of the cupboard. The girls' current enthusiasm was Weetabix, which sounded to Victoria like an animal in a children's picture book. She poured their bowls full, and put bread in the toaster and the percolator on the stovetop. "Girls!" she hollered when she saw that it was seven-thirty already. Pauloosie poked his head in from the kitchen porch when he heard her. Victoria waved at him resignedly. He resumed beating his fish.

When Justine and Marie appeared in the kitchen, Marie had a sweater hastily tugged over her head, but Justine looked like an airline stewardess, her hair pulled back, not a stray strand or visible pore anywhere. They sat down wordlessly and began eating their cereal. Victoria poured them both coffee and milk. Marie looked so tired, she might fall from her chair at any moment—purple-ringed eyes and lids drooping, head laid sideways on her hand as she directed spoonfuls of cereal inaccurately toward her mouth.

"Were you reading after you went to bed last night, Marie?" Victoria asked.

The girl nodded, did not look up from the cereal.

"What were you reading?" Victoria continued.

"The Chronicles of Narnia," Justine answered when her sister didn't.

"How late were you awake?"

"Two," Justine replied.

"It wasn't two," Marie said.

"Yes, it was."

"No more reading in bed, Marie. You need your sleep." The girl was too tired to argue. But that night she would.

Pauloosie came inside, a bitter draft hitting them all as the door closed. He began cutting slivers of flesh from the fish and eating it. Victoria watched him. It was what breakfast had been for her until she was ten—she was not disgusted so much as entertained by the eating habits of her son, although she detected the reproach in his rejection of all things Kablunauk. Marie and Justine assiduously refused to look his way.

What it must feel like for his father.

And then it was time for the kids to get off to school. Victoria bustled them into the porch, where the girls zipped up their nylon parkas and Pauloosie pulled his caribouskin parka over his head. He spoke often about quitting school, but this was the one point about which Robertson was not passive. Pauloosie would attend school, or he would sleep in the snow. It was a peculiarly southern approach to the matter, and so infuriated Pauloosie even more, but Robertson was unyielding. And then he left on another business trip to let Victoria make peace in the home.

Victoria watched them walk away into the night-darkness, Pauloosie striding quickly ahead of his sisters, and returned to the kitchen to begin washing up. She switched on CBC Radio. The chain-smoking morning host rumbled on with avuncular charm about Wayne Gretzky's strategic reimagining of the cross-rink pass. Since television had arrived a few years earlier, she, along with the rest of the town, had become educated in hockey, and the arena that had been built about the same time drew instantly zealous fans every weekend to watch the eleven-year-olds act out everyone's fantasies of their life being continuous with the world beyond this one.

It was a one-mile walk to the school. For the elementary kids there was a school bus that circled through the hamlet in the morning, but the older children were supposed to walk—this was the compromise reached after a loud debate about purchasing the bus. For those of Pauloosie's mind-set, the school bus was an embarrassment: Victoria's parents had dogsledded one hundred miles to attend a wedding once, and then come back again three days later. Emo, presumably, felt similarly, though was less inclined to argue the subject. Pauloosie would have said this was because the old man's sense of dignity would not permit it; Victoria would have said it was because he was indifferent.

The Robertson children arrived at the school a few minutes before the bell, Pauloosie still in the lead. Without a backward glance at his sisters, he disappeared in the knot of bodies streaming in the frosted-glass doors. After making his way to his locker, he stuffed in his parka—worse than an affectation in the minds of his classmates, an anachronism. When he got to homeroom, Mrs. Stevenson was drinking her tea and looking outside at the eastern horizon, where the sky was just starting to lighten. She saw Pauloosie slouch in and sit down. She set down her cup of tea on her desk and opened the class roll.

The girls made their way to the middle school section. They opened their lockers, which were across the hall from each other, and did not speak. The inside of Justine's locker was emblazoned with photos of David Lee Roth, Tiffany, Michael J. Fox, Def Leppard, Poison, Bryan Adams, Madonna (inevitably), Olivia Newton John, ABBA, the Cars, Tom Petty, Lynyrd Skynyrd, Huey Lewis and the News, Duran Duran, and the Eagles. These overlaid an earlier pastiche of Donna Summer, the Bee Gees, and the rest of the now-faded greats from the disco era.

Justine's musical tastes derived from late-night radio. In the winter she could pick up faint strains of commercial stations from Winnipeg and sometimes even Chicago. There was also a program on CBC, *Brave*

New Waves, that she was just starting to listen to late at night, in bed, when everyone else was asleep except Marie with her nose in a book. Usually she didn't take immediately to the stripped-down and often British music they played, but she had the adolescent's acute sensitivity for cool and she suspected that she was not supposed to be as enthusiastic a fan of Huey Lewis as she had allowed herself to become.

Justine's mixed parentage precluded her from being genuinely popular. Her preoccupation with unfamiliar music made her still more different—but gave her an aura of coolness that allowed her to exist on the margins of popularity. She was like a fourth-line center on a good hockey team—not exactly a luminary, but something. The boys would have understood this analogy: their lockers were equally emblazoned with posters of Gretzky and Messier and Anderson and Lowe and Fuhr—whichever Oiler played the position the locker owner did.

Marie's locker walls were bare. She hung up her down-stuffed, bright red nylon coat and slid her *Chronicles of Narnia* in with her schoolbooks. Her sister's quasi popularity did not extend to her. She was younger, and therefore less interesting absolutely, but neither did she have her sister's self-possession, and she was not conversant in popular music. She read novels that the aging librarian passed on to her like a secret. She was too skinny, too boyish, and looked too much like a Kablunauk, with her white-white-white skin under blue-black hair and sad gray eyes. In another context, she would have been considered more arresting even than her sister, but no one in the Maani Uluyuk Middle School had ever heard the word *goth*. And anyway, she wanted to be unnoticed, left alone to read her books. Which isn't quite the same thing as saying she was glad she had no friends. But if she had to choose.

Johanna Stevenson, Pauloosie's homeroom teacher, had come to Rankin Inlet the year before, after her separation. That was a common story among the teachers and nurses here—something had to give them sufficient velocity to propel them so far.

Her friend was Penny Bleskie, who arrived a few months after Johanna, right out of university and full of enthusiasms. Johanna enjoyed her. The two of them walked to school together in the mornings from the government apartments they had been provided. That morning Penny told her more cautious friend about the dog team she had bought, the caribou-skin outerwear and the rifle she took out with her on the land, as she was learning to use the dog team. Pauloosie's grandfather was teaching her how to handle the dogs. Johanna was tempted to mention this to the boy, as an invitation to conversation, but he had withdrawn to the back of the class, and then all the other kids filed in, and she let the moment pass, again.

Johanna enjoyed Penny's adventures vicariously. She felt like she was straddling two ages in her life: too young yet to be as bitter as the other divorced teachers, but just a little too old to be as reckless as Penny. She might not ever have been young enough to be quite as daring as her friend, as she remembered Penny's account of having become entangled in her dogs' harness, the seven of them rolling around together on the sea ice like a slapstick outtake from *Nanook of the North*. She couldn't really see how Penny had connected with Emo, Pauloosie's grandfather. Johanna found the old man frightening when she saw him moving through the aisles of the Northern Store. She predicted that Pauloosie would be dropping out of school any month now. Just like all the other boys here.

The bell rang and the kids in her homeroom dispersed. Her first class of the day was grade eleven language arts. They were reading Nordhoff and Hall's *Mutiny on the Bounty,* an instance of the southern curriculum falling pretty wide of the sensibilities of these kids, who did not quite engage with the idea of tropical oceans and Polynesian islands. She and the other English teachers had discussed this. "But is it any more familiar to the kids in Etobicoke?" she had asked. "Books take you to faraway places. That's the point."

She read aloud to her eleventh-graders and looked up as they either dozed off, nodding their heads toward their desktops, or grimaced at one another. Kids. In suburbs or little Arctic towns, wherever—how do you really get their attention? She had been reading aloud to rooms full of mostly bored kids for a decade now and had developed the ability to both disguise her own disengagement and to daydream even as she stood there, narrating Fletcher Christian's frustration with his captain. What she daydreamed was that she was ten again, and lying on the dock at her parents' cottage north of Toronto. Summer heat, and her whole body glowing.

At the end of the school day, Johanna looked around for Penny, but she had taken off, presumably to tend to her dogs. Johanna walked home alone in the dark, unlocked her door, and took off her parka. She sat down at the institutional kitchen table that had come with the apartment and looked at the grading she had to do that night. Suddenly she felt so lonely. This spare and bland box she lived in had hardly been marked by her. A couple of Matisse prints on the wall, and the inevitable soapstone carvings on the coffee table. She had been here eighteen months. With Penny down on the bay ice there was no one in the building she knew well enough even to visit. When she left here, she'd be forgotten in a minute, another one of the long series of Kablunauk teachers, nurses, engineers, who came up here for an adventure and then returned south with stories and prominently displayed artwork of the indigenous peoples. She wished she had some wine.

Without thinking about what she was doing, she found herself picking up the phone and dialing. She listened to it ring, listened to it ring, listened to it ring. She was setting the handset back into the cradle when she heard a voice and lifted it back to her ear.

"Hello?"

"Hey," she said.

"Hey, it's you."

"What did you do today?"

"I sold a new Chev truck, nine thousand dollars."

"That's great."

"Yeah, I'm on a bit of a winning streak here."

"Well, in that department anyway."

"What about you, what did you do today?"

"Listened to Penny tell me about dogsledding."

"With that old guy?"

"No, she's trying to start doing it by herself."

"How's that going?"

"She's got some work to do."

"The dogs just don't know how to take orders?"

"You don't know the half of it. They are so ornery."

"Mean?"

"Yeah, they can be."

"Does she have a whip, like in the movies?"

"Yep."

"Wow. She's hard-core."

"I kinda see what she likes about it all, though."

"Careful, honey."

"You don't like that thought?"

"Johanna of the North. Lice-ridden and flinty."

"She goes out by herself on the sea ice every weekend. Last month she saw a bear."

"Who feeds her dogs when she's at school?"

"She gets up at five to go out on the ice to feed them."

"What is it that you like about that idea?"

"I like the self-sufficiency."

"Well, you got that in spades."

"Yeah, well."

"Now, anyway."

"Doug."

"Sorry."

"So, are you dating anyone?"

"No."

"Would you tell me if you were?"

"No."

"Why?"

"Because I'm hoping you'll conclude that I will pine for you until you decide to come back."

"What if I do that and some Trixie is sharing your basement apartment?"

"Trixie will hit the road."

"I can't tell you how comforting that is to me."

"For you, anything."

"Well, on that note . . ."

"What do you need?"

"Good food, all of a sudden, and badly. Red peppers in oil, pesto, fresh garlic, some Camembert, cardamom, thyme . . . like that. I can't eat one more can of Campbell's soup."

"I'll go to David Wood's shop."

"That would be wonderful. I'll pay you back."

"Hey, I sold a truck, remember? This is on me."

"Okay. Will you express post it?"

"You bet. You're sure you don't just want to move back down here?"

"I can make it if I get some decent pesto."

"So my motivation in all this is where?"

Victoria walked home from the Northern Store with four bags of groceries pulling down on each arm. She stopped every hundred yards to rest her shoulders. She had run low on vegetable oil and tomato sauce. Normally the nonperishables came up on the barge in the summer in a great pallet of prepaid tins and vacuum-sealed foil, but it is impossible to judge exactly the annual requirements for everything from Band-Aids to Pop-Tarts, and every year a few things ran out. The girls had acquired the habit of cooking themselves spaghetti when they got home from school, and so the tomato sauce had run low. And what had she been thinking when she decided that five liters of cooking oil would do them? Though they wouldn't run out of bathroom tissue until the year 2000. Which was itself a comforting thought.

The front door swung open as she leaned against the handle, and she staggered in. She turned on the lights with her shoulder: at three in the afternoon, the sun was setting and soon it would be dark. She lifted the grocery bags onto the kitchen table. She studied the room closely: something was odd here. She walked around her cupboards, sniffing the air and scanning the room. She scouted the hallway, eyes darting warily about, and then at the same moment as she smelled him, she saw that Robertson's office door was ajar. He was sitting at his desk, reading from the pile of mail she had stacked there while he was away.

"I didn't realize you were home."

"Well," he replied, not looking up from the letter in his hands. "Yeah."

She turned back to the kitchen, and despite how long things had been like this between them, she felt a sadness so familiar and worn into place as to hardly be a sensation at all, except in the way that the lungs feel air enter them or snails feel the weight of their shells.

She turned off the lights as she retreated, and then stood in the kitchen. The house, and the land all around it, was almost perfectly dark. From beneath his office door a thin bar of light shone—otherwise, nothing.

In the storeroom she picked onions out of the bin; a single fifty-pound sack had not been enough and next year she would order two. The onions were soft and mostly sprouting. They should have a cold room for these, and the potatoes. Which wouldn't have been a problem at all—witness the tuktu carcasses stacked on every visible rooftop—but what onions and potatoes actually want is a "cool" room. That would take more thinking, since "cool" was about seventy or eighty degrees warmer than what prevailed outside the house. She felt the bulbs for the firmest ones and carried her selection out to the kitchen, where she began cutting them.

On the local radio phone-in show, Emeline Kowmuk was discussing how messy the streets had become. Something really had to be done. Madeleine Makigak suggested that some people could certainly start by not letting their dogs loose to tear open everyone else's garbage bags. Georgina Kapuk suggested that some people might want to consider making some actual wooden garbage bins like everyone else did, and that way, if just once someone's dog chewed through his lead, there might not be boxes and boxes of filthy magazines, with pictures of she-wouldn't-want-to-say in them, spread all over the road, for the children to look at. Emeline, I don't know where those magazines came from, but they're not really the point, are they? We're talking about how messy the streets are, and how some people have no problem letting their dogs just run free, through everyone else's private business and garbage. Emeline, what we're talking about is the mess in our town, and you're right, it is a problem on the roads, and everywhere else too. So . . . on to a new subject. Has anyone noticed how high the tides have been lately?

Then the language switched to English for the hourly news, and Victoria listened carefully as the newscaster spoke of the war in Nicaragua, and the anti–nuclear weapons protests on Hampstead Heath, in Britain. Famine in the Ogaden. The Montreal Canadiens continued their winning ways and Reaganomics was starting to trickle down at last, the administration insisted.

When her husband spoke, she jumped.

"Oh my God," she said, inspecting the tips of her fingers for injury.

"Are you okay?"

"I think so."

"I thought you heard me."

"I was listening to the radio. Was there something you wanted?"

"I just wanted to tell you about my trip."

"Okay."

"Well, it was interesting."

"How?" she asked, resuming her onion chopping. "Is the hospital going to be built?"

"Well, it looks like it might, eventually."

"So what's new about that?"

"I think there is going to be a diamond mine built."

"Really." Not a question.

"Why not?"

"Who ever heard of diamonds in the Arctic?"

"Well, they found some."

"Did they?"

"Yes."

"Where?"

"Up by Back River."

"Huh."

"George Miller wants me to help them out in Rankin."

"How?"

"As an adviser."

"What kind of advice do they want?"

"About local politics and whatnot."

"Sounds like a scam."

"Nobody's asking me for money."

"Who ever heard of diamonds here? Diamonds come from Africa."

"And Siberia."

"Really?"

"Yeah."

"Huh."

"They've found them."

"Who's behind this?"

"South Africans."

"Huh."

And that's how they were standing—he, leaning against the hall wall; she, with her back to him, cutting onions—when Marie and Justine pounded up the steps and through the porch door.

"Hi, girls," Robertson said. They were as surprised as Victoria had been to see him there but more welcoming. They both grinned, Marie especially, and, kicking off their boots, ran to him as he spread his arms. His daughters engulfed him, their parkas leaking melting snow on his shirt and trousers, and he squeezed them tight, enveloped in down like animated pillows.

"Okay, girls, get your homework out," Victoria said. And the girls backed out of his arms and went to the porch to hang up their outer clothes. Then they sat down across from each other at the kitchen table and began working through their arithmetic. A minute after they had settled, the porch door opened again and Pauloosie banged his way inside, stomping the snow off his kamiks and swinging his caribou-skin jumpa over his head and onto a nail. His father and mother watched him.

"Hello," Robertson said.

Pauloosie looked up, as if only noticing that there were others in the room.

"How have you been?" his father asked.

"Okay," said the boy. He disappeared down the hall and then came the click of his bedroom door shutting.

"You have to straighten him out when he talks to you like that. You're his father," Victoria said. "No one ever spoke to my father like that."

Marie and Justine looked at each other dramatically.

"Stop it, you two," their mother said, and they dropped their heads and went back to their schoolwork.

"I won't be raising him the way your father raised Tagak."

"Which is how?"

"What would have happened if Tagak had mouthed off to your father, exactly?"

"It never happened."

"I'm sure it did, when you weren't around."

"You seem to be quite the expert on what my family was like when you were still living in England."

There was the faintest trace of a smirk on Justine's lips. But Marie always looked panicked when her parents argued, and almost immediately she was on the verge of tears.

Robertson stalked out of the kitchen. Victoria's knife stuttered its way through another—the fifteenth—onion. The girls reopened their schoolbooks. Eight multiplication exercises later, a pan of liver, bacon, and many onions fried; a brief essay on the history of the British North America Act; a long fantasy about stalking a wolverine—and then Victoria called her family to eat.

Robertson emerged silently from his office, neck straight and eyes flashing—the boy did not challenge his father again that night. They ate quickly, quietly, and the sense of imminent peril prevailed until Marie caught her father's eye and winked at him. In a moment of inattention, he softened, his anger dissolving.

"Who taught you that?" her mother asked, detecting the sudden easing in the room and seeking to further it.

"Stacey Smith," Justine answered for her sister.

"Who's that?" her father asked.

"Better ask Pauloosie," Marie said.

Pauloosie purpled.

"Pauloosie?" Victoria asked, enjoying this now.

He bent over his mashed potatoes and ate like a grain auger.

"Someone's a little sensitive about something," his father observed. "Maybe we should let him alone." And the boy looked up with relief and met Robertson's eyes.

"Well, it isn't like you haven't learned a thing or two from Stacey Smith yourself," Marie added to Justine.

"Shut up!" her sister squealed.

Teasing broke out like August rain on a peat fire. Robertson's snoring. Victoria's halitosis. Pauloosie's brooding. Marie's solitary habits. Justine's rock goddess aspirations. The kids threw themselves into it, drawing in their parents. They understood that they were what kept these two in the same house now; what remained of Robertson and

Victoria's love was the mutual love they felt for their children. Which was a thin substitute for passion and tenderness. But was not nothing, and was enough to still draw them together occasionally, as it did now.

When the dishes were done, Justine retreated to her bedroom. She dropped her homework on the floor and turned on her shortwave radio. It was time for the BBC World Service rebroadcast of *Top of the Pops*. It was the end of Boy George's time, Culture Club in decline after ruling the Limey charts for six years. He didn't sound or look like any man, singer or not—though she thought he had probably listened to a lot of Smokey Robinson. And he could not be loved, or anyway desired, at least not by her. Later, when he was a junkie, and fat, she would mourn along with everyone else. But in his first youth he had soared, and she couldn't help but soar with him, a little way at least, as he swung into the chorus. *Brave New Waves* came on later, and the Ramones and Iggy Pop and really very little Duran Duran dominated that hour. "Twenty-, twenty-, twenty-four hours to go-oh-oh. I wanna be sedated. Nothing to do, no where to go-oh, I wanna be sedated."

"Justine!"

She took off her earphones. It was Marie. She wanted to go to sleep. She was in her pajamas, and in bed. Justine turned off the radio, and the light.

"It's nice having Daddy home," Marie said.

The boy cleaned his rifle again slowly, running gun oil down the barrel and sighting through it at his light. The riflings and the landings all looked fine. He screwed the trigger assembly back onto the stock, and then the barrel and action. It moved together almost silently. He admired the burled walnut and held the rifle to his shoulder. He aimed at the light. Click. Click again.

School. In the morning—a chemistry exam. Click. Not very interesting, or important. Click. His grandfather remembered watching his own father make a bow out of tuktu antlers and driftwood—what he would have given to own a rifle as fine as this at Pauloosie's age. He could probably make such a bow himself. Wouldn't that be something? Stalk in close enough to be in arrow range. Hard to believe anyone could be good enough at that to feed a family. Umingmak, musk oxen, were different—they didn't run away, but circled defensively, the calves in the center, as if every predator were the wolf and vulnerable to their hooked horns. He'd like to hunt umingmak. Click. He had tasted it once. It was interesting. Not as good as tuktu, but what was?

"Hey." Victoria stuck her head into Robertson's office, hours later. He had not reappeared for the late news.

"Hey," he said, not lifting his head from the form he was reading.

"The kids are all in bed. I'm gonna konk out too."

"Good night."

"Robertson?"

"Yes?" Not looking up.

"Night."

He undressed in the dark, hanging his shirt on the back of a chair and emptying his trouser pockets, then folding them and putting them on the chair seat before slipping into bed. She lay motionless, facing away from him. He studied her long, grooved back and remembered again what he had felt the first time he saw it.

"Victoria," he whispered. "Victoria?"

He couldn't tell if she was asleep or just pretending to be. He thought she was probably awake. He was right.

Two weeks after she had asked Doug to send her food, Johanna still hadn't received his parcel and she was beginning to consider the matter as another item on the long list of ways he had let her down. Her next trip to the post office she saw the plywood crate and bit her lip. When she got it back to her apartment, there was more inside than she ever could have imagined. There was a whole prosciutto, as dark as currants, as aromatic as smoked cheese; a whole prosciutto. She extracted it from among layers of newspaper cushioning and laid it out on the counter. *Prosciutto di Parma*. The scent that rose from it was unlike anything she had smelled since she had come to Rankin Inlet, so many boxes of Kraft Dinner ago: it smelled of pepper and the Mediterranean Sea, and fresh nutmeg and cloves and dark wine. "We bring the worst part of what we are up here," she had said to Penny the day before, when the younger woman had happened upon her in the Northern Store gazing at the racks and racks of fried cornmeal snacks.

There were three one-liter bottles of marc wedged into corners of the crate and wrapped in flannel sheeting. In the fourth corner was a forty-year-old bottle of Lombard balsamic vinegar. There were tins of truffles and a wheel of Asiago cheese, fresh walnuts and smoked duck and a box of Newbury Pippin apples, leaves still green on the stems, the fruit orange and red and yellow like a package of sun-melted crayons. There were wooden boxes of pine nuts and gravlax and capers and jars and jars of Italian pesto. A bottle the length of her forearm and labeled in Serbo-Croatian was filled with olive oil and roasted red peppers, charred bits of skin still clinging delicately to them; there were sun-dried tomatoes and Roquefort and figs the color of chocolate. A canvas bag full of fresh basil was miraculously unfrozen (Doug had stuffed an electric sock warmer inside the clump of basil, and then stuffed that into a thick woolen toque minutes before nailing the crate shut) and cumin and turmeric and whole nutmegs and vanilla pods and jars of chipotle peppers.

Johanna's eyes ran steadily as she extracted these treasures in succession and laid them out on her kitchen counter. She cut open the cloth bag containing the prosciutto and then sliced off the thinnest wafer and set it atop a piece of Asiago cheese on an Alexander's water biscuit, which she had extracted from a tin the size of her head. She bit into it and flavor washed over her like surf. She had to sit down on her kitchen floor and shut her eyes; she was afraid to swallow for long minutes. She opened her eyes and more tears ran out of them.

She had been given a ptarmigan by Penny a couple of days before and had wondered what she would ever do with it; declining the gift had not been possible. She took it out of her refrigerator now and studied it. From her plywood crate she pulled a bundle of fresh rosemary. She broke some needles off in her hands and smelled her fingertips, the scent of the rosemary oil rising in pungent waves. She liked that and so she continued, chopping the rosemary into small pieces on her cutting board. When she was done she examined the little gray-green mound she had made and, moving rather like an abstract expressionist painter, eyes not altogether focused and limbs seeming to operate according to their own ambitions and intentions, she reached into the crate again and pulled out a bulb of fennel, a glass bottle of heavy cream, and a lemon.

She cut the lemon in half and rubbed it all over the bird. Then she poured salt onto her palm and followed the contours of the bird's flesh again. She held a pepper grinder over it and applied a third layer of flavor within and without. The dark flesh of the ptarmigan glistened. She stuffed it with bits of onion the size of cherries and rubbed the flesh with the chopped rosemary, sage, and olive oil. She pulled off a bulb from a braid of garlic and peeled cloves as big as her thumbs and pushed them inside with the onions. Finally she cut up an apple and laid the slices alongside the bird in a small roasting pan and placed it in the oven.

It was late by the time her kitchen began to smell of ptarmigan and apple and garlic. She poured herself a glass of marc and, a little after one o'clock in the morning, extracted the roasted bird from her oven. When the lid came off the pan, the scent intoxicated her. She stood like one of the airport grandmothers clutching a new grandchild, eyelids sagging and eyes fluttering. The wild rice was ready as well.

She set her table with a cloth and a plate and a knife and fork. She lifted the little bird onto her plate and laid the cooked apples alongside it. She ladled the drippings from the bird over it and the wild rice. She poured herself a larger glass of marc. She sat down to eat, pausing to wipe her eyes with every third or fourth bite.

The first thing they tell you is how sick someone is. If they are vital, pink, and smooth, their possessor is either well or only recently unwell. Chronic illness of any sort causes them to whiten steadily with the diminution of vitality: this is leukonychia, or simply, white nails. It always bodes ill.

But what they reveal may be more specific than that. Lung cancer, for instance, induces a gecko-oid swelling of the ends of the fingers. The nails heap up in compound curves, as if some better instinct within the body was seeking to escape the coming disorder, but got lodged in these, the terminus ends. Chronic hepatitis produces the same effect, as do holes in the heart that leave their possessors blue and breathless. This is called clubbing, and when it is caused by trouble, the trouble is serious. Confusingly, however, sometimes it just exists, without any reason except perhaps to temper young doctors' certainty.

When Victoria returned to Rankin Inlet, her file did not accompany her and did not get sent north for almost a year. I had no details about her medical treatment in the sanatorium. Clearly she had had a thoracoplasty— I knew that much from looking at her. And she had been gone long enough to have completed the year and a half of antibiotic therapy and was now only a little underweight. She didn't cough.

I was among the first to notice her friendship with the Hudson's Bay man. At the time there were a total of nine of us from elsewhere living in the town: me, the priest, the Mountie, the five Bay Boys, and her.

She lived in a kind of internal exile in the community. She could be seen most days in summer and winter walking alone along the edge of the bay, perfectly erect—the nuns, and their preoccupation with posture—loneliness rising off her like scent.

As a doctor one can keep out of trouble most of the time by being cautious. It is not necessary to make precise diagnoses with any great facility so long as one is able to recognize the presence and the severity of trouble. Rashes in people who feel well, for instance, will tolerate leisurely investigation and treatment; rashes in people with fevers are an entirely different story. So long as one is clear about these sorts of things, there will be no conversations with local licensing authorities.

Victoria used to spend a lot of time down by the bay, a distance from town. We could all see her. We all watched her. I was supposed to follow up on the returnees from the sanatorium, make sure that the treatment held. She came to my little office whenever I asked her to, and she was healthy, she said, but not with the relief I might have expected. She looked at the books on my shelves at length. She asked me if I had anything she could read. At the time I had only textbooks, but I wrote to a friend and asked for some novels.

When they arrived I went looking for her, and of course she was sitting on the beach. I watched her for a time to make certain she was alone and not waiting for anyone. Then I watched her watching me approach.

"I have something for you." And she looked up at me with disappointment.

"Catcher in the Rye. It's about growing up in the city. And A Passage to India and The Magic Mountain." I handed them to her. She hadn't seen these before. She was pleased then.

"Is there anything else?" she asked.

"No, that's all there was in the package," I said. "Maybe when you're done with these, if you want, I could get you more."

She seemed to be waiting for me to say something. I was embarrassed, of course. I couldn't think of anything else to say, and I walked away. From then on, whenever the forms from the TB people came, I wrote down "unremarkable recovery" and didn't bother her about them.

Short black streaks running parallel with the finger and lodged at the terminal ends of the fingernails are called splinter hemorrhages, appearing like mahogany slivers lodged under the nails. They look painful, though they are not, and indicate infection in the heart, especially on the valves. The communication between the center of the body and its extremities is striking: this is the idea of this book, after all—that the edges reveal the center. It is as true in anatomy as it is in geography.

Splinter hemorrhages occur when small aggregates of bacteria and fibrin break free of the infected heart valves and flow out into the arterial tree, lodging at the ends of the fingernails, where they streak out into lesions. Clumps appear also in the retinae, where they are called Roth's spots, and on the palms of the hands—Janeway's lesions. And on the finger pads—Osler's nodes. They enlarge the spleen and cause micro-infarctions in the kidneys, the brain, the bones. But the fingernails are almost as revelatory as the eye, a place where we may also observe the havoc that is otherwise concealed.

When the thyroid is deranged and running unchecked, the body's thermostat cranked too high, the nails peel away from the nail bed. This is called onycholysis: splitting of the nails. They lift up and yellow, and it is unappealing to look at, though in the mania of hyperthyroidism, the afflicted may be unconcerned or, alternatively, preoccupied by them.

When pits appear all over the nails, like divots out of a driving range, it can be the only sign of psoriasis, or the only sign except for active and erosive arthritis. When someone comes to you with a throbbing knee and you dwell upon scarcely visible irregularities in his fingernails, it takes some work to persuade him he is not in the presence of an idiot. But the information is useful, and reveals the nature of the arthritis. The edges, again, in their revelatory mode.

I began every examination I ever performed on Victoria by examining her fingers. There was always a long minute of silence as she watched me inspect the lunulae of her fingernails, the texture of the nail beds, the angles between the skin and the nails. I held her hands in mine and ignored her quizzical smile. I can assert with quite uncharacteristic certainty that she never displayed any evidence of endocarditis or recent cytotoxic chemotherapy. She will have suspected that I was only looking for an excuse to hold her hand for a moment, a few times a year. She was insightful that way. But she never did say a word.

Plumbism: think of plumb bobs plumbing the depths and lead pipe benders and cinches and metalsmiths sickening—the lines of lead deposit themselves in characteristic streaks called Meese's lines. Argyria is what the silversmiths get; here the lines and the skin itself become blue and, famously, the tip of the nose as well. Chemotherapy shatters the body systemically and systematically; it leaves its traces in parallel brown lines.

And here the beautiful art of physical diagnosis runs up on the shoals of artifice. So many lovely signs and tests and names to know: Castell's technique, the dripping puddle sign, pistol-shot femoral pulses, retro-ocular bruits, Kernig's sign, Leopold's maneuvers—almost all of them important only as arcana, only for the poetry in their names and the history of their evolution. Physicians without CT scanners find a pathology on autopsy and imagine they could have detected it early enough if only they had felt the liver's lower edge as the patient had exhaled as hard as he could. The alchemists had books of arcana as well, and these books, and all the names and complex theories, made them feel proficient too.

The Journal of the American Medical Association publishes a series of articles called "The Rational Clinical Exam." In them, the various techniques of physical examination are assessed objectively for the sensitivity and specificity of their findings. In almost every instance, whether it is the accuracy of auscultation compared to echocardiograms in sorting out heart murmurs, or the usefulness of feeling the abdomen in an attempt to discern an enlarged spleen, the imaging studies have revealed that these hallowed techniques are dishearteningly unreliable. It would be easy to become cynical about the physical examination, to conclude that the most useful thing for a doctor would be to commence every encounter with a series of scans and proceed from there. As compelling an argument as that might be in the abstract, no patient would want a doctor who behaved in such a fashion, and no doctor would want to be such a clinician. It is necessary to preserve certain rites. Necessary to persist in our faith.

There is information crowded and stuffed into every aspect of the world: arcana and pith, straight goods and counterfeit. When I have been defeated, it has usually been because I failed in the task of prioritizing it, of giving relative weight to contradictory sources of varying reliability. When I have made my worst mistakes, it has been here.

But it remains true that the best way for a doctor to begin a meeting with someone who is sick is to shake their hand and hold it and look them in the eye and feel the texture of the skin between his fingers. And as he studies the opacities in their corneas, feels the tiny xanthomas running along their tendon sheaths, they will settle, will feel less frightened. As will the doctor. When the fear subsides, the truth becomes twice as apparent.

chapter six

The church had been built across the street from the water reservoir, a giant tank that dwarfed any other structure in town. The church had the good fortune to lie in the wind shadow of the tank, which sheltered it from the prevailing westerlies. In winter it generally sat in a trough surrounded by snow piled high on both sides. Visiting priests, novitiates from America and France, claimed tiresomely that this was evidence of the Lord's favor upon this blessed building, but Père Bernard was never guilty of such magical thinking. He had built enough iglus on the tundra to understand the effect an obstacle had on airflow and snow deposition.

The day that Justine and Marie were to be confirmed, Winnie proudly led the family up the steps of the church. Bernard stood there in his robe to greet them, watching the sky. As the children removed their wind pants and parkas, he consulted Emo on the weather. The old priest's Inuktitut was unaccented, more sophisticated and illustrative than that of most of the young adults in town. Winnie said that anyone she knew who had attended high school through to completion spoke Inuktitut like a child, with crude and obvious sentences stacked upon one another without music or subtlety.

But old priests such as Bernard had studied the language and practiced it with one another and their congregations until they could not only recite the liturgy in this language but capture a soul with it too. That was the difference, in Winnie's view, between the way these old men thought and the way the new doctors and schoolteachers thought.

It seemed these newcomers had decided they shouldn't learn the language of this place, should never stay long enough actually to be recognized, to have an effect. They were more interested in the effect the place had on them—as if they really could be much affected by a place with a language they did not bother to learn.

Tagak joined his father and the old priest on the steps. He was married to a woman named Catharine, who, uniquely among the women of the town, liked Victoria. Tagak listened to the older men discuss the weather and did not offer his opinion, which wasn't sought in any case. Tagak was considered an unlucky and inexpert hunter. This was painful for Emo, but he had given up on trying to sharpen his son's skills and concentrated on bringing his family food himself.

When Catharine and their two daughters arrived on the church steps, Tagak turned away from the men and led his family wordlessly inside.

Bernard had built his church of stone he had pulled off the tundra over the course of three sore-shouldered years. He had recruited a small body of helpers, men he had found eccentric and difficult—but no one else ever showed up on the work site in the morning. He and his taciturn helpers had hauled stoneboats full of rocks to the church site and had lifted them up the scaffolding hand by gnarled hand, unassisted by cranes or winches. As the church neared completion, more and more helpers accrued to the team, each one odder than the last. Lifting stones became easier, but he'd had to settle more conflicts, calm more anxious outbursts. He came to suspect that half the men helping him would be under psychiatric care, and benefiting from it, had they lived in the south.

From his position on the steps, Bernard saw Simionie Irnuk approaching the church. He was one of the men who had helped build it. Simionie was not volatile or given to bizarre declarations, but he was as intense as any of the others, the priest thought. Simionie had profound reservations about southerners, refused to speak Kablunuktitut, and accepted the priest only as a necessary part of the project and because he spoke Inuktitut so well himself. Bernard had not seen him much in the years after the church had been finished. He had concluded that Simionie's faith was shaken, or that he was drinking, both conditions the priest had thought he had seen the seeds of in the time they had worked together. As Simionie came up the steps of the church on communion day, trailed by a straggle of the more devout or lonely of the parishioners, the priest nodded to him. Simionie nodded back. The group followed the priest inside and Simionie took his place in a pew a few rows behind Victoria and her family.

Victoria saw Simionie walk in the door as she was surreptitiously sucking on a Tic Tac. As her eyes widened, her throat did likewise and the breath mint lodged itself sideways in her larynx. She gasped and turned deep purple as she coughed, the veins in her forehead distending. She inhaled deeply but felt as if she got almost no air, and when she tried to speak she couldn't, uttering instead a whistling sound that originated somewhere between her trachea and her diaphragm. She thought her chest might just burst out of her shirt—but then unconsciousness supervened and she felt abruptly much better.

As her chest struck the pew on the way down, the breath mint flew out of her mouth, high into the air, its trajectory describing a perfect and quite beautiful arc into the priest's beard. He felt it lodge there, stuck to his chin hairs. As she lay on the church's stone floor, Victoria got her breath back and gave a huge gasp. Subtly struggling with each other for primacy of position, Robertson and her mother knelt to tend to her, the others crowding in at their backs. When Victoria's tunnel vision opened up and she could take in the cast of dozens hovering over her, she heard herself croak, "Jesus, Mary, and Joseph."

■

Every Saturday that winter, Penny Bleskie and Emo went out on the land with their dogs. For the first three months he led and after that she did, winding out along the Meliadine River and into the barrenlands. She carried a map, she told everyone, but the truth was that she refused to unfold it, preferring to stop and consult with Emo as often as was necessary to memorize the layout of the country. Penny was from Alberta, and her idea of orienting oneself on the land rested on the idea of dim purple mountains hanging low and always to the west, an obvious and reliable landmark. When she became disoriented on the tundra, which was frequent, she quickly had no idea at all of where she was and which way was north. She had only to lose sight of the sun, or of the river valley or ridgeline they were following, for an instant to become hopelessly lost. The old man helped then, pointing the way without hesitation. Slowly, over the course of these many weeks, she went from having to ask him where they were every thirty minutes to going hours between consultations.

This morning she had risen at five and was out on the sea ice with the dogs at six, brushing and feeding them. The only other movement she noticed was Pauloosie's snow machine, twinkling its way north, out of town. The small number of those who spent a lot of time on the land could recognize one another's snow machines and komatiks from a distance. Though they went out partly to escape other humans, it was reassuring to spot a friend in the distance. Another person was so rare out on the land, you studied them carefully and soon knew the particular cadence of a dog team's trot, the pitch of a rattling exhaust manifold, the faded yellow hue of a snow machine engine cover.

She chained her team with the hunters' dogs, on the ice in the little bay abutting the town. The dogs were considered dangerous, not pets at all, and better kept away from the children. Serious maulings were common and in one or another of the nearby towns, most winters, a child was eaten after having strayed too close to the animals. There was a lingering sense that dogs were a part of life in the north, and that living so closely with them was both normal and perilous. They were no longer a necessity, but they remained essential to the way the people thought of themselves. And so the dogs were still tolerated. The day was coming when the only dogs that would be allowed in Rankin Inlet would be pets—castrated standard poodles and slobbering Saint Bernards that leapt playfully upon couches and laughing six-year-olds. In the meantime, the menacing creatures were pushed steadily farther out to sea. The other advantage of chaining teams on the sea ice was that in the spring the tide washed away the winter's accumulation of dog shit in one lunar heave.

The old man had been an effective instructor. Penny had learned how to kick apart a dog fight and untangle the intertwined traces of writhing and snapping animals. This frightened her the first time she tried it, but when she saw the glint in the old man's eyes, she never hesitated again.

Within six weeks she had grown bored with making endless loops around town and out to the floe edge and back. She pressured Emo to take her deeper into the tundra. He agreed without comment and on a Saturday two weeks later she found herself following him down the Meliadine River, her dogs panting with pleasure as they padded their way over the snow. In the midafternoon he stopped and let her catch up with him. He told her that if they wanted to get back to town before sunset they would have to turn around then. She told him she had no problem with staying out overnight. She had a sleeping bag on her sled.

He nodded and lifted up his snow brake, his dogs surging forward at the same instant.

When the sun began laying itself out along the southwestern horizon, Emo pulled to a stop and a few moments later Penny caught up with him. They hadn't stopped running all day long and she was euphoric. Her dogs were happy and exhausted, and even Emo's dogs looked relieved to stop—the first time she had seen that. Emo pulled out his panna and began probing the snow. He found a drift he liked and without saying anything at all began cutting out snow blocks. He stood within the circle he assembled and spiraled it up slowly over the course of the next hour. It was growing dark quickly now. Penny untied the dogs from the sleds and stood the sleds on edge, then brought the kit bags from the sleds toward the iglu-in-formation. Emo did not look at her. She watched him as he worked in the dying light, finally reaching over his head and laying in place the top block of the iglu, sealing himself inside.

His panna began sawing out an arch at the base of the iglu and his foot followed a moment later, kicking the snow out of the entranceway. Penny passed him their gear and then crawled in after it.

After that first overnight, they met every Saturday morning and traveled as far as they could in a chosen direction before sunset. The following day they made their way back to town. They always made slower time coming home, partly because the dogs weren't as fresh, but mostly because neither of them wanted to.

Pauloosie stopped his snow machine four hundred yards downwind of the tuktu, thirty of them chewing away at exposed lichen jutting out of the snow and hardly responding to the racket of the two-stroke engine or the reflection off the plastic windshield and hood. The sun was bright, doubled again by the glare off the snow. He wore leather pilot's goggles beneath a wool-lined scalp-hugging cap, and he slipped the goggles up on his forehead as he swung his leg off the machine, keeping it between him and the tuktu, crouching now to retrieve the rifle wrapped in a blanket and oilskin in the komatik he dragged behind the snowmobile. He untied the frozen cord around the oilskin, taking off his mitts to pull the knot apart with his fingers. The knot yielded to him just as he lost the ability to move his fingers in the cold. He slipped his hands back into his mitts and breathed quietly as the ache of their revival ran through him. Around his eyes were discs of white skin. Naked, he looked as if his face, neck, and hands had been dipped in teak oil, with slices of cucumber, perhaps, over his eyes, where his sun goggles sat.

Watching the deer, Pauloosie drew back the bolt of his rifle and then pushed it forward, rotated and locked it. The rifle round was seated in the chamber. He fell to his knees in the slow motion of a movie action hero and then onto his elbows. He crawled forward and up the slope of the ridge the deer stood upon.

The tundra is as much rock as it is snow, and any doubt on this point is dispelled by an attempt to crawl on it. When it is studied close up, it resembles a gravel parking lot with inadequately crushed stone, punctuated by eskers: great stony ridges that appear, wind sinuously across a couple or a couple hundred miles, and then disappear. Over this is laid the thinnest of layers of snow, spread clumsily. Where the tuktu have been pawing, there are exposed grasses and moss, dried and frozen and as nutritious-looking as a mouthful of sawdust. The deer must range so widely to find even the smallest amounts of forage that their wide cloven-hoof marks are found anywhere there is wind-pressed snow.

Winter for the tuktu is an exercise in deficit spending: they cannot hope to consume as many calories from the frozen mosses as they expend staying warm and running from the wolves. They earn their living in a three-month sprint of frenetic activity bracketed by clock watching. In the summer, the tundra is a green and voluptuous feast. In hollows, the grasses rise to midankle and the tuktu proceed through it like mowers lined abreast. The sun shines most of the day and the rest of the time there is twilight. By August, their bellies bulge and their necks appear like swollen wineskins appended to their trunks.

Which is the miracle of these animals—that they stand out here in wind and cold so complete, it freezes exposed skin instantaneously, yet so long as they have had enough to eat, they do not freeze, do not simply succumb, but paw on without cease, scraping their teeth against the rocks to break free flakes of lichen, stalks of grass, bits of shrub.

Between this thin soup and the fat they wear around their bellies, they endure the winters and a whole chain of existence is constructed upon that improbability. The wolves follow them, and feast on the calves and the animals gut-shot by inexpert hunters. Behind the wolves come the foxes, which scavenge the cracked bones, the shards of sinew and hide left by the wolves. Behind the foxes come the ravens, studies in endurance equal to the deer themselves, the only large bird present year-round in the Arctic, and which quixotically retains its black coloration in an otherwise monotonously white landscape. The ravens fly above the herds of deer, looking for spots of motionlessness within the sea of movement—an aborted calf, a senescent bull finally given in.

The tuktu, the last of the large herding land mammals in North America, exist in enormous herds that disperse and regroup, to calve and to mate and move from summer forage to winter: a hundred thousand animals each and growing steadily for the last forty years, as man has retreated to the edge of the tundra and the climate has warmed. The sparsest the caribou ever were was in the last years of man's presence on the tundra. There was famine then, which was part of what propelled the hunters into the hamlets. Just as that movement of people reached the point of no return, the caribou reappeared and have multiplied steadily faster ever since. Every extra frost-free day increases calf survival measurably and the herds are now astonishing things: masses of vitality in a landscape of icy stone.

What the tundra feels like, as it grinds itself across one's belly, is cold and pointed. Pauloosie pulled his rifle along with him exactly as his grandfather had taught him, with sights turned into and protected by his arm, the stock lying within the crook of his elbow. He watched the deer constantly as he crawled, and at the first shiver or suggestion of anxiety, he froze.

When he was in range he stopped. He pulled the rifle up to his face and raised it to his cheek, his elbows in grooves between the rocks. As he breathed, the rifle slowly rose up and settled on his shoulder and he watched the fattest buck walk closer to him. And. Finally. Pause. He tried to calm himself. *Pow*.

He missed. The bullet hit a rock and whined into the air. The caribou shuddered collectively and then stared intently away from the boy, off in the direction the bullet had headed. As they did so, they edged closer to him, looking backwards as they advanced. *Pow*. He missed again. The caribou stutter-stepped as Pauloosie yanked back the bolt of his rifle and slammed another round in the chamber, then dropped his head to the sights and aimed generally at a fat doe that was standing broadside to him, looking in every direction. Panting, he missed again. Abruptly acquiring some sense, the tuktu erupted in a mad dash down the hill at a right angle away from where Pauloosie lay, and he got up on his knees and fired again with the reasoning of a losing card player— luck like this couldn't just go on. He missed again. He jammed the last round into his rifle and, casually, almost as an afterthought, fired at the tuktu, running now as if they were airborne, legs stretching ahead and behind them nearly the lengths of their own bodies, little kicks of snow flying up in arcs as high as their heads. One of them fell. And then bounced back up and flew off with the others.

A part of the boy wanted to believe the doe had simply slipped on the snow and had recovered her feet as quickly as she had fallen, then jumped up and rejoined the rest of the sprinting herd and disappeared over a ridgeline as he stood there, kicking at the nearest stone for his stupidity at taking that last careless shot. But he walked back to his snow machine and started it, and set off on their trail.

At the top of the esker, Pauloosie stopped. The caribou were half a mile away now, and still running, none of them trailing. He turned his machine around to pick his way down the slope he had ascended. Then he ran the length of the esker to the valley the deer were in. When he was on the plain where he had last seen the caribou, all there was were tracks that led to another ridge a mile away. He followed them.

Three hours later it occurred to him that it was growing dark and that he had become so preoccupied with the task of finding the caribou he had shot that he was not entirely certain where he was, except vaguely west of town and north of the Meliadine River—maybe fifty miles out. But it was four in the afternoon and the sun was setting.

He stopped his snowmobile. He opened his pack and withdrew his steel panna, and walked in enlarging circles around the snow machine, probing the snow periodically. When he found snow that was packed yet penetrable he stopped and cut a small block from it. It would do, he thought. He had watched his grandfather do this many times, but he had never done it by himself. He began by summoning up a memory of the old man assembling blocks and placing them around himself, cutting the blocks to fit in an ascending spiral. The sun was already dipping toward the horizon when he realized that his iglu was taking the shape of an upside-down ice cream cone. He tried to lean his panels of packed snow in more aggressively as he rose, but nothing like a sphere emerged. By the time his walls began to meet one another, he was reaching as high as he could. He hunched down within the dark space, felt the wall in front of him, and found a joint. He carved out a crawl hole just large enough to admit his shoulders and emerged into the dusk. He collected his pack from the komatik and pulled it inside the iglu. There was not enough room to spread out the sleeping bag and so he sat in it, his head hunched over his knees. He had been very frightened but felt better now.

That Friday night Penny hadn't telephoned the old man to discuss the weather and to arrange a time to meet in the morning. After her supper of rice and smoked fish she had crawled into bed at eight and fallen asleep. She walked to her dogs in the purple and frigid darkness the next morning and when the dogs smelled her approaching they began yipping to one another, the neighboring teams replying with their own agitated cries. Soon the whole bay was echoing with high-pitched cries of dogs flinging themselves skyward against their chains in air so cold it seemed to fracture a little with each strangled cry.

She rounded the hills above the bay quickly, running alongside the dogs, their paws squeaking on snow so light and dry, the komatik seemed to float rather than ride on it. They ran easily in the darkness, so comfortable in the cold that they would not have wished it even ten degrees warmer, feeling able to run forever at this pace if they could so choose, or if this woman running beside them would for once decide not to turn back, carry on instead toward the horizon and whatever lay past it, never again returning to the long heavy chain frozen into ice on either end and surrounded by a baffling array of odors and antagonistic and ill-mannered dogs.

Two hours later Penny was still running and wondering to herself if it was dangerous to feel so light. The dogs' exuberance had swept through the air, through the rind of white and frozen hoarfrost clinging to her parka hood, and into her lungs and bloodstream. She reminded herself to watch the time to ensure she turned back early enough in the day. The dogs yearned for just the opposite, and a struggle occurred as they ran, the dogs willing her to shut her careful mind off, to lift her feet higher and stride with them longer and faster toward the distant-most ridge and the one past that. The sky was now lightening in the southeast and it was possible to make out such landmarks as there were with little effort. Penny was struck by how much easier this was when she was alone with her intrusive and impudent dogs and their incautious urgings, and not relying on Emo's expertise. She kept a running fix of her position in some part of her brain—it felt like it was just behind her left ear—and she never wondered for a moment where she was.

And then she rose over a ridge and she saw a snowmobile glinting on the horizon. As she approached, she recognized the old man's parka.

His machine was twenty years older than any other in the hamlet and she had never seen him use it. She was worried that he had come looking for her, and she prepared to apologize. She had just kicked out her snow brake when he asked her if she had seen anyone else on the land, any tracks at all. She said no, and he told her his grandson, Pauloosie, the boy from Johanna's math class, had not come home from hunting the night before.

Penny's dogs noticed the protuberance on the horizon before she did. She simply steered them in the direction they were determined to go in any event. She could see the snowmobile with its hood opened, engine exposed. There was an El Greco version of an iglu beside it, conical rather than spherical, ludicrously tall and narrow.

Penny poked her head inside the iglu. In the dim light she saw a figure curled up motionless against the wall of the iglu. She reached out to touch it—and Pauloosie stirred and rolled over. "Good afternoon," she said. "Everything okay?"

"My machine won't start."

"I could give you a ride."

"That would be great."

She backed out of the odd little iglu and he followed her. They stood up together. He was taller than she, and was smiling more than she had ever seen him do at school.

"Your grandfather is worried."

"I know."

"He's out looking for you."

"I thought it would be him that found me."

"I've never been on the land by myself before."

"Me either, much."

"At least you know how to build an iglu."

"If you call that an iglu."

"It kept you warm."

"It didn't keep me that warm."

"It must have been a long night."

"I didn't sleep much until it got warmer this morning."

"Probably a good idea."

"It wasn't really a decision. I wasn't very comfortable."

"I would have been scared out of my mind."

"I was pretty sure my attatatiak was coming to get me."

Pauloosie sat down on the sled and Penny called to the lead to get going. "Hee, hee, hee," she called, turning them to the left and back to town.

"You know what?" Pauloosie called to her.

She kicked out the snow brake and stopped the dogs so she could hear him better.

"What?"

"Actually, we say more, 'Hey, hey, hey.' "

"Thanks for the tip."

"I just thought you'd like to know."

"Your iglu back there, it looked pretty comfy."

"I was making plans for it."

She smiled back at him and grunted at the dogs, who took off with a lurch.

They met Emo at the lake three miles west of town. He had seen two forms running alongside the sled, and so by the time they met his relief had already given way to an impassive, barely detectable anger.

"Hello, Emo," Penny said.

"Hello," the old man replied, not looking at her but rather at his grandson, who looked only at his feet.

"His machine broke down. Could have happened to anyone."

"Jump on, boy." Emo indicated his snow machine with a nod of his head, not prepared to debate the boy's actions with a Kablunauk woman, even—especially—this one.

"Thank you, Miss Bleskie," Pauloosie said, and sat down on the snow machine.

Emo pulled the starting cord. It coughed but did not start. He looked up at Penny, the winter's intimacy that had grown between them scattering like ground drift. He pulled again. It caught. He nodded to her. The boy nodded to her. She nodded back. They roared away.

chapter eight

Dr. Balthazar stomped his way up the stairs leading to Robertson and Victoria's kitchen door. Even sitting in her living room, Victoria knew who was coming by the shaking of the floor. When she went to let him in, she found Justine there ahead of her, swinging the door open. Frozen air swept knee-high through the house.

"Victoria, good to see you," Balthazar said. "I hope I'm not too early."

"You're fine, Keith."

"Your house is looking nice," he called to her as she ducked into the pantry to gather enough potatoes from their burlap sack.

"We've been cleaning it all day," Justine interjected.

"It looks like it." Balthazar gave Justine one of his big loopy grins, which endeared him to his youngest patients despite the doubts of their elders.

"Is Robertson home?" Balthazar asked.

"Dad'll be here in a few minutes," Justine said, and slipped down the hall to her room. Victoria began peeling the potatoes. She opened the oven to check on the roast and closed it again. The scent of cooking meat filled the air.

"How is Pauloosie doing?"

"Still a little rattled, I think, not that he'd admit it. My father was in worse shape."

"Having a child lost on the land must be the most terrifying experience."

"Well, every son pretty much does that eventually, I think. I wonder if we didn't overreact a little. Pauloosie says he wasn't ever lost, just that the snow machine broke down and it was late in the day. He built an iglu and was fine all night."

"Well, he has a point then."

"Still. I was pretty worked up."

"What about the girls?"

"Justine just kept saying, 'I don't know what you're so excited about. He's on the land. He knows what to do.' "

"It's natural to be worried."

"The children and me, we're Inuit, is the thing. Being on the land shouldn't be the most frightening thing in the world for us."

"The boy is seventeen, Victoria."

"My grandfather was fifteen when he was married."

"That was a different time."

"Maybe it shouldn't be that different."

"Pauloosie would agree with you."

"Yes."

"What do the girls see themselves doing, do you think?"

"Justine wishes she were Pat Benatar. Marie wishes she were Justine. Who knows?"

"That's pretty cute."

"It isn't in the morning." And she hummed a snatch of "Love Is a Battlefield." "Hey, how is your family?"

"Everyone is okay. My mom is retired in Arizona now, and my brother and his family have moved to Newark. It's nice having him nearby—I'm close to my niece, Amanda. I've mentioned her before—she's just a little older than Justine."

"And what about your book? How is that going?"

Balthazar winced. No one else in the hamlet except the priest would have asked him. He kept a journal in which he wrote about his days there—mostly about the medicine. His habit was discussed in the community more than it would otherwise have been only because he refused to comment. Given his reputation, the prevailing question was: What could he have to say?

This was not exactly Victoria's point of view, but she knew she enjoyed a certain license with him that others didn't, and she couldn't resist teasing him. He almost liked it but still sidestepped the question.

"Have you painted in here since I last visited?"

She grinned. "No."

The door opened and Robertson came in, unzipping his nylon jacket. He was known in the town for his habit of wearing a light nylon coat even in fierce winds. He had confided to Victoria that heavy coats made him feel claustrophobic, but she had long suspected that he liked being known both as a man who could stand the cold and as a man who didn't have to. It was like the architect walking through a job site wearing a tie. It was also just about the most predictable of conversation topics and so was seized upon by Balthazar.

"Heavens, Robertson, I don't know how you don't just freeze solid in that jacket in this weather."

Robertson looked at him as he unlaced his boots. "Good to see you, Keith. Long time."

"Yes. Almost a year, I think."

He stood and held his hand out. Balthazar shook it.

"Kids! Dinner!" Victoria hollered.

"Hi, Marie," Balthazar said as the girls came in.

"Hi," she answered dutifully.

Pauloosie followed, a measurable beat later.

"Hi," Balthazar ventured.

" 'Lo," the boy answered, and slunk to a chair at the kitchen table. The children knew Balthazar well enough to not be interested in charming him.

Justine said grace. Victoria passed the roast to Robertson, who carved it as the girls dished themselves potatoes and mixed vegetables. Robertson pushed the serving platter into the center of the table. Each of the children drew it in turns closer to them and picked out a few slices. Robertson tsked at their manners but held his tongue.

"How are things at the clinic, Keith?"

"Oh, they're fine. Every year seems busier, of course. But the nurses are great."

"I think the funding for a hospital might finally be coming through."

"I don't even know whether to hope it's true. Twenty million to build, they say, and staffing would be another issue."

"Well, some things are happening."

Balthazar detected a note of insistence he had not heard in Robertson on this topic before. He looked up from his plate. "What have you heard?"

"I heard they might be prepared to let a contract in the next six months."

"How long would it take to build?"

"That's more a question of capital financing than anything else. The government has agreed to provide operating funds, but they say they aren't able to put the thing up, which is convenient. Still, it could be built in a summer if the money was all in place."

"Is there any reason to think that the money might be in place?"

"Yes."

"Why?"

"I can't say." Not-quite-silent chewing filled the pause. Robertson regretted having said as much as he had. Balthazar was alarmed by Robertson's certainty.

Robertson tried to move the conversation to medical matters, not money. "So how many beds would you say the hospital should have?"

Balthazar chewed slowly and swallowed. He looked at Victoria. "The thing is, truthfully, I don't think a hospital will make much difference here. I know everyone thinks it will, but we'd still have to fly people out for surgery and CT scans and things like that. There are a small number of things we would be able to treat: some of the bronchiolitis and croup, maybe, and pneumonia. But staffing the hospital will be a huge problem: we can't get enough nurses to work here now. How will we get twice as many?"

Robertson sawed at his meat as he listened to this. "Why do people in small towns in the south have their own hospitals and we don't? They aren't looking at a five-hundred-mile trip to the next nearest hospital either."

"I know."

"It's so hard to do anything new up here."

"If you say so."

"Who is threatened by a hospital, for crying out loud? I can sort of understand why people reflexively oppose every mine and resource development, but a hospital?"

"Hospitals paralyze health care. They suck up all the money in a flash and seem to be a solution to everything, but mostly they aren't."

"Keith, listen to me." As Robertson grew impassioned, his Northumbrian accent grew steadily more prominent. "You might be a little more influential on this subject than you realize. What you say might be listened to. So, you can't really allow yourself the luxury of your usual timidity."

Balthazar colored. "Well, that's one way of looking at it."

"So," Victoria interjected, "who would like more potatoes?"

"I would," Pauloosie said. He looked at the doctor. "Would you say that the hospital will require more Kablunauks to live up here?"

"Yes."

"How many?"

"The hospital in Churchill employs a hundred people, from janitors to doctors."

"A hundred jobs," Robertson said, "rather than assistance checks."

"So those people would come here and need houses."

"Yes."

"Where are those houses going to come from?"

"The hospital would have to make some arrangements as part of its recruiting strategy," Robertson said.

"Why don't they just build the hundred houses now? There's people that need them."

"It's complicated," Balthazar answered, eyes on his plate.

"It isn't that complicated," Robertson said, looking at his son. "The houses are needed. The hospital is needed. The money to pay for them is needed."

"I think it's time for dessert," Victoria announced.

■

chapter nine

A couple of weeks later, Balthazar stumbled out of his cab in front of his apartment building in Yonkers. He had dressed that morning in Rankin Inlet and had disrobed incrementally in airplane and airport washrooms as his latitude had dropped. Now he carried a sweater under his arm, a pair of rolled-up wool socks in his trouser pockets, and a light jacket over his shoulder. The long underwear had been deposited in a paper towel receptacle in Winnipeg. As he got out of the cab, his shirt was pulled away from his neck and displayed great perspiration stains under his arms.

It was summer in the city and raining in a hot, steady drizzle. The water hitting the pavement around him steamed as it fell and carried the street dust out of the alleys in an orange slurry of cigarette butts and plastic soda bottle caps. The air, however, was washed clean; in this heat it would otherwise have smelled like a charnel house.

Balthazar's fur-lined parka, poking out from his canvas pack, caught the cabbie's eye, and the scent of the untanned sealskin kamiks deep within his luggage caught his nose as they unloaded the cab. Balthazar paid the fare, gave a twenty-dollar tip, and pulled his trunks to the doorway and out of the rain. The doorman emerged from his office apologetically. His name was Samuel Tillman and he was accustomed to Balthazar and his travels. He hauled the trunk out of the lobby and into the elevator. As they rode up, he inspected Balthazar's gear silently. "How cold is it up there right now?" he asked, a bit of a ritual with them.

"Fifteen below."

"Heavens."

"It isn't so bad. It's getting warmer every day."

"The AC in my apartment is out and I haven't slept in three days. I wasn't thinking that there was anything bad at all about the idea of fifteen below."

"It's easier to stay warm there than it is to stay cool here."

"I believe it."

Then they were at his floor. They made their way to his apartment door, swaying and banging and staggering with the weight.

"Did you ever think about getting one of those dolly things?" Balthazar asked.

"And render myself immediately dispensable?"

Balthazar dug his keys—unused for three months—out of his pocket. When the door was open he gave Tillman twenty dollars and then they lifted the trunk onto the throw rug in the front entrance. Tillman backed out, Balthazar pulled the throw rug/steamer trunk aggregate far enough away from the door to shut it, and then he dropped everything he was carrying in a great mound.

He looked around his apartment. Apparently he had been in a hurry the day he had left. Apparently he had had a convulsion of some sort while holding most of the undergarments he owned in his arms. An unstable slope of letters and magazines had fallen through the mail slot. There were spiderwebs on every window sash and the hollow chitinous bodies of dead roaches scattered across the hardwood floors. He leaned over the mound of mail—veins of home furnishing magazines and medical journals running within a substrate of Audi pamphlets. Here and there were personal letters, which he picked out. The occasional bill— he had paid most of these in advance, but whenever he went up north he usually forgot something. He scanned for final-notice stamps.

As he walked toward his washroom he shed clothing. He ran the taps long enough to rinse out the carpet of dust that had grown in the tub. Then he ran the cold water until the tub was almost full and climbed in, nearly flooding his washroom in the process. For the first time since he had left Rankin Inlet he felt as if he could fully exhale.

After he bathed he walked dripping into his bedroom and extracted clean clothing from his dresser, the nonflannel textures feeling strangely supple against his skin, a cotton shirt and linen trousers sitting on him lightly. He stepped into a pair of leather shoes that had once been shined and, grabbing a handful of the more interesting-looking mail, walked into the night. It was almost midnight now, the city still accelerating.

At the Burger King down the street from his apartment—the empty cardboard boxes from a Whopper with cheese and onion rings in front of him—he leaned back and looked out the window at the night. There were no stars visible, no aurora borealis, only a dark absence hanging above him and the other ten million people around him on every side.

His brother, an English teacher in Newark, had written, inviting him to visit his niece. He seemed to be under the impression that a) his mail was being forwarded to the Arctic and b) there were no telephones up there. Balthazar had no idea how such a distance had crept in between them. He would have to speak to his mother about that, see if she understood. But he'd actually forgotten to tell her that he was going north this last time, and there was a succession of postcards from her retirement community in Arizona, chiding him for not returning her calls. His father lived in Seattle and had not written, as he had not in several years now. His mother asked Balthazar in one of her cards if he had any news from him. They were in trouble, Balthazar thought, if he had become the glue that held them together.

Simionie picked the kettle off the stove and poured the boiling water into a billy, the aluminum cylinder stained black from years of wood smoke and orange pekoe residue. Tea brewed in it was flavored like smoke. He stirred it with his knife as it steeped, staring at the tea bags swirling together in the water. Victoria watched him and the cloud of steam rising out of the billy in the frozen air and lighting up in the thin light poking obliquely through the window.

They spoke in Inuktitut, the soft, palatal consonants of that language lapping against the walls of the cabin. Simionie was telling her a story about his grandmother, who had disappeared off the boat. "She was walking with her first husband on the land south of Repulse Bay in 1945 and he slipped on a stone and broke his ankle.

"She carried him on her back, twenty feet at a time for two days and then she couldn't lift him anymore. He kept trying to get up and walk but his foot became more and more mangled and then it turned black. She stayed with him until he died and then she walked to the coast and found her uncle's fishing camp. She said she never felt right after that."

Victoria nodded and he poured the tea into their mugs. He added evaporated milk and some fly-specked sugar. He handed her a mug and sat down beside her on the bench beneath the window.

She said, "My grandfather used to help Dr. Moody in Chesterfield Inlet. One time a boy walked into town to get Moody, and he rode back on my grandfather's dogsled, showed them the iglu where his mother was having a baby. The baby was breech, and stuck. I guess they finally got the baby out, but the woman's uterus was so worn out by that point it couldn't contract anymore and she just kept on bleeding until she died. My grandfather slept with the baby on his chest that night, and carried him back to the town. He offered to raise him, but there were relatives who wanted the baby. He's in Chesterfield Inlet now, Ok-patayauk Iqapsiak—did you ever hear of him?"

"He moved here just a few weeks ago. Now he's living with Elizabeth Angutetuar."

"Really?"

"Yeah."

"Our parents must think we are children. The easy lives we live now."

"No."

"What, then?"

"Lucky." Simionie swirled his mug, watching the slurry of sugar and tea.

"They'd be wrong."

"Would they?"

"They're the lucky ones. Comfortable now, but not dependent on that comfort."

"There's only one generation that can be like that, though."

"Yes."

"Do you want more tea?"

"Yes, please."

The little cabin was now steamed up so thickly that the light was diffused as if through sea water. Simionie lit a cigarette to accentuate the effect. They both laughed. Then Victoria asked him to put it out because it would leave a smell. He did and they stopped laughing.

Robertson lifted Marie off the chesterfield, where she had fallen asleep watching *Hockey Night in Canada*. The Montreal Canadiens had beaten Pittsburgh and all was right with the world. She had begun breathing heavily in the third period. Victoria and Justine had long since gone to bed and Pauloosie was out on the land with his grandfather, learning how to build an iglu properly. Robertson was touched by his daughter's attempt to keep him company, and after he had turned off the television he watched her breathe for many minutes. As he leaned over her to kiss her, he paused to smell her breath, sweet and cool. Why did children's breath never take on the scent of what they've eaten, he wondered. He glanced at the half-full bag of ketchup-flavored potato chips on the coffee table beside them.

He carried her down the hall, past his and Victoria's room, past Pauloosie's malodorous den (they must speak to him about whatever he was keeping or curing in there), and opened her door with his sock foot. Justine was revealed in her bed, lying with her face turned to the wall and breathing lightly. He laid Marie down and pulled the covers up to her chin. She turned onto her side and coughed lightly. He touched her cheek. There was something wet on his finger. Even in the dark he could tell it was blood.

chapter ten

Robertson hated what he had been called here to do, and he hated the place where he had to do it. Layers and layers of gray Toronto skyline stretched out from the meeting room windows, devoid of any contour or texture except asphalt, yellow haze, and carefully aligned rows of nursery-planted and regularly replaced trees. He had flown through here in 1967 when he had immigrated, and had spent a week staying in a boardinghouse on Bathurst Street. In each of the interviews he had had with immigration officials, he was advised to stay on in the city—it was where the future lay, the jobs, the careers. Robertson had looked at these men and wondered how they could be so daft about their own country. Toronto reminded him of nothing so much as the postwar cities of northern England: stolid and sad and restrained, bars emptying at eleven with relief. He couldn't wait to get out of there.

It was a different place now, more different each time he returned. In the 1970s, the place had exploded with immigration. There was more color and far less melancholy in the city, and the scent of rotis and curries and jerked goat hung in the air.

As he had ridden in the taxi from the airport, Robertson found himself resisting his own reappraisal of the place and realized that he had become, in an important way, old. As if his interaction with his son hadn't already made that point. But more pressing to him was his concern about Marie. She had been his favorite for years. In her diffidence and solitary habits he recognized himself as a boy, and he saw for her a future that would take her far from her home, just as he had been propelled from his. He hoped it wasn't evident to Pauloosie and Justine how he felt about their little sister, but at the same time he knew that it probably was. The matter of favorites in families is complicated. In this instance, as usual, the favorite was the one who needed it the most. Pauloosie had been asserting his self-sufficiency since before he was born and Justine bore down on her own life like a train on a track.

On the walk from his hotel that morning he had thought about how elusive Pauloosie had become. When the boy was still young, Robertson had hoped that his son would continue to draw him into his wife's culture, and he would draw his son into his own. Instead, especially since the stillbirth, the two became steadily more mysterious to each other. Just as Robertson's own father had become to him, until Robertson had ebbed out of his birth family like the tide, impassive in the face of any special effort by his old man at Christmas or when he had come home from the pub especially drunk and affectionate.

Resentment is inherited as reliably as an accent. And Robertson's decision to leave the country entirely had been informed by this insight. And if he lost his doltish-sounding Midlands accent in the process, then so much the better. Pauloosie's speech had been formed only in the Arctic and knew nothing of northern England except for his rare habit of ending declaratory sentences with "what?" But the resentment had come through the line as immutably as his blood type.

On arriving in the financiers' offices, Robertson had been greeted by a South African geologist and an engineer—he had met these two in Yellowknife a month earlier and it was they who had asked him to come to Toronto. Their names were Van Rensburg and De Kock, and they were both in their early thirties and looked uncomfortable in their suits and new shoes. As they shook hands with him, he was reassured by their calloused hands. They showed him into a small office, where they settled him in and offered coffee. As he stirred sugar into his cup, the two of them looked at each other anxiously. "So perhaps we should start with you two telling me what you want me to do here," he said.

Van Rensburg was the designated spokesman. "Mr. Robertson, what we need from you is to allay the concerns of our backers about the local political climate. Especially as it concerns large-scale mining developments."

"How do you propose I do that?"

"They're worried about the land claims negotiations, and whether the Inuit advocacy groups might simply oppose any development in order to reserve the land for traditional use."

"Well, they might."

"Yes. Our question to you, then, is what can be done to persuade them otherwise?"

"Doing anything could stir up sentiment against the idea." He sipped his coffee. "You're foreign and talk funny."

De Kock shrugged, as if to suggest there was little he could do about that. "So whatever is to be done would have to be thought out well," Van Rensburg ventured, leaning forward in his chair.

"Yes . . ."

De Kock spoke: "I wonder if we could ask you to tell our compatriots that you will come up with an approach you could recommend to us. Them."

"I'm here to make it look like you've anticipated all the possibilities."

They answered together, "Yes."

Robertson nodded.

"If the mine goes ahead it could be very rewarding for your group. For you," De Kock said.

"I have some ideas about what you might do."

"Excellent." All three men looked at one another.

"Let's join the others," Van Rensburg said.

The two men showed him to an empty meeting room. Through the window, the largely residential parts of Toronto stretched out to the north in all their green and leafy expanse. He saw a cyclist making her way down Yonge Street. To the east he could just glimpse Lake Ontario, which, in its domesticated ease, couldn't have looked less like Hudson Bay if it had been filled with lime-flavored gelatin.

The financiers filed in, followed by another knot of engineers and geologists. They all sat down, and Van Rensburg introduced Robertson to the group. He smiled at each of the men in turn and watched them assessing him, taking in his cheap suit and wondering what to make of it, given who he was, where he was from. De Kock began the presentation. There was a flip chart and slides of the tundra, graphs of diamond prices, summaries of cost estimates from Siberian diamond mines.

The proposed site was located a hundred kilometers northwest of Rankin Inlet. The land there had been sparsely populated even by the standards of the Inuit prior to contact, then when the settlements were built it had been essentially cleared of humanity. The Back River dominated this landscape and ran heavily with char in the spring and, four weeks later, the autumn; but the forage was sparse and the tuktu smaller and less numerous than in other areas of the tundra. The Netsilkmiut, who had once lived along the banks of the Back River, had been drawn first to the sea and were now folded into the richer and more populous places around them. The people who had dwelt in the area of the mine had been dispersed among several different communities—Repulse Bay, Baker Lake, Rankin Inlet. There had been work done by anthropologists on these people, but what mattered to the miners was that they were hard to identify, and did not speak with one voice. Robertson revised his estimation of Van Rensburg's thoroughness: these people were not amateurs. The geologist sat down.

One of the financiers rearranged his papers. His name was Stumpf. He was thick and plethoric, and at ease in expensive clothes. Robertson detected in him an enthusiasm for the project alongside a certain impatience for the city, for the backwater he had had to travel to in order to discuss the proposal. As he looked at the notes he had just taken, his florid cheeks seemed to pulse slowly, and then he looked out the window, not meeting anyone's eyes. "Mr. Robertson, I would like to thank you on behalf of our organization for attending this meeting. As I think you understand, we are all extremely excited about the potential for a high-yield diamond mine near Back River. The engineering and techno-logic obstacles seem surmountable. What we need to learn from you is the nature of the local politics. Will your townspeople oppose such a de-velopment? What would win their favor? How ought we to proceed?" The older man sitting across the table from Robertson leaned back and clasped his hands together behind his head, looking at Robertson. Robertson decided to speak directly to him, clearly the real power in the room.

"My townspeople need jobs, Mr. Stumpf. Sixty percent of our young people are unemployed. Our territorial government runs an an-nual deficit of fifty million dollars on a population of thirty thousand and still there are not enough homes for people to live in. We need jobs, we need revenue, and we need this mine to be built."

"Is this view unanimous?"

"No."

"Who differs?"

"There are two camps you need to be aware of. One is loud but in-consequential: the environmentalist schoolteachers and junior civil ser-vants who are in the north briefly and remember the fun they had in college protesting logging on the West Coast."

Stumpf blinked uncomprehendingly.

"But they are not taken seriously, either in government or among the townspeople. Of more concern to you will be the independent Inuit land claims organizations, NTI and KTI. These are bodies set up to receive land settlement money from the government, to invest it and administer its dispersal. The influential young Inuit all work for them; they employ several bright and aggressive lawyers outright and they have three of the largest law firms in the country on retainer. Some of the locals feel that these organizations have been coopted, but there are not many who hold that view. NTI and KTI have money, is the thing, and they have lawyers. When they get wind of this, they will be all over you."

"What can we do about that?"

"Buy them off."

"Just like that?"

"Offer an up-front disbursement to every household in the area and publicize the offer at the same time you make it. There is no history of the kind of development money you are proposing being spent up there. Nobody will know in advance how much money is at stake. The faster you do it, the less it will cost you."

"How much will they require?"

"I don't know."

"Can you find out?"

"Yes."

"It goes without saying that everything will have to be completely legal."

"Of course. There's another thing you might do."

"Which is?"

"There's no hospital anywhere on the west coast of Hudson Bay north of Manitoba. The government is finally making plans to start erecting one over the next several years, but the capital funding is still being worked out. It could take years."

"We will build a first-class one by next summer."

The talk turned away from him, toward the size of the investment—about one billion pounds sterling in capital the first three years. *There really are diamonds in the tundra,* Robertson thought. Another five billion in the following ten years and the mine looking to be profitable by year four. Robertson wondered how he was going to pull this off.

He had time to kill before his flight. He headed to Queen Street West, thinking he might find gifts for Justine and Marie, music or a T-shirt or something for his older daughter. He was baffled by the array available. He asked a pubescent salesclerk for advice, who took in his suburban dress and suggested a Duran Duran shirt. Temporarily confident in the success of that mission, he found Edwards Books & Art and wandered in—Marie had asked him for *The Silmarillion*. Walking back into the warm night, he leafed through the book and marveled at the eccentricity his daughter had been able to cultivate in their tiny town. Pauloosie hadn't wanted anything from the city.

He stopped in the Horseshoe Tavern and drank a bottle of Labatt Blue. He ordered a bacon cheeseburger with extra pickles. He drank another bottle of beer. He looked around the place, and was surprised to realize that he was the oldest man in the bar and the only one not wearing jeans. He paid his bill and picked up his bag of gifts and walked back outside. There was a pay phone on the corner. It was an hour earlier in Rankin Inlet and he decided to call home. There was a long satellite pause.

"Hey," she answered.

"How are things?"

"They're okay. How did the meeting go?"

"It went very fast. I'm coming home tomorrow."

"Wow, you got paid a lot for one day's work."

"An hour and a half's work."

"Even better."

"What did Balthazar say about Marie?"

"He said the X-ray hasn't changed. There're still scars, from when she was sick as a baby, but nothing new. He sent her sputum off for tests. It's going to take a month for the culture to grow, he says."

"You told him she coughed blood, didn't you?"

"No, I kept that a secret."

Pause.

"You're pretty worried about her, huh?" she said.

"Yeah."

"I'm glad you're coming home early. I hope these tests turn out okay."

"I'll be in at eight."

"I'll pick you up."

"I left my truck at the airstrip. I'll just drive myself home."

"Okay."

Robertson walked back to his hotel in the summer heat, the kids passing him in T-shirts and gauzy skirts—so beautiful, these boys and girls. She said she was glad he was coming home. Clear as day.

That summer, Marie's and Justine's days stretched out in front of them in an elastic, almost infinite emptiness that matched the tundra horizons around them. They rose whenever it occurred to them—the sky was light for all but a few hours after midnight—then fed themselves and eventually made their way outside, where people laughed and spoke loudly at all hours. The children played street hockey at four A.M. with as much enthusiasm as they did at four P.M.

Marie had spent the previous summers out on the tundra gathering cloudberries and collecting specimens of flowers and insects. One year she had carried home a great winged monstrosity that none of the elders had recognized, though everyone from the south did: a dragonfly, not seen this far north before.

This summer, Marie had less energy, it seemed. She spent most of the time in her bedroom, reading. She was cold even when everyone else was warm, and she wrapped herself in sweaters and blankets. Sitting at the kitchen table, drinking tea with her mother, she seemed distracted. When questioned on the matter, she replied she was just daydreaming. Though she denied being sad, she was more withdrawn than anyone in her family had ever seen her. Discussing it with Robertson, Victoria attributed Marie's behavior to puberty, but she did not really believe this herself. It was such a long wait for the TB test results, and worry gnawed at her like a stomach ulcer. She recognized that look, that listlessness. She had studied it every morning for the six years after her baby was born dead. But Marie only said, over and over, that she was fine. And then got up and walked back to her room.

Pauloosie was out on the land with his grandfather the moment school was over. He returned at infrequent intervals with appalling laundry only to pack for another trip. Robertson was in the house hardly more than his son. Summer is building season in the Arctic, and every plan and ambition developed in ten months of winter must be realized in a few short weeks. Anyone trying to make the north more like the south has to sprint continuously—from the moment the pack ice breaks up to the first blizzard. Great ruts of grooved mud and berms of compacted muskeg stretched through the town during this time, and Robertson was standing in the center of most of them, watching the heavy equipment—preposterously expensive to operate here—chug and charge as they prepared foundations and swung shipping containers into position.

Victoria was the one constant presence in the house—though even for her, in summer there was little constancy. She ate breakfast alone at three A.M., slept in the late afternoon. She listened to the doors emitting and admitting her family during all hours, and gave up trying to keep track of who was where. Absent the solar metronome, individual tempos became improvised and idiosyncratic. The old people had always been suspicious of summer. It was hard to travel on the tundra when it was melted, and the season was so short, it was easier just to be confused for a few weeks and wait for it to be over.

That summer Justine fell in love, along with twenty million other North American girls, with Axl Rose, the lead singer of Guns N' Roses. Satellite television had come to town the winter before, and on MTV she watched the video of "Sweet Child O' Mine" and felt as if she couldn't breathe. She lay in front of the television, fantasizing scenarios involving, variously, airplane engine trouble, a full-up hotel, and her playing good Samaritan to the band. She'd cook them supper, laughing ironically about the isolation of the place they were marooned. "Oh, no, we know your work, well, some of us do . . . Care for another bottle of beer?" Then they would perform a special show at the high school and thank her publicly, and everyone would know how cool she was.

Still, she knew he was bad for her. For long hours at a time she was able to shut him out of her mind, but when it was night, and her sister was in bed, her parents in their opposite orbits, and her brother on the land, she turned the television on and waited for him to appear before her. She had subscribed to *Rolling Stone,* and now whenever a GN'R photo appeared, she meticulously cut it out and tacked it to her wall. The gossip pages made allusions to Axl's excesses, and she ached over these, forgiving him even as she learned of the binges, the rampages, all the women. "Sweet Child O' Mine." As supple as a seal.

Satellite television had arrived just at the moment when Justine's understanding of the world was coalescing. If it had been delayed another year she would not have been receptive to these images of the south, would have been too old to incorporate them into her idea of what was normal and desirable. But as it was, the pictures of Hollywood Boulevard and long, blond leonine hair, surfing beaches, and trees jutting from every unpaved and unpruned surface all sank into her just when she was maximally interested in the world. How lovely all that seemed to her, how these pictures thrilled her. And for the first time, she thought of the place she lived as sterile.

Axl's imitators only served to make more evident his own magnificence. Poison, Def Leppard, Billy Idol—all compelling in their way, but ultimately trivial beside the regal and disdainful Axl. Who ever imagined that a kilt could look so good on an American rock star?

Balthazar's brother, Matthew, lived so far south of the city that he had to drive to get there. He caught a cab to the garage where he kept his 1978 Thunderbird and took a moment to check the oil and to marvel that the car hadn't been stolen in the nine or ten months since he had last used it. When it started, it blew blue smoke for a minute before settling into a smoother rumble, and then he slipped it into gear and backed up. He struck a concrete pole. He pulled forward. He backed up again. The concrete pole was still there. He pulled forward again, and then he was free.

Driving south on Garden State Parkway, he watched the city transform itself from the downtown core of minimarts, pawn shops, and liquor stores into a stretch of franchise box stores and gas stations. Matthew was an eighth-grade English teacher at a local public junior high school. His wife, Angela, was a chartered management accountant, whatever that was. His niece was fourteen years old, played the viola, and attended an expensive private school. Angela's firm had transferred her to their Newark office from Sausalito two years previously with the understanding that it was only for two years, to bring the Newark office "up to scratch," as Angela drily put it. But there had been a number of changes in HR, and the economy was not what it had been, and the move back had been delayed. Matthew and Angela still had most of their furniture wrapped in packing material in a storage unit in California. They knew none of their neighbors. Amanda's school was a twenty-minute drive away and had been selected largely on the basis of the limited degree to which it would impart Newarkness to her.

Matthew met him on the front step and hugged him stiffly. "Hi, Keith," Angela called from the kitchen when he came into the foyer.

"Good to see you, brother," Matthew said as he closed the door behind him. "No peanuts?" Amanda had food allergies.

"Nope."

"Do you mind?"

"Of course not."

Balthazar formally pulled out his pockets, shaking them to dislodge any wayward M&M's that were not there after all, and then turned his pockets right-side in. Angela observed from the kitchen as the ritual was completed in its entirety, scanning with her own eyes for a glimpse of peanut butter cup wrapper.

Matthew sat down with Balthazar on the living room couch after he poured glasses of whiskey for both of them. "We've been meaning to have you over for ages."

"I'm sorry I'm away so much."

"How long are you in the city this time?"

"Well, I've been back about eight weeks now, so I'm looking at going up again in another three or four weeks."

"Brother, you're never gonna get a woman keeping up that kind of travel schedule."

"Well, I like it up there a lot."

"And it pays well."

"Reasonably."

Angela joined them then, with a glass of cranberry juice for herself, and tucked her legs under her as she sat down on the chair across from them. Amanda emerged from her bedroom, wearing headphones and carrying an electronic viola with ironic disdain.

"You know, I'm still surprised how you were transferred to Newark of all places. What unbelievable luck, isn't it? I mean, really?" Balthazar offered merrily.

"Unbelievable coincidence, absolutely," Matthew replied, nodding slowly.

"And it isn't like they gave me even one other option to choose from," Angela added.

"Destiny." Balthazar smiled. Amanda stood behind her mother's shoulder and waved at him with the tips of her fingers in a fourteen-year-old smart girl sort of way.

"Hey, Amanda."

"Hello, Keith."

"Uncle Keith," her mother said.

"Did you hear me playing?"

"You sounded great."

"Really?"

"Oh, yes."

"Because, I had turned the sound, like, off, and you could only hear it through the headphones."

"Amanda," her father said. She looked at Balthazar, the faintest suggestion of a smile on her lips.

"You caught me," Balthazar admitted.

"I know."

Then Angela, discomfited by the moment, as she was by many, many moments, stood. "Well, I think we should eat now." And Balthazar stood as his brother rose too, and they walked over to the dining room table, whiskies in hand, ice cubes clacking. As they pulled out their chairs before the lavishly laid table, not a misaligned napkin fold in sight, Angela apologized, "Our real silverware is still in . . ."

"California," Balthazar said, surprised by his own impertinence.

"Yes."

Amanda shrugged her headphones off from around her neck and arrived at the table half a beat behind the others. Her father glanced at her just as she slid into her chair and saw her navel sticking out between her jeans and too-tight T-shirt, and he flushed. Balthazar watched Matthew look away for a moment. "Since when do you come to the supper table half dressed?" her father asked her.

"Matthew, we can discuss this later," Angela said darkly and began passing around the peas with lemon butter and pepper in a taupe serving dish from the MoMA design store, with little silver curlicues embossed on the sides.

Matthew locked eyes with his wife, and what Balthazar wanted to do was run outside to his car and barrel his way down the street. What he did was dish himself some peas while exchanging glances with his niece. Telepathically, she told him, *I'm glad you're here.*

Telepathically, he replied, *I'm not.*

As boys, Matthew and Keith had endured their own parents' volatile tempers with widely different strategies. Matthew's recollection was that Balthazar spent much of his childhood facedown on his bed with hands over his ears. Their parents' passions had been more all-encompassing than those of Angela and Matthew, it seemed to Balthazar. Where Angela and Matthew were locked in a cool struggle, circling each other warily in between their periodic eruptions, his parents—when they weren't actively trying to destroy each other—felt a deep and evident desire for each other. The two types of fighting seemed to Balthazar diametrical opposites. Angela and Matthew were locked together like the deer he had seen on the Discovery Channel, antlers entwined, dying slowly even as they continued to struggle against each other.

Besides the fresh peas, which were set off nicely by the tang of the lemon butter, there were smoked salmon crepes and squash and wild rice. Angela must have been working on the meal all day, Balthazar thought as he ate his way through the servings. Angela had long ago generalized her difficulties with his brother to include him, and probably resisted having Balthazar over in the first place, but there was no denying the work she had put into this meal.

Duty. Resolve. Bafflement. Balthazar had never been married, had not even had a substantial romantic involvement since he had begun working in the Arctic. His own explanation for this—and the one he advanced to anyone clumsy enough to raise the matter with him—was that his divided life was the obstacle he faced. But the truth was that he was grateful for the excuse. He could not have faced the life his brother led, and every married person he knew confronted elements of his brother's struggles. Which was quite a price to pay to avoid simple stupid loneliness.

After supper, Amanda said good night to her parents and her uncle and retreated to her room, leaving the silence and the forced conversations of the adults behind her. Matthew and Balthazar cleared the table as Angela began filling the dishwasher. "Can these go in the dishwasher, Angela?" Matthew asked as he brought the serving dishes into the kitchen.

"You know they can't," she replied, shrugging, not bothering to disguise anything for Balthazar's sake.

"I'm just asking," he said.

"Why don't you two let me finish up?" she asked as she rinsed plates under the tap.

"Okay," Matthew said, and picked up a couple of fresh highball glasses and a bottle of Lagavulin scotch. Balthazar followed his brother out the kitchen door to the backyard. In the night the cicadas thrummed. The two men drank whiskey slowly and looked up at the night sky, glowing with city lights and punctured by only a handful of the brightest stars.

"In the north, on a night like this, the sky is just dazzling."

"I'd love to see that sometime," Matthew replied.

And then there was a long silence between them as they listened to street traffic and sirens. Matthew refilled their glasses and they drank more and they didn't lower their eyes from the sky until they heard the patio door open and Angela sat down with them, reaching for the whiskey.

They watched scattered low clouds sweep over them, glowing luminously. Balthazar began planning his escape.

"Keith, you always seem to me like the only one I know who's thought clearly about his life," Angela whispered into the warm, humid half darkness.

Balthazar, for the life of him, could not think of anything to say to this.

"We both work so hard, and we know none of the neighbors, and these days we hardly know Amanda. Most days, even each other," she said, nodding in Matthew's direction. Matthew's head turned at her uncharacteristic display of vulnerability.

"But you're up there, living this strange life in the north, and then you're down here in your apartment in the city, going to all the shows and the bookstores. God, you do exactly what you want, don't you?"

"I don't think any of us do, really. I think we all idealize what we don't have. You don't think I'd like something of what you have here?"

"Not really. And if you really do, you'll have it one day. You get everything else you want," Angela said.

"That's just not true."

"What don't you have?"

"I wanted to be an academic field researcher. I wanted to do an oph-thalmology residency, live in Boston."

They sat there, swirling their drinks. They could all hear Amanda talking on her telephone, the sound carrying on the humid air.

"We're made to be dissatisfied," Matthew said. "Unhappy people are the only ones who achieve anything. It's normal—it's what pushes us forward."

"It's not normal. Common, maybe, but not normal—it's not how we're supposed to live. Always pissed off. Always resenting something." Angela was emphatic.

"You two need a vacation," Balthazar said.

Unlike every other place, the Arctic does not tire of the sun, even in late summer. The low bushes and impertinent little willows remain green and push themselves upward until the moment when what they are pushing up against is snow. When it's warm, the place agitates itself without reserve; the tasks of reproduction and food storage are not so much completed as they are crammed as tightly as possible into the short amount of time available. That sometimes enough gets done, suf-ficient stores to survive the winter are accumulated, is demonstrated by the improbable reappearance of greenery again ten months later.

The snow geese showed up at the end of August, on their way south from the islands of the Arctic Archipelago, coalescing like weather for the great flight to their Texas wintering grounds. The same day the geese appeared, the first of the teachers returned to town.

Johanna met Penny in the teachers' lounge with a great grin of pleasure. She had just returned from a stint of teaching summer school in Vancouver and hadn't been sure if Penny would be back yet. Penny had disappeared in June—slipping out of the end-of-year party in the teachers' lounge before the liquor had even been opened.

Her hair was sunstreaked and her cheeks the color of oiled leather, and she grinned back at Johanna. "I stayed out on the land the whole summer!"

"No way."

"I got out to the Back River with my dogs and I set up camp and a net for char—a week later I realized I had all the fish I needed for the summer, so I spent the rest of the time drying and smoking char. I came back with eight hundred pounds of dried fish. I cached it at the mouth of the Meliadine River."

"Really?"

"It seems like a dream to me. Eight weeks I was out there."

"I'm not sure whether to envy you or to worry about you."

"Envy me, please."

"Did you see any bears?"

"No nanuqs that far inland, but I did see a barrenlands grizzly."

"Really? Did your dogs protect you? I guess they did, seeing you're here telling me about it."

Penny dropped her voice. "I protected them. The hide is in my freezer."

Johanna didn't know what to say.

"I shot into the air at first and then he killed Percy, the slow white one, remember?"

Johanna dropped her voice, whispering, as the chemistry teacher approached them to say hello. "Really?"

August 15, 1988

Dear Johanna:

Here are the sweaters you asked me for. I hope they fit. I included some socks because I think your feet must get cold from time to time.

I went fishing with my father last week, up the Moon River, north of Etobicoke. He showed me how to cast a fly rod. I caught two bass and a rainbow trout, and enjoyed myself way more than I thought I would. I've found myself starting to understand what that Penny woman likes about the Arctic. Afterward, we cleaned the fish and fried them in beer batter and ate them by the shore. I wish you and I could have done that sometime. Anyway, not to get too gooey here. I hope you are well.

Love, Doug XOX

August 21, 1988

Dear Doug:

The end of summer has come to the Arctic. The geese are migrating home and the other teachers are migrating here from home. The classrooms have all been cleaned out nicely and we met the new teachers yesterday—I think about a third of last year's staff left. Some we knew about, others left resignation letters in the principal's mailbox. I was relieved to find Penny still here; she spent the whole summer out on the land, along the Back River, fishing for and drying Arctic char. She looks like she's climbed Everest, her face is as sunburnt as any of the old hunters'. I hope she doesn't lose any more weight though, heavens.

I am perplexed by the degree to which I admire her. I wish I had been that confident when I was her age; I wish I were that confident now. It gives her a kind of self-sufficiency that I see as a real strength. You've pointed out that that can be a two-edged sword, and you are right about that: being too self-sufficient can look a lot like lonely. I don't see that happening to Penny, though. I see her as living more richly than anyone else I know.

At the same time, I suspect I am getting a little caught up in all this. What she does—living out on the land for weeks at a time—is not for most people, probably not for me, and is, anyway, only a difficult thing. We all do difficult things. Living with me, for instance, the last year before I left was probably very difficult.

Doug, the day after I mail this letter I'll start looking anxiously for a reply. I spent the summer in Vancouver teaching summer school. I had an instinct that it would be better if I didn't come back to Ontario unless I knew what I wanted to say to you. And I didn't. Don't. But I do like hearing from you.

Thank you for the lovely sweaters, and yes indeed, my feet do get cold up here, so thank you very much for the socks. Thank you as well for your patience. If you ever see a good hunting knife, could you send it to me? Penny took me out tuktu, sorry, caribou hunting and I admired how deft she was with hers. One more respect in which I fantasize about being her.

> All my love,
> Johanna

September 1, 1988

Dear Johanna:

Apparently the Finnish knives are supposed to be the best, and at Central Knife and Cutlery they suggested this one. It has a groove in it that lets the blood run out. Which paints quite a mental picture, if you ask me.

It might be the end of summer there but here it is still very hot. Do you remember that fan you made me go out and buy in the middle of the night three years ago when we couldn't sleep? I sleep beside it every night these days. Some things come in so handy, huh?

If you sent me a picture of your friend Penny I could do my best to dress up like her if that would help you decide to come home.

> XOX
> Doug

Near Coats Island, south of Coral Harbour off the coast of Hudson Bay, are offshore treeless islets, rocks, really, the color of brick, upon which walruses rest and sun themselves. The iviaq see very poorly, but their sense of smell is almost extrasensory. Emo turned the Peterhead miles from the island so he and his grandson could approach from downwind. It was the very end of summer and the animals were obscenely fat, great rippling waves of flesh sloshing with each movement. Pauloosie studied them as they approached, and studying turned to staring and then simply transfixion. Iviaq weren't often seen as far south as Rankin. The local seals were more typically a hundred or two hundred pounds. These behemoths were like nothing he had seen up close.

They had fed earlier in the day, diving hundreds of feet and more to the bottom of Hudson Bay, there to swallow great gulps of mud for the shellfish within, like mining pistachio ice cream for the nuts. The mussels sat in their bellies now, holding their shells as tight as they could, but weakening from the stomach acid and the enzymes. All the walruses had to do was wait for the mussels to exhaust themselves and release their grip. When hunters killed a walrus, the first thing they liked to do was slit open the stomach and dig out the opened mussels and swallow them, still warm and bloody and steaming. This is called qalluk, and is considered one of the best things there is to eat in the Arctic. Emo had told Pauloosie what it tasted like as they motored up the coast.

In the summer on Hudson Bay there is always fog, which is much more of an impediment to men, who can see, than to iviaq, who would prefer that nothing else could either. When the lapping of waves upon rocks became audible, it was necessary to shut off the engine so they could glide closer. The odor of belched half-digested shellfish was as good as a beacon. They carried .303 rifles and military ammunition. The bullets did not mushroom on impact, and so penetrated deep into the layers of blubber, the lungs and heart. Emo and Pauloosie had already chambered their rounds and held their rifles level with the sea as they

peered into the fog. They could not see the beasts but heard the snuf-
fling of calves sucking at their mothers.

When the mist cleared they were within fifteen feet of shore, in
front of mounds and mounds of walrus flesh and hair and tiny beady
eyes, muzzles like fat old bewhiskered men's and shining white tusks
idly scratching, rubbing, nuzzling.

Gunfire exploded for a long minute. Each time Emo and Pauloosie
fired, they looked for the walrus just shot, seeing the blood spurting
from its chest—or was that its neighbor? Firing again, leveling the rifle, pulling back the bolt, firing. Then there was nothing to shoot at, the
walrus all gone in great barely noticed splashes into the sea, all except
three, bellowing, roaring: two young bulls and an old cow, probing the
air with their tusks, waving and thrashing and coughing out a red mi-
asma that drifted out over the boat, more desperate aching protest, and
then, slowly, the sound of wet loud breathing for a long time and then
nothing at all.

Simionie was watching the kettle boil, hunkered in front of the fire.
Victoria sat at the table and watched him watch the kettle. She had not
wanted to make love today, and this was the first time she had ever said
that to him. She assured him that nothing was the matter. She was just
a little stressed out. School had started and Marie still didn't look right
to her and they still didn't have the test results. The girl seemed more
and more withdrawn and listless.

"I think that may be how teenagers are," Simionie said. "On the TV,
they are, anyway."

"Yeah, I know what you mean. Still, I can't help thinking something
is the matter."

He didn't contradict her. Sallow and thin, Marie had hung around
town that summer like an underfed caribou calf: all limbs and joints and
wide eyes. Nobody outside her family ever heard her speak.

"How's Pauloosie doing?"

"He spends all his free time with his grandfather. We hardly see him. I think he's this far from quitting school."

"Well, your father knows a lot. He's a good teacher."

"How about you—what are you doing lately?"

"I've been out hunting a bit. And I've been going to that Attatatiak Committee whatchacallit. Okpatayauk and his friends."

"What's that about?"

"Okpatayauk thinks that all this talk about a new mine is based on something." He stirred the coals.

"Yes?"

"He thinks Robertson is involved in it and wants to know why."

"I don't know much about Robertson's businesses."

"I know. But when Okpatayauk and his friends get together, all they want to talk about is this mine and why they don't know anything about it, but he does."

"You two close? You and Okpatayauk?"

"We have coffee sometimes."

"I didn't know that."

"I think maybe we don't need a diamond mine on the tundra," he said, turning from the stove at last to look at her.

"Well, there should be a discussion, if there is to be one."

"There won't be. It will just be pushed through. And all the jobs and money will go to Kablunauks. Like your husband."

Victoria sighed and crossed her legs. Through the window, the clouds were perfect cumulus cotton balls, each nearly the same size as the other, stretched out at regular intervals from one horizon to the other.

"Simionie, I don't want you to get involved with Robertson, okay? He's not a bad man."

"Why should I be the one that keeps out of his way?"

"You just have to be."

"We'll see."

"Simionie."

"I said, we'll see."

Balthazar awoke from his sleep in the early afternoon. Around him, the disarray of his apartment pressed on him with a familiar and sallow weight, its hairy belly hanging on his face with malodorous gravity. He stirred himself and the thing on his face was his stiffened terry cloth bathrobe and, free of it, he could breathe after all. There was a knocking at his door. He swung his heavy legs over the side of his bed. Pulling on sweatpants and a T-shirt, he made his way to the front door and unlocked it. There stood Amanda.

"Samuel let me up," she said. "He remembered me."

"I see."

"Can I come in?"

"Of course," he said, moving aside.

She took in his apartment, which she had visited before. There was a moment as her eyes scoured the place—the stacks of pizza boxes and junk mail and unfinished meals. "Keith, they're called M-O-L-L-Y, Molly, M-A-I-D, maid. Mo-oo-ll-y," she said, enunciating this laboriously, "Mai-yuhd."

"What are you doing in the city?" he asked.

She launched into a cheerleader routine: "Gimme an 'M'! Gimme an 'O'!" but broke up with laughter. Balthazar thought for a second that maybe she was high. But she wasn't.

"What are you doing in the city, Amanda?"

She stopped laughing, slowly decelerating like a windup toy. She wiped her eyes and looked at her uncle.

"Will you let me stay with you for a while?"

"What? No."

"Pleee-ase."

"What's going on, Amanda?"

"My parents are going crazy."

"Oh, dear."

"I want to live here until they get their act together."

"Has anyone hit you or anything?"

"Of course not."

"Well, then you have to go back. Imagine what your mother would say if you told her you were moving in with me."

They both shuddered.

"You mean it, huh?"

"Yes," he said, his voice rising unintentionally.

"Will you take me out for lunch then?"

"First, we're phoning your parents."

"Oh, God."

There was no lunch, not after talking to a frantic Angela. Balthazar and Amanda walked to the garage where he kept his car, stretching out her reprieve. He felt guilty—for what he was doing and for what he wasn't doing. A problem without an obvious solution.

When Robertson walked into the kitchen, Victoria looked up at his anxious face and found herself smiling at him. "The sputum came back negative for tuberculosis. The nurse just phoned and told me."

"Thank God," he breathed.

She had been holding on to the good news all day, waiting for him to get home. "Yes," she said, and hugged him.

His eyes widened at the feel of her arms around his waist. He rested his chin on her shoulder, a once-familiar sensation. How could he have forgotten how pleasant this was? "Did anyone have any ideas about why she coughed blood?"

"Not really. She said that bad bronchitis can do that." They breathed together and thought about that, and about the fact that they were touching each other.

"In a kid?"

"I don't know."

"It doesn't sound right to me."

They stood there, still holding each other for the first time in so long. She was thinking, *It's good we can be kind to one another, even though we've become what we have.*

He was thinking, *Things can get better, after all.*

the patient predator

The creature arrived in the Arctic in the same way it spread itself around the world. It lay dormant in the lungs of those apparently healthy enough to undertake such a journey, and then, when he was weakened, perhaps by hunger, or cold, or simple loneliness, it revived explosively. The sailor, or the missionary, or the trader found himself febrile and coughing paroxysmally, in some little iglu or tent, the bacteria streaming through his blood to all his organs—and then a local Inuk had the misfortune to enter the shelter.

In Rankin Inlet I knew a woman who carried the descendants of the creature within her. She was my patient and we were acquainted for most of three decades. Mostly we had quiet consultations about such things as contraception and bladder infections, but what dominated her medical chart were the pages and pages that describe the ordeal she endured as a young girl as a consequence of tuberculosis. She had been evacuated to a dismal hospital in the south for six years. She has been beautiful as long as I have known her, with an incandescent energy that I've always been inclined, however unreasonably, to attribute to her illness. The febrile and gangly beauty of consumptives has long been a trope in Europe. All I knew was that Victoria stirred me more than any New York City fashion model could.

In my early days there, Rankin Inlet was populated by eighteen hundred people, almost all of these Inuit, and its houses clung to the low rocks that stretched into the Arctic Ocean. The wind scoured this place. Everyone here knew everyone else and most of their problems.

There have been outbreaks of tuberculosis here ever since the first coughing sailor or missionary arrived, the infection smoldering on long after the advent *of antibiotics. The disease is firstly an expression of poverty and its consequences—especially crowding—and in the Arctic, these were usual. Latent infection endures in almost everyone older than forty—the creature has its hand on these people still. By the time a new outbreak is recognized there are usually dozens of new infections, some apparent, most already gone dormant. Victoria did not know from whom she caught her illness.*

When she was diagnosed, half her left lung had been taken up by a giant cavity full of the organism. Every time her sputum was analyzed in her first year at the sanatorium, it was packed with the little rods of Mycobacterium tuberculosis, *which stain crimson when examined under the microscope. She coughed constantly and became so thin that she was cold even huddled in her bed, wrapped in blankets. After months of unsuccessful treatment with antibiotics, she underwent savage deforming surgery. The scar on her chest looks like a mauling.*

The bacteria inside the cavity in her lung had walled themselves within the surrounding scar tissue; blood did not flow there, and so antibiotics and the two arms of the immune system—white blood cells and antibodies—did not reach it. The operation Victoria underwent is called a thoracoplasty, and it involves excising ribs in order to collapse cavities of infection within the lungs. After the Second World War, with the development of effective antimicrobial therapy for these infections, chest surgeons were thrown out of work en masse (only to have their futures brightened anew by the postwar rise in cigarette smoking and consequent lung cancers). Such operations are almost never done now. Many experienced thoracic surgeons in the developed world today have never had to operate on a tuberculous lung. This is an astonishing and improbable state of affairs, really: chest surgery was born of tuberculosis, and occupied itself almost entirely with the problem until fifty years ago. A chest surgeon then would not have believed the problem could disappear for good, so quickly. He would have been right.

Among Victoria's friends in Rankin Inlet are always a handful of men and women who have developed resurgent infection. They endure their coughing and weight loss for a time and then they come into the nursing station, seeking attention. By the time they do, they've already infected a few dozen of their friends and family members. We track them down and treat them too. No one pretends that we find everyone. And every year, around the world, in this lingering brushfire of a disease, we identify more and more strains of the bacterium that are resistant to the available antibiotics. There hasn't been a new antituberculosis drug released since 1968. And the frequency of resistance had increased tenfold in that time. There is trouble brewing——here and all over the world.

Viewed over any time frame longer than the last half dozen decades, tuberculosis is the most common cause of death among young adults anywhere. It remains a principal killer——is still the single most common infectious cause of death, certainly——throughout most of the world, and two billion people, a third of those living, carry TB, alive and waiting, within them.

Tuberculosis infection has been so common for most of our history, it has been almost a normal, if periodically lethal, part of the human bio-niche, like a taste for intoxicants, perhaps. Modigliani died of tuberculous meningitis, infection of the linings of the brain. Keats, a former medical student, remarked famously on the foreboding bright red color of his sputum. Chopin, Orwell, Vivien Leigh: all dead too young of TB. Then, for a mere fifty anomalous years, in North America and Europe, it ebbed back and a lingering cough became no longer cause for immediate terror. In retrospect, the complacency with which rich people have viewed tuberculosis is difficult to understand. When the enormous historical toll of the disease is considered, it becomes almost incomprehensible.

We claim to have forgotten it——the appearance of pallid coughing men and women, the idea that even the young and wealthy may sicken and die—— but study the perfume ads: these are not archetypes of beauty formed de novo. These are Katherine Mansfield and Modigliani: so young, so thin, so pale. "Love us now, for soon we will be gone" is what those faces say to us. "And while you're at it, buy some of this cologne," they add. "It comes in this nifty spritzer bottle."

Patients suspect that their doctors objectify them, reduce them to a compilation of symptoms and diagnoses, and in this they are wholly correct. ("I'm sending you an acute stroke," conversations with my colleagues will begin.) Each of the different diagnoses carries a certain characterization. The vascular diseases are clean and lethal; the cancers, darkly menacing.

Smoking- and obesity-related processes are viewed with a certain impatient contempt. The psychiatric diagnoses are all considered in their own light. TB is different somehow, has always been different—though it would be as perilous to love a patient because of her diagnosis as it would be for any other reason.

Everything about her is special, different; just watch the way she holds herself, head high even as she is ignored by the people around her. Her perfectly erect neck as she turns to me at the grocery store and those black eyes shining. But knowing her as I do, it seems only expected that her illness was this storied and anachronistic malady that refuses to submit even when antibiotics are thrown at it by the fistful.

Mycobacterium tuberculosis *is descended from similar organisms that have inhabited cattle for eons. Four thousand years ago, about a week and a half after cattle were domesticated, the organism spread to humans. It has since adapted to us, tweaked its genetic arrangement to optimize its capacity to spread and persist. Its virulence is largely a consequence of the thick, waxy cell wall that surrounds it like a rind, making it substantially resistant to the effects of the immune system. When the organism is inhaled, white blood cells called macrophages ("big eater," from the Greek—one pictures a pie-eating contest) engulf and bathe the invaders with toxic chemicals like hydrogen peroxide and protein-dissolving enzymes. Despite the macrophages' attempts to poison it, the creature often survives because of its thick rind, and will slowly replicate itself until the macrophage is so full of tuberculosis bacteria that it bursts and dies. The daughter organisms drift on, to be engulfed in turn. Most of the time, an equilibrium is attained: about as many organisms are killed as survive, and the spread of the creature is checked. This is the latent phase, which can last decades, until for some reason, or no reason at all, the balance is tipped.*

Perhaps the immune system is weakened by stress, or by pregnancy, or by another infection—especially HIV—or by starvation, or simply by age. In any case, when the balance does tip, the bacteria overwhelm the immune system. They begin to fill the adjacent alveoli and block the transfer of oxygen and carbon dioxide to and from the blood. The patient notices that she is more easily winded than normal. The increasing concentration of foreign protein within the lungs stirs the immune system to maximal activity and the quantities of not-quite-toxic-enough poisons inflame the walls of the airways, which come to bleed easily. The patient develops a fever, and she notices streaks of blood in her sputum. Initially, as Keats knew, this blood will be dark red and venous; later, as infection erodes its way into arteries, it becomes bright crimson. If the affected artery is a large one, this may be what doctors dryly describe as a preterminal event. Katherine Mansfield expired in a great geyser this way. Keats, crediting his instruction, foretold his own death as his sputum became brighter and brighter.

Even if the artery isn't large, now the seed is in the wind and the creature in the blood—it swims to every organ system: the brain, the kidneys, the intestines, the bones, the ovaries, the skin, the uterus, the heart. The modern understanding of organ systems and how they fail was largely gained through observing the consequences of their involvement by Mycobacterium tuberculosis. Failure of the adrenal glands, called Addison's disease today, was then a consequence of tuberculosis eroding the adrenals from within; this is what killed Jane Austen. Any medical textbook more than a generation or two old lists tuberculosis as a possible cause of almost any organ dysfunction, and usually high up on that list. Pott's disease was tuberculosis of the spine, which most commonly affected hunchbacks such as Victor Hugo's bell ringer of Notre Dame. Lupus vulgaris was infection of the skin; the systemic wasting syndrome was consumption, or phthisis. The history of medicine, until fifty years ago, was largely the history of tuberculosis.

One of the great calamities for all mankind, tuberculosis was simply the worst thing that ever happened to the traditional Inuit, and to indigenous Americans more generally. Nobody knows why it has been so bad among them. There are many potential explanations: the small, crowded snow and skin dwellings they lived in, the coexistent lung diseases from the smoky fires they lit their dwellings with, a genetic vulnerability, and most persuasively, the chronic, recurrent famine that lurked on the edge of the ice floes.

The Inuit called it puvaluq, or "bad lung," and it infected most of them. Across the continent it killed many millions more Aboriginal people, contributing to the clearing of the American Plains. When settlers spread out across them in the late 1800s, they commented often on the wide open and *fertile grasslands, uninterrupted by signs of human habitation. But for the effects of the creature (and its other infectious companions), those plains would have been alive with children and hunters and women growing corn. One hundred million people lived there before the plagues came.*

Where I worked, the Inuit were compelled by the Canadian government to move into the desperate little settlements it erected on the shore of Hudson Bay, largely to facilitate attempts to control the infection. Throughout the 1950s and 1960s, ships with mobile X-ray units visited every summer, and men, women, and children found to have active disease were evacuated to sanatoria in the south. The cultural disruption that ensued from these years-long exiles interrupted the thousands of years of traditional teaching and knowledge of the land that enabled the people to remain independent of southern culture. The children, returning to parents they barely remembered, were often unable even to speak to them, having lost their language in the south. By the late 1960s, the last of the nomadic hunting families had come in off the land to settle in the clapboard houses provided them by the government, there to begin the cycle of acculturation that continues today.

When I left the Arctic, in 1992, there were then active epidemics in the hamlets of Coral Harbour and Arviat. Five years before that it was Repulse Bay; a few years before that, Chesterfield Inlet. The historic exposure rate is so high that TB outbreaks can be expected to arise from reactivated latent disease for decades to come.

It is difficult to overstate the menace that Mycobacterium tuberculosis *is to humans. Like a storm forming from the coalescence of several different weather systems, it is the perfect pathogen in many respects: it has a long latent asymptomatic phase, allowing it to dwell on in populations; it spreads invisibly, in the air; and when it takes hold it erodes every single organ system: the brain, kidneys, the gut, as well as its principal residence, the lungs. Its perfection is preserved most of all by its ability to shrug off our poisons.*

In North America we imagine this to be a disease on the margins—of history and geography. But the story of HIV is illustrative: suffering does not localize. Trouble on the edges moves to the center. The economy globalizes and, at the same instant, so does our epidemiology. Strains of resistant superbugs,

tuberculosis isolates resistant to all known medications are identified
in Russian jails and six weeks later they show up in Brooklyn. Our
reacquaintance with the old antagonist is already well under way. And,
whether we like it or not, we return to this problem that so preoccupied
our grandparents.

The idea of latency is worth thinking about. Biology rewards patience.
Mycobacterium tuberculosis understands this. It establishes its toeholds and
then it becomes dormant. And in this restraint it demonstrates the full extent of
its power. It is not necessary that every thirst be slaked. In not acting upon a
desire, that desire is diminished neither in intensity nor in merit. Priests fall in
love with parishioners and display it all the time—we read about this in the
newspapers. What we do not read about are the times, over and over again,
when those words are not said, those kisses are not offered, or solicited. But such
unexpressed love does not amount to nothing. When we love it is because we
have seen especially clearly. And a clear view of human beauty is a treasure
that endures for as long as the possessor of such insight breathes. And
endurance is the final measure of importance: of ideas and of organisms.

Love lies latent sometimes, as tuberculosis does—but, as any
epidemiologist will tell you, latent is nothing like gone.

She used to obsess over whether her children had puvaluq. Everyone she
saw—the nurses and the other doctors who worked with me there—who didn't
know her story dismissed her worry with a wave. They were all from the south,
those shining faces, where the creature had been pushed away, for a little while.
How could they know?

∎

chapter eleven

Victoria heard the hoot of the tug in the bay and looked at her calendar. Third week of September. She had been late with her barge order and so her groceries hadn't been on the first two, which had arrived earlier in the month. She wondered again if she had ordered enough food. Pauloosie was the variable. Every week his appetite seemed to double, but at the same time he was increasingly strident about eating country food, insisting on cutting up his own frozen char while the rest of the family ate roast. Still, she wished that Marie had even a portion of her brother's appetite. These days Marie did hardly more than stir her food around on her plate. Char, fish sticks, toast, beans, roast: nothing moved her to eat. And she looked like it too. The teachers all commented on how skinny she was when she went back to school.

That afternoon Victoria drove down to the warehouse where the barge orders were being unloaded, wrapped in polyethylene and labeled prominently with the name of the person who had placed them. If you were lucky your order came off the barge first. Johnny Ingutar, one of the warehouse men, met her as she stepped out of the truck. "I don't think you're supposed to be here," he said, smiling broadly.

"What do you mean?"

He pointed. Robertson was already here, which surprised her. He had left two days earlier for Yellowknife and he wasn't due back yet. But there he was, directing the placement of enormous crates on the hamlet office's flatbed truck. Victoria walked up to him.

"I thought I'd pick up our groceries," she said, touching his shoulder.

His face fell as if he had been caught in the act of doing something dreadful. Then he went various shades of inarticulate and stammering purple. Finally she asked, "What's the matter?"

"I have a surprise for you, but you can't see it yet."

"Okay," she said, and walked back to her truck and drove home.

Victoria didn't see Robertson for what remained of that day or the next. She thought that he had gone back to Yellowknife, that the surprise had something to do with the hospital. Perhaps they were going to begin construction that fall, or something.

A full week later there was a knock at the door. She answered it, expecting to see her father back early from walrus hunting, and saw her husband there, frowning anxiously.

"What?" she asked.

He motioned her to his truck.

"What?" she asked again.

"Just come!" he yelled, startling her. Who knew what this was about? So, okay, she would go look at the first pilings of the hospital, or whatever it was that he was so sure she wanted to see.

She climbed in and he took her down to the head of the bay, on the very western edge of town, where she had collected shells as an awkward and lonely seventeen-year-old just returned from the south. There was a new house there, a two-story affair of raw cedar logs, with a wooden roof and new tiles and doors and triple-paned windows, like nothing else north of the tree line. Robertson pulled to a stop in front of it.

"What's this?" she asked, wondering whether Robertson's consortium had built a new government office building, or what.

"It's your new house."

Victoria gaped. She bent her neck to see under the sunshades, her mouth still open. They got out of the truck.

"I had to hire every man in town who could be trusted with a

Skilsaw," Robertson said. They climbed up the front steps and he insisted she be the one to open the door.

She took in the shining kitchen cabinets and the hardwood floors and the clean bright paintwork, the skylight in the ceiling. She was speechless. There was a dishwasher and a new stove. Even a maple block island, just like in the magazines. She opened the doors to the pantry and there was her barge order, already stacked inside.

The kitchen gave onto the living room, which featured, of all things, a windowed cast-iron woodstove. There was a large color television in an entertainment center, and new loveseats and a chesterfield in matching dusty rose arranged around it in a horseshoe. The bedrooms—one for each of the children—were twice the size of those in the old house. When she saw the en suite toilet in the master bedroom, she stopped and couldn't go on.

And then she began weeping and couldn't see anything else anyway.

She ran to the kitchen door and outside. She kept on running down to the bay, away from the truck and that huge house, until she was standing with her feet almost in seawater, and shivering with cold. After a long time Robertson appeared on the front steps and walked down to her. They both stared out at the sea.

"I was hoping you would like it," he said.

"It's a great house," she said.

"Do you like it?"

"It just feels like you're trying to buy something, Robertson. Like that disbursement for the diamond mine."

He walked away from her and up to his truck. He drove off and she stood there by the sea, trying to divine her own future. It was snowing. The tug in the bay began pulling up its anchor to take the empty barge back to Montreal.

When the telephone rang, Balthazar expected it to be the cab company; his duffle bags and suitcases were beside the door and he was still panting from the effort of panicked stuffing.

It was Amanda. "I just called to see how you are doing. I haven't heard from you in a while."

"It's going pretty well."

"When are you going north again?"

"Twenty minutes ago."

"Why didn't you call me, Keith?"

"I'm sorry about that. I know you've been struggling."

"I'm not struggling. I'm just pissed off."

"At who?"

"You, for not returning my calls. My parents, because of the way they're acting."

"They're still having a hard time, huh?"

"You should hear them."

"I can imagine."

"Can you?"

"I think so."

"My mom says you've never stuck around long enough to face a problem in your life."

"I'm not sure how she would know that, since she only met me after she married your dad."

"She says she has your number."

"Does she?"

"Dad says he's not you."

"Well, that would be difficult to argue with."

"Mom manages."

"That sounds rough, honey."

"It's awful," she said, her voice softening almost to inaudibility.

"Is there anything I can do?" Balthazar felt a twinge as these easy and false words came out of his mouth.

"I think we've established that there isn't, really."

"I'm not going to abduct you, Amanda."

"You're not gonna stand up for me to my psycho parents, you mean."

"There isn't anything I can do to solve their problems."

"Well, how about if you just answer the damn phone sometimes."

"Yes."

"It's awful, Keith. They go at it until two in the morning, fall asleep for a few hours, and then wake up to fight some more."

"Has anyone hurt you?"

"You keep asking that. Whaddya think? Listening to your parents shrieking at each other all night, d'you think that's doing me any good?"

"I'm sorry."

"The thing is, if you and I just went to them and I said that I was gonna live with you until they made some decisions, they might get their act together. It's not like I'm four."

"I'm sorry."

"You are, a little, you know that?"

"I do, actually."

"Yeah."

"Hey, my taxi is here," he said, looking out the window with relief.

"Really? You're going now?"

"Yeah."

"You're not just making this up?"

"The cab just honked."

"So you were gonna leave without calling?"

"I guess so."

"I see."

"I'm sorry I'm not what you want me to be, Amanda."

"Let me know when you're back?"

"I will."

He hung up and did not lift his head for a long moment. Then he picked up his bags.

In the boardroom at the Rankin Inlet Hotel, Betty Peters stubbed out her cigarette after a sharp look from Robertson. It was the first time the Ikhirahlo Group had met in months. Increasingly, Robertson dominated the workings of the partnership; it remained in his interest to have the affiliation of the group, which included two Inuit because an individual stirred up individual resentments. Robertson's success was reaching the point at which he was vulnerable to a backlash from the community. There could be no more gestures like the new house.

The small group was formed as a way of corralling local support for government-funded construction projects. The idea was that if everyone in town with enough organizational ability and financial know-how to put together a bid worked together, then when the inevitable contracts were let, they would be in terms that would benefit the whole group. To begin with, it was an informal arrangement, and then, as the pace of development had accelerated, they had incorporated as the Ikhirahlo Group, a name they had chosen one especially cold Thursday night as they had sat in this room in the hotel and drunk together. *Ikhirahlo:* very cold. The name had acted as a goad to the people in the town ever since it was chosen. Great that it should be an Inuktitut term, and great that they should include the Killimeet brothers, but just in case there was any doubt that it was southerners making all that money, the name rubbed it in: imperialists complaining about the inclemency of the land they'd stolen. Robertson had regretted the witticism ever since.

His five partners, pleased with profit statements that steadily swelled, let him run things. They had only heard whisperings about the mine but had begun to question him about his role. He had not told them any details so far because he did not trust them to be discreet. But things had advanced too far now to be derailed.

Robertson closed the door, a rare gesture at group meetings. Melvin Anders and Josie Killimeet stopped talking and looked at him expectantly. Robertson sat down.

"Well, I have very exciting news. The Back River Diamond Company, a subsidiary of Boer Gems, has offered the Ikhirahlo Group a small position in its mine, in exchange for ongoing professional consulting and public relations services. If you all agree, we will own one quarter of one percent of the mine, doubling the book value of our corporation."

His colleagues sat back at that.

"It sounds too good to be true," Betty Peters said. "What about liabilities, Robertson? Have you thought about that? Say the mine explodes in some environmental catastrophe—would we be on the hook for that? Even a quarter of one percent's worth?"

"The South Africans have insured the whole process through Lloyd's of London—it's a comprehensive underwriting. You can have a look at the document if you like."

"I will," she said. But she wouldn't, and everyone there knew it.

"I'll bring a copy to you tomorrow."

"So, Robertson," Melvin Anders asked, scratching his long beard, "what exactly would we do, in return for this?"

"Well, I've been meeting with them fairly regularly now for several months, and am already advising them on the local political terrain. I've promised to continue to do this. Their principal concern is the campaign Okpatayauk and his friends have launched to stop the development."

"Could they stop the mine from going ahead?"

"Probably not. They already have Orders-in-Council from Yellowknife, explicitly permitting them to operate. But the South Africans have been very clear that they have no interest in operating a mine in the face of local hostility. They have some experience with that and they've found it expensive. Plus, with their political situation with apartheid and everything, I think they don't have much enthusiasm for more negative publicity."

"So what would happen if opinion goes Okpatayauk's way?"

"Nothing immediately, I think. But they would downscale their plans and then, if the local sentiment is clearly against them, try to find a buyer."

"And the problem with that would be?"

"They're the people who know how to run a profitable diamond mine. They're who we want up here, for all our sakes. There will be three thousand jobs building this thing and a thousand running it. Imagine that."

"So how do we get town opinion to go against Okpatayauk?"

Robertson paused. "I have some ideas."

Balthazar sat in Bernard's living room, listening to "Saturday Night Fish Fry" on the priest's 78-rpm record player. Whenever Balthazar was in the city, he picked up records for the priest, whose passion in this arena revolved around late-1940s blues. He had found this one in a shop in Chelsea. He had other presents: a braid of garlic, a wheel of blue cheese, and a case of Armagnac. The priest's eyes had lit up most at the music.

When the new dormitory had been built behind the church in 1973, Bernard had had to abandon his cabin and move into it. He had rankled at the indignity of living like a seminarian again but had not protested. He was aware of the lack of housing in the community and of the likelihood that any other single man should be given a cabin to himself. And there were upsides to the new arrangement. He did not have to fuss with the toilet or, on the many nights cold enough to freeze all manner of plumbing, the bucket. He also thought he was better off to be surrounded by visiting priests and novitiates to offset a certain isolationist streak in himself. And then, in the last few years, the health board had rented one of the unused apartments in the building for Balthazar.

Their friendship had not been immediate. The priest had known of the man for some time before he began appearing in the morning in the hallways, lumbering to the showers and yawning and scratching without modesty. And Bernard had shared the town's reservations about him, or had no reason to dispute them. But, as their arrangement went on, he had become fond of Balthazar in a way that he had not antici-

pated—a union of two equally antisocial introverts with an obligation
to safeguard the welfare of the town. In the winter, they were usually
the only two residents of the dormitory for months at a time. Bernard
had propped his door open, and the music poured out into the empty
building for all, that is, no one, to hear. It felt daring to both of them to
play music at such volume in a public place. Balthazar was in his late for-
ties, and Bernard had to have been sixty, anyway. But that night, they
felt like twenty-three-year-olds, intoxicated by dangerous scratchy music and Armagnac.

When the record was finished, the priest rose to pour them another
and to cut up the cheese. "Robertson built his wife a new house, a real
château. Have you seen it?"

"No."

"Apparently, it was a surprise even to her. The only log house I've
ever seen north of the tree line."

"Well, there's the old hospital the priests built in Chesterfield."

"Well, yes. And isn't that a treat to heat?"

"Did Victoria like it?"

"She's refused to move in."

Balthazar looked at him quizzically.

"Well, why do you suppose he built it for her in the first place?"

"He wants her to love him."

"Of course."

"I see."

There was a short silence as they both thought about Robertson's
position in that marriage. Both Balthazar's and the priest's sympathies
usually gravitated to Victoria, but this night they couldn't help feeling
sorry for the man.

Balthazar decided to change the subject. "What else happened
while I was away?"

"The schoolteacher, Emo's friend, was out on the tundra all summer, up by the Back River, camping alone. The hunters checked up on
her. I think they enjoy her spirit."

"Certainly Emo does."

"Well, that would be gossiping. How does your book go?"

"Well, it isn't really a book, Bernard—you know that. It's just some thoughts I've written down."

"Did you work on it this summer?"

"Not too much. I meant to. But I got distracted."

"By what?"

"I saw my niece a few times. She told me where to find these records."

"You two are close, yes?"

"Not exactly. But we seem to be more patient with each other than any other two people in my family."

"The Inuit understand this better than southerners do. How children are supposed to be raised by their aunts and uncles and grandparents too."

"Well, I'm not up to raising her, exactly."

"But perhaps that would change if only you did, a little."

"My brother and his wife aren't doing well. I think they're going to split up."

"I'm sorry to hear that, Keith, but I'm sorry for your niece, mostly."

Then Bernard put on *Slim's Jam:* tenor saxophone and oblique 1940s references to marijuana.

They both leaned back, eyes half closed as they listened to the music, the priest laughing into his Armagnac. When it was done, the needle scratched its way rhythmically around the center of the record until Balthazar rose and lifted it off. They had listened to all the music he had bought that summer. "So, Bernard," he asked as he poured more brandy into their glasses, "do you think it's harder for people to keep marriages together than it used to be?"

Bernard did not open his eyes and Balthazar thought that the priest had fallen asleep. Then he answered, still without moving his eyelids. "If people are different, then their marriages will be different too. Marriage has changed, the people in them have changed."

"Up here too?"

"Everywhere is the same as everywhere else—that's the lesson of the end of the twentieth century. You're talking about your brother and his wife, no doubt."

"Yes. My niece ran away from them, to me. She wanted to live with me until they figured things out."

"What did you say?"

"I avoided the issue."

"Tsk."

"You disapprove?"

"I'm not criticizing you, Keith."

"They fight like they hate each other."

"That's an old story."

"Yeah."

"And so is relatives helping out."

"That part isn't so much the case now."

Robertson and Victoria sat together on the steps of their old house. The girls were inside doing their schoolwork and Pauloosie was sharpening a knife. Victoria smoked a cigarette, which she had not done in front of Robertson in twelve years.

"It's just that I love this house. You should have talked to me about getting a new one. I've raised my children in this house and—I just don't know what you're trying to do here."

Robertson rubbed his knees. "Victoria, there is nothing you will let me do for you."

"I think we've been living alongside each other, rather than with each other, for way too long."

"So can we fix that?"

"I don't know."

"I'll never be an Inuk, you know. Is that the problem, at the end of the day?"

She shook her head and drew on her cigarette, tears welling like water off an icicle: hanging and then the long drop. She took off her glasses and wiped her eyes.

The *Appetite for Destruction* tour pulled into Madison Square Garden for three shows, October 7, 8, and 9, 1988. Amanda bought tickets with Emma, a friend from school, and together they spun a story for their parents about taking in a dance performance. Emma and Amanda met at the mall. They changed in one of the washrooms in the food court, trading their jeans for miniskirts and applying makeup so heavily, their skin took on the texture of sparkly Play-Doh. Then they took a bus to the Port Authority and walked to the Garden. They were both so excited, they skipped as they walked, recovering their composure only as the Garden hove into view.

Their seats were high up in the arena. Even before the show started the girls were enthralled by the noise and the smoke and the electric sex in the air. They were a little younger than most of the people around them, but they were pretty, and many smiles were sent their way. Even as the warm-up band was taking their bows, Amanda was consulting her watch and calculating when they would have to leave to catch the last bus home. Then Axl Rose strutted onto the stage and Slash followed him and the two of them launched into the introductory verse to "Welcome to the Jungle" and that was it, Amanda was standing on her seat and writhing like every other person in the building—eighteen thousand of them—and there was no more discussion of late buses.

A boy stood in front of them, tall and lithe and, in the heat of the show, naked from the waist up. He turned to the girls, and he was very, very high, and he handed them a joint without asking and they each smoked a bit of it, choking and coughing before handing it back. Then they all went back to dancing. The show only got better.

The boy's name was Lewis and after the concert was over he drove them back to Newark, where he lived too. He dropped Emma off in front of her darkened house. Amanda guided him to her parents' place and after he pulled to a stop on their cul-de-sac, he leaned over and kissed her as she was reaching for the door handle. She was astonished. But then she kissed him back, for a long time, fumbling, conscious of the saliva building up in her mouth. He kept giggling and she thought he was laughing at her, but it was only that he was so high. Finally she wrote her phone number on his hand, then slipped out of the car and ran up the sidewalk.

Okpatayauk was twenty-nine years old and had lived for two years in the south, studying at the University of Ottawa with a view to becoming a lawyer. His pride undid him. At school in Rankin Inlet he had been considered a sort of prodigy, from grade two on, the object of constant praise and pointed comparisons with other students because he read books for enjoyment and listened in class. His first semester at university had almost shattered him. He struggled on for a bit, then gave up and returned home, sullen and angry, and had spent the nine years since working as a casual clerk in the government offices. Over and over again his superiors told him that he could have a bright future in the civil service but for his attitude. People with such attitudes typically respond about as well as Okpatayauk did to this admonition.

He had heard the same gossip everyone else in town had—some of Robertson's colleagues were too talkative—and found himself responding to the subject of the mine in a way he had not responded to anything before. He began asking his coworkers if they thought the mine would be a good thing for the Inuit. The prevailing view was that not much of the money from such a venture would find its way into Inuit hands—the lion's share of any windfall would no doubt drift toward Robertson and the Ikhirahlo Group—and that, anyway, the idea of diamonds under the tundra was a little silly.

Okpatayauk lived with his girlfriend, Elizabeth Angutetuar, who had a government apartment and was another Inuk who could have a

bright future in the civil service. It was either live with her or room
with a half dozen other single men in one of the houses set aside for
them. The smell of spilled beer was the least of it. And meanwhile, the
Kablunauk Robertson wore wristwatches that cost as much as a truck,
he had heard.

And so Okpatayauk formed a committee to oppose the mine. Soon
there were thirty people coming to his and Elizabeth's apartment once
a week to talk about what was happening, and to discuss what they
might do to stop it. Okpatayauk thought that it was not in his interest,
at this stage, to make the protest a race-based matter. He thought that
would muddy the issue, and alienate the schoolteachers who had had
some experience in forming movements such as this.

He had persuaded the town council to hold a meeting about the
mine. Robertson and his colleagues in the Ikhirahlo Group had expected this and had not expended political capital opposing the suggestion. A date was picked and the hockey arena was booked. In the weeks
beforehand, posters began appearing in town—on the announcement
board at the Northern Store, the church corkboard, and, in an unprecedented act of effrontery, taped to the light posts along the streets. They
read, THE CARIBOU LIVE THERE NOW. IN TWO YEARS, THEY WON'T.

Every night of the week before the meeting, Okpatayauk's committee gathered in his apartment. The members made more posters and
the Kablunauks talked about how logging had been stopped in the old-
growth forests in British Columbia. The Inuit listened and spoke less
stridently but with more weight. The tenor of their objection: What if
we don't want it to change that much?

Penny did not normally participate in town politics, affecting a kind
of macho impatience with anyone who proposed to speak of the land
who couldn't themselves build an iglu worth sleeping in. But the mine,
and the people who appeared to be associated with it, struck her as
something that needed to be addressed. She thought about the farmland
north of Edmonton where she had grown up: thick with oil heads rock-

ing up and down, the mixed farms gone now, leaving behind three- and five-thousand-acre expanses of rapeseed stretching in monotonous yellow to the horizon. In the absence of working livestock, the sloughs had all been filled in. Where hogs were still kept they were housed in enormous sheet-metal natural gas–heated and dimly lit enclosures, twenty thousand animals jowl by jowl, the odor blasting out like some Dantean wind onto the prairie. She thought of the mine in these terms—as proceeding inexorably to the diminution of the land and the people involved with it.

Apart from her intense and complicated relationship with Emo, she had almost no friends among the local adults. She was known to the community and she was aware of this: the Kablunauk woman musher who spent her weekends and holidays alone on the land. It was a big deal when she finally decided to go to Okpatayauk's apartment.

"I'm Penny Bleskie," she said at the door, shaking Okpatayauk's hand. Inside, she nodded to Elizabeth Agutetuar, Madeleine Tuktuk, Jerome Nappigak, Uluyuk Tartuk, the social worker, the two nurses, and the three teachers who were there, all of whom knew who she was and had spent long hours speculating about her and the old man.

She sat down on a pillow. The smoke in the room was thick, and her eyes stung so much that when Pauloosie Robertson walked into the room five minutes later, she didn't recognize him at first. She had not seen him since she had found him on the tundra. His attendance at school had become steadily more sporadic, and it had been assumed that he would stop attending altogether soon. Still, here he was at the meeting, and it could only be because he was concerned about the mine—the principal advocate of which was his father.

He sat down on the floor against a wall. He and Penny and Okpatayauk were the only people present under thirty. He regretted coming immediately but realized that leaving would only make him more of a spectacle. He didn't know any of the Kablunauks except the teacher with the dogs and he couldn't remember her name. Okpatayauk was talking about the mine as some sort of power struggle. Between Inuit and Kablunauks, Pauloosie supposed. Why were there Kablunauks in his apartment, then? His grandfather had told him that the first mine here changed the way everyone lived. People left the land then; now they hardly even went out onto it.

Everyone but Penny understood that Pauloosie was also there as a gesture of defiance to his father. His father, who had learned Inukti-tut, and how to shoot straight and how to dig in for bad weather, and now refused to acknowledge any familiarity with these skills at all. It was worse than mysterious to Pauloosie—it felt like a repu-diation.

"The thing is, we have to get people to understand that this is our land," Okpatayauk said. "These southerners come up and they see a way they can make money by wrecking it and they just go ahead and do it. So many people here in town think they have nothing to say about it. But they do."

"I think maybe things are changing," Elizabeth Agutetuar said. "In the grocery store today, five people came up to me to talk about the town meeting, and why it was good we are doing all this."

"So who wants to head out now to put up the last of these posters?" Jerome Nappigak asked.

Pauloosie put up his hand. Anything to get out of here. So did Penny.

"How are your dogs?" he asked as they stepped outside, each hold-ing a bundle of yellow posters.

"Fine, thanks—yours?"

"I need a new lead."

"I heard Apilardjuk has one for sale."

"He wants five hundred dollars."

"When did dogs start going for five hundred dollars?"

"When they started getting fashionable."

"When did that happen?"

"You tell me."

"Your Ski-Doo working better these days?"

"Yeah."

October 15, 1988

Dear Keith:

How are you? I am fine. I hope it's not too cold up there. Ha! Ha! I wish you were still here. If you were, I'd play my new Guns N' Roses album for you. Sad to say, but my interest in the viola may be ebbing. Don't tell my mother. Speaking of which, things on that front are only getting crazier. My dad is starting to drink too much. The other night I came home from music lessons late and he was loaded. He was kinda sweet, though, all apologetic and everything. Mom wouldn't even talk to him.

Anyway, if you were here, I'd also have some questions for you about birth control. Write back when you have a chance!

Love,

Amanda

Woodchopper's Ball, by Woody Herman and his orchestra, was more mainstream and much more mannered than the priest's usual fare; nevertheless, since Balthazar had found the original recording in the city, Bernard was prepared to enjoy it. Beauty runs in many rivers. Less deeply, perhaps, in all-white orchestras led by an egomaniac like Woody Herman, but one of the lessons of art is that, despite themselves, the blind stumble across sublimity too. And then, in the break, the clarinet—that was gorgeous. He could see why people liked it. One of the lessons of God.

"You seem distracted tonight, Father."

"I've been thinking about the mine a great deal. Several people have asked me to address the subject in church."

"Are you going to?"

"Good heavens, no. The church of St. Peter has not endured for two thousand years by being topical."

"But what do you think of the whole plan, really?"

"I think that if it had gone ahead ten years ago, there would hardly have been any discussion."

"And now?"

"The Inuit have changed."

"Are you sorry to see them more politically assertive?"

"Of course not."

"But you reject the worldliness that assertiveness demands."

"*Bien sûr*. And who could but mourn that? Must we all be exactly alike?"

"The church has had a hand in that, Father."

"Oh, I know it."

"I'm surprised that you're liking the Woody Herman."

"I am too, to tell you the truth. Just don't be coming over here with any Glen Miller, if that's your plan."

"Don't you worry."

"So how is your niece these days? You haven't mentioned her lately."

"I got a letter from her just the other day. It sounds like she's growing up quickly. Her parents are the same, though, it seems."

"Poor child."

"I think she's got a handle on things."

October 25, 1988

Dear Amanda,

I'm sorry that your mother and father are still struggling so much, and that your father is drinking. That is, actually, a bit of a habit among the men in our family. Your paternal grandfather had the same problem, as did his father. But your father has not drunk excessively, to my knowledge, until now, and presumably this has to do with the fighting between him and your mother. So what I'm saying is, when that gets resolved, as it must, soon, then I think he will stop drinking. Though I can only imagine the effect that behavior has on your mother.

You know, if you wanted, you could come up here to visit me sometime. In the summer, you might find it especially beautiful, when the tundra flowers are all out and there are caribou and musk oxen everywhere. It can be quite gorgeous. I'm sorry I wasn't able to help you when you asked for it just before I left. I still regret that. Do you know what you want for Christmas this year?

Love,
Uncle Keith

The town meeting was scheduled for three in the afternoon on a Saturday in early December. The weather was gorgeous all that week, and everyone involved in the anti-mine movement had felt buoyed by the sunshine and warmth. If two hundred people requested it at the meeting, a plebiscite would be arranged for the following month, they had learned from the hamlet lawyer. It could all go so well. Penny and Pauloosie and Okpatayauk and the others had been all over town, extracting commitments to attend, and were looking forward to their triumph.

Dawn broke beautifully on Saturday, around ten A.M., and Penny awoke as it streaked through her window. Her first impulse was to leap to her feet and head out onto the land. And then she remembered that it was the day of the town meeting and turned over in bed. She hoped this wouldn't be the last of the good weather.

She dressed and walked down to the sea ice to feed her dogs, the sky glowing orange with the morning sun. Most of the dog teams were already out, and her own dogs were agitated beyond soothing that they were still chained. Not that it stopped them from devouring the seal carcass she had brought for them. She turned around and made her way to the hockey rink. She'd volunteered to get there early to help set up for the meeting at three.

The town was oddly quiet for a weekend. The Northern Store should have been bustling and the street traffic ought to have been incessant. But it was as if it were summer or something.

When she arrived, the rest of the committee were already there, unfolding chairs. Okpatayauk and Elizabeth Angutetuar were huddled together beside the podium, reviewing his speech. The last few days, in the grocery store, you heard hardly anything else discussed. *There could be fireworks today,* she thought. Penny hung her coat on a chair and set to work.

By two o'clock the arena was ready and the committee members could hardly contain themselves. The chairs and tables were all laid out, everyone knew how the meeting was going to be structured, and they knew when they were to applaud and when not to. The Ikhirahlo Group directors were the first to arrive, Robertson and Betty Peters and Melvin Anders. They stood in one corner of the room and watched their opposition chatter gleefully with one another. At two-thirty, members of the town council began drifting in. The mayor, who was to moderate the discussion, arrived last, breathless and windburnt. He brought news that had escaped the notice of the committee. The beautiful weather had brought the caribou out of the central river valleys to forage wildly in huge numbers. They had been spotted within twenty miles of Rankin Inlet. "I've never seen so many tuktu so close to town. You should see them, thousands of them! Clive Akpalik got six fat bucks in ten minutes. Practically the whole town is there."

By three, no one else had arrived. There were more people sitting at the table on the stage than in the audience. Père Bernard sat beside Dr. Balthazar in the front row. Johanna was behind them. At ten after three Pauloosie burst in, breathless, his face wind- and sunburnt. He started to apologize to Okpatayauk, who just cut him off. "I know. It doesn't matter."

At four, the mayor declared the meeting canceled due to lack of interest. The committee members began folding up the tables and stacking the chairs. They hardly spoke.

It started snowing that night and by Sunday a full blizzard sat on the place and just howled. Everyone made it back into town okay.

Johanna's telephone rang as she was returning to her apartment on the following Friday afternoon, her arms full of book reports and exams. She dropped them in a great cloudburst of paper and picked up the receiver.

"You sound flustered," Doug said.

"I just got in."

"Everything okay?"

"Yes. Hey, can I call you back in five minutes?"

"I'm not at home."

"The office?"

"Nope." His evasiveness irritated her.

"Where, then?"

"The Rankin Inlet Airport?"

"What?"

"Surprise!"

"You're kidding."

"Nope."

"I'll come get you."

"Whew."

"Place has you a little frightened?"

"A little. There's an archway made of caribou antlers outside the airport door here."

"I've stopped even noticing that."

"You should hurry."

"I'm on my way."

In the airport Doug was sitting on one of the benches, wearing an enormous bright yellow down coat that ballooned off him as if it were inflated. When he stood to greet her it hung below his knees. And he held his arms out akimbo like a child in a snowsuit. Johanna smirked.

"I said, 'I want the warmest coat you have.' 'The very warmest, sir?' he said. 'The very warmest,' I said. 'It won't be cheap or fashionable.' 'I don't care,' I said."

"What are you doing here?"

"I thought I'd drop in for a visit. Spontaneous-like."

"What did you think I would say if you had asked me beforehand?"

"No."

"So maybe this is a bit of an intrusion."

"I was hoping the coat would inspire some pity for me."

"Do you have luggage?"

"Right here."

"Let's take it to my place."

When they stepped through her doorway, Doug whistled as he took in the items lying on the kitchen table: her sealskin boots, rabbit-fur hat, and windpants. A VHF radio was charging in a wall outlet, and a fishing rod stood in one corner, a large, green and malevolent-looking lure hanging from its tip.

"It's about what I pictured."

"So let's talk about why you are here."

"Impulse. Same reason you are."

"Except that you're here because of your impulses, and I'm here because of your impulses."

"Those damn impulses."

"Well, I would agree."

Then he stepped forward and kissed her, his mouth just touching hers, barely perceptible but felt everywhere, all at once. She breathed in and was done for. He pushed himself closer and they were up against the door, and near parboiling themselves in goose down. She was hungrier than she had allowed herself to understand, and when his hands reached her hips, she bit her own lip and then, when that didn't work, she bit his.

From a distance it would have looked like violence. He held her wrists above her head, her arms straight up and against the wall; she lunged at him and her forehead struck his lip, splitting it, blood running down his chin and over the front of his throat. He kissed her hard, and when he pulled away blood was streaked over her mouth like an angry welt. Her lips chased his as he arched his neck backwards; she caught him by his bloody throat, and kissed him there, where the windpipe dives under the sternum. He let go of her wrists and wrapped his arms around her shoulders, shuddering, as she bit him again and again.

In the coffee shop the following afternoon they sat not speaking, staring stuporously at one another. They each had bruises along the length of their collarbones and the pressure of their trousers on the front of their pubic bones was painful. Everyone in town knew that Johanna had a visitor. The teenagers crowding the coffee shop studied him and, especially, they studied their teacher's look of exhausted satiety, a look the kids knew well, being young and living in a place with limited diversions.

When they got back to her apartment the door had only just clicked behind them when they began pulling each other's clothing off again, shaking their heads as they did so. They paused only to fish out the tube of personal lubricant from Johanna's coat pocket, which they had picked up at the grocery store. Evidence of more foresight than she would have guessed her benumbed brain capable.

She put him on the plane the following day. They said almost nothing to each other as they walked from her car to the airport. When his plane was loading he turned to kiss her and the next thing they knew an apologetic flight steward was poking him on the shoulder. She felt so happy, she had become stupid. Her thoughts did not extend beyond the intense and unprecedented pleasure of this moment. She felt bite marks all over her body, the muscles along the inside of her thighs ached, and her shoulders and knees were made of gelatin.

As his airplane took off she felt as if a film had been pulled off her. Off her entire body, and from her mind, or whatever portion of it houses desire.

The Igloo Hotel in Baker Lake had been a thumping, slamming, and flatulent particleboard-paneled box for the week that the construction crew had been in town. Balthazar had groaned inwardly at the noise and imposition of having to share his lodging with enormous chain-smoking Albertans who smelled of wheel-bearing grease and spoke of only one thing: the prohibition on alcohol in this and all the other hamlets along Hudson Bay. When he returned from the nurses' station after work on Friday to find the building disgorging itself into three awaiting GMC crew cabs, his pleased surprise was soon displaced by the silence of the hallway as he walked its length to his room.

He had to stay on in Baker Lake for the weekend to attend clinics scheduled for Monday and Tuesday before he could return to Rankin Inlet. And he would have nothing to do. The nurses were accustomed to not having a doctor in town, preferred it actually, and he knew they would not call him in over the weekend for anything less serious than a decapitation.

He had been looking forward, he realized, to the prospect of grumpily listening to the inane conversation of the Albertans as they played cards and chewed tobacco and told obscene stories about women of their acquaintance in Yellowknife. Now he was alone in the hotel, and would only be joined for a few minutes at mealtimes by the cook, Martha, an elderly Inuk who spoke no language he had ever heard and delivered white ceramic plates of sodden mashed potatoes and pork chops as resilient as Tupperware to his table. By the time he had set down his stethoscope on the bed and begun to contemplate the two days stretching before him, he heard her slamming the door as she left for home. It was five-thirty. The manager, Brian, who surfaced from time to time during the middle of the week, was out on the land, fishing. Through his window, Balthazar could see light snow beginning to fall obliquely in a rising wind.

He wandered through the darkened hallways, turning on lights. In the kitchen he found a plate of turnips and corned beef hash with a sheet of Saran Wrap over it, a little cloud of condensation in the center, with a similarly filmed pitcher of orange Kool-Aid beside it. He carried his meal into the dining room, sat down at the long table, and wearily peeled off the Saran Wrap. He probed the food with a fork, then ate it, in the absence of any alternative, and drank the Kool-Aid as if it were medicine. The squeaking of his knife and fork on the plate echoed through the empty dining room. There was a television mounted on the wall, but Balthazar could not find the remote, so he moved a chair underneath it, climbed up, and reached for the controls. Perched on the chair on tiptoes, he cycled through the satellite package until he found the news. He climbed down and resumed his efforts against the corned beef hash.

Ronald Reagan was having his final meeting as president with Margaret Thatcher. The two of them looked like desiccated mannequins carved from weathered walnut as they grimaced out at the news photographers from the podium. The broadcast shifted to English soccer hooligans brawling in Marseilles and then to floods in the Mississippi Valley.

Balthazar went into the kitchen to boil some water in order to make instant coffee. He put his dishes in the sink and walked back to his room, carrying his coffee mug. He turned the television on there. He was agitated with boredom and it was only Friday evening.

He opened his suitcase and found his medical journals. Every time he turned a page his eyes rose and he surveyed the room. If he could, he would have simply lost consciousness until it was time to get up and go to work Monday morning. He could happily do without the next two days of his life.

Restless, he shoved his journals back into his suitcase and got up to pace. In the shadowed hallway, the night glow shone in through the small square windows, built high up on the wall so that they wouldn't get covered with snow in the winter. Outside was an opaque swirling mass: a storm rising quickly. It had stormed twice a week since the fiasco of the town meeting. Everyone was happy that they had enough meat. The Ikhirahlo Group had announced it was holding a special Christmas party that year, flying in Stompin' Tom Connors as entertainment. The paltry attendance at the town meeting had been taken as acquiescence to the mine's going ahead, and the South Africans had been delighted. Stompin' Tom was the least they could do.

Balthazar watched the storm coalescing through the window and his spirits sagged. He wished he had scheduled this trip differently, wished he were back in Rankin Inlet, listening to obscure music with the priest. There it was: his principal companion in life was a priest who scarcely knew him, whom he knew even less.

He brooded on the state of his apartment when he had returned home last time and, worse, when he had left it again. He lived like an adolescent. What could be so difficult about the idea of washing all the dishes in the sink before leaving town for three months? Or even, for God's sake, draining the dishwater from it?

The wind rose higher and Balthazar thought about the hotel manager, out on the land this late in the year. He did not know whether Brian was with one of the local families or whether he even had a tent. He assumed he must. Storms happen all the time and people mostly survive them. Then the whole building shook and he thought, *But how?*

A storm as big as this meant that nothing would happen in the nursing station for several days. When the wind settled and the air cleared, there might be business: hunters and fishers caught by surprise, straggling in with frostbite.

In moments such as these he had long been in the habit of contrasting his brother and sister-in-law's life to his own. He had always thought of them as exemplars of competence and structure, and had wondered why order should come so easily to them and not at all to him. They got up in the morning and started looking around for bills to pay, laundry to wash. He woke up in the morning and wished he hadn't.

This time that picture didn't hold. He tried to imagine his brother drinking, Angela yelling. But still. They both went to work, they kept their house up, attended the parent-teacher meetings. What was the difference between him and practically everyone else he knew?

Back in his room, moving robotically, he unzipped his toiletry kit and unwrapped a leather case. Inside was a handful of plastic syringes and ten vials of morphine sulphate, some alcohol pledgettes, and a rubber tourniquet. He tied the tubing around his bicep as if he were performing a religious ritual. He tore the alcohol pledgette open with his teeth and swabbed the crook of his elbow. His brachial vein bulged purple in the weak light. He stripped off a syringe wrapper and broke open the glass morphine vial. He drew out ten milligrams, holding the vial to the light and flicking the syringe, watching the bubbles in the cylinder break loose and float up toward the needle. He pushed on the syringe until all the bubbles, and a thin stream of water and morphine, sprouted from the needle point. By this time his arm was starting to feel cold. He straightened it and slid the needle into his skin. There was a dimpling, which Balthazar watched, anticipating what was to come, and then the needle pushed through and into the vein. He could feel a subtle popping as the tip of the needle found its place. He drew back on the syringe and a crimson flower opened in the barrel of the syringe. He slowly pressed on the plunger and watched the blossom crumple, fold in on itself, and disappear. Even as the syringe was half empty he felt a metallic taste in his mouth, and then there was a warmth settling over him, crawling up his arm and sliding down his chest, filling his skull. Happiness was upon him.

He stood in the darkened dining room of the hotel and listened to the storm on every side. If he had been less high, he would have wanted

a sweater. He thought a little more about Amanda. He was sorry to
know that her parents were fighting so much, but neither was he surprised. He knew his brother too well to imagine that it was mostly Angela's fault. He pictured his niece lying in her bed at night, holding
pillows over her head, and was dissolved for a moment by the sympathy he felt for her.

There was a sodium yellow streetlight outside the entrance of the
hotel. Martha lived across the street, and Brian the absent manager
lived in a locked room adjacent to the kitchen. When the snow blew
hard it stretched out in long yellow streaks across the night sky. Balthazar was drawn to the window, staring out at the very absence of anything to see. He pressed his nose against the glass and held it there,
feeling the aching cold spreading into his face, and then the ache diminishing as his nose became numb. Still he stood there, his breath misting
up on the glass and freezing, a widening butterfly-shaped spot of ice extending on either side of his face. He leaned his forehead into the glass
now and felt it slowly become numb.

Balthazar blinked. It was morning. Or midafternoon, more accu-
rately, he judged from the dimming light. He rubbed his face and then
he stretched. He was no longer high. He still had most of the weekend
to pass here. He closed his eyes for a long minute.

He opened his eyes again and reached into his travel bag and pulled
out a thick spiral-ringed notebook with a yellow cover that read
SCHOOL DAZE and had a cartoon of a boy fishing. He felt around the bottom of the bag until he found a pencil. He opened the notebook and began rereading the last thing he had written. He touched the eraser of
the pencil to his lip. He narrowed his eyes. He scratched out a sentence.
He wrote out a phrase, *opiate addiction,* and then crossed it out.

The line crackled with satellite interference, and each of them
leaned into their telephones, to hear the other's breath:

"I felt like I was nineteen again. Like I was drunk."

"Me too."

"Why don't you come up next weekend? I'll pay."

"How about the one after?"

"Oh, you have plans."

"It's just the short notice."

"Doug, are you still seeing people?"

Satellite hum.

"Doug?"

"Why do you ask?"

One evening in 1973 I took one of the medical journals to which I
subscribed home with me from the clinic where I worked in Rankin Inlet. I
liked to spend the evenings reading about far-off developments in the hospitals
I had trained in——it made the isolation a little less acute and made me feel a
little less like an imposter. It was my first job, and every day I wondered when
someone was going to see right through me. (This is not a concern that has
ever entirely resolved.)

I read late into the night, about the utility of beta-blockers and bile salt
sequestrants. Just as I was about to go to bed, I came upon Abdel Omran's paper
advancing the idea of the epidemiologic transition. The next time I looked up
from the page it was dawn, and I had come to understand human illness and
history in a way I had never considered before. I was like a second-year sciences
student coming to terms with relativistic motion. I knew how physicists must
have felt at the beginning of the last century when the patent clerk had started
publishing in obscure journals.

Omran's epidemiologic transition rests on the idea that the way we live is
revealed fundamentally by how we sicken and die. When changes that are truly
important occur in the way we eat and fight and raise our children, then they
always show up in the way we die.

The skeletal remains of paleolithic humans bear the stigmata of the
threats they faced while living: skulls scored with teethmarks, fractured long
bones and necks, and the hallmarks of starvation: pitiably small children lying
with older adults. The marks on those bones are the clearest indicators we have

about what those lives were like. From them, we learn that there was always a struggle to find enough food and all around there were predators—great cats and wild dogs looking to pull us down by our necks. For millions of years, humans died mostly of those two causes, and what we adapted ourselves to was bleeding, and hunger. Six million years we spent walking on the Serengeti, living and dying that way. The Inuit lived exactly like this until the Second World War, walking and hunting and keeping an eye out for bears. Many of the old men I treated claimed to still long for that harder life, and the dignity they thought it lent them.

When humans began planting seeds—initially in Mesopotamia—everything changed. We grouped together for the first time in stationary villages, in numbers that no hunting-gathering society could support. We domesticated animals and produced enough farmed food to support specialists: potters and metalsmiths, priests and soldiers. One effect of all this was that, grouped together in cities and towns, humans become vulnerable to infections in a way we had never been as wanderers.

Nomads suffer no epidemics because they are dispersed, their populations too small to sustain a cycle of infection. A society smaller than half a million people, for instance, is not able to sustain endemic measles and consequent population-wide adult immunity. When pathogens enter a small population, everyone dies or becomes immune at once. Mostly what they do is die. The Icelanders demonstrated this, to their great cost, when North Atlantic trade resumed after the Dark Ages.

Indeed, the only transmittable infections of any sort that hunter-gatherers suffer from are insect-borne—malaria especially, but also dengue fever, yellow fever, and the various encephalitides. The Inuit, whose mosquitoes were frozen solid every September, suffered from no transmittable infections at all. None. This was subsequently to change.

With the Neolithic revolution, tuberculosis learned to infect humans, and within the crowded little homes of the early farmers it became as ubiquitous as the rodent vermin that adapted itself similarly and moved in off the fields to seek out man and his leavings. We find the evidence in the bones that are dug up, the cold abscesses and the characteristic patterns of osseous infections.

Influenza leapt to us from wild birds, and syphilis from the unlucky sheep domesticated by Neolithic farmers.

These were all features of the second phase of the epidemiologic transition, a change that revolved around the development of agriculture, a time that also saw the rise of tyrants and of armies. Permanent populations adjacent to cultivated fields could spare enough men to send off to war. Hunters and gatherers living alongside these civilizations simply melted back into the trees and were progressively confined to nonarable spaces. Still, their bones are revelatory: the nomads were better fed in their less-organized bands than the peasants of the settled tribes, whose populations expanded in Malthusian fashion to the limits of supportability as rapidly as the food supply grew. And it is the civilized bones that bear the marks of sword cuts and shackles—seen nowhere among the hunters, for whom war is usually a relatively nonlethal pastime.

These were the prevailing circumstances from the rise of the Mesopotamian civilizations to, in Western Europe, the early nineteenth century. Life expectancy remained at about forty years throughout this period, in every society. The principal causes of death were TB, homicide, dysentery, starvation, and, beneath fifty degrees of latitude, malaria.

What changed everything, ushering in the third phase of the epidemiologic transition, was the rise of engines. For Europeans this corresponded to the Industrial Revolution. As both agricultural and manufacturing techniques industrialized, the population movement into cities and off the fields coincided with a rise in availability of mass-produced food and with increasing crowding in the tenements. Accompanying this movement was an unprecedented human exposure to chemical toxins, the appearance of occupational lung disease, an increase in the consumption of animal fats, and a decrease in fiber intake. Tobacco and alcohol use became significant limiters of health too. The Dickensian horror that was Victorian London was replayed in successive years in Berlin and Paris and Ankara and St. Petersburg. Following these: Delhi and Mexico City and Beijing. Bodies mangled in industrial and road accidents while food comes in from the countryside at a steady clip. Tired workers stumbling home to gorge themselves on cheap manufactured food.

The diseases of affluence—heart disease, cancer—gained a foothold then, and for the first time there were important threats to humans other than starvation, violence, and infections. One of the most important insights gained through examining the epidemiologic transition is this: there is nothing inevitable about the sicknesses of our time. Heart attacks are not just what happens to people who manage to survive into their fifties and sixties. Before the Industrial Revolution, coronary thrombosis, as heart attacks were initially called—myocardial infarctions, as they are called now—had not been described. By this time, vaccination for rabies and smallpox had been developed; the causative organisms for malaria and tuberculosis had been identified; the developments of aseptic surgery and anesthesia made operations survivable. Medicine was young but not blind. Heart attacks were unknown because they hardly ever happened, even among those who lived to be old. Before bleached flour became widely available at the beginning of the eighteenth century, colon cancer was as rare as it is in Africa now. Throughout the Industrial Revolution, as it unfolded in Europe, and a century later, in India and China, these illnesses have appeared with monotonous predictability. Cancer and heart attacks and strokes are what will most likely kill anyone wealthy enough to know what those words mean. Alongside these ran the infections, especially tuberculosis, but before useful treatment was developed the death rate was already falling, as apartments and houses became less crowded and the food supply more reliable. Violence continued, of course, and the homicidal spasm of the first half of the twentieth century was like nothing else history has seen. Food may pacify hungry babies and holiday diners, but it does not soothe the martial instinct of nations.

The fourth phase of the epidemiologic transition began after the Second World War. It saw the dramatic impact of medical therapies such as antibiotics on infant mortality. With these, and better obstetrical care, life expectancy soared by two years per decade, to the mideighties, in Japan and Scandinavia. For Asian and South American societies, the fourth phase trailed, but not by much. These treatments are cheap, and so these technologies—especially the vaccines—have been readily exported to developing nations. From this point forward, a certain amount of overlap exists between societies at varying levels of affluence. Populations may be affected by the availability of antibiotics and vaccinations while they are still dependent on subsistence farming. Starvation may persist notwithstanding the (imminent, and astounding) eradication of polio.

The effect of antibiotics, even on the rich societies, is difficult to overstate. Long lists of sanatoria closed as consumptives regained their color and were pushed out into the world. Heart disease and stroke, increasingly important killers since the advent of the cotton gin, began to decline in lethality in the mid-1950s, when it became possible to treat hypertension. Cancer deaths too have declined under the weight of billions of dollars' worth of research and therapy. Health care in America now consumes three times as much wealth as the military. One hundred years ago it was one tenth, but in those days, babies whooped themselves to death every night in every neighborhood, and now they do not.

Our prosperity has grown enormously in this time; we have become richer even more quickly than our riches have made us sick. Our wealth has allowed us to hold at bay the diseases of affluence, allowed us to believe that we are becoming innately healthier. Look at our children's height and the robustness of their aligned incisors. The old idea of the essence emerges; the Victorian consumptive's TB was an expression of himself. We are taller and more long-lived, we assume, because we are essentially stronger and, one supposes, cleaner. It is the centerpiece of Omran's idea. The Greeks wrote plays about this sort of thinking.

Although Omran did not describe it, a fifth phase of the epidemiologic transition is becoming evident now. As death rates from vascular disease have declined under the effect of beta-blockers, cholesterol-lowering drugs, and ACE inhibitors, every developed society in the world has grown fatter. And for those who are fat enough to develop diabetes and the metabolic syndrome that is its precursor (40 percent of adult North Americans), there has been much less progress made in the mortality rate from heart attacks.

The societal effect of obesity is now beginning to outweigh technological progress in treating vascular disease: we are fatter than our drugs can compensate for. We have not grown steadily healthier at all, but rather less healthy, less robust, and vastly more indolent—though we have for a time disguised the effect of this with our pills. But the essence of us seems indeed to have changed rapidly and recently. Cars have been widely available to Americans—the fattest of all, and the fastest-growing—for half a century, but lately it appears we walk much less than ever we used to. People point to joggers in the park, but they are mere window dressing on the great immobile mass that we have become. For the bulk of us, the truth of our bulk is revealed by the numbers: the incidence of diabetes, adjusted for age, is growing faster than any other lethal illness.

More people in South Africa die of diabetes and vascular disease than of HIV. In Malaysia the prevalence of childhood obesity in 1980 was half of 1 percent. By 1999, it was 5 percent—a 1,000 percent increase in twenty years. In America, it increased from 3 percent to 12 percent between 1989 and 1999—a 400 percent increase in a decade. In most illnesses, and especially infections, these sorts of increases plateau quickly after their prevalence becomes commonplace. But the growth curves for obesity are accelerated. Obese children in America have the arteries of forty-five-year-old smokers. This, despite all the money and technology in the world being thrown at us. Perhaps because of all the money and technology in the world being thrown at us.

A plague is coming to us. Already the sailors in Constantinople are falling ill.

It is important not to distort the matter with nostalgia and sentiment. The Inuit led harder, more painful lives when they lived on the land, and this is why they have chosen not to return to it. The children died one after the other and their mothers sobbed with grief undiminished by the regularity with which it was summoned. Hunters who were merely affectionate fathers, imaginative storytellers, and tender husbands—and not adept trackers and good shots—could not feed their families. It was not a romantic life. It rewarded only a narrow set of attributes: focus, endurance, and distance vision.

And yet. Something about the way we have constructed ourselves now leads us, and anyone who tries to live like us, to immobility and engorgement.

Our habit of staring into lit screens is part of it. But more generally, we have become laden with fear. The young Inuit are withdrawing from the tundra, forgoing even weekend trips in fine weather, to the dismay of their parents. In New Jersey, parents nervously scan the sidewalks and parks, will not push their children out into them, draw them instead into their bedrooms and keep them there with glowing boxes. Fear. And why shouldn't we be afraid? We have so little experience with genuine peril: all the threats were defeated years ago.

part two

eskimo poetry

I will walk with leg muscles
Which are strong
As the sinews of the shins of the little caribou calf.
I will walk with leg muscles
Which are strong
As the sinews of the shins of the little hare.
I will take care not to go towards the dark.
I will go towards the day.

Recorded and translated from the Inuktitut by
Knud Rasmussen, *Report of the Fifth Thule*
Expedition, 1921–24

chapter twelve

■

It was the construction of the ice road from Rankin Inlet into the mine site that made it clear that the mine was something other than pure abstraction. Work began in earnest just after Christmas, 1988. Tractor-trailers—an unprecedented sight in the eastern Arctic—shuttled between the port and the road camp, which a week into the project was already five miles into the tundra. The sound of the trucks was audible throughout the town. Multiple flights arrived at the airport simultaneously—a new thing—disgorging twenty construction workers at a time. From the steps of Balthazar's apartment building at night, he could make out the track of the ice road winding its way inland, headlights twinkling along it like bioluminescence in nearly still water.

Ice roads depend on the innumerable lakes and rivers that cross the barrenlands and freeze with the onset of winter. For the duration of the cold, they make the country quite passable, even for heavy-wheeled vehicles. As the ice rots in June and July they are abandoned for the summer. Gravel sinks cloudily to the riverbed; the road signs float downstream to wash up in an oxbow someplace, or to the sea. The portions of the road built on muskeg and rock are more enduring, and can be seen from the air during summer, looking like dashes interrupted by glistening dots of small lakes, a Morse code message reaching across the land: Poor Drainage Here.

If the ice road is renewed the following winter, these portions of the road will be used again, and this much, anyway, of the effort is cumulative. The muskeg is more easily graded each time, as the ratio of

gravel to ooze slowly increases. After a number of years the gravel remains distinct in the summer—a ribbon of gray abutted by damp
greenery on either side. The engineers describe such a roadbed as "ma-
turing."

Each night, Balthazar looked out the window above his desk at the
twinkling headlights extending to the northwest in a line straighter than
anything that had been imposed on the tundra in the previous twenty
centuries of human habitation. Though he was generally disposed to ap-
prove of knowledge and capability, this manifestation of technology of-
fended his eye. The straightness of the stream of flickering headlights
held his attention, like a glimpse of something obscene.

Penny wondered every day whether she should ask to be transferred somewhere farther north, less exposed to the effects of industry
and ambition. What dissuaded her was her affection for the sullied land
itself. She had learned the sinuous curves of the Meliadine River and
Ferguson Lake and Wager Bay. She knew where to find caribou and
char. Her dogs did too. She imagined spending as much time as it had
taken her to know this country over again, on Baffin Island, where there
were mountains and glaciers, far more narwhals but fewer caribou, and
higher tides—she would be nearly as much a child as when she first
ventured out here with Emo. So she stayed.

In the summer of 1989, a succession of rust orange barges floated
up the coast to Rankin Inlet, depositing bulldozers and dynamite and
cases of food and radios and lumber, prefabricated buildings, and as
many tons of goods as the entire town would have required to survive
for several years running. The work camp became another, newer and
more moneyed, version of the town itself, with its own dispensary,
cafeteria, and rows and rows of bunkhouses. The mining company's pol-
icy was to attempt to limit the distorting effect it was having on the local economy and hire more Kablunauk workers, who shuttled directly
from the airport to the mine site and back again.

The sound of blasting rang out along the length of the Meliadine

River valley that summer, and the caribou did not appear to graze there for the first time since the famine thirty years earlier.

The ice road to the mine site was functioning by early December 1989. The enormous quantity of stores that had been laid in by the mining consortium—far too many reels of steel cable, forty-gallon drums of gear oil, and bundles of two-by-fours to fit in any warehouse, stored instead under huge tarps on the land—were then hauled out to the mine site. Every journeyman of any sort in the town was hired that winter—and for wages that were hard to believe for those who had not been. When they returned to the town on breaks or upon the completion of their contracts, they emptied the Northern Store of rifles and snowmobiles in successive waves. Every two weeks men and women rotated in and out from the mine site, cooks and welders and mechanics and electricians crowding the Northern Store with their unparticular tastes and limitless credit cards. Those who did not work in the mine found themselves unable to buy almost anything substantial, which compounded the less tangible but more toxic issue of jealousy. Soon the town was full of men and women seething at absent friends and cousins.

When the first North American diamonds appeared for sale in the Antwerp auctions, they generated excitement quite out of proportion to their quality or number. The diamond buyers were less interested in them as a mineralogical fact than as a public relations issue: the word *blood* had been glued to their product by newsmagazines (not referring to crimson fancies). With the wars in Africa generating steadily starker photographs, these new, more palatable Canadian diamonds were good news.

The people of Rankin Inlet had no way to judge how successful the mine was. A privately held consortium, it issued no public annual reports. Rumors abounded: one month they had found gold in the ore too and would be tripling the size of the development. The next month, the mine was a bust and the South Africans were leaving entirely. Waitresses and assistant managers at the grocery stores became acquainted with the politics of Namibia and the international diamond cartel that sustained and dictated the valuation, production, and marketing of the gems around the world. At work they exchanged opinions derived like sports page expertise on hockey, opining on the future market in diamonds the way furniture salesmen in Edmonton held forth on Grant Fuhr's butterfly stance.

Okpatayauk and his group did not fold after their failure to stop the mine. They continued to meet every Saturday afternoon (except the sunny ones), and the attendance at these meetings slowly grew as people became irritated at not having landed a job on the mine site. Older hunters began coming, to express their anger at what was being done to the land. Only the hunters, and mine employees, had actually seen that, and what the hunters described was awful. Great towers of spotlights illuminating a pit sunk steadily wider and deeper into the land. Pumps spitting out a gray slurry of melted permafrost and snow into fantastic shapes on the frozen soil.

But, at the same time, what most of the townspeople knew was that their houses had suddenly doubled in value. And lots of their kids had stopped wasting their time in town and started apprenticeships at the mine. Which made for more room in their parents' crowded houses. So there was no easy consensus to be had. As time progressed, those who abhorred the mine did so more violently. But the rewards to those involved in it grew, and so did their gratitude.

There were building sites all along the edge of the community now. Wherever there was a clear spot of tundra adjacent to a road, a bulldozer appeared. The pace of construction was such that no one had the time to try to make their building distinguishable from anyone else's. The buildings sprouting up were all the same prefabricated white vinyl-sided model shipped in bulk to the port in the summer. From the view of a plane flying into town, the settlement looked like a crystalline fractal, expanding outward in unpredictable but ordered multiples of identical little units. There was a white vinyl-sided VCR rental store now, and a white vinyl-sided optician's and a white vinyl-sided adult lingerie and marital aid store. The hospital arose almost without anyone noticing.

Robertson walked every day from his new house on the bay out to the road where the hospital was being built. He watched the pilings being sunk into the rock, the concrete being poured, and the steel floor joists being laid.

In the architect's drawing it was a beautiful building. Two stories, with an operating theater and a delivery room adjacent to each other, a lab, an X-ray department, a library, and a huge outpatient clinic. Happy-looking pencil-sketched children played in the waiting room and there were implausible-looking trees beside the entrance, with bicycles parked alongside.

When construction began, Balthazar had called the Ministry of Health, asking if it wasn't too late to redirect the money into housing for the people who didn't work at the mine—or to community health programs. The voice on the other end was astonished at the idea. In the ministry they considered the hospital in Rankin Inlet their principal accomplishment that year and, better yet, done with the private funding. They had never felt so smart. Who was this man Balthazar, anyway? How long had he been working for them?

Robertson was home much more now. The center of his business was no longer in Yellowknife or Toronto but on his own doorstep, and he was now the one conducting eager-to-please strangers into meeting rooms, or across the tundra and out on the ice. He was called "the fix-it man" by the mine's leadership, and this is what he did. When one of the geologists got drunk at the hotel and got into a fistfight with the mayor's son, it was Robertson who smoothed things over, arranging a job at the mine for the newly gap-toothed son.

It was his habit to rise before anyone else in the house. In the early summer the sun was up at three and this morning Robertson was up by five, sitting on the porch steps of their log house, drinking coffee.

Victoria appeared, her own coffee cup in hand. "Hey," she said as she sat down beside him. He looked at her in surprise.

"What's up?" he asked, the smallest bit of alarm in his voice.

"Nothing," she said soothingly.

"Can't sleep?"

"I'll put tinfoil over the window today."

"It's nice out this morning."

"This house is growing on me."

"I'm glad you changed your mind. When did Pauloosie say he was getting back?"

"Maybe today, if not, tomorrow. Dad thought the weather would be good."

"Is his ATV working better?"

"I bought him a new one."

"He liked that?"

"Seemed to," she said.

"Good. Maybe he'll decide I'm not a waste of air after all."

"Don't get your hopes up."

And then Robertson realized that, for the first time in years, he and his wife were joking with each other. He looked at her and then he looked out at the tundra glowing beneath the climbing sun and he thought to himself how beautiful this land was.

Tagak's wife, Catharine, walked through the frozen meat section of the Northern Store and groaned inwardly at the price of the roasts. Her husband was out hunting again, but he usually had bad luck. His father brought them meat periodically, but there was tension between Emo and his son on that point. Most of the old man's spare meat went to Victoria's family—her Kablunauk husband could not be expected to hunt competently—while Tagak . . . what was the matter with him, anyway?

At that moment Tagak was climbing a ridge on his ATV. He had thought he had seen tuktu grazing on the crest, but as he came closer, he realized that it was only black boulders jutting into the sky. He stopped his Honda and let it idle. He reached into his pants pocket and pulled out a package of cigarettes. He bent over his lighter, trying again and again to light it in the wind that swirled all around him. He faced north. He faced south. Finally he pulled his arms inside his jacket and tucked his head inside, and in the darkness he lit his cigarette. He became aware that his beard was on fire as he was exhaling that first deep drag. He stood up off his ATV and ran blindly until he tripped on a rock and fell over, facefirst onto the tundra, and the fire was extinguished as it sizzled into his chin.

Catharine was hefting a forty-dollar roast into her cart when Victoria touched her on the shoulder. *"Qanuipiit?"* she asked at the same instant that Tagak sat up and thrust his head through the top of his parka, still pulling on the cigarette and rubbing his face.

"Not so good," Catharine said. "Tagak hasn't caught a caribou in two months and the assistance check barely covers the heating bill." She held up the roast she had just put into her cart. "And forty dollars for a piece of meat this size."

"Pauloosie shot two caribou yesterday. I'll have him bring one over."

"Thanks. But who wants to be always asking for help?" Catharine shook her head.

"Do you think Tagak would take a job with the mine?"

"Oh, he would, whether he wanted to or not."

"Really?"

"Yes."

"Let me talk to Robertson."

Robertson visited the mine twice a week. After the helicopter set down he met with Vangelis, the site director, and together they reviewed the perception of the mine in Rankin Inlet, the adequacy of the support services, and the plans and needs for shipping the next summer. Robertson kept these conversations short and efficient and this was appreciated by the Greek engineer, who hardly seemed to stop moving.

Vangelis had worked for two decades in the Botswana diamond mines and in Sierra Leone. Robertson liked him, detected in him a sensibility he largely shared, which had to do with the nature of the work and isolation each man had constructed as a sort of shield. In the summer of 1990, the second year of the mine's operation, Robertson had noticed a perceptible warming of the Greek's demeanor. He surmised it had to do with better-than-expected progress at the mine, which had won Vangelis the appreciation of his employers. He led Robertson to his private office, a warm den incongruently furnished in hardwood paneling and Iranian carpets. The Greek shrugged as Robertson took it all in. "I spend all my time on the site and I need to have one place to come where it is beautiful." It was late afternoon and the weather had delayed the helicopter's departure; Robertson would have to sleep on site. The Greek poured him a tall glass of whiskey and they sat down in leather chairs that would not have looked out of place in a private New York club.

"Everyone here seems in good spirits," Robertson said cautiously, taking a sip of the whiskey.

"The mine turned a handsome profit this year."

"Yes?" Robertson said, though he knew as much already.

"Yes, a very satisfactory one. We were all pleasantly surprised."

"As I am."

"The miners all seem pleased as well."

"The year-end bonuses were generous."

"I have been asked to talk to you about your own circumstances. Your status is a little ambiguous—you are not an employee, but we feel you are a part of our family."

"Thank you."

"And therefore entitled to a share of our good fortune."

"Oh?"

The Greek passed him a cloth bag. Robertson emptied from it seven large uncut diamonds. They looked like sea glass, opaque and irregular pebbles he would never have remarked upon if he had picked one of them up on a beach somewhere.

"None of those are less than three carats."

"I don't know quite what to say."

"It is only what you deserve."

There was a pause as Robertson held each of the stones up to the light, admiring them.

Vangelis said quietly. "The rules of accounting are such that they cannot, of course, show up on any income statements."

"I understand."

Marble Island lies just north of the mouth of Rankin Inlet, looking out onto Hudson Bay much the way Manhattan looks out onto the Atlantic. It has a melancholy history. Because of its perfectly protected harbor, successive expeditions of explorers and whalers chose to over-winter there in the last three centuries; the Knight Expedition slowly starved to death in 1719, after their vessels were crushed by ice in the lagoon. The crew dragged their stores ashore and thought they would wait for the Hudson's Bay Company to send a rescue ship. None arrived for three years. When finally a small trading sloop, searching for copper, landed on Marble Island, all that remained were graves and a mound of coal salvaged from the wrecks.

The Inuit regard Marble Island with caution too. The tradition is to climb up past the high waterline on one's knees in deference to its ghosts. They must have had their share of calamities too on that blasted spot.

In 1990, the crosses that still marked those graves overlooked Emo as he steered the boat in circles within the lagoon, Pauloosie kneeling in the bow, holding his grandfather's .30-06. The whales had been down now for long minutes. Emo was about to conclude that they had gotten away when a great streak of white appeared in the center of the lagoon, sounding a deep resonant gasp, then descended again. The whale's pod-mates followed, and when the third whale blew Pauloosie had his rifle leveled at the spot. He fired and a cloud of red appeared in the water. The whale he had hit remained on the surface, swimming in tightening circles. When Pauloosie fired again the whale shuddered and stopped moving and began slowly to settle in the lagoon. Emo raced toward it as Pauloosie reached for the harpoon, throwing it with a shout into the water. Both men exhaled in relief when they saw that it had lodged in the sinking whale. Pauloosie made the harpoon line fast on the boat and Emo steered toward shore.

When they had beached the boat, they leapt into the water and began hauling on the harpoon line. The whale had sunk deep in the water now and it was all they could do to move it even a few inches. The leather trace they pulled on stretched tight as the two men staggered backwards, grip-ping the gravel bottom with their kamiks, slipping and heaving.

Slowly the line shortened. When Pauloosie caught the first glimpse of the whale's snowy bulk he shouted to his grandfather. It was a bull, the biggest he had seen. Emo nodded and kept pulling, and did his best to re-main upright. When the animal was within six feet of the beach Emo reached out and laid his hand on its back, grinning. Then the animal gave a great shake of its powerful tail and struck Pauloosie, throwing him into the water on his back. As he struggled to regain his footing, Emo was left with the full weight of the whale on the harpoon tether. He dug in his short legs but was pulled steadily deeper into the water by the thrashing whale. He was up to his chest when a shot rang out and a parabola of whale brains was sprayed across the still lagoon. Pauloosie set down the rifle and gripped the tether again, pulling until the whale lay motionless and limp on the shore. Emo dropped the tether and, gasping for breath, he stumbled up to the high-tide line and sat down on a rock, looking more wan and exhausted than his grandson had ever seen him.

"That. Is a really. Big. Whale," Emo said.

"I've never seen a bigger beluga," Pauloosie replied. "It's hard to be-lieve they used to hunt bowheads in qayaks."

"It's hard to believe I used to do that." Emo was hoarse.

And then, for the first time, Emo sat and only watched as Pauloosie eviscerated and cut up the whale, removing the muqtuq in great foot-thick slabs, like heavy squares of red and white sod, and placing it in green plastic garbage bags on the floor of their boat.

Balthazar walked into the drug room in the nursing station while a patient waited in his examination room, clutching her aching ear. He found the large bottle of amoxicillin and he poured out a handful of pills onto the medication tray. He counted them out, three two-hundred-and-fifty-milligram tablets a day for ten days. Thirty tablets. He reached for the stickers printed in Inuktitut summarizing the commonly prescribed regimens: *Take after each loose bowel movement to a maximum of eight per day. Complete the entire course of this prescription, even if symptoms begin to resolve. Avoid grapefruit products while taking this medicine.*

He picked the appropriate label for the amoxicillin and stuck it on the bottle. He listened to the noise outside. It was the end of the workday and people were leaving. There was a box of morphine on the shelf above the amoxicillin. It had already been opened. He looked inside. He removed a package of a dozen ten-milligram vials. He put it in his lab coat pocket. He closed the door behind him and walked back to his examination room. One of these days they were going to start counting narcotics, just like in hospitals in the south. He wished they would start now.

Pauloosie stooped and picked up another rock the size of his head. He carried it clasped against his abdomen and staggered back to the river.

Forty years earlier, there had been a char weir here and the outlines were still evident on the streambed: the rocks themselves had been scattered by successive spring breakups, moving ice, and marauding bears. The weir had been maintained for most of a thousand years by the Inuit who had inhabited this area. It directed the char as they swam downstream into a stone enclosure, which surrounded them with acute angles that spoke to them of further confinement rather than escape. Instead of simply swimming out the way they had come, they stayed.

After two days' work, Pauloosie was nearly finished. He had rebuilt the walls three feet above the water level, tightly enough that no fish large enough to eat would escape, but loosely enough to let the water run through. That had been a lesson he had learned over successive attempts. After he placed the last rock on the weir, he removed the piece of wood blocking the trap's entrance and waited.

The char run was on and every few minutes he saw a red and silver fish flash by, but over the two hours he sat there expectantly, none entered his trap. He decided to take a walk, and picked up his .22 in case he saw a rabbit. When he returned, the water in the weir boiled with motion. He dropped his rifle and the ptarmigan he had shot and stood grinning beside the fish trap. There were dozens of fish in it, some as long as his arm, circling madly within.

He untied his kavitok from his pack and stood beside the weir, watching the fish. One of the larger char approached him. The spear flashed and it was caught and he carried it to high ground and removed it. He walked back to the weir. The sun was shining brightly and with the work of spearing and carrying the fish, he was soon hot. He removed his sweater. The fish seemed to enter the weir as quickly as he removed them. He figured out how to fling the fish in such a manner that they were piled, jumping and writhing, far enough from the river that they were not able to bounce their way back to it. His long wet hair flew around his head as he twisted his torso and worked his spear. His shoulders and back stood out in the oblique afternoon light, his skin as white as a beluga's beneath the unfamiliar sun, shining like wet polished ivory.

When his arms became rubbery, he hunkered over and slowly caught his breath. There were as many fish in the weir as when he had started. The mound on the bank still squirmed collectively, and was as high as his kamiks. He set down his spear and lifted a rock out of the enclosure. The fish began swimming through the channel he had created. Soon they had rejoined their brethren and the weir was empty.

Pauloosie began cleaning and splitting the fish he had caught. He erected laundry racks he had bought in the Northern Store and laid the fish open-bellied in the sun and the wind. He had brought ten laundry racks but hadn't quite enough room to lay out all the fish.

Tagak surprised everyone with his ability as a bookkeeper at the mine's purchasing office in town. He was less surprised himself—he had always suspected that a job involving methodical patience and a well-defined set of problems would suit him. As a hunter he had been considered lazy, but he was not. He demonstrated this now in his new job, working late into the night and arriving the next day before anyone else in the office.

As a hunter, his problem had been that he was too inclined to be thinking about where he would go next. Over the course of his hunting years, thousands of caribou had scampered over ridgelines as his distracted gaze had passed over them unawares. Seals had slipped into and out of their alus as he thought about how quickly his grandparents had abandoned their old gods, nanuqs had padded away from him as he wondered what the hunters had thought the first time they saw a rifle, and char darted across riverbeds while he imagined how the lives of his daughters would unfold.

His inability to empty his mind and simply observe betrayed him as a hunter but made him unusually capable in his new job. He wondered and reflected upon problems that arose constantly, simultaneously, and found himself reaching conclusions and thinking of solutions in a steady stream that matched the attempts of the mine's suppliers to bill twice for the same services, to overcharge and undersupply with ruthless avarice. Tagak, whose contact with business had been limited to avoiding the bank manager when he spotted him in the Northern Store, was soon in charge of the office, a step every Kablunauk in town who hadn't found work with the mine attributed to his race. The mine operators thanked Robertson repeatedly for having recommended him. The first few times, Robertson apologized.

∎

chapter thirteen

Already the snow should have been deep. It was falling heavily at last, and Emo watched it with a pleasure that snow had never occasioned in him before. It was still dark at six and very cold. He had fed his dogs and was walking home to eat breakfast with Winnie when the silver flakes appeared in the sky, moonlight glinting off them. He studied the moon, which was full and bathed the town and the bay in a light that seemed to him unprecedented in its intensity. He blinked his eyes. The moon had been halved. The right side of his face was no longer cold. He tried to rub it and his forearm hit his ear. He fell. He was unable to move his right arm or leg. Every time he attempted to rise, he turned in a circle in the accumulating snow.

Penny sat on the floor in her living room and slowly ran her hands along the leather dog harnesses, inspecting the swivels and the stitching. They had been gnawed in spots, and she clicked her tongue as she ran her fingers over them. They would do as spares. She unwrapped one of the new nylon harnesses she had ordered from Minnesota and lifted it approvingly. It weighed half of what the leather harness did and would, she hoped, be less appealing as a chew toy. She had food packed into her two rucksacks and her rifle was oiled and lying in its case beside them. She had been holding her breath all summer, waiting for this.

On the bay, her dogs leapt in the air when they saw that she was carrying gear and not just food. The nylon harnesses were unfamiliar and the dogs sniffed them as they were attached; they did not seem appetizing. The dogs attempted to express their disapproval to Penny even as she was clipping them onto the sled lead. She ignored them. She lashed the packs down on the komatik and picked up the ice hook. The dogs took off and the komatik flew forward.

In the blue half light, the ice appeared even more textured and uneven than it was. Shoulder-high ridges burst up from it regularly, among shards of pack ice of smaller dimensions. Penny turned the dogs north when they reached the mouth of the inlet, and they followed the coast another twenty miles before heading inland, where an Inukshuk marked the beginning of a little river valley that stretched westward.

She and the dogs ran for hours, until they came to a fork in the river. There was a char weir there now, and this was what she was watching for. She stopped her dogsled in a sheltered bend near the river. She began assembling her tent, hoping at the same time that there would soon be enough snow for an iglu—which would be so much warmer.

Pauloosie's dogs smelled the other team long before he saw them. They called out to the dogs and were answered. The baying of the two teams of dogs drew them nearer, call-and-response growing closer and closer until there was no distinction at all, and when the cacophony became constant, Pauloosie spotted the dome of Penny's tent. He drew close and tied up his dogs several lunge-lengths away from the other team. He set his sled on its end and untied his rifle and his pack. He bent down and unzipped the entrance of the tent.

Yvo Nautsiaq found Emo as he walked home from an all-night house party. He thought Emo was dead at first and began weeping as he stood over his motionless body. He rolled him off his left side and when Emo lifted his arm and grunted, Yvo leapt back as if he had been electrocuted. He noticed then how one side of Emo's face had fallen, and concluded—with notable astuteness, given his level of intoxication—that Emo had had a stroke. He picked him up on his shoulders and carried him to his home. When he knocked at the door and hollered for Winnie, she at first refused to acknowledge him, having listened to decades of gossip about the man's drinking. But she detected something urgent in Yvo's voice and finally opened the door to see her husband hoisted up on Yvo's shoulders. He carried Emo into the living room and deposited him on the chesterfield heavily.

Emo's eyes were open and Winnie leaned over to tell him she was calling the nursing station. He rose up at that, gripping the back of the chesterfield with his good left arm, shaking his head as he roared gutturally. This frightened Yvo again and he shrank back to the door. Winnie said then that she was going to call Victoria. Emo reached over with his left arm, grabbed the phone jack, and yanked it out of the wall. He lay back, gasping for breath. Winnie's eyes were wide with fear and she began crying. Emo rumbled at her. This frightened her more and she cried louder. He swung his left arm and hooked it around her waist and pulled her into him.

They lay alongside each other all day. Emo fell asleep after an hour, but Winnie remained awake, wondering to herself what she would do now, what her life would be like if Emo remained unable to walk or speak. When the sun finally set in the southwest, she fell asleep.

When Emo awoke a few hours after sunset he was surprised to be lying with his wife on their chesterfield. The first conclusion he reached was that they had gone drinking the night before, something they hadn't done in twenty years. Then he remembered Nautsiaq's weeping and then he remembered his collapse. He shifted his shoulder under Winnie's weight and, as he did so, he realized he could move his right leg again. He kicked it a few times to make sure. It was still weak, certainly clumsier than the left, but he could definitely move it. He lay there, wiggling his toes in his boots, and tried to squeeze his right hand. He felt the fingers moving.

"Oh, thank Christ," he said aloud, waking up Winnie, who started to admonish him about his language and then stopped as he stroked her

face with his right hand. She laid her face down on his chest and began
crying again.

Just before supper that night, Victoria and Justine and Marie sat together on Victoria's bed and looked at the lumpy little bag in front of
them. Robertson was away on a rare trip to Yellowknife. Justine had
asked Victoria how the miners found what they were after and Victoria
thought she would show the girls what raw diamonds looked like. She
realized that within the desire to educate her girls about mineralogy she
harbored an unexpected motive—she wanted her daughters to be impressed by their father. When she opened the cloth bag and upended it,
the cloudy misshapen rocks spilled out onto the bedspread. Marie
picked up one of the larger ones. "How do they make them shine?" she
asked.

"They cut and polish them."

"How much is this one worth?"

"I don't know. A lot."

"As much as a truck?"

"Maybe."

"Even though it doesn't sparkle?"

"I think so."

Pauloosie said goodbye to Penny and waved as he took one fork of
the return path and she took another. They were ten miles north of
Rankin Inlet. Their dogs looked over their shoulders at the other team
growing steadily more distant. Penny's trail led her into town from the
north; Pauloosie's trail came in from the southwest.

As he pulled onto the ring road, the runners of his komatik began
to scrape as they ran over the sand and gravel that had been laid on the
snow to render it less slippery. He jumped off the sled then and ran beside the dogs, holding the trace in one hand, lest some Kablunauk's
wayward poodle catch their attention. He led the dogs down onto the

ice where the teams were chained. Penny's team had already settled into the accumulating snow, their tails over their noses. Her sled was standing straight up and neither she nor her gear was visible. He chained his dogs to their line and unpacked his own sled. He put his pack over one shoulder, picked up his rifle with his other hand, and walked toward home.

When he entered the kitchen he did so quietly, because he was happier than he had ever been before. He removed his boots and eased the door shut, enjoying even the little click it made as the lock caught. He shook his head at himself and laughed quietly. When he passed the open door of his parents' bedroom, he saw Justine and Marie and Victoria sitting in a circle on the bed with a pile of cloudy semitranslucent pebbles in front of them. He stopped. His mother looked up at him, then Justine and Marie did too.

vascular access

If mammals moved as slowly as trees, they would not require hearts and the complex web of vasculature feeding into and out of all their organs, their muscles, this always hungry tissue. But because they do sprint, and think, and love, they cannot rely on seepage for the circulation of their nutrients. There is a price for needing blood and blood vessels: when we are pierced we bleed to death. No gradual upwelling of self-sealing sap or starfish juice for us. Teeth and projectiles and damaging collisions free our blood to slide into lungs and belly, or out onto the ground, growing crimson beneath our shuddering forms.

When the injured survive long enough for a doctor to treat them, one of the first priorities is to place tubes in the injured person's own tubes: intravenous cannulae, to pump salt water in, replacing the volume of blood and giving the heart something to pump. The best places to do this are the brachial veins, thick and close to the surface of the straightened elbow. IVs the size of pencils are shoved quickly in, and connected to bags of saline, wrapped in turn by blood pressure cuffs—squeezing the fluid in, optimistically, as fast as it escapes.

But when the injured have bled a great deal, and are in shock, blood pressure falling and the skin mottling, there is too little blood left in the system to distend even the lax veins of the arms, and it is sometimes impossible to insert such tubes in the arms or anywhere. With children, whose bones are still growing, the right thing to do then is to hammer a hollow metal spike into the shin bone and leave it there. Fluid pumped into the body through this route joins the vasculature quickly through the rich plexus of veins feeding the child's marrow. Nobody ever does this without the taste of fear in his or her mouth. *Imagine the faces of the child's parents as you do this. (Imagine the mauling severe enough to prompt it, the shredded tendons, the violation.)*

There are people in whom the veins aren't close enough to the surface of their skin to be felt. Apart from the severely volume-depleted child, there are also the chronically unwell, who have had so many IVs started that all the visible veins have become scarred and nonpatent—cystic fibrosis kids are like this, and patients receiving chemotherapy.

But the most difficult people in whom to establish vascular access are the IVDUs—the intravenous drug users. These are regular attenders of every city emergency room. The same habit of mind that inclines them to stick needles in their arms seems also to put them in the path of knives, at the mercy of infections and in septic shock, requiring intravenous antibiotics and fluids.

Their bodies are battlefields of penetration. The arm veins are dispensed with, typically, within a few years of the habit, and then the feet, the hands, the neck, the groin: all marked by linear puncture scars, tracking the path of this corrosive appetite. Men take to injecting themselves through their genitalia. This strategy is unavailable to women, though pregnant addicts commonly inject the distended veins in their breasts. By this point, the ignominy of the habit has long since become an abstraction. The use of surprising injection sites matters little beside the betrayal of every other single thing in the addict's life.

There are deeper, larger veins that feed blood directly into the heart, called the central veins—the femoral, jugular, and subclavian veins in the groin, neck, and shoulder, respectively—which form the superior and inferior vena cavae, the vessels that join directly to the right atrium of the heart.

The Seldinger technique is how large catheters are placed in these vessels. A needle is fed under the collarbone, or into the side of the neck, or beside the femoral pulse, as the piston of the syringe is drawn back. When blood flashes into the barrel of the syringe, the syringe is removed and a wire is fed through the needle. Then the needle itself is removed, leaving the wire in place. A thicker plastic cone-shaped cylinder is then fed over and around the wire, dilating the tissue surrounding these deep veins, and then is drawn back.

A venous catheter is then fed over the wire into the vein. The wire is then removed, leaving the catheter in place. When it has been placed well, the tip of the catheter will lie just outside the heart.

There are many things that can go wrong with this operation. The lung can be punctured by the needle, causing air to leak into the pleural space surrounding the lung. As air accumulates here, it compresses the lung and the vessels feeding through it into the heart. Suddenly, the already troubled patient is blue and pulseless and has not been helped at all. A chest tube will then have to be hurriedly inserted into the chest to release the air, but if things were tenuous before, now they will be dire. Most problems don't lessen when another is stacked on top of them.

Along every great vein also lies a great artery, and in the initial blind-but-hopeful placement of the needle, it sometimes enters the associated carotid, subclavian, or femoral artery. If the blood is not recognized as being arterial, rather than venous, too bright and too vigorously pulsing, and the procedure continues—the dilator expanding the hole in the artery—this becomes an even more serious problem. If the vessel punctured is the carotid, or the subclavian artery, under the collarbone, then it cannot be compressed while waiting for a clot to form. The right thing to do is to leave the catheter in place and make an embarrassed call to a vascular surgeon, with a view to having the vessel sewn up.

Addicts love these lines. When they are feeling well enough to walk around again, they slip into washrooms and car parks beneath the hospital to inject effortlessly, for once, their preferred balm. This agitates their doctors and nurses, who feel as if they are facilitating the terminal process that brought the patient into their care in the first place. At the same time, it's probably safer for them to inject one of these lines than their armpits and groins. Very quickly, the lines are infected anyway and must be removed, usually over the objections of the addict, who would leave them in place until the end.

In every large hospital there will be a number of physicians who do not wonder about what motivates people to stick needles in their arms for relief. Vials of morphine and fentanyl and hydromorphone flow through operating rooms in large and poorly counted quantities. Anesthetists, in particular, develop this habit. Driving home one day, they discover a mislaid vial in their pocket. Clean needles being as available to physicians as bad marriages, they find themselves in their little apartment, surrounded by pictures of estranged children, and they discover relief.

Doctors are the hardest to identify of all the junkies; they do not develop hepatitis and AIDS, generally. They do not share or even reuse their needles. By long training they are fastidious phlebotomists, cleaning and preparing their injection sites. Weeping infected ulcers do not appear in their arms and hands, their heart valves are not shredded by infection, and so they are able to sustain themselves and their habit without such visible damage for far longer than street users. They find their solace alone, in secret, and are thus less likely to have a knife thrust into them by a suddenly agitated friend. They use drugs of known potency, and understand enough of pharmacokinetics that they do not die of overdose.

But betrayal is as much a feature of their lives as it is of the lives of all junkies; anesthetists administer half-dose narcotics to their agonizing patients in order to have more drugs for their own use. Internists and surgeons write illegitimate prescriptions they fill themselves in pharmacies where they are not known; they rifle through the drug cabinets on the wards where they attend. The only thing about them that is genuinely purer than other addicts is what they inject into themselves.

They baffle their colleagues, these men and women. Why would doctors feel such a void that they would be inclined to do this in the first place? Look at what they do for a living.

This question contains its own answer. The novitiates of the various priesthoods are the most devout. In some that faith is maintained. In others it isn't.

The most stressful thing in the world is boredom. Trauma surgeons are not the ones who become morphine addicts. What they do is dangerous and fast and dramatic; they do not get worn down the way the rest of us do, forgotten family doctors in small towns and anesthetists facing a lifetime of hernia repairs. We

are designed to be confronted by difficulties that often surprise and sometimes
defeat us. In the absence of that, humans wither. Or rather, they swell.

When I came here I was twenty-seven years old and skinny. Everyone I
knew here was as skinny as I was. There was food then too, available at the
Northern Store. Canned bacon and white bread and all the things that make
men fat. But no one was. I was not yet so lonely, and the families were only
freshly off the land, and still spent months at a time out there. Bear maulings
and drownings were common.

Now the people I treat, especially the ones that need me the most often,
have withdrawn from the land, and live like my brother and his family do, in
Newark. They work under fluorescent lights and eat prepared food, recoiling
from imagined dangers with a zealousness that looks each year a little more
like simple cowardice. Everyone in town wears a helmet when riding a quad
and the dogs are kept well away, out on the ice. One is not allowed to use a
rifle, or even buy ammunition, without a firearms safety course. All of which is
reasonable. I do not see the head injuries and the dog maulings that I used to.
Many of the young men I know who have good jobs in town don't even own a
rifle. They marry Kablunauk women who worry, rightly, about their children
shooting themselves. Together they all waddle in to see me, and together we all
talk about how we might control our diabetes better.

My niece is insanely allergic to peanuts; even a glancing contact with a
peanut shell will raise red welts on her skin. Her parents live in terror of the
ill-considered spring roll. She has asthma too; both these diseases are increasing
in prevalence and severity in American cities in a time when other serious medical
problems are in decline, as we all grow richer and better doctored.

The problem is that our bodies are meant to struggle as much as our
brains are; children's immune systems expect to have to beat off infections.
When the immune system is never called upon, it behaves the way underworked
soldiers do and makes trouble. If it's not finding infections, then it must not be
looking hard enough. So it looks harder, and starts to detect infections that
aren't there: thus the terrible toll of autoimmune disease rises steadily in our
era of antiseptic floors and single-child families.

But the real trouble is what people's minds become when they are never called upon to fight off a predator. Gelatinous gray goo. Middle-aged fat man looking out his window at people walking in the snow, dressed in his underwear at two on a Sunday afternoon, teeth unbrushed since Friday morning, a litter of alcohol swabs on the floor and empty pudding cups stretching to the walls.

I made a deal with myself that I would never do it on weekdays or more often than once a month. And although stealing the morphine was itself a transgression, I was able to limit that transgression to these bounds. I wondered about that often, even at the time: if I was able to control it all, why didn't I just stop? And if I couldn't stop, why didn't I become a daily user, with the attendant ongoing catastrophes for my patients and my eventual firing?

The answer, I think, is twofold. First, either would have been too decisive a course of action for a man of my nature. All my life I have equivocated, puzzled most of all about what it was I wanted, what I should be striving for. I came to the Arctic for a summer to pass the time and make a small bit of money after my exams. But this is where I ended up spending my professional life, out of habit and out of what became an increasingly narrow range of options. I didn't actually choose the place until I had spent half my life there.

And too, there was my overfondness for secrets. I was pleased that there was something unapparent about me, something not evident at a cursory glance. The people who divined my secrets and chose not to reveal them, they were bound even closer to me as a result. So my loneliness was assuaged in two ways: by the drug sliding up my arm and by the complicity of my friends. Potent thing, loneliness.

chapter fourteen

When Victoria picked up the telephone, she knew it would be Simionie and she felt guilty immediately. Guilty for not having called him in weeks, and guilty for talking to him at all. Yes, she would meet him, she said, wincing even as the words echoed in the telephone receiver.

The cabin was cold and neglected. They sat at the table and drank tea. He leaned over to kiss her.

"I've missed you too," she breathed, her hand on his chest, fingers splayed. He slid his mouth down her neck. She pushed against him gently. "I can't," she said. "It's my cycle." He kept kissing her, smelling her skin, pulling her to him. She pressed back, just a little harder. He stopped kissing her then and looked at her. She turned to the billy and poured more tea into their cups and stirred in sugar.

"Robertson is home so much more than he used to be. I don't know what to do. It used to be he didn't seem to be able to think about anything but business, but with this mine, the amount of money involved is almost frightening. The other day he came home with a bag of uncut diamonds, a thank-you gift from the mine manager. God knows how much they are worth, but it's just an example of how crazy things are. And then there's this new house he made me move into, as if a dishwasher and shiny countertops could make me love him." She felt ashamed about what she was saying but wasn't able to stop.

"I shouldn't have said anything about the diamonds. You have to promise not to mention that to anyone."

Simionie leaned back and looked out the window of the cabin. He fished a cigarette out of his pocket and lit it. "Sure," he said.

Emo and his grandson walked out in the morning light to the dogs. Pauloosie's were eager to see him, but Emo's team was frantic. From a distance, they had not been certain at first who he was; his gait and posture were different. Then they smelled his particular scent in the wind, even though that had changed subtly, and they became airborne, launching themselves to the limit of their leashes, and crashed back down on the ice. They were skinny, and they had been fighting, and their fur was clumped and torn out in spots.

Emo's face grew bright with shame, but in the wind, it was hard to see this. Pauloosie had fed the dogs while the old man had been sick, but had not taken them out on the land because Emo had not asked him to. Could not have asked him to. The other men who owned dogs had watched Emo's team grow thin, and they suffered when they saw this but could not bring themselves to intervene. Pauloosie had cut up frozen char and seal and fed the dogs, not saying anything, but food is the least part of what dogs and men need. Chained to one spot for weeks, they were half mad with agitation and had spent as much energy fighting over that food as they gained from eating it.

Pauloosie began unchaining his dogs and tying them into their harnesses. Emo began attempting the same, but with much less success: his dogs jumped up on him, staggering the old man. To quiet them, he struck them about their heads and shoulders. They cringed at this but did not settle.

Pauloosie's dogs were the inferior littermates of his grandfather's, given to him one by one as he had shown himself adept at their care. He took in the proud arcs of their backs, the curled tails held upright and eager, and he glanced over at their sisters and sires, clawing and climbing up his grandfather's chest. And then he saw the old man fall. Pauloosie was sprinting across the ice before Emo's shoulders had even touched the snow. But the dogs were on the old man in an instant, their reflexive response to weakness engaged in a flash of slashing teeth.

Pauloosie sent dogs flying through the air to land in a tangle of whimpering thuds. He pulled his grandfather away from them, the heels of his kamiks drawing two perfectly parallel lines in the snow, blood dribbling between them in a third parallel and crimson line.

They had just gotten clear of the dogs when Pauloosie felt his grandfather struggling. A great flap of skin and hair hung down over his eyes, and Emo pushed up on it to see better. His nose had been caught by a tooth as well, and a flap hung down where his right nostril had been. Pauloosie could see the old man's facial bones, like snail shells through the wounds, and he blinked and looked away. He helped Emo to his feet and the two of them walked to the nursing station, the old man pressing his mitten into his face.

The on-call nurse was accustomed to repairing and stitching up most of the lacerations that came in herself, but the extent and severity of the old man's injuries took her aback. Reluctantly, she phoned Balthazar. Pauloosie listened to her repeating herself, more loudly, persuading him to come in.

When Balthazar arrived, he looked as if he had just woken up. He read and reread the old man's thin medical chart for long minutes as Emo bled into the dressings the nurse had laid over his flayed face.

As the doctor finally leaned in to inspect the old man's wounds, he told Emo that the lacerations were deep and complex and would likely leave a large scar.

"I don't care very much about scars."

"That's fine. We'll get started then. Were you knocked out at all, sir?"

"I don't think so."

Pauloosie shook his head.

"Did you hit your head at any point?"

"Not that I remember."

Pauloosie shrugged.

Balthazar rolled up his sleeves and washed his hands. He had the old man lie down on a stretcher and he positioned a bright lamp to shine on his face. He cleaned the exposed muscle and fat with sterile water. He tried to identify the cut ends of the muscle belly, looking for edges to rejoin. Dog teeth are pointed but they are not really very sharp: the wound was a scramble. Every other stitch he placed had to come out again. Steadily, layer by layer, Balthazar worked, consulting a manual of facial anatomy beside him. It took hours.

He had nearly finished when he lifted up the sterile drape covering the old man's face and asked him how he was.

"I've changed my mind," Emo said.

"About seeing a plastic surgeon?"

"I don't want the girl to go."

"Which girl?"

"My daughter. She should stay here. We'll take care of her."

Balthazar looked over at Pauloosie.

"*Attatatiak . . .*" the boy said.

"That's my decision."

"Okay, sir, don't worry about anything, nobody's going anywhere."

"I'm sorry for changing my mind like this. But we'll lose her anyway, if she goes south for that long."

"Okey-dokey . . . just about done, here."

"Everything is all right, Grandfather," Pauloosie said.

When Balthazar pulled the last drape from Emo's face half an hour later, the old man lay quite still with his eyes closed. He appeared to be asleep—or worse—and Balthazar and Pauloosie were both starting to panic when he opened his eyes.

"How are you feeling, sir?"

"*Nahmuktah,*" Emo answered.

"He's okay, he says," Pauloosie said.

"Excellent. Well, there isn't much else to do here. We'll give you a tetanus shot, and in about a week we'll take out the stitches. If there is any sign of infection, like increasing pain or fever or discharge, you should come back, of course . . ."

Pauloosie could not take his eyes off his grandfather's face. Balthazar had done a fine job, but neither the nurse nor Pauloosie knew what to say. The scars were long, it was true, but the man's face had been flayed open, and now he appeared nearly normal, albeit swollen and bruised, with fine nylon stitches running in jagged lines across his face.

Emo looked at himself in the mirror above the sink and pronounced it satisfactory. *"Koyenamee,"* he said to the doctor.

"You're welcome," Balthazar said.

The old man and his grandson left. Emo did not speak Kablunuktitut again.

Pauloosie stood with his friend Pierre Karlik on the ice with Emo's dogs, who clambered around them. Pauloosie fed them seal meat, which they gobbled down in great eager mouthfuls. The lead, Kanyak, held back from the meat, and stood alongside Pauloosie's leg, stiff and dignified and solemn. She did not climb up on him as the others had, neither did she shrink from him. The side of her chest lightly touched his knee. He did not trust himself to speak. Karlik asked Pauloosie again if every musher in town had turned the dogs down and Pauloosie nodded yes. They were too closely bonded to the old man. They would likely not accept another leader, and Kanyak herself was too old to be worth bending to a new owner. And there was the matter of their neglect and undernourishment. And the mauling. Even before Pauloosie had approached the first owner, a consensus had been reached.

Karlik reached into the komatik they had towed out with them behind his snowmobile.

"Not just yet," Pauloosie said.

At Okpatayauk's apartment, the door opened and closed steadily, admitting Penny, Simionie, Mariano Kringyurak, and finally Pauloosie.

Okpatayauk had spent the afternoon on the phone, asking everyone who had been involved in the committee—excepting those who had subsequently taken a job with the mine—to come by his apartment that night. He was deliberately mysterious about the urgency of the meeting. This, he found, was a useful tactic in reigniting the fading interest of his friends.

"In two months, the annual general meeting of the Kivalliq Mining Commission will be held," he announced when they were all assembled in his living room. "This is the regulatory agency that oversees all mining activity in this part of the Arctic, including the Back River mine." He paused and let everyone take a sip of pop.

"By statute, these meetings have to be open to the public. Last year I attended it, and was one of four people there. Yvo Nautsiaq showed up because he heard there would be drinks. The other two I think were ringers the mine owners sent for some reason. They had suits on, anyway, and wore galoshes. I haven't seen them in town again.

"I've learned something about the relationship between the mine owners and the Ikhirahlo Group that might turn out to be a bombshell. I want everyone here to start encouraging all their friends to show up at the meeting. It'll be held in the hotel. Tell people there will be snacks."

Waiting in the line by the cashier at the Quick Stop to buy tea, Pauloosie saw Billy Tootoo and Clive Akpalik, who told him there was a party that night. It had been months since he had spoken at any length with anyone his own age. After he paid for his tea he tucked it into his jacket pocket and joined the boys.

They walked over squeaking snow to the house of a friend, the son of one of the men who ran a dog team, Frank Kapoyee. The father was fastidious with his dogs, Pauloosie knew, and had to be appalled at how his son lived. There was one piece of furniture in the house, a chesterfield with cigarette burns so thick that the thing functioned better as a testimonial to the effectiveness of modern fire retardants than as a source of back support. The stuffing protruded out of it in a dozen places, and the springs had been bent back to avoid snagging on clothing. People sat on the curling-up linoleum floor under a pall of purple cigarette smoke so acrid and substantial that the windows had been opened and minus-forty air blew through the house and everyone shivered. They were all drinking, sharing bottles of Seagram's Five Star purchased from the bootlegger. In the kitchen three men and a woman were hot-knifing hash.

Pauloosie wandered through the house, looking for someplace to stand where he would feel comfortable. He ended up in the kitchen, watching the hash smokers at their solemn ritual. When the toilet paper tube was handed to him he stepped up to the stove and watched, fascinated, as the tips of the knives grew red. Tim Kaput nodded to him and took one knife and touched it to a spot of hash. Then he squeezed the tips of the knives together as Pauloosie sucked in through the toilet paper tube. The smoke seared its way into his lungs, and after a long, hyperinflated pause he whooped out a lungful of blue smoke and staggered backwards, coughing and shivering with the combined effects of the draft and the sensation that his lungs had just sloughed off most of their lining. Cindy Adams looked at him in a concerned manner as his face bulged and grew purple. Then she took the toilet paper tube from his hand. "That might be enough for you," she said huskily, and took her place at the stove.

Pauloosie stood back gratefully. By the time he took his third step he was so stoned, he no longer understood why his chest throbbed with pain. By the fourth, he would have been unable to describe what that sensation was. Or what his chest was, exactly. He felt like a duck paddling his feet in a pond filled with Jell-O, and being propelled through the house by an unseen Jell-O current. He looked at Cindy, who was leaning back from the stove now, and grinning at him. "Quack, quack," he said.

"I bet you say that to all the girls," she replied.

He rose up above himself and lay over the room, his enlarging back against the ceiling. He watched himself circle through the house, smiling vapidly and happily.

And then he was wandering outside, unable to remember why he had come out in the first place, and unable to find the house party again. It was only good fortune that he hadn't bothered to take off his parka at the party, and now he pulled it tight around his shoulders. He wandered up to the government workers' apartment building, where he found Penny's name on the buzzer. He pressed it. It was midnight. Normally he would have been asleep for three hours, as she had been by now, in preparation for an early morning on the ice with his dogs.

Penny ignored the first few minutes of buzzing, interpreting it as another late-night attempt to exchange a soapstone carving for bootlegger-destined money. Then she rolled out of her bed, stepped over her rifle case and backpack, and stabbed the intercom.

"Go away!" she barked.

"Hello," he whispered.

There was a long pause.

"What?" she asked. She stared at the intercom, understanding that she wanted to wake up but not certain why.

"Are you going?" He breathed in and out a few times. "Out on the land in the morning?"

Pauloosie was down there, where he could be studied by anyone. She did not want that, could not have him viewed that way. "Come up," she whispered, and buzzed the door open.

He wound his way up the staircase and peered down each darkened hallway in turn until, on the fourth floor, he spied her open door.

There were no other open doors, though Penny did not know how many cocked ears had listened to their exchange, how faithfully their voices were transmitted through every piece of particleboard in the building, how every insomniac and alienated Kablunauk had lain there listening.

She pulled him in and shut her door. He stood in her kitchen and she saw that he was not himself. She made him tea and sat him down at her table.

"You're really stoned, aren't you?" she asked, gazing into his red eyes.

"I'm tired, but I feel really good," he said.

"Uh-huh."

"Hey, tell me something."

"Yeah?"

"I've been thinking about going out on the tundra for a long time. Maybe a year."

"Really?" She stirred her tea, trying to decide how much of what he was saying was hashish-related.

"Do you think it would be possible to carry enough gear to do that? What would you take?"

"Uh . . . you'd have to have really good hunting to pull it off. You'd want to cache enough seal meat for the dogs. And in the summer you'd need a heavy char run. You wouldn't be able to carry enough store-bought food to last. You'd be better off carrying a fishnet and lots of ammunition. Maybe take a twelve-gauge, for the spring geese."

"That's what I'm thinking too. You'd have to be stingy with the lamp fuel."

"Really? Do you mean this? Do you think you really might do this?"

"I think I have a choice here, we have a choice, about which way we'll head."

"I know exactly what you mean."

"I figured you would, was why I came here."

"Are you going out on the land tomorrow?"

"Yes. First thing."

"We better get some sleep then."

When a high-pressure system hangs over the land in midwinter and the air stops moving, it becomes very cold. Eventually a low-pressure system will move in to raise the wind and the temperature, but for a time—sometimes for weeks—it is as if the air itself has hardened and sits on the rock and ice like frozen glass pressed against one's eyes. The leads in the ice freeze over and new ones are not formed. The ice is not pushed apart by wind and waves. Those who need to travel leap at the opportunity and snowmobiles and dog teams charge out across the ice, confident for once that they are not likely to pitch forward into the sea the moment their attention wavers.

For the sea mammals, however, this is trouble. The seals tend their breathing holes in winter, and keep them open with their periodic nosings. But the white whales and the walruses dive under the ice, looking for places where they might breathe, the whales chirping out their echo-locating cries and listening carefully for the sound of open water. As the leads close, the whales' options diminish and they collect in those that remain. One lead, kept open by an unlikely combination of local weather patterns or ocean current, will attract dozens of belugas gasping into the air after each deep dive, reaching out under the ice as far as they can, calculating with infinite precision the moment when exactly half of their endurance has been reached, and then surging their way back to the lead they had left. There might be walruses there as well, and together the great breathing beasts of the Arctic Ocean line up behind one another and take their breaths and dive optimistically, determinedly, and wait for a storm to stir the ice.

All of this unfolds without urgency or panic, and is responded to with patience and energy-conserving (and oxygen-conserving) attention. There is plenty of air, after all, and each animal needs only a few seconds at the surface to fill its lungs with many minutes' worth. All of this unfolds easily—that is, until the bears find the lead.

Nanuq, *Ursus maritimus,* the polar bear, is two thousand pounds when grown and able with one great swipe of his enormous paw to hook the spine of a beluga whale and pull it to the ice edge. Then, like some enormous steroid-infused weight lifter, it straightens and pulls back and hauls such a whale right up and out of the water.

Then the scent of blood is in the air and all the bears—usually frat-
ricidally antisocial—converge. They line up at the open lead and they
swipe until the water is a crimson froth. The bears stagger backwards
under the weight of the walruses and whales, and collapse, sometimes
killed by tons of flesh falling onto their chests. More often, they roll
gamely out of the way and eat themselves into catatonia, dying whales
all around—those on the ice and unknowable numbers of others,
frightened into diving in search of leads. They gamble long past the
halfway point that there will be others, and anyway, all that can be done
is to continue, and listen, and hope. And get away.

chapter fifteen

■

The Inuit are, at their essence, a maritime people. The Thule culture re-
lied on the hunting of sea mammals, and it is this culture that dashed
across the Arctic about the same time the Norse arrived in Greenland.
The Norse imagined themselves mariners without equal, but the Arctic
reduced them steadily and they withered in their little fjords facing
south into the Atlantic. But the Inuit prospered, pulling their living
from the sea without iron spearheads, without compasses, and without
any dependence on traded timber from far-off cities. There were off-
shoots among them, the Padleimiut and the Ihalmiut, who traveled inland in search of caribou, but they remained, first, men and women of
the ocean. Though the government ships and the Hudson's Bay Company barges had made obsolete their own tradition of open-water voy-
aging, on summer days when the fish were not running, the people still
looked off to the edge of the ocean.

Sometimes that ocean horizon was marked by small sailboats. Most
of the sailors who poke their way into Hudson Bay do not linger but run
back before the ice closes in. Every few years, however, a boat will attempt the Northwest Passage. This will involve wintering-in, either at
Iqaluit, or, as Amundsen did farther west, in Gjoa Haven. Some of the
boats choose to head for more southern harbors in Hudson Bay, but this
adds hundreds of miles to the length of the passage and so sailboats are
less commonly sighted south of Repulse Bay.

Therefore, when a steel ketch anchored in the inlet at the end of
July in 1991, most of the town came out to watch the little man who

rowed ashore from it. His name was Simon Alvah and he had welded his boat, the *Umingmak,* together in his backyard in Juneau over the course of four long years. He had spent the previous winter in Gjoa Haven, had broken out a month ago with the melt and made his way here. He had read of Marble Island and the long history of sailors who had been frozen in for the winter there, and had decided he wanted to pass a winter just like that. It was an odd ambition and, if questioned, he would not have been able to explain it. Nevertheless, it was what he wanted to do. He had studied the charts of the area for years, and now took in each promontory as if he had passed many years on this coast. The place drew him.

The following spring he intended to return back through the Northwest Passage to the Bering Strait and home. He had sailed around the world four times in other boats, had overwintered on Elephant Island and waited out cyclones in mangrove swamps, and now he was trying this. He found living in cities difficult, he told anyone who asked.

He was forty-eight years old and looked sixty. His beard was dreadlocked and the same steel gray as the sky. He had the appearance of men who have abandoned the company of women: not neglected, exactly, but clearly combining aesthetic decisions with ease of maintenance, an ethic he never allowed to prevail when it came to his boat. His hair was clumsily trimmed, and in the uneven and scalloped edges one caught a touching picture of the man awkwardly holding scissors as he leaned in to his shaving mirror. His clothes were patched and sewn with waxed sail thread that stood up proud in tight, even stitches as thick as light cord; none of the seams was parting, but the effect on the eye was not subtle.

As he pulled his tender ashore he looked around impatiently, as if he felt crowded, which was strange to observe in someone who had just been a month by himself coming down the coast from Gjoa Haven. When Inuit families came in off the land after very long trips, they acknowledged everyone they saw; solitude was understood as an unavoidable imposition but never as a thing to be sought. Alvah was plainly mad, however much one might admire his capacity for endurance.

In order to overwinter on Marble Island, he planned to use some of the coal left behind by the whalers to heat his stove, then get going again in early July the next year. He figured that would give him time to get back out into the Pacific again. He did not ask anyone's permission about anchoring there, or using the old coal. He wanted to be in Gjoa Haven again by the end of July, would have to, if he was to get around again to open sea against the prevailing winds and current. The older men who spoke with him about his plan concluded it was as insane as he was. Then one of them said, in English, "We're sure you know that water better than we do."

In the Northern Store hardware department, Alvah spent long hours looking at the array of wrenches and arc welders, solder and crimping tools. The way in which he weighed the decision to buy each tool testified to how short his money was—if that point wasn't made clear enough by his determination to remain on his boat even after it was frozen in for the winter, and eat rice and tinned fish and listen to the radio, rather than live in the town or fly home to wherever it was he belonged. He represented a disconcerting challenge to those who imagined themselves confined to this place. Here he was, after all, broke, and still making his own way around, not acquiescing to anything. It would have been more comfortable simply not to have known about him.

The territorial mining commission had expected ten people at the hearing and prepared for twelve. The boardroom in the hotel had sixty people in it. Men and women in parkas stood along the walls. They had been promised some interesting developments and they waited impassively. Robertson and the other members of the commission had realized something was up the moment they had arrived and seen faces they had never previously seen anywhere but on the land, or in the Northern Store.

Okpatayauk stood first when it was time for questions from the public. Robertson looked to the people on either side of him, then finally said, "Yes, Mr. Iqapsiak?"

"Mr. Robertson, I wonder if you could tell me why you have been accepting illegal disbursements from the mining corporation?"

Nobody moved. The people lining the walls had not expected anything so personal. They all looked at the floor or the ceiling, uncomfortable to the point of agony. If it had been possible to leave unobtrusively, they all would have in an instant.

Robertson looked at his wife, sitting in one of the chairs around the table, waiting to pick him up so they could go shopping after the meeting. She had wondered what Okpatayauk was talking about, but with that look from Robertson she knew.

"I don't know what you mean, Mr. Iqapsiak. The Ikhirahlo Group is contracted in an advisory capacity and is remunerated for that."

"What I'm asking is, have you accepted bags of uncut diamonds from the mine manager, Mr. Robertson?"

Robertson looked at him.

"Is there, as we speak, a bag of diamonds worth one hundred thousand dollars or more in your dresser drawer at home?"

"No, there is not."

"All right, Mr. Robertson, is there a bag of diamonds worth any amount of money in your dresser drawer at home?"

Melvin Anders intervened. "Okpatayauk, this is slander."

"No, Mr. Anders, it is not."

Victoria sought out Pauloosie, standing on the other side of the room, but he did not meet her eyes. Simionie was sitting beside Pauloosie and he stared resolutely at the floor. Okpatayauk said he had more questions, and turned the page in his notebook.

Betty Peters and Melvin Anders were both looking at Robertson, who stood gulping for air, his face completely flushed.

Victoria ripped her son's bedding off his bed and carried it into the kitchen. She opened the door and threw it out into the snow. Then she emptied the porch of his gear—his kamiks and dog harnesses and his sleeping bag and his harpoon and rifle and the boxes of ammunition—

and threw all this out into the snow too. The wind picked up the corners of his sleeping bag and stirred it, and the snow drifted over the
rifle shell boxes, the cartridges spilled out and glinting. One of the
kamiks rolled over in the wind, tumbling slowly, making its way to
the sea ice. She looked at it, blinking through tears, and then she shut
the kitchen door and locked it for the first time in her life. Robertson
had left the meeting room without speaking to her.

She had been unable to determine who was the architect of this. He
was more certain. Neither Pauloosie nor Simionie had looked at her,
and she blamed them both. She had trusted them, and had been betrayed. The trust was the mistake, and so she withdrew it. As it had been
withdrawn from her.

chapter sixteen

Amanda was supposed to meet Lewis at the North Garden Mall in South Newark, at the food court, in front of Lung Fung Wok. He was waiting there, sitting at one of the table installations, as he referred to them, reading *The Lord of the Rings,* when she walked up. She touched his shoulder and slid into the seat opposite his. "Hey," she said.

"Hey to you." He brightened when he looked up from his book. "You look great."

"Thanks." She was wearing acid-washed jeans and a cropped jacket over a tie-dyed T-shirt. She did look pretty good. "Whatcha doin'?"

"Reading *Lord of the Rings* again."

"How many times is this?"

"I lost count."

"You should check *The Guinness Book of Records.*"

"There would be a fair amount of competition for that particular honor."

"But would they be the sort of people who'd be checking *The Guinness Book of Records?*"

"Meaning?"

"You know, übernerds."

"Uh-huh . . ."

"Not that you're one, exactly . . ."

"Uh-huh . . ."

"Or, if you are, you are in a totally different way."

"What is it, exactly, that you're trying to say about me?"

"I mean, uh, sexy, gorgeous, brilliant."

"Shaddup."

"You shaddup."

They walked to the cineplex.

After the movie, they made their way down the escalator with the rest of the afternoon movie-going crowd, sweatsuited and moonfaced. They stood blinking in the abruptly bright light and dispelled the images of spurting mayhem from their retinas. They did not talk for a long time, and were comfortable in this silence, as the escalator rumbled down and people all around them made small talk.

They had nothing to do with other people; they lived a separate, purer life. They saw more clearly and would not lie to themselves about stupidness everywhere. Lewis knew what she meant. She knew what Lewis meant. She leaned against him and he rested his fingers on her bony hip.

"I don't know when things went wrong with us," Matthew said, leaning forward on his chair, hands clasped between his knees, eyes on his feet. "I think maybe it became obvious when we moved here from California, but the trouble started before that."

"What do you mean, Matthew?" Dr. Kernaghan asked. There was a long silence as Angela looked steadily at her husband, whose breath was coming to him in short, barely audible gasps.

"I mean, from the beginning, even before Amanda was born, I knew I would be the subordinate parent, just as I was the subordinate earner, the subordinate everything. I feel as if the role I play in the family is more like that of an older son, or an uncle. I don't make any decisions—I just reassure Angela that she's not neglecting Amanda, or me, that she keeps a well-run house, that . . ." His voice had grown hoarse and strangled, and he stopped talking. His mouth opened a few more times, like a fish gulping water, but no more words emerged.

Angela didn't wait for Dr. Kernaghan to respond. She spoke rapidly and evenly, with measured logic. "Matthew, your passivity is why I make most of the decisions. I ask you what color of wallpaper you prefer, and you just shrug. Pizza, Greek, Chinese—you'll eat anything. You want someone to take the lead on everything. And when you're with Amanda and she's acting up, your only response is to tell me about it. What do you expect from a situation like that?"

"I think we should take a moment here and try to think of what it is you both really want," Dr. Kernaghan offered, but Matthew had found his voice.

"The problem is, whenever I do voice an opinion, if it's not exactly what you want or believe, there's an instant explosion. There's no such thing as a conversation. If I insist on any point and you do give way, which hardly ever happens, then you punish me for three weeks. But usually you just dig in, say anything you think will help you win the point, draw on any ammunition from past arguments that have nothing to do with the one at hand. There's no such thing as seeing my point; there's only victory or defeat. And you find defeat humiliating."

"We need to remember that both points of view are valid," the therapist said.

"You imagine you're this man of opinions and positions." Angela was glaring at him. "And that if only I wasn't standing in the way of you, you'd be doing all these things, making what you want happen. But if I wasn't around, you'd still be living in that squalid college student's apartment you had when we met. I'm the reason we have a house, a daughter, a life. I carry you through it. And all you do is resent me."

"Let's try to concentrate on our own feelings, and let the other describe theirs."

"And all you feel for me is contempt."

"Maybe this would be a good time to take a break, collect our thoughts for a moment."

"But I didn't use to."

"Me either."

"We can't fix this."

"I know."

"I have an opening next Monday afternoon. I have some exercises I'd like you to try out."

"This is going to be awful, isn't it?"

"Yes."

Later, Amanda and Lewis sat in an all-night pizza joint on Garden Avenue and Lewis talked about the conventions of slasher movies, about how they all depicted sex but punished characters who actually did it with wicked vengeance. *Texas Chainsaw Massacre, Nightmare on Elm Street, Halloween,* it was a constant theme—the devil will make you pay for your sins. Amanda was delighted by Lewis's impish curiosity, by the irony implicit even in the notion of considering Freddy Krueger as a literary figure. Much later she would understand how hard he had been trying to seem smart, but for now she felt as if she had been released from her house of old angry people and tossed into another place, where people made jokes and thought hard.

"Remember the concert where we met—was that your all-time favorite?" she asked, stirring the crushed ice around in the bottom of her paper cup.

"With GN'R, if the show does actually go off, you know it's gonna be great. It's all a question of how much Axl and Slash have had to drink, though."

"What's that about?" she asked, worried by how straight she sounded. "Why are they so messed up on drugs—why aren't they just enjoying their success?"

He leaned on his hand and mused. "Part of what we're buying is the repudiation of our parents. If our parents disapprove of drinking a lot, you know that the bands we like will do that."

"That just sounds juvenile."

"That's the point," Lewis said, and leaned over to kiss her, the smell of pizza all around, fluorescent lights flickering overhead. The short bored man behind the counter turned his back to them to watch ethnic television.

Seventeen-year-old Terry Umiak was walking in the alley behind the Northern Store, late for his shift at Red Top Convenience. He looked where he put his feet, avoiding the late-autumn proliferation of puddles and new snow.

When he slipped and fell over the body, he landed in an ice-limned puddle, mud splashing up over his arms and face. He blinked the water away and saw that the man was still alive, gasping for breath. A rivulet of blood was running into the puddle now occupied by the boy. Terry Umiak looked quickly around, to see if there was anyone else who could help, someone who had seen this happen, or made it happen, but there was no one. He tried to lift the man but couldn't. He had never heard of anything like this happening where he lived. He tried to lift the man again and dropped him. He had blood all over his clothes and he tried to wipe it off. The man on the ground blew blood out through his cut throat like a lung-shot tuktu.

Terry Umiak ran to the nursing station.

Susan Pazniuk was there, peering at a wee child's bulging eardrum, when the boy burst in through the heavy metal doors. Everyone inside—the child and her adolescent mother and father, the supervising grandmother, and the other children and parents scattered around the waiting room—looked up at the boy who seemed to have just cut apart and crawled inside an iviaq, finding something horrifying in there.

Pazniuk called Balthazar at home and told him to come immediately. From the tone of her voice it was clear that something terrible had happened. The first thing he asked her was whether there were any other doctors in town. "If there were, I wouldn't be calling you," she snapped back. "I need you now."

When he arrived, there were Royal Canadian Mounted Police standing around the entrance of the hospital and bystanders gathered at the steps. As he puffed his way through the front door, the second on-call nurse gripped his elbow and propelled him into the emergency room.

The man lay on his back, thrashing and spraying blood in a scarlet mist from his throat. He made no sound but gurgling. Pazniuk and the ambulance attendants had an oxygen mask over his face and were bagging him, trying to drive oxygen into his lungs. Balthazar pushed himself to the head of the bed. When he recognized the man as John Robertson, he felt for a moment that he himself could not breathe. Then he lifted the laryngoscope. He passed the endotracheal tube between Robertson's vocal cords without difficulty, and exhaled with relief as he reached for the ventilation bag. But when he squeezed oxygen down the tube, a brisk bubbling appeared at the front of Robertson's throat, where his neck had been sliced open.

Balthazar watched, fascinated, for a moment as the bubbles rose through the myriad of tendons and nerves and vessels, all emitting dark purple blood in a slackening stream. A part of his mind started to identify the structures lying before him: the sternocleidomastoid muscle, the hyoid, the thyroid isthmus, the trachea, the common carotid, the internal jugular vein, the vagus nerve somewhere in all that, the platysma muscle, and the scalene too. Then he noticed the impatient faces around him and he gripped the endotracheal tube and tried to push it deeper down the trachea into the lungs, below the laceration. He deflated the balloon cuff that sealed and fixed the tube inside the trachea and attempted to advance it. He pushed a little harder and it moved down. The nurse attached the ventilation bag to the tube and then tried to squeeze air into Robertson's lungs. The tube curled upward out of the front of Robertson's throat, blowing bits of fat and cartilage as it did, like a surfacing sea mammal. Around the tube, they could hear Robertson breathing, sucking in blood and exhaling noisily. And then he stopped.

Balthazar sat down heavily on the chair in his office. His spectacles were spotted with blood. He breathed in and out and then he called Victoria.

"It's your husband, Victoria," he mumbled.

"What?" she said, wondering who this was.

"He's been stabbed."

"Who?"

"We don't know—he was just found a few minutes ago behind the Northern Store."

"What are you talking about?"

"I know it's hard to believe."

"Who is this?"

"Balthazar."

"Keith, what the hell are you talking about?"

"Robertson."

"Okay, speak louder. What about him?"

"You'd better come to the hospital."

"Okay . . . like right now?"

"Yes."

When Victoria arrived she pushed through the crowd of people who had gathered around the place, standing silently in shocked horror. Since the community's inception forty years earlier, there had been fights and stabbings and a few shootings, but this was the first murder. Death was common here, and everyone who descended from the land lived by its dealing, but murder was a thing that happened, singularly, in old stories, or with extravagant multiplicity in action movies—but not at all in the intimate confines of small Arctic hamlets, where people were vastly more likely to tie extension cords around their own necks as an expression of their anger.

Victoria took the stairs two steps at a time, and when she burst in through the front door, the nurses and the RCMP and the ambulance attendants and Balthazar all turned to look at her and then quickly away. She walked up to Balthazar and grabbed him by the arm. "Where is he?"

He took her into the trauma room and together they surveyed the gruesome sight before them. "Oh, my," Victoria said in a little girl's voice. She walked over to her husband and picked up his hand and held it. Tears ran down her face in a steady sheet.

Justine was sitting in the living room of what they still called the new house two years after they had moved into it, listening to her Walkman, when her mother came home. She sat down at the kitchen table.

"Is that you, Mom?" Justine called from the living room.

"Yes," Victoria said.

When Marie returned from the library she came in the kitchen door to find Victoria holding Justine on her lap, the first time she had seen that in years. She ran to her mother and her sister.

"You heard?" her mother asked.

"How did it happen?" she asked, sobbing.

"I don't know—they're still looking into it," Victoria said.

"Was it fast?" Marie asked.

"Yes."

"Good. Another stroke would have been awful."

Victoria lifted her head. "It isn't your grandfather, Marie."

Constable Bridgeford had heard about the exchange of accusations at the mining commission meeting. After Susan Pazniuk called him and asked him to come to the nursing station, he supposed there had been a fight. The sight of Robertson's slashed-open throat froze him—as much for Robertson's sake as in grief for the person who had done this. In gentle places, murders are committed by friends, kin, lovers.

The constable sat down on a stool in the trauma room and wound back the film in his camera, listening to the squeal of the flash. The son was an obvious choice. He had been kicked out of the house after the meeting, and was sullen and silent and hardly talked to any Kablunauks in town. Everyone had seen that side of him. And his father a white man.

Or one of the man's business partners, feeling betrayed, perhaps. But who, in business in the north, was as naive as that? He'd start with the boy. The statement from Terry Umiak didn't seem very helpful. And the puddle Robertson had been found beside was a streak of blood and meltwater, making for the sea.

Pauloosie was walking down Water Lake Road with two of his dogs, headed out of town, when Bridgeford stopped the police ATV beside him.

"Good afternoon, Pauloosie."

" 'Lo," he replied, and continued walking. Bridgeford put the ATV back into gear and rode along beside him.

"Pauloosie, I'd like you to set your rifle down on the ground."

He stopped. "Why?"

Bridgeford set his hand on his pistol and unsnapped the strap over it. The sound punctuated Pauloosie's question.

"Pauloosie, set your rifle down."

The boy stared at the Mountie for a long minute. Then he opened the action of the rifle and revealed it to be unloaded. He leaned it on a stone carefully so that no snow or moss would get in the action. Bridgeford stepped forward and picked it up. "Come with me, please." The boy looked at him with curiosity.

When Balthazar met the priest in the hallway, Bernard was carrying a teapot up to his room. Balthazar told the old man how Robertson had been found with his throat slashed. As the words settled on Bernard, it looked as if he might collapse.

"Ah," he kept repeating as the story unfolded, aging a bit with each detail. When Balthazar was done, Bernard looked crumpled and beaten.

He sagged against the wall and dribbled tea out of his teapot. "So many lives," he said. "What will Victoria do now? And her son, and that youngest girl? Ah." He shook his head.

Balthazar watched the priest climb the stairs to his rooms, shoulders stooped, and dribbling tea as he went. He considered whether Bernard would be okay, and then he considered whether he himself would be. He closed his door behind him, shrugging off his parka, and sat down in his living room. Out the window the lights of the town twinkled all around.

Later that night the priest knocked on Balthazar's apartment door. The doctor bade him enter and together they listened to Dexter Gordon play the Horace Silver ballad "Darn That Dream." When it was finished they listened to the turntable go around and around, needle scratching soothingly, both lost in thought. And then the priest stood, nodded good night to Balthazar, and padded back to his apartment.

At the funeral, Victoria stood beside her father and clutched his arm, supporting the old man, who seemed to believe that he was attending the funeral of his decades-dead brother. He hissed to Victoria that he thought his sister-in-law would be remarried in a month. She nodded sadly. "It's okay, it'll be better for the kids," he said, patting her arm.

As he read the service, Father Bernard looked drawn and tired. Balthazar sat in the back and listened as his friend read out the liturgy in Inuktitut. The priest's unaccented Inuktitut was a marvel to Balthazar, who, in his twenty years in the north, had accumulated maybe a hundred words. It was as unthinkable that the priest would maintain an apartment in the south as it was, apparently, for the doctor to learn the language of his patients.

Balthazar was struck once again by the old man's air of gravitas as he intoned from his pulpit. It had never been clear to Balthazar how Father Bernard had felt about Robertson. He was fond of Victoria, that much was clear—the two men smelled it upon each other—but Balthazar could not recall the priest's ever offering an opinion about her husband. And it wasn't as if he didn't have opinions about people in the community, or that he was reluctant to express them. In the priest's grief, Balthazar had seen an affection for the man he had not been aware of. But now Father Bernard stood straight and recited from Job to the assembled, his personal feelings suppressed so as not to impose on those who might have need of him. He was inspiring to watch, Balthazar the atheist thought. That was probably the idea.

When it was time to sing, Balthazar stood with everyone else and hummed as the translated hymns rung out in polyphonic and at times imperfect harmony. Justine and Marie wept quietly and Victoria struggled to hold back her tears. No one from the Ikhirahlo Group was at the church.

Simon Alvah sat in the back row and watched solemnly. He wore a black suit that he had produced, miraculously intact if redolent of kerosene. He bowed his head and prayed aloud in Inuktitut with the rest of the congregation. No one asked him what he was doing there. Pauloosie sat in the same pew, accompanied by Constable Bridgeford and beset by torments everyone present was prepared to offer an explanation for. His mother had not acknowledged him. His sisters had reached out for him when they saw him, only to be pulled past by their mother.

Justine perched on Oiltank Hill overlooking the harbor. In the bay was the year's last barge, just arrived from Montreal ahead of the ice. A tug was maneuvering it alongside the wharf. In the afternoon light, the collection of men and forklift trucks gathered there seemed to vibrate in anticipation. Around her were ripening cloudberries growing through sphagnum moss and Labrador tea. Mice scurried through the moss, making small shivers in the green; circling in the sky was a snowy owl looking to feed on these sensibly hidden creatures. She had been here since just before dawn.

When she had got up, her sister had rolled over and watched her dress. Even in the dark Justine could see Marie's dulled eyes opening and she shushed her quietly. The younger girl did not speak, and after her sister had gone, she turned to face the wall, breathing slowly but without ease.

Justine crept out through the kitchen, where the dishes were stacked haphazardly, pots half full of pointlessly heated soup. She pulled on her shoes and a windbreaker and eased out the kitchen door. The sky was pale in the east, the breaking light illuminating the moss and rocks enough for her to pick her way out to the shore, where she sat down and looked at the water.

What she thought was, *This place is falling apart.* She was surprised by how shattered she felt. She had not known her father well, had not felt well known by him. Since she had been old enough to reflect on these things, it had always seemed to her that she was next on his to-do list, after Pauloosie, and whatever it was that was happening at work at any given moment, and the ongoing salvage attempt on his marriage, and even Marie. But with his death, she felt her whole world shift from under her.

When he had been living, but absent, his work had been the thing that took him away all the time, and the work seemed to Justine both uninteresting and oppressive. She hadn't thought about it much except to resent it. Now, it seemed important to her to understand whether it was true that he had been corrupt, what role he had played in bringing the hospital to Rankin Inlet, what he had done for the mining consortium. His smell was vanishing from the house, the memory of his tired, sadly smiling face—gray benignity—supplanted by the frozen white grimace she had last glimpsed. His work would endure long after these impressions of him had evaporated, she knew.

The ocean hung gray and cold across the eastern sky. Winter was coming any minute. She shivered. She could not remember her father's ever having once raised his voice to her. She recalled her Charlie's Angels Barbie, which he had brought from Yellowknife. She shut her eyes and cold rain began hitting the tundra all around her.

Pauloosie and Bridgeford sat in the police station, facing each other across a coffee table.

"So, Pauloosie, I have to tell you again that if you can't prove where you were the morning your father was killed, if you can't come up with someone who saw you there, then I can't eliminate you as a suspect in his death."

"I didn't kill my father."

"Someone did."

"Did you think about the Kablunauks he was in business with?"

"Is there something in particular you want to tell me?"

"No."

"Do you know where the diamonds came from?"

"Which diamonds?"

"The ones he had in his dresser drawer."

"I don't know anything about those."

"Are they still there?"

"I don't know."

"Pauloosie."

"Yeah?"

"Where were you?"

"Hunting."

"Anyone see you out hunting?"

"No."

"Where were you exactly?"

"You asked me all this already."

"I know."

"North bank of the Meliadine."

"Funny, we've spoken to three people who were fishing the river that morning and none of them saw you, or anyone else, out there."

"I didn't see them—why would they see me?"

"Let's say, for a moment, that you were somewhere you're embarrassed about—with a girl, say—no one needs to know that. All you have to do is tell me, and if I can prove it, then everything stops there. No one finds out, not her dad, or her employer, no one."

Pauloosie sighed and stared at the ceiling. Bridgeford leaned back in his seat. The wind rattled the windows. The constable began again, at the beginning.

"Can you tell me what you know of your father's business dealings in the month before his death?"

Outside the window, the season's first heavy snow was falling.

Pauloosie was released on his own recognizance after two days of questioning, mostly to get him out of one of the police station's two cells so that he wouldn't be able to speak to the next two men to be questioned, Okpatayauk and Simionie. There are no roads out of Rankin Inlet, and it was easy to ensure he didn't get in an airplane. Pauloosie made his way immediately to Penny's apartment.

She was waiting for him. He pulled his pack out of her closet and stuffed his sleeping bag in it.

"What are you doing?" she asked.

"Going," he said.

■

chapter seventeen

Constable Bridgeford sat across the card table from Okpatayauk. "Do you know why I brought you in?"

"Why don't you tell me?" Okpatayauk had his fingers interlaced on the table in front of him.

"I'm interested in what you can tell me about Robertson's death."

"I'm not interested in saying very much about that."

"People tell me you weren't friends."

"You and me, we're not friends."

"I'm not dead."

"There hasn't been anyone killed by an Inuk up here since the town was built." Okpatayauk was alluding to the more violent dispositions of the Bay Boys, and the habit of frightened young Mounties—indoctrinated by American police dramas—to pull their pistols when confronted by drunken hysterics.

"What are you saying?"

"It would be the first, if you're thinking I did it."

"You don't seem to be trying very hard to convince me you didn't."

"It isn't my job to tell you who did it."

Bridgeford rolled his eyes. "Why don't you start by telling me you didn't?"

"Why should I?"

The phone rang.

Bridgeford, relieved at the excuse to get away from Okpatayauk

and let him stew a bit, picked it up. Okpatayauk watched him lift his
eyebrows with surprise.

Bridgeford turned away and dropped his voice. "Yes?" he said. There
were loud chirping sounds from the telephone receiver, and he held it
away from his head until they stopped. "If you have anything to say, I'm
happy to listen." The chirping noises recommenced.

When Bridgeford sat down he said, "That was your girlfriend, Elizabeth Agutetuar."

"She's not my girlfriend."

"She tells me you were with her all morning, in her apartment."

"Well, she would."

"She says two of her neighbors came over for coffee and saw you
there."

"Uh-huh."

"And one of the schoolteachers."

"Oh."

"And when you went to leave, in the afternoon, you stopped outside her door to talk to the priest."

"Yeah."

"Get out of here."

Simionie had suffered insomnia for many years. This was not widely
known. He was thought to be a phlegmatic man, not given to anxiety
or outward displays of anything. This idea of him—held to a certain extent even by himself—was destroyed when he was brought in for questioning about Robertson's murder.

He had watched so many late-night and early-morning detective
movies on television that he expected to be beaten within minutes of
sitting down. He drummed his fingers nervously as Bridgeford made
tea. "You want some tea, Simionie?" the constable asked.

"No," Simionie spat.

"What's the matter?" Bridgeford looked up as he stirred his Earl
Grey.

"Let's just get it over with," Simionie said, trying unsuccessfully to affect world-weariness.

"Okay," Bridgeford said, sitting down at the table across from him. "So what do you know about Robertson's murder?"

"Nothing."

"You seemed pretty worked up about it. I thought maybe you'd have more to say."

"I don't."

"What were you doing that morning?"

"I was home."

"Anyone else there?"

"My parents."

"You live with them?"

"Yes."

"So what were you doing that morning?"

"Watching TV."

"What were you watching?"

"Gilligan's Island."

"What episode was playing?"

"The one where the Howells discover their wedding wasn't valid and she decides not to remarry him after all."

Bridgeford shook his head. "See, I was home that morning too, and that wasn't it. It was the one where the professor makes a radio out of Gilligan's fillings."

Simionie opened his eyes widely for a moment and then he laughed. "They teach you that in detective school? Check it out. It was the Howells' marriage crisis episode. I was watching it."

Bridgeford drank his tea. "I love the one you're talking about. The idea that what everyone assumed to be eternal is not."

"You think even Gilligan ever thought marriage was eternal?"

"Maybe not."

"That radio in the fillings one is pretty funny too."

"Yeah."

"You got some interpretation of that one too?"

"Something to do with the incongruence of technology in primitive settings."

"I guess."

"I'll think about it a little more."

"Can I go?"

"Yeah."

Simionie got up and walked to the door.

"Simionie?"

"Yeah?"

"Who do you suppose killed him?"

Simionie stopped. "I dunno. This never happens here."

Okpatayauk knocked on the door of the police station. Bridgeford opened up. "Yes?" he said.

"I want to confess to the murder of Robertson."

"You've been drinking," the constable said, and closed the door on him.

Okpatayauk pushed it open. "No, I haven't. I cut him across the neck with my knife because of what he's stolen from the Inuit."

Bridgeford looked at him. "What about your girlfriend and all those people who saw you at home that morning?"

"They're lying to protect me. I can't stand the guilt."

"The priest is lying to protect you?"

"Yeah. You never heard of a priest lying before?"

Bridgeford sat in the kitchen of the police station, talking to Anna Kowmik, the dispatcher. Okpatayauk was reclining comfortably in one of the cells. "The thing is," Bridgeford said, "if we just blow him off, and we find a better suspect, Okpatayauk's confession will be seen as reasonable doubt unless he recants."

"So what do we do?"

"We proceed to charges and sentencing and wait for him to lose his nerve."

"You don't think he did it?"

"No."

"How come?"

"He's a thinker. He's not explosive."

"Why is he confessing then?"

"Attention. He's making some sort of political point."

"Are you sure?"

He shrugged. "I've been wrong before."

"What if he doesn't recant?"

"Then maybe I'm wrong."

"Do you think Pauloosie did it?"

"I don't know. I don't think so."

"He is family. And that cut was deep."

Nodding. "Whoever did it knew him enough to hate him."

"I have to say, I got that vibe from the boy."

"Me too. I'm not saying he couldn't have done it. Hey, you were off Saturday morning. Did you watch *Gilligan's Island*?"

"Yeah."

"Which episode did they show?"

"Ginger and Mary Ann have the beauty contest."

"You sure?"

"Yeah."

"Huh."

"What?"

"What do you make of Simionie?"

"He didn't do it."

"Why do you say that?"

"Look at him."

"I know. Wouldn't that be a surprise, though, if he did?"

"He didn't."

s w e e t   b l o o d

When I first came to the Arctic I was told by the other doctors I worked with how different medicine was here. There was rabies in the foxes and every year we gave vaccinations to trappers who were unwary; bear and dog maulings were common; there was still endemic tuberculosis; and "seal finger," an infection acquired while skinning seals that involved an unusual bacterium unresponsive to conventional antibiotics. The Inuit also smoked heavily, and had since the whalers from New England started coming a hundred years ago and paid the Inuit hunters for being crew with tobacco. That completed an interesting circle of exchange of that little weed: Indians to Caucasians ("Kablunauks" up here, meaning "hairy eyebrows and bellies," as a tribute to New Englanders' hirsutism) to Inuit. And so we treated emphysema and lung cancer, just as in the south.

But there was no diabetes, except among Kablunauks, and almost no heart disease or stroke. This in a people who, until twenty years ago, confined their diets almost exclusively to animal fat and protein, except when they ate the stomach contents of the caribou and musk oxen. (Which sufficed to prevent scurvy, but surely could not have been their favorite part of the day.) Almost all their calories were animal fat. For years the Rankin Inlet Clinic kept bottles of clot-dissolving thrombolytics on its shelves to treat heart attacks and yet the drug was never given.

The absence of vascular disease in this part of the Arctic is an astonishing thing for a physician trained in the south. Working here is like walking off a noisy city street into a silent cathedral. Vascular disease kills a hundred million people every year. The worldwide toll from banal and familiar heart attacks and strokes exceeds that of wars and malnutrition and AIDS by a factor of eight. Fifty-five percent of us will die of atherosclerosis, hardening of the arteries, in one or another of its manifestations: the strokes and heart attacks mentioned above, but also peripheral vascular disease and blood clots, and atherosclerotic kidney disease and abdominal aortic aneurysms. This affects every single one of us. The minority who do not succumb to vascular disease directly avoid it only by dying of malignancies and pneumonias first. Every old person who grew up among automobiles and plate glass has this disease. But none of the Inuit does.

Our blood vessels tighten into wiry strictures; our limbs grow progressively cooler and die in blackened gangrenous agony, just as our hearts and our minds do when the lumina of those blood vessels finally occlude completely. And yet we are inured to it, understand it to be "normal," an essential expression of who we are and what we must endure, like consumption was in another age. Living in the south, it is an easy mistake, to think that vascular disease is the unavoidable conclusion of a life spent on this earth. Then one comes to the Arctic and immediately wonders why it is so noisy outside.

The thrifty gene is a concept that describes the changes seen among hunting-gathering peoples as they are acculturated. It exists both as an idea and as a sequence of nucleic acids; the genetic trait is common to most of the indigenous peoples of North and South America, and to most Pacific Islanders as well. It represents an evolutionary response to the problem of recurrent famine, altering the way fat tissue and the brain communicate with each other, prompting people to eat aggressively whenever food is available and to avidly store those calories as fat. Clearly, heading into famine with an extra fifteen pounds under the belt is a helpful thing, and the Darwinian pressure in favor of such a trait must have been significant on the islands of the South Pacific and in the Indian settlements in the taiga of the North American Subarctic.

But what was an adaptive trait in a traditional setting has become profoundly maladaptive in the era of unlimited cheap calories. All through the tropical Pacific and the native settlements of North and South America, obesity, as well as the consequent diabetes and vascular disease, is exploding in prevalence. These are peoples who were devastated by European diseases; tuberculosis, smallpox, and influenza all killed millions in waves of epidemics that swept through these places over the last five hundred years. But the worst *thing that ever came from the contact between traditional and European cultures is turning out to be Spam. And Cheez Doodles. And Cherry Coke. All available in little stores on tropical islands and Indian reservations and small Arctic communities for a bit of money and no physical effort at all.*

These are bodies designed to anticipate extraordinary stressors in the coming rainy season or freezing winter. These are bodies prepared for the need to work to the point of muscle-shaking exhaustion on a few hundred calories of chewed sinew or dried taro root. The problem of limiting caloric intake is not one that has previously arisen. For millennia upon millennia, there was no such problem as too much food.

Until the late 1970s, diabetes was still uncommon among the indigenous peoples of the Subarctic, the Cree and Dene of Northern Ontario, Quebec, Manitoba, and Saskatchewan. Research efforts were undertaken to understand why the Cree, for instance, seemed relatively immune to diabetes. Then the disease appeared like a pall in the desperate reservations in the taiga. Now half of adults in some reserves are diabetic. The dialysis population doubles every three years. The immunity proved relative indeed.

There are two types of diabetes. Type I, sometimes called juvenile onset diabetes, though it need not develop in childhood, consists of a failure of the pancreas to secrete adequate amounts of insulin, usually as a consequence of an assault by the body's own immune system. This used to be by far the most common type of diabetes, and was the type that Banting and Best addressed by administering insulin derived from pig and cattle pancreases. It is not related to obesity, is not really preventable, and its incidence has changed relatively little over the last century.

Ninety percent of diabetics today, in every developed society, have Type II diabetes. This disease is not really a variant of the other but a distinctly different circumstance, as different as obesity is from anorexia. It ought to have a different name. Here, the pancreas is initially healthy, and produces insulin as it should, but the insulin receptors in fat and muscle cells are resistant, numb, to its effect. The body is dependent on the activation of such receptors to be able to take sugar up from the bloodstream and metabolize it into energy, or store it as fat. When it can't do this, the sugar levels in the blood rise, and the pancreas senses the elevated glucose levels and so pumps out more than normal

amounts of insulin. By pumping out steadily increasing quantities of insulin, it
is able, for a time, to overcome the increasingly benumbed insulin receptors and
to maintain appropriate levels of sugar in the blood.

But, like the heart that pumps for years against too-high blood pressure
and then dilates and fails, eventually the pancreas becomes overburdened and is
no longer able to secrete enough insulin to maintain normal blood glucose.
Indeed, when the pancreas fails, it often ceases to be capable of secreting even a
normal quantity of insulin into the blood. The problem in the late stage of
Type II diabetes is insufficient insulin combined with insulin resistance. The
body is hit from both sides of the equation, like a bushfire in drought—there
is the problem and there is the absence of what you need to solve it.

Eight percent of North Americans have diabetes as it has been
traditionally recognized—by elevated blood sugar levels. Five times as many
have insulin resistance—the metabolic syndrome. Essentially every obese
hypertensive is insulin-resistant and, today, the majority of American adults
are overweight. The prevalence of diabetes is increasing logarithmically—as is
obesity and insulin resistance, its precursor states.

It is an appalling and demeaning illness; ulcers develop in the cold and
unoxygenated feet and progress steadily, rotting off limbs—modern-day
leprosy. Diabetes is the most common cause of amputations anywhere it is
prevalent. The high concentration of sugar in the blood paralyzes the white
blood cells and infections of every sort arise: bladder infections and yeast
infections and, especially awful, stinking skin infections caused by fungi and
bacteria and anything at all that wants to eat sickened sweet flesh. The odor of
a person with longtime poorly controlled diabetes is like rotten milk. The
ability of too-sweet blood to cause blindness and the swelling malaise of kidney
failure comes as no surprise to anyone who understands the disease's character.
Diabetes is the commonest cause of these indignities anywhere people are fat.

Rankin Inlet possesses two parallel cultures that are steadily becoming one.
The Kablunauks are here briefly as individuals—the Mounties for three or four
years, the nurses for two, the teachers for maybe five or six. (The doctors: usually six
months or a year.) Nevertheless, every year there are more of them and, ludicrously,

more cars and trucks too—even though the town is less than a mile across and there are no roads to any other place. Recently, the school system had school buses brought in on the summer barge to carry the children to school in the winter.

Every southerner who has ever affected concern for the people here declares the Inuit to be damaged by their contact with the south. It is a little like city dwellers worrying about the last stands of old-growth forest after they've cut down an entire ecosystem to build their subdivisions. The indigenous peoples of the entire New World have been swept aside without a thought, and if they have had the misfortune to inhabit valuable land, the sweeping away was completed generations ago. But when it comes to the Inuit, who live in a place no sane southerner would ever covet, we affect concern for our acculturating influence. As if they aren't aware. As if they aren't embracing their own self-abnegation with exactly the same rigid-jawed determination as we have.

Insulin resistance begins and ends with obesity; if there is no obesity, there is almost no Type II diabetes. As insulin levels rise, the desire to eat is increased, and so the obesity and the insulin resistance and the insulin-induced overeating worsen. It is a dreadful sequence of problems.

Human beings will eat what is available. Obesity is a problem to some degree wherever famine is not, and it is not confined to those with the thrifty gene; Americans, who for the most part do not descend directly from hunter-gatherers, are the fattest people ever to have existed, and the number of them with diabetes is unprecedented: eighteen million, at least. Obese humans of any genetic heritage are effectively unable to limit their own dietary intake; none of the myriad of diets advanced is effective over any length of time at maintaining weight loss because no one sticks to them. Wherever people stop working, stop sweating and gasping and running for their living, they grow fat. And then they start falling apart from within, and dying.

The Inuit are the last of the indigenous peoples of North America to come in off the land. When one speaks to a fifty-year-old such as Yvo Nautsiaq, who is still young and vital, one must recall that he was born in an iglu and grew up eating caribou and whale and walrus flesh. Farther south, the indigenous peoples of North America don't know their own languages anymore. Among the Pacific coast tribes, teachers come from the universities to instruct the children in Haida, or Coast Salish, as a gesture of some sort. The indigenous languages of the Americas are dying faster than can be recorded—whole ways of thought, of seeing the world, vanishing with the last breaths of old men and women. But when you walk on the frozen beach of Coral Harbour, avoiding the children playing hockey on the sea ice, the cries are full of q's and k's that mean nothing at all to anyone from the land of cappuccino.

These peoples came here about the same time that the Vikings were settling Greenland. The Thule culture, with its lithe little sealskin boats and its elaborate technology revolving around sea mammal hunting, spread in the course of a few generations from the Beaufort Sea to the east coast of Greenland, just in time to meet the hairy bellies of that era, in longships and waving steel swords. The Norse were gone within a few generations of climatic cooling, after the medieval warm period ended. We presume. The Inuit endured, supplanting the Dorset people who preceded them in the Arctic, either absorbing or slaughtering them. By the time Europeans were exploring the Arctic in the 1800s, only the Thule Inuit were found, the ones with the beautiful skin boats and harpoons and lances sufficient to kill bowhead whales: forty tons and they killed them in thirty-pound boats armed with sticks tied to sharp rocks. They invented the iglu and developed the dogsled. Relentlessly nomadic, with these skills they made voyages thousands of miles long across the sea ice and they inhabited—in the qualified sense that any part of the Arctic allows itself to be inhabited—every place south of Ellesmere Island.

What the Inuit were was a miracle. They lived in a land without trees, in houses made of snow. When there was no driftwood to be had, they made sled runners out of frozen fish wrapped together. Their technologies—the qayak and the toggle-headed harpoon and the seal-fat lamps—were the most elegant solutions to the problems of living in this land, and the finest expression of their wit and sense of beauty. What the Inuit are is us. And what they achieved in the Arctic was the clearest expression of human ingenuity and tenacity. They— we—prospered in the hardest place there is, and achieved magnificence.

But no one lives there anymore. From the edges of the little towns on the coast of Hudson Bay, you can look out on the tundra and guess at some of the difficulties involved in pulling a living from a land such as this. Rock and lichen, snowbound ten months a year: no wonder no one lives there anymore.

■

chapter eighteen

October 21, 1991

Dear Uncle Keith:

I finally got your letter. Mom gave it to me today when we met for lunch. I'm sorry to hear about your friend. It sounds to me like everyone's taking it really hard. Murder must be so much more personal a thing up there. Everyone knowing each other and everything. Here everyone's more used to it. It's always on the news, you just hear about it more. When it happens to someone you know then, it's not such a big surprise.

So things are pretty much the same around here. I'm still seeing Lewis. He's really smart. Mom and Dad don't like him, natch. I'm actually not as bothered by them as I used to be. I think everything is gonna be okay. They might not be, but I will.

So you should get yer butt down here to visit me sometime soon! I have lots more to tell you.

Love,
Amanda

The people Lewis drew to himself were as fascinating as he was. Amanda's friends at school had always been conventionally timid girls who regarded the world as an opaque and ominous place, the only shelter from which was their parents. She compared those sweater-wearing clarinet players to Kat, whom Lewis brought along one afternoon when they met at the mall, skin like white latex and blue-black hair. He was thin and long and erect, dressed in anarchist regalia, and almost entirely mute in any group larger than a pair. Kat knew the members of every hard-core band in the city, and was preoccupied with anime and graphic novels. He sat with them at the food court and flipped through his comic books and when Amanda asked him about them, he described the nexus between western and Japanese animation, and how it hybridized ideas of sex and submission and irony into a thing that struck all concerned as intriguingly alien. A part of her wondered if he had read those words somewhere, but she was stirred by the effort he put even into posing. And when he smoked his Camel Plains and laughed through his teeth, she could not take her eyes off him.

The three of them were at a house party when the boys stepped outside to smoke a joint. Amanda stood against one wall, feeling the music throbbing in her chest and listening distractedly to the conversations around her. She was just learning to smoke pot herself. That night she felt a thin sliver of anxiety that had to do with her father's inevitable departure and had thought better of getting high and letting that anxiety free to roam.

The girl sidled up to her as if she just wanted to lean against that part of the wall too. It was very dark and Amanda was nodding to—being nodded by—the music and the next thing she knew the girl was asking her if both the boys were her boyfriends. Amanda laughed, flattered at the daring that had been imputed to her. No, just the muscular one, she said, though no one other than besotted Amanda would have so characterized Lewis, only marginally less stringy than Kat. "They're both so cute," the girl said. "I'm Beth."

"Amanda." And she closed her eyes a little and nodded to the music. "Do you wanna go smoke some pot with them?"

"Where are they?"

"Outside, in the back. Go ahead."

When the three of them, Lewis and Kat and Beth, finally came back inside, they were giggling circularly and so short of breath, they could hardly speak. They walked up to Amanda arm in arm and looked at her.

"Well, hello." She felt so cool.

"Uh, hi," Lewis said, smiling so widely it looked as though his face might just split. "D'you wanna stay here or go?"

"It's pretty heavy."

"We could go."

"This is Beth."

"We met." Beth smiled soporifically at Amanda.

In the course of a weekend it became winter, thirty below in late October. The dogs panted their way across the tundra, the squeak of the komatik's runners on the fresh snow a kind of musical counterpoint to their breathing. The interplay between these rhythms and harmonies caught Penny's ear and held it. The sun glistened off every crystalline shard of snow and ice and it simply could not have been brighter or colder than it was.

She wore sheepskin booties over her kamiks and curled her hands into fists inside her mittens. She watched the texture of the snow, alert for any sign of candling, of the snow beginning to form jagged and miniature stalactites that would abrade the dogs' paws until they bled. But for that to happen it would have to warm up. For now, it was so cold that the snow had the consistency of coarsely ground cornmeal, and it erupted into clouds as the dogs' feet collided with it. Every time she inhaled, her teeth ached. Under everything else, she sensed dread like another forty degrees below zero.

She had an idea where Pauloosie might be. Twenty miles down the Meliadine was a valley with steep sides, through which a tributary of the river ran fast and deep. It had good fishing even in winter. The valley walls would provide some shelter from the wind, and the snow packed nicely there too. It was one of his favorite campsites, he had told her, because no one else seemed to know about it. The snowmobilers are careful with river valleys and fast water. With dogs, one goes slower and so is more certain of the footing.

When she reached the fork on the Meliadine she turned toward the tributary she sought and started scanning the sky for smoke, even though he would be more careful than that. Still, when a wisp of snow blew up in the air, for a moment she felt like she couldn't breathe. There had been dogs through here too, she saw, but not for a while, and she kept going. It was her third night out. She was missing work. Even if she turned around now she wouldn't make it back before the end of the week. She had lost her job then.

She stopped on a bend of the tributary where the bank was close to the ice and provided good shelter. The snow wasn't yet deep enough to make an iglu, and so she erected her little white dome tent and pulled her gear inside with her, thinking of the last time he and she had been inside that tent. She hacked frozen meat off the caribou in the komatik and threw it to the dogs. She checked each of their feet in turn, and then she peed in the snow. She crawled into her tent and pushed her Primus stove out of it and lit it. She boiled water for tea and drank it while she heated a can of stew. The dogs smelled the food cooking and whined at her. She fed them some more and they still whined. She too heard the wind rising.

An iglu is a surprising thing for most people to contemplate. For instance, the Dorset Inuit, the predecessors of the Thule culture Inuit, struggled with the Arctic the entire time they lived there, scratching out a living in skin tents heated by low smoky fires. Neither had they the dogsled, the toggle-headed harpoon, or qayak; any contention that technology inevitably demeans humans falters on considering what must have been the misery of that life.

Penny had occasion to contemplate such misery—the difficulty of remaining warm and dry in a tent when the wind reaches sixty miles an hour and freezing rain hits the fabric with such velocity that it blows through the wall in a frigid mist of atomized ice. Melted snow formed puddles at the base of the windward wall and then trickled the length of the tent, running downhill and wicking its way through everything fabric.

After the blizzard there was more snow. She lay in the tent for four days, eating quietly and settling her dogs. When the wind finally lifted, every track she had seen coming to this place was gone, her own and those of the dogs she had been following. A slender, even a false hope, is still a hope, and when she emerged under the bright sky to see the tundra scoured bare of any evidence of movement, she sagged. Her dogs emerged from the mounds of snow they had become, shaking their great curled tails and rumps and then throwing themselves against their tethers toward her.

She headed inland, south and west, because she knew that there would be fewer hunters there, and he would know that too. She crossed the great rivers one by one, noted the fording sites the tuktu used and tried to remember their Inuktitut names. Her dogs charged across them successively, pausing only to note the scent of tuktu and to glance back at her, wondering.

She shot a fat buck they came upon when they rounded a hilltop. She had her rifle out and was kneeling down, her elbow planted on her thigh, when he turned to run parallel to her and afforded her a lung shot. She led him by a foot, he was running so fast, and when she fired she blinked her eyes and when she looked up again he was somersaulting onto the snow.

She drove her dogs down to the young buck and stopped them fifty feet away, tying the sled to an ice hook planted firmly in the tundra— as she had seen the old man do a hundred times. The dogs leapt forward at the smell of the blood leaking out over the snow from the deer's chest. She approached it. It seemed not to be breathing, but when she was close enough she saw its eyes were open. She squinted her own, and then she drew out her hunting knife and cut its throat. Blood

flowed forward like a river in flood and the dogs whined like puppies.
Still he looked up at her. She thought to herself that if she had cut both
the carotid arteries, and clearly she had, then he must be unconscious.
But the eyes were not glazed, were unmistakably gazing up at her, and
there is no denying the fact of another creature studying you, especially
when it is doing so in pain or malice, and so she raised her rifle and shot
it in the head and then the eyes were shattered and what remained of
them froze quickly. As she flung the tongue and the liver and the heart
and lungs to the dogs, she wondered if it might be too much food for
them, after eating so sparsely for the last week. But her dogs harbored
no such hesitation. The fattest, strongest dogs ate deeply and well and
then staggered away and the older and younger dogs snarled over the
steaks she continued to fling their way. At least, she thought to herself,
she knew that she could find food out here, could remain here until she
found him or until she or the dogs were hurt.

She had crossed the Thelon River and was staring along its length,
studying it for tracks, for abandoned tent or iglu sites, when something
about the sinuous curve of ice resonated with her. It was only a few
miles downriver of where she and Johanna had camped after the bush
pilot had dropped them off, the summer before. She smiled at this recollection, but then the contrast between the memory and this circumstance was too much and she had to push the picture of Johanna
laughing into her tea from her mind. Instead, she reduced the memory
to a series of abstractions in order that she might find what was useful
to her in it. Fact: there was a cabin upriver from here, the pilot had told
them, built by three Englishmen before they starved to death sixty
years ago. One was a boy, Edgar Christian, seventeen years old, rowdy,
and unloaded by his parents onto his adventuresome and impetuous uncle, Jack Hornby, who had proposed that they cross the Canadian tundra together. With Hornby's friend Howard Adlard, they had reached
the Thelon from the west, after coming up the Mackenzie River to Yel-

lowknife. From there they had walked and canoed their way east, and had prepared to spend the winter on the Thelon before completing their journey the following spring.

Nobody understands, really, what winter is like on the tundra. Every book ever written about men wintering over in small cabins with caches of food has left the lingering misimpression that it is principally a question of resolve—with a few large sacks of flour, and some ammunition and determination, inexpert but strong men may attempt this confidently.

But there is no wood. Thus, there are no wood fires, no wooden shelter, no forests to break the wind, no trees from which to fashion skis or snowshoes, or to collect the snow in sufficient quantity and depth to require them. Tuktu exist only in proportion to the scant forage: they are as sparse on the ground as their food is, and when they disperse, after the rut and after calving, they are thin on the ground in every sense.

She had not seen another deer since she had shot the fat buck. Now she recalled how cavalierly she had tossed the organ meat to the dogs, and winced.

The Hornby party had had the Bay leave their order of plankwood and flour for them and they had found it easily enough, but they had underestimated how much they would need: how much flour, wood, coal, oil, and sugar three men will use over a very cold winter. Their supplies had given out before the solstice. They had thought they would use the flour to batter the chops, but there were no deer since the autumn river fordings. The boy's diary describes the erosion of their strength, the five-day-long hunting expeditions that generated only a single rabbit. In the accumulating foreknowledge of their deaths, there was a kind of equanimity in his writing that had surprised Penny, familiar as she was with boisterous seventeen-year-old boys. She had ordered a transcript of the diary from the Hudson's Bay Company archives, in Winnipeg.

When it had arrived, wrapped in brown paper, it had been accompanied by a handwritten letter from the archivist, reading: *Thank you for your interest in this material. I should be honored to be of any further assistance whatever. We remain, Mickey Reid.* Penny had imagined a woman librarian drunk with the richness of her wares and simultaneously baffled by the absence of crowds at her door.

She found the Englishmen's cabin and thought to herself that it was a grand title for what was not much more than a lean-to. It was collapsed, the graying timbers sticking up above the snow like the stumps of rotten teeth. There were no signs of anyone having camped there that year—or the twenty prior.

She built her iglu quickly and perfectly. After about thirty of them, she had found the knack, and had learned to recognize the best snow for making them. Puka, Emo had called it when he had shown her, sticking his panna in halfway and pausing to demonstrate its texture, the incomplete resistance it offered the knife. Pauloosie had given her the same lecture once, using the same words and the same sequence of gestures, and she had bit her lip in amusement but had not said anything to him. Pauloosie. She was certain he would not have returned to Rankin Inlet yet. It was still early winter and he would have hunted more successfully than she had. His anger at his family and at the town had lodged deeply inside him, born of grievances certain to inflame themselves with more contemplation—and there was only ever more time out here, alone and in the cold, for more contemplation.

She was out of ideas by now of where he would be. Her thought was that she would go south, to the ruins of the Padlei settlement, and then she would turn northwest and farther inland to arc back around to the ruins of the Wager Bay encampment. This would take her through the least traveled portion of the tundra, and perhaps one of them would see the other's tracks. Beyond that, she did not know her own intentions.

Padlei was an abandoned plywood-sheathed hut with two smaller outbuildings already collapsing into themselves. She had been two more weeks getting here, had shot and eaten one old doe, not enough food for her dogs, but some, anyway. There had been no other visitors to Padlei since the snow had fallen.

The days were growing short now, and, deducting the hour at the end of the day she needed to make her iglu, she could travel for only five hours or so. It meant that she had too much time by herself, lying in her sleeping bag and imagining finding him. Her favorite scenario involved coming upon his camp when he was very tired, and the dogs (improbably: this was a fantasy, she reproached her excessively realistic self) not noticing her, sneaking into his iglu and waking him with a kiss, explaining to his delighted cries how she had sought him out, had brought him tuktu tongue and rifle cartridges and found a place on the Kazan they might camp together.

She imagined sliding into his sleeping bag then, his running his hands over the frostbite scars on her face, hands, and feet. His hands on her shoulders, down between the muscles on either side of her spine, fingers splayed out along her ribs, silently sliding along her skin, over her breasts, her arms, her shoulders, pushing her down. She imagined this. It's what solitary travelers do when they are far from company. They become so lonely, they cannot resist their yearnings.

She had resisted her own yearnings all her life. Coming out on the land was the first extravagant thing she had ever done. She was strong and therefore had constructed checks within herself to guard against self-pity. Her reflexive response to self-pitying words and thoughts was the appearance of her father's skeptical face in her mind. She imagined her father's reply to the contention that she had only once been extravagant and wondered if she wasn't on an eccentric orbit, being propelled farther and farther from the center with each revolution: first from the farm and then to the Arctic and then into the Arctic in pursuit of the boy. That would be how it looked to her father, she supposed. And now, certainly, to everyone at the school, even Johanna, though she was not as certain about that last. It would be Johanna's inclination to give her the benefit of any doubt. She had caught the scent of the other woman's admiration a few times. Though she might be seen in a different light now. How does one know when one has gone crazy? Don't the insane always consider themselves simply courageous?

She was tired. Her hands slid back up along her abdomen, imagining themselves to be his hands, and then she folded her fingers together and lay on her side.

In the morning she rose, struck camp, and hitched her dogs up to the trace. She turned them north and headed for Wager Bay.

December 20, 1991

Dear Amanda:

Well, things here in Rankin Inlet just get stranger and stranger. The son of the man I told you about, the one who was killed, has disappeared, with his dog team. Everyone figures he has gone out on the land. But he has been gone for almost three months now. We're all worried about him. I delivered him, when I first got here.

One of the schoolteachers, who happens to own a dog team herself, has gone missing too! You can imagine what everyone is thinking. I don't know either of them well, certainly not well enough to know what their relationship to each other was. But it is difficult not to draw inferences. Could either of them have had anything to do with the murder? Well, one thing is certain: they won't stay out on the land much longer. Soon it will be midwinter, and the days even shorter. Tonight it is fifty degrees below.

It would be remembered for years after as a difficult winter, heralded by an awful autumn. In the final two weeks of her journey Penny traveled barely a hundred miles. Her dogs were exhausted and so was she. Their paws had been cut by ice shards until they became bloody stumps. She had had to carry three of them on the komatik with her gear the last three days. It had been five days since any of them had eaten—two rabbits that she had shared with her dogs. She hadn't seen any caribou in a month.

She thought he might now be making his way to the Back River, where his grandfather had hunted as a young man. She had taken a route he had once marked on her map, and several times she had come across what appeared to be dog tracks. She wondered now if they might have been small wolves or large foxes.

No, they had been dogs. There were sled-runner tracks with them. Still no sign of a recent camp.

She was very tired. There had been two days of storm for every one of fair weather for the last month. She wondered how he was doing. Her dogs started to die.

She could not travel anymore. She climbed out of her sleeping bag and cut the dogs' leads, and then she returned to her sleeping bag. She undressed within it, peeling away the oily woolen underwear she had been wearing for weeks now. When she was naked she ran her hands over her body, her breasts, still growing even as the rest of her became so thin, skin sagging from her throat, her ribs, her almost empty abdomen. Her womb, the only other part of her body not shrivelled nearly into absence.

■

chapter nineteen

When Pauloosie saw her iglu he thought that it had been built by a hunter out of Baker Lake, come north looking for umingmak, musk oxen. After watching for three hours he had established that there was no activity there; then he drew closer and studied the response of his dogs. They did not smell fresh scent from other dogs. He saw gear strewn around the iglu, and from the chewed-open packaging and mittens it was clear that foxes had been through the camp.

"*Qanuipiit!*" he hollered hoarsely, after his dogs had drawn to a stop. There was no response from within the iglu. He looked again at the mittens in the snow and recognized them.

He bent low and crawled into the entrance. He saw her. She was the first human he had seen in four months. Frost ran around her nostrils and had collected in her eyelashes. She lay on her side, curled within her sleeping bag. Her skin was almost as white as the walls of her iglu, made precisely in the fashion of his *attatatiak*. Her hair was stiff with frost, and when he swept it from her eyes, it bent like waxed thread. She was so thin, the bones of her cheeks jutted out like armor, her shoulders standing out like knobs on a stick, her belly tight against her spine. Still, she looked strong; her thighs were grooved and powerful. Her little stove and kit bag lay neatly beside her. He was grateful to the foxes for not eating her. He kissed her forehead. He ran his lips along her eyebrows. His tears fell onto her frozen skin and melted the faint crusting of frost, running down in short rivulets before they froze themselves and stopped.

■   ■   ■

Amanda and Lewis lay together in Lewis's bedroom in his father's basement. She stared at him. He was so beautiful, his narrow shoulders rising and falling as he breathed deeply, his wet hair hanging in curls around his forehead, the nape of his neck. She ran her hand over his chest, her fingertips curling between his ribs. Harder. He smiled but did not move. Harder. Along the grooves in his abdomen she ran her fingers, as he shivered, the sensations of arousal battling those of being tickled. She saw this and grinned.

His father had painted the room the same turquoise he had long ago painted his baby son's room. When the strategy of duplicating the boy's mother's house failed to move Lewis, others had been employed; there was a home entertainment center in his room, with a wide-screen television and a new IBM personal computer with a dramatic 640K of RAM and its own 20 MB hard drive. It was a convenient place for Amanda and Lewis to come when his father was at work and they wanted someplace to hang for a little while. Lewis almost never slept here, could not deal with his father's beseeching attempts to curry his favor, and they were careful to be gone before he came home. (At least the boy remained involved with him, his father thought when he smelled the pot, saw the strewn bedclothes.)

This afternoon it was raining in New Jersey, had been since the end of November. The cool gray afternoons hung over them, the effect of the weather growing more obvious as they retreated from every other stimulus, until it was only them, the two of them, and the meteorological facts of the moment.

They had fucked three times and were exhausted. It was four in the afternoon and Amanda had skipped school. She had realized that she was immune to the administrative remonstrations of the vice principal; her grades had remained excellent, even as she had aroused concern in one teacher after another. She looked an inch shorter than she had at the beginning of the year, though if she stood straight she revealed that she had actually grown two. She rarely stood straight, over concern that attention might be drawn to her breasts, whose increase horrified her. This grotesque body of hers, swelling and stretching in such obvious and public ways—she wanted to be blind to it. Only when Lewis discovered the beauty of her body did she feel, in the moment, lovely. She stretched, her arms reaching back over her head, and watched Lewis watching her, and she smiled as he moved closer. Long, glowing, and exquisite, she curled into him.

He was working these days at Garden Avenue Videos. He did not attend high school any more but was pursuing a correspondence diploma with the support of a private high school specializing in just his sort of circumstances. His father thought his mother had poisoned him with her anger, as she had poisoned herself; his mother thought his father couldn't have made it any more apparent that he didn't give a shit about anything but himself. They had joint custody. Lewis moved between his parents at will, evading every boundary with skillful maneuvering. He had stopped going to school in the end simply because he couldn't be bothered. He could go back anytime, he told her. One of these days he might.

It was his mouth she liked to stare at the most. It was perfect. Tight little lips, wry grin always hanging on them. She could look at his mouth all day long.

She liked that he was smart and she liked that he was trouble. She wanted badly for him to think she was smart too; she wanted him to admire her. Her mother and father, on the basis of one blinking introduction on her front door stoop, were appalled by him and she liked that too.

Her parents' arguing had reached such a crescendo that it felt like they could not possibly go one more minute without rupture, but they did, on and on, screaming that had become the eye-rolling joke of the neighborhood. There was talk among the neighborhood wits of taking up a collection either to insulate their walls better or send them back to California. When she was home, Amanda huddled in her room. She was home less and less.

She looked up at Lewis's dropped-tile ceiling. So many dots. He was rolling a joint now. The Monks' *Bad Habits* was playing on the stereo, so loudly the dots shivered; she felt the bass line of "Nice Legs Shame About the Face" rippling through the bed and into her. She watched him roll the joint. His fingers moved precisely. It was four in the afternoon and they still had hours to themselves.

Pauloosie carried her to the riverbank, where there was a gentle rise that exposed the ground and the rocks around it. He lay her down facing the river and placed her rifle alongside her, and he made a row of large flat stones around her form. It was difficult to dig the stones out of the frozen dirt; he had to pry them loose, one by one, with his hatchet. He ran another ring of stone around her on top of the first layer, but leaning in. By the time the sun began to settle on the southwest horizon, he had finished three layers. He crawled into her iglu and rolled out his sleeping bag. He could smell her scent in there, in the snow and the few things that remained. As he waited for sleep he wondered whether it was possible anymore for men and women to live on this land, whether the land itself had changed, become no longer accommodating.

Slowly the stones rose in the shape of an oblong cairn. It took him two days to finish it. Before he lifted the final stone onto the top row above her face he leaned into the gap. It was dark inside, but he could still see the outline of her jaw and forehead, a trace of hair. She had not thought herself to be beautiful and had so persuaded others of her assessment, but this was a mistake. She was beautiful. She had ached for something she couldn't have described with any precision, but it had something to do with a place like this—cold, hard, unyielding—and the sort of heat a place like this requires one to generate. She wanted to be the kind of person who could have lived here. And she could have been.

Pauloosie, grunting, lifted the final rock up and onto the last row of stone. She was now immune for all time to the depredations of foxes and even of bears. He tipped her sled on its edge beside the cairn. She had had some ammunition and fishhooks, which he took. Then he loaded his sled and hitched his impatient dogs to it and headed south. He thought he might go to Padlei to see if there were any tuktu there. He would be unlikely to run into another hunter in that part of the land.

Victoria sat at the kitchen table, drinking tea and smoking. It was after eleven already and neither Justine nor Marie was home yet. They were supposed to be at a party at Johnny Apilardjuk's house. Victoria had called there a few minutes ago and there was no answer. She was not going to call the police. She could not talk to those sons of bitches one more time.

When the door squeaked open and her daughters laughed their way into the kitchen, they didn't notice her at first. When they did, they stopped laughing quickly enough.

Victoria's mouth was tightened in a manner they had never seen before. Her lower lip was drawn half into her mouth and the muscles of her chin stuck out in protruding radiations. Her eyes—they had seen her eyes like this, but not until six months ago, when it seemed to them that everything had started falling apart.

"Mom, don't be angry, it's not late," Justine said.

"You've been drinking."

"No, I haven't."

"For God's sake, you smell like a brewery."

"Well maybe just a sip—all the other kids were having some and . . ."

"And did you give your little sister liquor too?"

"Mom, we were just having a little fun . . ."

"Is that a hickey on the side of your neck? Oh my God!! You were drinking and having sex . . . Marie's just sixteen years old!"

"Don't go crazy, Mom, I was not . . ."

"Just shut up! Shut up, both of you!"

They cringed in silence. Each hoped Pauloosie and Robertson would creep in from whichever shadow they had been hiding in, to settle things down. Victoria felt as if she sat within a cone of sadness and grief, her husband dead and her boy gone from her. Her fault, all of it. She tried to speak and a sob broke out before the words, falling over them like a breaking wave. She slid from her chair onto the linoleum, her legs jutting out from her like a three-year-old's.

Her daughters looked at each other, still shrinking from the fury their mother had displayed. And now she was collapsed, which frightened them even more. They sidled past her to their room, closing the door behind them, their mother's sobs echoing through the house.

Three times a year it was court week in Rankin Inlet. The Justice Department flew in a judge, a stenographer, a prosecutor, a defense attorney—all the necessary players. They stayed in the hotel and met every morning in one of the conference rooms. Portable chairs were brought in for the public, and these chairs were always full. Common assaults were the principal fare, but there were attempts to smuggle in alcohol, a few drug-trafficking charges as well—a kilo of hash being so much easier to carry in than the equivalent, five hundred cases of beer. There were domestic abuse situations, and petty thefts at the various government offices. Occasionally a miner came up on an attempt to pocket a stone, but these cases were rare—the security and searches of the mine site were so thorough, no one thought very hard about risking his lucrative job for the slim chance he would get away with stealing a raw stone of undetermined quality.

Court week was a snapshot of impetuous and destructive acts performed many months earlier and fading already in the memories of the perpetrator and the aggrieved. It was a ritual almost everyone directly involved would have been as happy to avoid, and the appearance rate of witnesses rarely exceeded 40 percent. For the uninvolved, on the other hand, it was incomparable theater. Every elderly woman in the community made her way to the hotel on court days, to perch on a metal chair and nod impassively as the victim impact statements were read.

The week Okpatayauk was to be tried, everyone in town spoke of the matter. It was generally agreed that he was being absurd, confessing to an act he so clearly had not committed. Elizabeth, his girlfriend, had placed a succession of calls to Constable Bridgeford, asking him over and over again if he genuinely believed that Okpatayauk did it. Bridgeford pled that the matter was in the hands of the Crown now, and that she should talk to Okpatayauk about this, not him. When Victoria called him and asked if she could visit Okpatayauk in his cell before the trial, Bridgeford was stumped. "Victoria, why would you want to do something like that?"

"I want to ask him some questions."

"I don't think that would be a very good idea."

"Just ask him if he'll see me."

"Okay."

Okpatayauk had shrugged.

"Is that a yes or a no?" Bridgeford had asked. "You know you don't have to."

Another shrug. "I'll talk to her."

When she appeared at the police station, Bridgeford stopped her at the door and asked her to take off her parka and kamiks. He hung these carefully on his coathook and studied her for bulges. "Victoria, I'll be just over here. I'm afraid I can't allow you much privacy."

"I don't care."

She sat down on the chair Bridgeford had pulled up for her. Okpatayauk looked at her evenly. She studied him. He hadn't killed her husband. She could tell.

"Why are you doing this?" she asked.

Shrug.

"You have to tell me why you're doing this, because it affects me."

"How?"

"It means the real killer won't get caught, and it means I have to go through a trial I know is for nothing."

"It's not for nothing."

"I'm not really very interested in your political agenda."

"I am responsible for your husband's death. I'm saying that. And I will go to jail."

"You aren't taking responsibility for his murder—you're taking credit for it. Even though you're lying."

Contempt spread across her face. He turned away from her. She sat there, looking at his averted eyes. Finally Bridgeford had to tell her to leave.

Pauloosie rode his sled to the top of a rise southwest of Baker Lake and studied the horizon. He was disappointed that he could not see the beacon from the Baker Lake Airport. It was late in the day and he thought he might see lights; it had been months now since he had talked to another person.

He descended the rise with his dogs and as he did so he decided it was time to make shelter. There was good wind-packed snow here and an iglu would not take him long. He had found the tuktu scarce in recent weeks, but coming south he had seen a herd of musk oxen, which were rarely seen this far west. Their strategy when threatened remains geared to the wolf: the adult males line up in a circle facing outward while the calves and females huddle in the center. It is a useful strategy when threatened by gnashing teeth. For the .30-06, however, it is rather less effective. Pauloosie took down a bull with a heart shot. It was enough meat for many days, for him and his dogs. Already they looked stronger. He chopped off slabs of frozen meat with his axe and threw it to them, and then he made an iglu. He boiled water for tea and settled inside as it grew dark.

When he heard movement, his first thought was that he had been foolish to come so close to a settlement, that he had been spotted and

these were now the police. He looked at his rifle, listening. He had not
heard an engine, and until he did he could not be certain it wasn't a barrenlands grizzly. Then his dogs rose as one to cry, but they did not
launch themselves at the air the way they would have if they had smelled
a bear. It was other dogs they were greeting. Pauloosie removed the
round from the rifle's chamber and let the firing pin click down on air.
He slid the weapon back in its case and watched the entrance of his iglu.

When the hood of a parka inserted itself, Pauloosie sat up. A hand
reached up and pulled the hood down and it was Simionie, or a version
of what had been Simionie, thinner and windburnt, and smiling widely.
"Qanuipiit?" he asked Pauloosie.

"Qanawingietunga," Pauloosie replied. "Would you like tea?"

"Yes, please."

"When did you leave town?" Pauloosie squinted at Simionie in the
dim light—judging from his weight loss it had been some time.

"The day after you did."

"How come?"

"I figured it was pretty clear they were gonna charge someone as
soon as they could for killing your dad. I thought I was the obvious one."

"Did you kill him?"

"No."

"I wouldn't care if you had."

"I didn't."

"Oh."

"I guess that means that you didn't either, eh?"

"Nope."

"So who do you think did?"

"No idea."

"You really wouldn't have cared if I had killed your dad?"

"No, I would have. I just wanted you to tell me."

"You're like them RCMP, huh? Tricky."

"Yeah," Pauloosie said, laughing and pouring the tea. "They taught
me some things."

"See anyone else out here from Rankin Inlet?"

"Yeah, the schoolteacher, the one with the dogs."

"Your girlfriend?"

"Who told you that?"

"I forget."

"Okay."

They stopped talking then, each lapsing into his own reflections. They drank the last of the tea and then Pauloosie invited Simionie to spend the night. Simionie thanked him and turned onto his side. There was barely enough room for both of them to lie down. Their legs and shoulders and hips touched each other.

Tagak decided to order a new suit from the Northern Store catalog. Every other manager at the mine wore expensive suits to important meetings. He had never owned one in his life, and was too embarrassed to discuss this with his wife. The catalog described the relevant dimensions it required. He had measured himself, naked in the bathroom, with a tape measure he had brought home from work for the purpose. The metal tape measure had difficulty gauging the circumference of his neck, so he used his belt then laid it flat and measured that. The belt was not quite large enough for his chest, so he switched to a length of tooth floss. Then he measured his belly, and needed a much longer length of floss, and his hips, just as was marked on the figure in the book. His inseam. His outseam.

At the end, Robertson had worn suits at work. Tagak had noticed how the frayed and ancient sports jackets had given way to crisper clothes when the mine began to turn a profit. He had watched too as the way the other men spoke to him changed. He was not sure what was the cause and what was the consequence, but he wanted to be treated with regard too. The suit would cost him as much as a new rifle.

He looked at the floss he had used and thought it was a pity to waste it but threw it out anyway. There's frugal and then there's silly. He shook his head. He was thinking more like a Kablunauk every day. Soon, he'd be flying to Winnipeg just to watch a hockey game.

Emo asked Winnie whether Victoria had enough deer meat. He was sitting across from her at their kitchen table. He wore a spotted white T-shirt and blue jeans many sizes too large for him. He was losing weight quickly. On the plate in front of him were strips of bacon Winnie had fried, which he had not eaten. She looked at him, and away from her needlepoint. "Yes, she's fine of course."

"That husband of hers is no hunter."

"He's dead."

Emo looked surprised. "How did he die?"

"A *nanuq* ate him."

"He was out on the land?"

"It came into town and caught him just as he was taking a leak out back."

"Really?"

"Yep."

"You have to be careful with those things."

"Yep."

"Anyone catch the bear?"

"You did."

"Did I?"

"Yep."

"What was the hide worth?"

"A hundred bucks."

"Did you sell it for just a hundred bucks, a good *nanuq* hide?" he asked, starting to rise from his chair.

"No, you did."

He put his head in his hands. "Why did I do that?"

"I dunno."

Victoria sat on Marie's bed. It was morning and Marie said she felt sick. She had eaten nothing the day before and did not want any breakfast. Her ribs stuck out against her pajamas even more prominently than Victoria's had when she had been sick. She held a cloth to her daughter's forehead, but Marie pushed it away, saying it was cold. She coughed dryly.

"Honey, you can't lose any more weight," Victoria whispered.

"I know, Mom."

"I don't think I was ever as thin as this."

"Why can't they figure out what's wrong with me?"

"I'll get Dr. Balthazar to send you to a specialist."

"Okay."

Victoria ran her hands over Marie's forehead, sweeping her hair aside. She leaned over to kiss her and was struck by how papery her daughter's skin had become, how fine her hair, how white her nails. She studied the bruise on the side of her daughter's neck.

"The idea isn't actually to bruise each other, Marie."

"I know, Mom. It's just for fun. Everyone laughs about them later."

"Really?"

"You take it too seriously."

"I really want you to eat some soup now, okay?"

"I'm really not hungry, Mom," she said, and rolled away.

"Honey, how come you're never hungry?"

"I'm just not."

"When I was sick, I remember being hungry. I could never put on any weight, but I was hungry all the time."

"Well. I'm not."

"I know."

"Do you think I'm dying, Mom?"

"Shhhh, don't talk like that."

Victoria and Marie sat in Dr. Balthazar's office. He had draped his parka over the back of his chair and held a mug of tea in both hands.

"The thing is, Victoria, we've done more than twenty sputum cultures for TB and they've all been negative. There's no doubt she had it when she was small, but we knew about that then. We know the organism was sensitive to the antibiotics and we know she took a full course."

"So maybe it was killed then, but she could have caught it from someone else again, at school, maybe. Is that possible?"

"Absolutely."

Victoria leaned forward. "So, she could have *puvaluq* . . ."

"Her sputum would be positive if she did, though."

"Maybe we're just not doing the right test."

"I can send her to Winnipeg to see a pediatric respirologist, if you like."

"What would he do?"

"Have a look down inside her lungs with a bronchoscope."

"Does that hurt?"

"No. They do it under sedation."

"We can't just do nothing."

"While she's there, I'd like her to see a psychiatrist."

"Why?"

Balthazar looked at Marie, feeling clumsy at having started this conversation with the girl present. "I wonder if she isn't depressed."

"So you think this is all just in her mind?"

Marie looked at her mother with wide eyes and shook her head desperately.

"Of course I don't, but sometimes illnesses bring about behaviors that make weight loss worse, and sometimes chemical abnormalities in the brain, like in the rest of the body, can make people thin. The psychiatrists are down there, is the thing, and if there's nothing they have to add, then that's—"

"I don't think she needs to see a psychiatrist."

"It's just that, as long as she is down there—"

"No. We're not crazy, here."

■   ■   ■

Justine put down her homework and answered the knock on the door. She opened it wide because at first she didn't see anyone. Then she saw Simionie, standing out of the light.

"I saw you in the window. I thought you were your mother," he said.

"Do you want her?"

He nodded yes.

"Mom!"

Victoria appeared at the door. "Oh good God," she said. "It's you."

"I'm okay," he said. "A little skinny, but okay."

"Come in then, and tell me what you know."

He walked into the first wooden house he had entered in three months. As he smelled the odor of cooking and laundry, he was overcome.

"Where have you been?" Victoria asked him as he turned away from her and blinked away tears. "Have you seen Pauloosie?"

She walked around him to see his face. He reached for her.

Justine and Marie were right there and she started to push him away but then she saw his expression and she held him.

When Penny's emaciated dogs started to appear in town, circling warily among those chained up on the Bay ice, there was a discussion among the hunters of what this meant. They soon concluded she had to be dead. The RCMP came out to look at and photograph the animals, and then the animal control officer was called to dispose of them before they attacked someone. To the other hunters it seemed unfair that these dogs, which had been very good dogs indeed, should meet such an end because of the impetuousness of their owner, who had not understood the land as well as she thought she had. But the dogs were bad luck now, so none of the hunters were willing to accept them.

Johanna came home from work to find Penny's lead, Norbert—at least a hollower, more frightened version of him—sitting beside the entrance to their apartment building, wagging his tail. Penny had brought him into her home sometimes (alarming her Kablunauk neighbors), and he had come looking for succor. Johanna knew what his return meant. She let the dog inside and took him up to her apartment, opening the door and trying to shush him in before any of the neighbors noticed. He looked down the hallway at Penny's door, whining. Johanna pushed him in. She unthawed a steak in her microwave and let him eat it. She did not stroke him and she held a large wooden pepper grinder in her hands as he ate, and chewed on the inside of her own cheek.

When he had eaten that steak she unthawed another and watched him eat it too. There was a rump roast at the back of the freezer she had forgotten about. He ate that. Then he looked up at her and she looked at him. He walked to her door and pawed at it. She took the key Penny had given her and they walked down the hall to Penny's door and went in.

Johanna had been watering the plants for months now and the apartment was thick with foliage in a way it had never been when Penny was here. Her things were as she had left them in her hasty packing. There was a box of rifle ammunition on her kitchen table. Her shotgun lay in its case on the sofa. A box of freeze-dried meals she had deemed excessive (and had longed for, subsequently) sat beside it. Johanna had been picking up Penny's mail too, and it sat in a large mound in a box she had placed beside the door. Johanna stooped to sift through the mail, looking for letters from Alberta. She found one. Penny's father. Johanna sat at the kitchen table and copied down the address.

She wrote to him that she thought Penny was probably dead now, that she had been watering her plants and everything but there wasn't likely any point in paying the apartment rent anymore. She could pack up her things if he wanted, and send them to him. Penny lived pretty lightly; she didn't have much. Once she gave away the food, there would probably be only a few hundred pounds of possessions here. She wrote that she had admired his daughter a great deal. She wished she could shed more light on her decision to go out on the land like she had, so abruptly. She thought she might have been in love with one of the local hunters, who had also gone out on a long trip, and she wondered if she had meant to join him. Everyone in town thought he was dead too. On the other hand, maybe she had meant only to make a slightly longer trip than usual and had an accident out there. There was no way of knowing, really.

They had made a canoe trip the summer before, she wrote. Penny had spoken of him, of growing up on the farm with her father and grandfather and of how much she loved those two men. Johanna didn't know what else to write except that she understood how wonderful his daughter was, understood the extent of his loss. He mustn't think that she met foul play with this hunter. She knew him a little and was certain nothing like that had happened.

Johanna folded the letter and then found an envelope in one of Penny's kitchen drawers. She addressed the envelope and licked it shut. She looked around the disheveled room and cried for a little while. Then she stood up and took Norbert back to her place.

Tagak sat in his office on the mine site. He spent four days a week here now, and the fifth in town, interviewing prospective employees. He had bought several suits; he was getting rich. He read the morning mail and thought at the same time about his sister and her troubles. His wife had called him again, to say that Victoria looked like she was having a meltdown, that his father was wandering incoherently and aimlessly through town dressed in a housecoat, and that his nieces had everyone worried. Marie looked like she had to have puvaluq and the older one like she thought she was a TV actor or something.

The four days a week out at the mine were a not unattractive aspect of the job. Tagak spent them in the company of men who had not known him as a boy, or as an awkward, inadequate young hunter. He had become a friend of the Greek manager, who was sorry about the death of his brother-in-law. Sorrier, it seemed, than Tagak was, though Tagak found himself more interested in and admiring of Robertson now than when the man was alive. The Greek reminded him that the mine was

partly Robertson's work, and the wealth that flowed into the community as a consequence was partly Robertson's gift.

Gift was not the word Tagak would have chosen. He had known
Robertson for many years and had never known him to be noticeably
generous with his money, except to Victoria. Tagak lived with a difficult
woman too, and thought he could guess at some of the things that had
been said in that house. The Greek had mentioned that he had eaten
supper there, which had surprised Tagak; his own wife would have told
the entire town if she had cooked for the mine manager, and Victoria
had not mentioned it even to her brother.

He was grateful to Victoria, nevertheless, and by extension to
Robertson for having arranged this job, which was the first thing he
himself had ever done well. That was the thing about this life of the
Kablunauks: it was possible to be good at something other than one
thing. The young men—Okpatayauk and his friends—romanticized a
way of life that would swallow them whole in a second if they chose to
pursue it. They were too thoughtful, too sensitive, too impatient, those
young men so knowledgeable of legal terms.

He decided that he would ask his mother and father to move into
his home. He knew that Catharine would protest, but ultimately she
would understand. Someone—probably Catharine—would say that
Victoria, with no husband in that big house, should take them in, but he
would reply that they were doing better than Victoria was, which would
provide Catherine with a moment's pleasure. His father had been disappointed in Tagak his whole life. Perhaps he would become more lucid
with regular meals, surrounded by children and company. Tagak would
like it if, during even one moment of lucidity, his father would say thank
you. He daydreamed about this scene for a moment and then he picked
up his telephone and called his wife back and initiated the process. In a
few days he would call his mother. She would only be relieved.

He had been invited by the Greek to eat supper with him that night.
He was making something called dolmades. Tagak had looked this up in
his dictionary. There were grape leaves involved. He had not known

they were edible. Grapes were available at the Northern Store in Rankin Inlet, and at the cafeteria at the mine; why weren't the leaves more commonly available, if they were good to eat? Were only special Greek grape leaves edible or were all grape leaves? This launched another thought: Where had he gotten them? Had a friend mailed him some from Greece? Where exactly was Greece, anyway?

Simionie sat in the RCMP office with a Styrofoam cup of coffee between his hands and Constable Bridgeford across from him.

"The thing is, when people disappear like that immediately after we've questioned them about a crime, after we've told them to remain available, we pretty much conclude that they've got something to hide," Bridgeford said.

"I did not kill Robertson."

"You keep saying that."

"It's true."

"Then why did you disappear?"

"Because I thought you were going to blame me."

"Well, if you're so innocent, why not stick around and show us that?"

"How many men left after that murder? Two? Me and Pauloosie. Do you think we both killed him, or do you think we each concluded that you were probably going to blame us one way or the other?"

"Where were you again, that morning Robertson was killed?"

"At my parents' house. They were there, as you know."

"And when was the last time you saw him alive?"

"At the mining commission meeting."

"And did you oppose his work for the mine?"

"Yes."

"Did you tell Okpatayauk about these diamonds he supposedly received?"

"No."

"Who did?"

"I don't know."

"Where is Pauloosie?"

"You tell me."

"Did you two talk about going out on the land before you did?"

"No."

"It was just coincidence that you both left within twenty-four hours of each other?"

"I heard he left and I thought that sounded like a good idea, so I did too. Took my father's dogs."

"Why did you lie to me about watching *Gilligan's Island?*"

"Do you think I killed that man?"

"No."

"Then I'm going to go now."

"You didn't happen to run across him out there, did you?" Bridgeford closed his notebook.

"No," Simionie said, and Bridgeford stared at him for a moment and knew what Simionie looked like when he lied.

"Did Robertson know about your relationship with his wife?" Now the constable knew what Simionie looked like when he was ashamed.

"Didn't you convict someone of all this a while ago?"

"Why do you suppose Okpatayauk pled guilty to the murder?"

"I guess you don't think he did it?"

"It doesn't make a lot of sense to me."

"Nothing about this does."

When Tagak appeared in the Greek's apartment for supper he was surprised to see boxes lining the walls. Supper was ready, Vangelis told him, and led him to the table. "Are you moving?" Tagak asked.

"The business with your brother-in-law has embarrassed my employers. I am being sent back to Africa."

"I'm sorry."

"Have you noticed how cold it is outside? I am not sorry in the least. Do you drink ouzo?"

He filled two glasses. Tagak nodded, having no idea what he was being offered.

"It has been a pleasure working with you," Tagak said.

"I have found this interesting as well. I am still a little surprised, to
tell you the truth—diamonds in the Arctic? But it remains, the mine is
a success."

"It seems unfair that you are being punished for doing what you
were asked to."

"I was asked to do something discreetly, and in the end, discretion
was not preserved." He shrugged in his thick black fisherman's sweater.
"We all understand the rules. The South Africans had to do something
to distance themselves from the scandal."

"Will you tell me something?"

"Yes."

"If my sister were to try to cash those diamonds in now, how would
she go about doing it?"

The Greek smiled and toasted Tagak and they drank. Tagak choked
and the other watched him recover.

"It tastes like licorice."

"It tastes nothing like licorice."

"Well." He swallowed again and looked at the liquid remaining in
his glass.

"I didn't think Robertson would try to sell them himself. Not for
many years, anyway."

"He probably wouldn't have."

"I never attached a cash value to them when I gave them to him."

"What are you saying?"

"They are large stones, but industrial grade. They aren't worth
more than a few hundred dollars."

"Really."

The Greek looked at the ceiling. "Yes."

"You thought he was stupid."

"I thought he would be impressed with the gift. Which is why I gave it to him. And he was."

"A few hundred dollars for his life."

"Yes. It's all quite awful." The Greek drank his ouzo. After a pause, he continued: "Your brother-in-law was a skilled businessman. He would not have been out of place in Africa, it turns out."

"What do you mean?"

"He understood how much local influence he had here."

"And?"

"He sought to use that to his advantage."

"He wanted a larger position in the mine."

"He did."

"You gave him the diamonds to set him up. You told Okpatayauk about them."

"No. I gave them as a present. I knew their value, but these sort of gifts are commonplace in the business. I would not have been part of setting him up. I have made my views on the matter clear to my employers. Which is why I will now reside in Botswana."

Tagak set his drink down and walked out of Vangelis's apartment. The Greek remained seated as he watched the other man leave.

Marie and Justine sat together in the hockey arena and watched the boys play. There was a tournament, and Baker Lake, Repulse Bay, Coral Harbour, and Chesterfield Inlet had all sent teams. Justine had asked Marie to come with her, a gesture unusual for her; she usually tried to distance herself from her strange, sticklike, and melancholy little sister, the way any older sister would.

For her part, Marie had been too astonished to refuse. Halfway out of the house she realized it was a mistake, that Justine must have some agenda, but by then it was too late. Justine shouted their destination out at their mother as they passed her bedroom doorway and did not wait for a reply.

Marie had no enthusiasm for boys as of yet, was actually still inter-ested in her dolls, although she was ashamed of this and played with them alone, speaking quietly enough that she would not be heard either by her sister or her mother. Oddly, the only person who had known of this had been her father; he had seen her when they had been alone in the house together and her door had been ajar. She had looked up at his smile and had waited to be mocked. But he hadn't. And then he had died, taking her secret with him.

The last Christmas before he was killed he gave her a beautiful wooden dollhouse he had bought on a business trip to Toronto. Victoria and Justine had rolled their eyes at how out of touch he was. Was he even aware that they both bled? Victoria had hissed to him the night when he brought the dollhouse home.

God. I hope not, they both thought, listening through the wall as they lay in their own beds, wondering what had occasioned that particularly horrifying question: Justine twisting with the idea that he knew the truth; Marie, with the idea that he misunderstood it. She had started having her periods, and had told her mother, but then they had stopped, and her relief could not possibly have been more potent.

The boys hurled themselves at one another on the ice with an en-ergy never evident in the classes the girls shared with them. It was a strange relief, to see them moving with such enthusiasm. The girls had thought their classmates to be silent and immobile automatons, unfeel-ing and barely alive. Among the older, smarter boys there was more promise, Justine had decided. There were even a few who spoke of go-ing to college in the south when they graduated.

"Marie, how come you never eat?" Justine asked her after long min-utes of silent hockey watching.

"What do you mean? Shut up," Marie replied.

"I think you have the ano-rex-ia ner-vosa," Justine said, pronounc-ing the phrase carefully. She had never heard it said aloud.

"What's that? I do not." Marie stared fixedly at the hockey rink, finding sudden fascination in the power play unfolding in front of her.

"Where girls stop eating because they think they're too fat."

"Well, that's not me."

"I bet it is."

"I'm not fat."

"That's for sure. Have you looked at yourself in the mirror lately?"

"Justine, if you keep talking like this, I'm going to go home right now," Marie said evenly, much more evenly than she felt. She was horrified and outraged and violated by her older, intrusive, imperious, and incredibly obnoxious sister.

"I really miss Pauloosie."

"Me too."

"Yeah?"

"Which has nothing to do with being a little thin."

"Okay."

"Do you think he's okay?"

Justine shrugged. "He's been gone for months. Anything could have happened to him."

"*Attatatiak* thought he knew his way around out there."

"*Attatatiak* doesn't know much these days."

"Shhh . . . don't say that."

"You know what I mean," Justine continued. "Why does everything have to be a secret to you?"

"Shut up."

"He was determined to get away from here. One way or the other."

"I know."

"Do you think he'll come back?"

"No."

"Hello?" Doug asked when he picked up the phone.

"Hi," she whispered.

"Hey, it's you."

"It's me."

"Long time, no hear."

"I know."

"I signed all those papers your lawyer sent me, if that's why you're calling," he said.

"Thanks."

"Is anything the matter?"

"Penny is dead."

"Oh."

"The one with the dogs."

"Yeah, I remember. What happened?"

"She went out on the land and disappeared earlier in the winter. Her dogs showed up in town the other day. There was some business with one of the local boys here."

"You think he killed her?"

"No. I think she wanted to find him. Or for him to find her."

"And he didn't."

"I don't know."

"She was young."

"I'm having a really hard time here, Doug."

"I'm sorry about that, Johanna."

"Maybe the hardest time ever."

"You were pretty close to her, eh?"

"It isn't that."

"No?"

"Everyone will say now that she died doing what she loved out there. That she lived for that adventure."

"Didn't she?"

"I suppose, a little. But she didn't really. She was cringing from the world, every time she went out there. She was so determined to be self-fucking-sufficient."

"Uh-huh."

"And she couldn't—it crept up on her in the end."

"A bear, or something?"

"No. Need."

"No need for what?"

"Doug."

"Yeah."

"Will you come up here?"

"What?"

"Get on a plane, like you did that time."

"Do you know what kind of shit I was in at work when I got back?"

"No."

"And how much it cost?"

"Yeah."

"A lot."

"I just think, we're all too hard on ourselves. And one another."

"I signed those papers your lawyer sent, like six months ago."

"I know. He told me."

"So what else is new up there. How is work."

"You won't?"

"Johanna. You can't just call me up like this, order me up there."

"So you can come up here on a moment's notice only so long as you haven't been asked to, is that it?"

"Why do you want me to come up there so badly?"

"Oh, Doug."

"What's the matter?"

". . ."

"Why are you . . . ?"

"I'm not."

"Yes, you are—I can hear it."

"I just think that sometimes we do everything we can to stop ourselves from being happy."

"Oh, sweetie, it's okay. Shhhhh."

"I never wanted to be this alone."

"You're not alone. Take a deep breath."

"I don't know what I'm going to do."

"Shhhhhhhhhhhhhh."

February 18, 1992

Dear Ms. Stevenson:

Thank you for your kind letter. I received Penny's effects a few days before it and had wondered if she was moving home, but now I've learned that the news is much worse than that. I've spoken to the RCMP in Rankin Inlet and they told me that until they find a body they can't say anything definite but in their own minds they have little doubt.

Penny had mentioned you a few times and called you her only friend up there. I am glad you knew her. It would be much more painful to think that she had lived as isolated up there as she died. We will be having a memorial service for her in a week. If you come upon anything else in her apartment, anything that might have the address of her mother on it, would you call me right away with it?

Yours truly,
Ed Bleskie

Marie packed her own clothes prior to flying south. She had protested that this trip was unnecessary—what were they going to do, for heaven's sakes, that hadn't already been done a hundred times over? Were the little pots into which she would spit somehow better down there? But Victoria watched her bony shoulders protrude as she leaned into this argument and any possibility of compromise evaporated. She was going.

Marie was frightened. She thought she might really have some form of TB after all—the few photographs of her mother at her age showed exactly her face, tight and large-eyed—but she wondered how well it could be treated by the usual drugs if none of the usual tests seemed able to find it. She did not want to have to go through surgery like her mother did. She thought about the scar and she shuddered. The invasion.

Her misgivings about all this had to do with her suspicion of Dr. Balthazar. She asked Justine what she thought of him and her sister had just shrugged. To Marie he seemed the essence of gross: his thick lips and the perspiration on his forehead that accompanied the least exertion, the damp hair, and the white white white skin. Every year he was larger, folds around his neck now. His arms could no longer hang straight at his sides.

Marie had watched enough episodes of *St. Elsewhere* to know that he could not be considered representative of the medical profession, but at the same time, for her, he was. In his furtive, hesitant manner, she detected something dark, possibly malignant. Here he was sending her off into the arms of his colleagues, and she could not help feeling deeply anxious about that.

Her mother was awash in her own anxieties, trying to summon up the resolve to pick up the telephone and book a ticket south to Winnipeg, to accompany her daughter. She had not been out of the community since she had come back to it in the Norseman, decades earlier. Her memory of Winnipeg was through the lens of her ten-year-old self, gawking at the department store on Portage Avenue, escalators of moving stairs propelling themselves steadily upward and downward. Then she had been propelled to the hospital, where she had watched children die, so alone, far from their parents and everything they knew, the sweet little boy Abraham geysering blood from his lungs like a lung-shot tuktu, and then his sister, Faith, turning away. She wept silently so that she would not interrupt Marie's packing, shuddering into her hands. She would stay in a hotel room. She did not have TB anymore, she was an adult, and she would come back with her daughter just as soon as the tests were finished. She picked up the telephone. She set it down.

When Amanda walked down the sidewalk, coming home from school, she saw from a block away that her father's car was in the driveway. She thought for a moment that he had come home sick from work, but as she approached the house, she saw him through the living room window, moving quickly, and she realized that whatever he was doing, he wasn't lying on the couch. She walked up the steps and opened the door and saw his suitcases open on the living room floor. He was shoving shirts into one of them. He looked up at her and began filling another case with trousers. Angela was standing in the kitchen, not speaking. Amanda stood there and watched. Neither of her parents addressed her. She went to her bedroom.

Kat and Beth were with them, in Lewis's father's kitchen; they had the elements on the stove heated to blazing red and butter knives wedged into the coils, the tips scarlet. Kat had a razor in one hand and carefully sliced small curls of hash off a larger chunk, pausing to roll the smaller bits into tiny balls. He wore a black leather jacket, which Amanda had never once seen him take off, and seemed to carry a knife in each of about eight different pockets. He was very eager to show his knives to people, which Amanda thought made him seem both less menacing and more wacko. He told her that at home he had a real samurai sword; he had stolen it from his uncle, who had been in the Marines. He was really into graphic novels, was she? He liked *Love and Rockets* the best. You know? He seemed lost and sweet.

She was so high, she wasn't sure where she was. She hadn't spoken to either of her parents in three days now. After her father had driven away she had waited another couple of hours to see if her mother needed anything, wanted to talk about anything, but there was no knock on her door. She heard her mother go into her bedroom and close the door. Then she got off her own bed and left the house.

Lewis was reading a comic book. Beth was standing close to Lewis and laughing with him over the pictures. Amanda felt herself being drawn into Joy Division's mournful grind, which was playing at maximum imaginable volume through Lewis's father's very excellent audio system. Lewis was commenting on the narrative trends in anime these days since Westerners had caught on to it—since *Sailor Moon* had started off as parody and then became coopted—God help them all, people actually thought that this is what it was. As if a desexualized anime could ever be genuine anime.

"Is Sailor Moon really desexualized?" Beth said. "I find her kinda hot." Lewis smiled at her a really long time. Amanda wondered what was taking Kat so long with the hash.

Kat and Beth and Lewis had quit school and all now worked in the same chain of video rental stores along Garden Avenue in Newark. They rotated among different outlets as the vagaries of employee absence and intoxicant habits dictated; in the course of this random mixing they had accreted to one another, recognizing some commonality. They all had the same look—colorless, consumptive, and dark—and they listened to the Smiths, Joy Division, Iggy Pop. But as well a shared sense of disdain and humor drew them to one another, a sense that the prevailing recession was not for them to struggle against, and that any country led by a man such as George Bush was not much worth investing in. They weren't politically informed; rather, their dismissal of that world arose from a considered and deeply felt anxiety about it. It was like having an unpleasant neighbor who was not worth knowing better. You just hope he isn't worse than he appears.

In Emo's view, it was a strange place for a man to live. But his view was not much sought. Which was okay with him. It was a little puzzling, anyway: what kept this place so warm, far too warm, and what fuel these lamps burned that lasted so long, days on end. There was fur on the floor but not from any animal he had ever hunted or eaten, nor would he wish to either, judging from the odor and texture of its hair. He did not understand why he was so tired, and so weak, and then he remembered that he was old. He thought to himself, *What a strange thing to have forgotten.* And then he wondered to himself whether he would have preferred not to have remembered. And then he forgot what he had been thinking about and stood up. Where had he put his rifle, his panna?

■

chapter twenty

Balthazar sipped his beer. He and the priest were listening to "Strutting with Some Barbecue." The priest had been reading an account by a Czech writer who had listened to this music as a boy during the Second World War. "They looked up the title in an English-Czech dictionary: 'Walking pompously with a piece of roasted meat'—what could it mean?" They both laughed. "When I was a seminarian, the priests learned of my affection for this music and they punished me. They told me it was carnal music."

"Have you watched MTV?"

"I have, briefly, while looking for the news, yes."

"What would they have said to that?"

"Their heads would have popped right out of their cassocks."

"I suppose you could argue that any music worth listening to is always carnal." The priest nodded at that. "People hunger for things. Rhythm and blues is about hunger, perhaps, more than it is about sin." He tapped his foot to the beat.

"Hunger—for liquor and women and dope." Balthazar leaned back, eyes shut and also tapping his foot, teasing the priest.

"Well, yes."

"Hard to imagine anyone enjoying this music who doesn't understand those hungers."

"Keith, if that's your clumsy way of asking if I've ever desired anyone, the answer is yes. I've fallen in love, in fact. Which is not the same as acting upon it, of course."

"Falling in love is certainly an act in itself."

"It isn't the definitive act. As you know."

Balthazar grinned uncomfortably at the sudden intimacy. "I'm sure anyone human has been in love."

"You know that isn't true, either."

"I suppose."

"Though one could assert the opposite: anyone who has been in love is certainly human."

"Well, here's to us humans."

There was a pause in the conversation as the priest examined what Balthazar had just said. Then he resumed nodding to the bass line. The song finished and then the priest put on Muddy Waters singing slow. "Are you still in contact with the person you allude to?"

"Yes," Balthazar said, and he could see Bernard deciding who it was.

"But you did not act," Bernard said.

"Not in the way you mean, no."

"That is better."

"I'm not sure."

"If you had, would you have maintained your other secrets?"

Balthazar was unable to speak, so Bernard answered for him.

"Either she would have known, and eventually revealed you, or she would have made it unnecessary."

Balthazar nodded. "Which would have been much better, actually."

"To have been content."

"And unafraid."

"Why are you afraid, Keith?"

"God knows."

"Maybe He does. Though He keeps His own secrets too, in my experience."

"Sacrilege."

Bernard laughed. "Hardly."

It was storming and Balthazar had been stuck in the priests' residence for four days, waiting for a flight to Repulse Bay. Father Bernard was near the end of his time there—as was Balthazar, it turned out. At some level, they both knew this. Hence, the revelatory nature of their conversation.

Balthazar stood on the shore of the frozen bay and looked eastward. Under his feet was an amalgam of gravel and frozen seawater that merged imperceptibly into the whiter and flatter sea ice, which stretched all the way to the floe edge. A thin purplish haze hung on the eastern horizon, as the seawater sublimated into the dry and frozen air hanging over it. He spotted a figure walking into town. As he stood there the figure grew slowly larger, weaving its way between ridges of soft snow and heaped-up shelves of sea ice. It walked unerringly toward Balthazar, and when the figure was thirty feet from the shore he lifted his hood off his head. It was Simon Alvah.

"Hello, Doctor."

They had never been introduced, but Alvah had been there long enough that they each knew perfectly well who the other was.

"Mr. Alvah."

"Out for a walk?"

"Nothing like what you've just been up to."

"Well, that's purely a function of circumstance, my boat being as far away as it is. If I were doing it over again, I'd have anchored closer to town. This trudge is getting old."

"Keeps one trim, I suppose."

"I'm trying to put on weight. Do you have any idea how cold a steel boat is, out here?"

"My technique: Cheez Doodles and beer."

Nodding. "Things still pretty nuts around here?"

Balthazar blinked. "Oh, you mean the murder and everything."

"Especially the 'and everything' part."

"Yeah."

"Does anyone around here ever actually talk about anything out loud?"

"Not to me."

"How long have you been here?"

"Twenty years or so."

"Do you think they talk out loud even to themselves?"

"No."

"So you actually got any of them Cheez Doodles and beer you mentioned?"

"Yeah."

"Wanna share?"

Justine had an appointment to see him, but when Balthazar looked
eagerly into the waiting room for Victoria, he was disappointed to see
only her daughter sitting there. He waved to her.

"Hi, Justine. Is your mom late?"

"She's not coming."

"Oh."

"Is that okay?"

"Sure, if it's okay with you."

"Good."

He closed the door behind her and sat down at his desk. She took
the chair beside it.

"So how are you?"

"I'm okay. You?"

"I'm fine. Your mom okay?"

"She's worried about Marie."

"Of course. You must be too."

"I am."

"Is that what you wanted to talk about?"

"Not really."

"Because, I can't really . . . you know."

"I know. She's told me everything anyway."

"So what can I do for you?"

"I want to start on the pill."

"Your mom know about this?"

"Not really."

He dropped his eyes to her chart. "Okay. You're going to need to have a Pap test and everything. I'll set it up with one of the nurses."

"Okay."

"Is there anything you need to ask about the various contraceptive options?"

"No."

"Okay." Normally the nurses handled this sort of work. And normally when he had this kind of conversation, the girl would be pawing at the door by now. Justine sat in her chair, looking straight at him, her eyes locked on his Adam's apple, it appeared.

"What's on your mind, Justine?"

She looked at him. "So, not talking about Marie or anything, how would someone know if they were going crazy?"

"You're having a hard time with all this, huh? Your dad's death and everything."

She nodded.

He leaned forward, his elbows on his knees. "See, that's the thing, we're all just about going crazy half the time. Anyone who's been through what you have lately is, anyway. Do you ever think about hurting yourself?"

She shook her head.

"That's all anyone can expect of you. And if you start thinking about that, it wouldn't be so surprising either. Just don't do anything about it. And come see me."

"Dr. Balthazar?"

"Yes?"

"It's okay with me if you tell my mother I was here."

"I can't see why the matter would come up."

"I'm just saying. I'm not hiding anything."

"I understand."

chapter twenty-one

Victoria stood over Simionie as he lay beneath her kitchen sink. "Can you hand me the big whaddyacallit wrench? No, the other one, the red thing."

Her father was no help anymore, and the plumber in town was long ago hired by the mine, along with every new one that came in to replace him. Tagak, whose skills in these areas were suspect, wore a suit every day now, even on the weekends, and simply would not have lain on his back under her cupboards. So she waited until she was alone and then she called Simionie.

He had told her over the phone that he knew next to nothing about plumbing. She said he should come anyway, see what he could do. He took this as an invitation, and though she would not have acknowledged this if asked directly, it was. He knew better than to ask her a direct question.

"So the drain just stopped working, all of a sudden, or did it gradually stop draining?" he called from within the cubicle of painted plywood, cleaning supplies, and mouse poison.

"It was acting funny yesterday. Took longer to drain than usual. I didn't think anything of it."

"I guess it's plugged somewhere, eh?"

"I was thinking that myself, yeah."

It was better that he did not see the expression that went with this. He banged on the pipe a couple of times.

"I don't suppose it's draining now?"

"No, you don't suppose right."

She could not see him rolling his eyes.

"I'm gonna try something here."

There was a loud clunk and the sink drained in an instant.

"Well, that appears to have worked," Victoria said.

"Jeezus Christ." There was the sound of an appalled mouth, spitting.

"You okay in there?"

"Hairball. Has someone been washing their hair in here?"

"Marie. It's like she's got the mange these days." Then bits of matted hair began appearing on the newspaper Simionie had laid down on the floor beside him.

"Where is she now, anyway?"

"Winnipeg. She left two days ago."

More wet hair slapping down on newspaper.

"Tests?"

"Yeah."

"Hand me the Teflon tape, please, the white stuff."

"Here you go."

"It's good that she's being checked out. She's been looking pretty sick."

"I know."

He wiggled himself out from beneath her sink, rose, and wiped his hands on a patch of newspaper. "All done here."

"Great. Thanks."

"Okay. I'll get going now," he said—asked—as he finished wiping his hands.

"All right."

He stopped at the door as he zipped up his jacket. "It's hard, eh?"

She held the door and, as she looked at him directly, slowly softened. "You know, it really is. It really is. You were the only one I could think of to call."

"Let me know what I can do to help."

"You could mop up this floor." He stopped zipping up his jacket, his face lighting.

"I'm just joking. Thank you."

She closed the door.

Amanda sat in Café Mogadur and looked out at the street as she smoked a Camel Light. She had woken up in Lewis's father's basement, Lewis nowhere around, and had put on her clothes from the night before and walked down to the Rockwood Diner, where they usually ate. He was not there, and neither was Kat or Beth, nor anyone else she knew. She found herself stepping onto a bus that would take her home, wondering whether her mother was still there. When she came to her stop she could see their house even as the bus started to slow and found herself unable to rise—to step off that bus and walk in through that door—even for the sake of clean clothes. It wasn't that she feared violence, say, or even violent speech, but rather the confusion and disarray that would be evident in the obsessed fussing of her mother. How long it would take for her to comment on how much weight Amanda had gained was anyone's guess. She could not walk inside that house.

So she stayed on the bus and rode it to the Port Authority, where she was obliged to exit. She caught a subway downtown. Tompkins Square was green and damp and cheerful in the warm spring morning. Amanda watched the cyclists flying past her.

She called her uncle on a pay phone, with the idea of having lunch with him, maybe accepting some money. She knew he was home, but there was no answer.

She called him again, over the following three hours, seven times.

"Mrs. Robertson? Dr. Hildebrandt here, from Children's Hospital in Winnipeg."

"Hello."

"I've been seeing your daughter Marie these last couple of days and I thought I'd discuss with you what we have found."

"Go ahead."

"Well, first, I don't think she has TB."

"No?"

"We've done a bronchoscopy, had a look inside her lungs, and taken samples and they're all negative. We did a CT scan too, and saw that she has scarring from when she had TB as a baby."

"Yes?"

"Yes, well, it's called bronchiectasis, and in her case it's fairly mild, but it is almost certainly what has been causing her to cough up blood. It's not dangerous, and it can be managed with antibiotics when she has a worsening cough."

"So she can come home now?"

"Well, I wanted to talk to you about that. Mrs. Robertson, I'm worried about how thin she is."

"That's why we sent her to you."

"Yes, I have Dr. Balthazar's referral note in front of me. I think we should admit her to hospital and get to the bottom of things that way. I wonder if she might have a malabsorption problem—that's out of my field. But if she's an inpatient, we can have different specialists see her quickly."

"I think I better come down there then, if she isn't coming right home."

"I think that would be a good idea, Mrs. Robertson."

"Okay."

"Mrs. Robertson?"

"Yes?"

"Is there anything you think we should know about your daughter that Dr. Balthazar didn't mention? Why do you think she's so thin?"

"I had TB at her age and was the same way—that's what I've been thinking it is. I don't even want to say this, but could it be some sort of cancer?"

"Well, we're going to exclude every possibility we can think of."

"Okay, I'm coming down there."

"I look forward to meeting you."

"The only reason I didn't before was it was just going to be a clinic visit and some tests."

"I understand."

"I'm sorry I'm not down there now. Is she frightened?"

"I would say that she is, a little."

"Is she there, can I talk to her?"

"I'm in my office now. She's up on the ward."

"I'll see you soon. I'm on my way."

Dr. Balthazar's office at the hospital was as lovely as the South African diamond money could make it. His window gave out on the sea ice, and adjoining his office was an examining room with a table and matte black German ophthalmoscopes, otoscopes, sphygmomanometers, shining rubber and stainless steel everywhere, reflex hammers and minor surgery trays laid out as if for imminent carnage. When he and the rest of the staff first walked through the building, they had all gaped.

On this day he was not scheduled to see patients and so he reviewed the piles of lab work that were waiting for his assessment. He had started a folder for the newly diagnosed diabetics, and every time an elevated blood glucose came back he filed it there, in order that the person be brought back for treatment and further evaluation. The file was now inches thick, and Balthazar sighed wearily as he shuffled another half dozen sheets of lab values into it. This disease had been unknown here when he first came to the Arctic. Kerry Nautsiaq, thirteen years old—heavens.

Marie Robertson's results were being copied to him, at first as a trickle and now as a deluge. Sputum sample after sputum sample was negative for acid-fast bacilli, however, and TB had been ruled out early. Nevertheless, they went ahead with the bronchoscopy—you go to see the barber, you end up with a haircut—and that too was negative. CT chest, abdomen, and pelvis were all normal except for the upper-lobe scarring from remote tuberculosis infection. A marked decrease in both visceral and cutaneous adiposity was noted on the CT scan report. The things they could tell now—soon the radiologists would be offering opinions on whether the patient's footwear clashed with their shirts. She was skinny, very, very skinny. That's why they did the scan. Here was the infectious disease service's consultation:

MAY 8, 1992

Miss Robertson is a sixteen-year-old girl of mixed Inuit and Caucasian (English-Scots) descent. She was admitted to hospital after being seen in the respirology outpatient clinic with a view to investigating her for active tuberculosis infection. This concern was occasioned by a long-standing history of mild hemoptysis and, more pressingly, by marked and progressive cachexia noted by her family doctor, Dr. Balthazar, in Rankin Inlet. Serial sputum studies were normal in Rankin Inlet, but given that she is known to have suffered primary pulmonary *M. tuberculosis* infection as an infant, it was thought that the likelihood remained high that she had reactivation infection. At age three she completed six months of directly observed isoniazid and rifampin therapy for treatment of drug-sensitive bacillus. She did sustain some right upper-lobe scarring and has been occasionally troubled by mild hemoptysis as a consequence of limited bronchiectasis; she has not been known to suffer extrapulmonary disease. She has not suffered from antibiotic-related toxicities.

Miss Robertson seems to be substantially emancipated. She presents here unaccompanied by her mother; her father died last year. The history obtained is therefore exclusively from her. She reports that she has always been thin, and that she has never thought she was ill, but that recently, "a lot of people have been riding her" about her weight. She thinks she has not lost weight lately but has grown in stature, and this accentuates her appearance of thinness.

Miss Robertson denies diarrhea or abdominal cramping; she has no personal or family history of inflammatory bowel disease. She has never suffered dermatitis herpeteformis, and she has not been anemic. She reports no recent fevers or night sweats; she has noted no changing moles or lymph nodes. She reports that there are occasional outbreaks of active tuberculosis infection in her school, and she thinks she has had frequent contacts with such patients since she was a baby.

She takes no medications on an ongoing basis. Her immunizations are up to date, and she does not smoke. She has no allergies, either environmental or pharmacologic, to her knowledge. This is corroborated by Dr. Balthazar's note.

On physical examination, she weighs 40.2 kilograms and is 1.72 meters tall. Her BMI is 13.9. Pulse is 54 and regular, temperature 35.1 degrees Celsius, respiratory rate 16. She appears profoundly cachectic, and rather anxious.

Examination of the head and neck demonstrates normal retinal vasculature, and unremarkable anterior chamber structures. The direct and consensual pupillary responses are normal. There is no lid lag or droop present. The oropharyngeal examination is unremarkable. The cervical lymph nodes are unenlarged. The thyroid is normal to palpation; she is clinically euthyroid.

Respiratory examination demonstrates the absence of digital clubbing. Breath sounds are auscultated throughout the lung fields; rales and ronchii are absent. The central arterial pulse volume and contour is normal. The jugular venous pulse is two centimeters above the sternal angle and falls physiologically with inspiration. The apical pulse is readily palpable and is undisplaced. The first heart sound is normal, the second widely but physiologically split, there is a soft flow murmur present, and the third and fourth heart sounds are absent.

The abdomen is scaphoid and her ribs and hips rise strikingly above her umbilicus. Normal bowel sounds are present, the liver and spleen are unenlarged, and both kidneys are easily palpated. A gynecologic examination was not performed. Examination of the extremities reveals extensive laguno, but no other abnormalities.

Review of the available laboratory data reveals no suggestion or evidence for active infection of any sort. One wonders whether an eating disorder might underlie her weight loss; she will be referred to the eating disorders clinic for assessment on an urgent basis. She will require hospital admission to expedite this, as clearly matters have not been able to be addressed in her home community.

The dry, information-packed language of the medical consultation brought Marie's face into sharp focus; that poor, poor, girl. Balthazar did not know why she was so thin; he wondered if it wasn't simply a grief response to her father's death and her brother's disappearance. Victoria had been so adamant that she was fine from a mental health point of view, but he was glad he had gotten her to the city anyway, where they could all have a look at her, see what they thought. He remembered the day she was born, in 1975, another one of Victoria's precipitous deliveries. Marie was smaller than the other two, but active; he remembered how she had squirmed in his hands as he passed her to her mother. These are the memories that keep old family doctors going. God, he hoped that little girl would be okay, that whatever was going on was treatable. He hoped he hadn't missed anything dreadful. Her body fat was 8 percent, for Pete's sake.

Feeling suddenly and deeply weary, he stood up at his desk. His chest was heavy with anxiety and he suspected he'd overlooked something pivotal. He squeezed his eyes shut. He walked out of his office and into the hallway of the echoing, nearly empty building.

His office was in the physicians' wing. As the sole physician there, he was without neighbors and so he walked up to the nurse practition-ers' offices and looked about to see if there was anyone having tea whom he might join. Here there was a hum of activity as children with scabies or colds or in need of annual immunizations were seen and weighed and assessed by the efficient women in this hallway. He was nodded at with a certain amount of impatience, and he retreated back to his office. The pharmacy was on his way and he stopped to look in; there was no one there. He opened the door with his key and walked inside. He looked for Tylenol. He picked out a bottle.

As he was leaving, Melinda Peterson, the new nurse-administrator, approached him. He smiled at her. Beside Peterson was a young bespec-tacled and serious-looking woman he didn't know.

"Are you needing something, Keith?"

"Just some Tylenol," he said, holding up the bottle. "Headache. How are you?"

"I'm well," she said. "I want to introduce you to Diane Richards, our first-ever pharmacist. Dr. Balthazar here has worked in Rankin In-let for more than twenty years. He knows everyone," she said as the new pharmacist held out her hand.

"Wow, this is turning into a real hospital. Our own pharmacist—soon we'll have to get some real doctors up here," he said. And they all laughed at that.

"So we'll be controlling the access to the pharmacy a little more rigidly," Melinda explained, "now that we have a real pharmacist. We'll be writing prescriptions and she'll fill them. Which should save you a lot of work."

Balthazar nodded.

"So maybe we should collect all the outstanding pharmacy keys, I'm thinking," said Melinda, as if the idea was just occurring to her now.

"Okay." And he detached his key from the key ring and passed it over.

"Thanks."

"You're welcome."

He walked back into his office and thought about that for a little while.

The phone rang and it was Milt Henteleff, a pediatric psychiatrist in Winnipeg. "Hello, Milt," Balthazar said. They had had a few patients in common over the years.

"Keith, I've just seen this Robertson girl you've sent us. She looks awful."

"I know, that's why I sent her. What do you think is going on?"

"Well, she'll hardly talk to me, but I gather that her father was killed up there last summer, and her brother was lost on the land this winter?"

"That family has had a terrible year, Milt. I've been wondering if the girl isn't depressed, but her mother doesn't want even to talk about that. And you've seen how voluble Marie is."

"Yeah. I dunno if she's depressed, Keith. Maybe somewhat. But she keeps herself up, you know? She isn't very neurovegetative."

"I'm just a country doctor, Milt."

"I know," Henteleff replied impatiently. "I'm wondering if she doesn't have an eating disorder."

"We never see those up here."

"Well, maybe you do."

There was a pause.

"It would be more treatable than cancer or some malabsorption problem," Henteleff continued.

"Which is one way of looking at it."

"Has she ever been sexually or physically abused, Keith?"

"Not that I know of, Milt, but who knows?"

"I know. It's a wonder we don't see more of this stuff, when you think about it."

"We see a lot of self-abuse—it's not like the theme of self-punishment is rare up here."

"Yeah. I'm gonna go talk to her some more. Thanks, Keith."

"You too, Milt."

He hung up the telephone and felt, as he always felt after talking to the city, clumsy and blind and inept. He laid his head down on his desk. And what was that Melinda getting at, anyway?

This used to be so much easier a job, he thought to himself. Then he thought, *No, it wasn't.*

Johanna was sitting in Penny's empty apartment, looking out her living room window. The days had grown long. The sun was setting in the west like fresh-cut char: pink and red and strands of orange. The snow glimmered pastel beneath all this, and Johanna wondered where Penny had died, whether she had gotten as far as the Thelon River where they had camped. She wondered what that place looked like, frozen and snow-covered.

Johanna had heard that the new teacher had been hired and heard his family was moving in here, but she still had not been asked for Penny's keys. She thought that once there was a family in here, with children running around, Penny would be gone forever. When she heard a knock on the door, her first thought was, *Oh my God, we've all leapt to a horrible conclusion.* Her next thought was, *Why would she knock on her own apartment door?* Johanna got up and opened it.

Doug.

"You weren't in your place and so I figured you might be here."

". . . ."

"They weren't very interested in giving me any more time off work."

"Uh . . . how . . . did you persuade them?"

"I told them if they didn't I'd quit."

"Oh, good." And she held her arms out and he walked into them and she squeezed him so hard, he could scarcely breathe. She began crying quietly, but he did not seem to hear this and she wiped her face on his arm so he would not see her tears. Norbert looked up from beneath the apartment window and wagged his tail carefully. He then settled his head onto his paws to watch this strange man, and tried to understand the agitating effect he had on his new mistress.

"You miss her, huh?"

"I miss you."

"Me too."

"Can you stay for a little while?"

"Yes."

"Let's get out of here," she said.

"Too many ghosts?"

"Too many bad examples."

They went back to her apartment. He had set down his bags in her kitchen. Nine of them. Rucksacks, duffle bags, and enormous suitcases, stacked in a pyramid.

"I'm surprised they let you on the plane with all that," she said.

"There was a substantial service charge."

"What's in them?"

"Everything I could think of and everything I couldn't throw out."

She looked at him. She felt as if she were standing on the edge of a high building, and the fear centered itself in her liver and spread across her abdomen. "Did you bring me any food?" she asked.

"I brought coconut milk," he said.

"That's good." She nodded.

"And fresh coriander and Pouilly-Fuissé, ginger marmalade, Calvados, reggiano-parmigiano, lemongrass, pine nuts, a braid of garlic, maple syrup, chipotle peppers, lox, smoked goldeye, kimchee, Roquefort, tarragon, balsamic vinegar, salami."

"Wow."

"And seeds for rosemary, thyme, eight kinds of basil, cucumbers, garden peas, butternut squash, carrots, and sage. I have a case of Wolf Blass Shiraz, and chevre and Worcestershire sauce."

"What have you been doing down there?"

"Not what you think."

"So it appears."

"You can't stay up here without decent food, among other things."

She finally got up the nerve to ask. "What did you mean, 'everything you couldn't throw out'?"

Johanna sat at her kitchen table as he made Thai curry. She watched him. The earlier conversation was held suspended in the air, tendrils of discussion floating frozen and still, while they both concentrated on trying to breathe. He was chopping the lemongrass. "I don't really know anything about this, you know," he said. "I just buy the things the man in the shop tells me are good. Try to make the food look like it does in the pictures in the recipe books." Out of breath, he turned back to the lemongrass.

"It's pretty much all anyone does."

He resumed chopping. "It seems to me that the Italians and the Thais understand something about it."

"Or did once."

"Shh. Don't say that."

"We're all so hungry for the authentic."

"What do you mean?"

"I don't know."

Pause.

"Did she say anything to you before she left?"

"Not much. She told me she was going out on the land for a little while. I was surprised, because I hadn't thought the principal would give her any more time off. She asked me to water the plants. At work everyone was as surprised as I was. I covered her class as well as my own for a couple of weeks and then the school board flew in a substitute teacher."

"Had she thought it out, taking off like that?"

"She'd thought it out, I think."

L'Hôpital Sainte-Thérèse in Chesterfield Inlet stands out as an anachronism among the younger buildings all around it. It towers above the hamlet of four hundred Inuit, and from its top story the floe edge may be glimpsed even in late winter, miles from the shore of Hudson Bay. It is the oldest building there and is constructed of thick wooden beams the size of ship timbers and has nearly cubic proportions, jutting three stories high into the Arctic wind. The buildings that surround it, the new houses and the interlocking government buildings, were shipped here prefabricated from Montreal or, by train and barge, from Winnipeg. They sit upon poured concrete pilings, and line the rock face of the coastline like aluminum-sided mollusks. When the wind blows very hard the new buildings all rattle and the snow blows right under the floors, between the pilings. In the morning, even with carpeting, it is necessary to wear shoes while dressing because of the cold seeping in from beneath. The old hospital, on the other hand, is like a hollow tree. It is imposing and resolute and of a time when the church was considered above suspicion, and when the idea of missionary work among indigenous people was not itself suspect. It was erected when such structures were built in the place they were meant to stand, of heavy timber and with thousands of man-hours' worth of labor.

It is the only building with a basement in the community. The permafrost and the rock face do not normally permit them. The priests that built the old hospital were wedded to temperate-climate architectures, however, and dug through the shallow soil to bedrock to lay the foundation of the hospital. In the basement is a bread oven that has not been used since the Oblate fathers, and the doctors they employed, left in the late 1960s. There is also an old

*workshop with a dusty lathe and drill press. A small room and a narrow cot lie
off to one corner—presumably for the baking priest's use—but are unused.*

*Once, there was an old priest visiting the hospital and he died in his sleep
in that bed. The last nun with medical training—my friend Sister Isabelle,
who kept the place going until her death—used to tell this story with a
conspiratorial gleam. You thought,* Next she's going to tell the story about
the monkey's claw. *But she didn't. She just walked on through the corridors
of the former hospital, reeling off the outlines of anecdotes like forgotten
genealogies. These things happened. These people existed. There was no attempt
to impress, and anyway it was all being forgotten. On the moment of her death,
in 1999, a whole history vanished.*

*Along with the bread oven in the basement, pieces of obsolete surgical
equipment lie about in odd corners, dusty and corroded. They have been unused
since the mid-1960s, when the federal government assumed responsibility for
health care in the Arctic and the church was eased aside. The old hospital, the
only one ever to function in the Kivalliq District, stopped performing surgery
then and stopped treating emergencies or providing any sort of acute care;
anyone requiring hospital admission was flown instead to the hospital in
Churchill, by this time a booming Canadian and American army town of five
thousand. There were military physicians there, with specialist surgeons and
anesthetists. It was probably a reasonable decision at the time. The military's
interest in the Arctic looked to be long-lasting, and anyway, there is a rail line
to Churchill; shipping supplies and people there is possible all year long and is
vastly less expensive.*

*When I was last there, the old hospital in Chesterfield Inlet was home to
a dozen handicapped Inuit children. There were eight to twelve patients at any
one time. They suffered the sequelae of meningitis, adrenoleukodystrophy,
cerebral palsy, and various genetic and idiopathic neurodegenerative disorders.
It was sad to see them there, as it is to see such children anywhere, but the care
they received was extraordinary. Some were fed through surgical feeding tubes;
others could be fed orally but only by dint of tremendous patience and
affection. Bedsores—a constant problem in the care of such children in most
centers—were very uncommon, testimony to the fastidiousness and tenderness*

with which these children were turned in their beds, and washed each day, and sung to.

They were cared for by a handful of women led by Isabelle, who was then eighty-five years old and had possessed as long as I had known her a vitality and fresh-aired enthusiasm not commonly seen in urban settings except among the deranged. The first time she took me fishing on the ice floes I watched her bounding out over the several-foot-wide leads in the ice as if there were no possibility at all of ever slipping or, worse, falling in. I gingerly held a foot out, trying to span the gap, and she hollered at me from the other side, "You just have to throw yourself across. It's all about momentum!"

The other women included at any one time at least a few nuns—usually two—and two middle-aged Inuit women who lived in the old hospital on the patient ward, in stark plastered rooms with cots and plain wooden crosses on the wall. Isabelle was one of the last nursing sisters still working anywhere and certainly the only one in this part of the Arctic. The others helped at whatever they could, but the truth is that it was, and had always been, pretty much up to Isabelle.

She knew her children so well that without lab tests she usually could tell when the anticonvulsant drug levels were too high. The doctors who visited from time to time admired her deeply. We were none of us as dedicated or as selfless as she. She would pass the prescription pad, and as I took dictation, we chatted about her childhood in the Qu'Appelle Valley in Saskatchewan. Her accent was still lyrical and full of long vowels, and I could only imagine how isolated her family was, that she did not learn English in 1940s Saskatchewan until late enough in her adolescence that an accent still endured at her age. She told me once how she decided to become a nun, after working outside the home for a year, at a bank, I believe, and she was unhappy and lonely and wanted community. When I first met her, at sixty, she was tall and thin and disconcertingly beautiful; as a young woman, I think she must have been painful to look upon.

Until very near the end, she walked every day from the old hospital to the airport, ten miles out of town, even on the coldest days, which, on the tundra in January, are a different experience altogether from what is usually meant by the word cold, requiring, really, their own term, one that better contains the ideas

*of unwelcome pain of searing immediacy. The manager of the co-op store, which
buys carvings and furs and sells ammunition and Cheezies, thought that she was
insane. He fished and hunted with the old men as avidly as any southerner had,
but in January he stayed inside and watched satellite television and worried
about her when blizzards blew up quickly. She dismissed his concern with a
wave. Or rather, she did until the very end of the millennium. Then she learned
that she was sick and would soon be unable to continue working.*

*I have not been to Chesterfield Inlet since this terrible news. I can only
think that she must have been irritated by the insistent concern of her friends
and colleagues. And with the manager of the co-op. I imagine that she was
terrified by the question of what would become of her children and the old
hospital. This would have weighed on her like a clamp. Isabelle was an
anachronism as much as the old wooden building is. There are few young nuns,
and the initiates no longer often choose to study nursing—that is no longer
the province of religious orders, at least in this part of the world. But neither
are there nurses who will work here and accept being on duty all the time, and
rarely take vacation. Nor are there such doctors, for that matter. There is a
nursing station run by the Nunavut government in town, but the nurses there
seem to change every six months and nobody knows how to persuade people to
stay in that job. Which pays well, and involves holidays.*

*It seems inevitable that the old hospital will close. The facts of its history are
less relevant than the fact of its age, and the extraordinary expense of heating it.
Several years ago it was pointed out that there was no sprinkler system in the
wooden building and that this was the least that could be expected of a place
where handicapped children are cared for. Funds were found somehow. There are
other renovations in its future, to meet future building code amendments, but
buildings may be modified only so much before it becomes more practical to
simply build new. This is true in cities and more true in the Arctic, where supplies
for renovations are shipped thousands of miles and it would be no more difficult
to send up a barge with a new rectangular aluminum-sided building on it. But
that part is not the obstacle. The problem is the matter of who would work in the
new rectangular box. This problem seems to have no solution.*

Selfless devotion to others is not as much seen among my generation as it was among Isabelle's. None of my doctor and nurse friends are prepared to be on call all the time, except in brief, well-remunerated spurts, and it is unthinkable that any of us would work that hard in anonymity. If any of us wants to work for free we will go with Médecins Sans Frontières, to some topical and equatorial disaster, where there will be other concerned Western doctors and nurses and maybe some sort of social life. Nobody I know would go up to the old hospital, over the long run, to replace Isabelle.

There is an idea contained in the massively constructed hospital, of resoluteness and faith, which I admire but do not quite understand. I have no faith myself, have never attended any church, and I find the nostrums of organized religion facile and unpersuasive, mostly based on mind tricks to assuage the fear of death. That's what I think. But there is something else in there that I wish I had access to. The religious sense of agape, of not just concern for, but of personal obligation—to the point of ongoing sacrifice if necessary—to one's fellow humans. There is self-righteousness in this, certainly. The evangelical sentiment that lies within most missionary efforts is, faced squarely, fairly repugnant on one level. As if these people didn't have gods already, and ones better suited to this fierce climate. But whatever the contradictions of the ethos that brought Isabelle to the Arctic and kept her there, it did—and the children she cares for are not anonymous residents of some chronic care ward on the southern prairie. They live their short lives in the Arctic. And their parents may visit them. It is much better that she was there, that someone did what Isabelle did. She died May 15, 1999, in a convent in St. Boniface, in Winnipeg.

I remember eating caribou roast with Isabelle, and listening to her stories about her first years in the Arctic, and I imagined for a moment that I chose to stay with her. I imagined reading long-anticipated mail in the dining room of the old hospital underneath kerosene lamps, baking bread and doing surgery and delivering children. I imagined forgetting all about trees and cities and coming to love the formidable taste of seal meat. I imagined focus and devotion on a scale that I have no experience with. For just a few moments I had a sense of what might have sustained her. And then it passed. A few days later I flew south, to New York. I rented a resort cabin on Long Island and slept late and then went swimming in the ocean every day.

chapter twenty-two

Marie sat on the edge of her bed on Three West, one of the inpatient pediatric wards of the Children's Hospital of Winnipeg. The resident and the intern had already been in to see her, she had had more blood-work, and then this tube was put in her nose and now she was being fed through it. When she closed her eyes the humiliation of the scene only got worse. They didn't want her even to shut her door. And she couldn't wear her own clothes, had to give them to the nurse and put on this awful hospital gown and she was cold in it, and there was no one she knew and they wouldn't even let her play her music until she got headphones and, and, this is what the world does to people like her, whom no one looks out for, her mother still at home and her sister only ever embarrassed by her and her brother who hadn't noticed her in ten years, and she had thought up there that she couldn't possibly feel lonelier, but she was wrong. She could. And she could with a tube shoved in her nose.

A young woman knocked on her door and came in. "Hi, I'm Carol James. I'm a dietician and your doctors have asked me to come talk to you about your eating habits."

She wore a teal cardigan pulled tightly across her narrow frame and her manner was simultaneously halting and impetuous. Marie looked at the woman blankly. Good God in heaven, there was a tube in her nose—surely she had drawn some conclusions about her eating habits.

"You're looking a little bowled over. I understand. Most of the girls do when they come in the first time. A big part of what I do is education. And the best way to start that is to talk about what you eat. Can you tell me about when your eating habits started to change? Was there something that happened about the time you started worrying about your weight?"

Her words rushed on, undaunted by Marie's determined blankness. "Hey, it's gonna be okay, honey. They tell me you're from the Arctic. We've never had an Inuit girl here before in the eating disorder unit; everyone thinks that's really interesting. You know, I should tell you, if you have any dietary preferences, like char or caribou or something, we could get some flown down for you, no problem. We do it all the time for the older folks. Do you think you'd like that? Not sure? Well, let us know if you would; it would be easy for us. I suppose you might just want to tie into some hamburgers and fries, or something else you can't find up there, anyway. Feel free. I mean it: feel free.

"You know, I've always been interested in the Inuit. It seems incredible to me that you people ever lived up there without wood, making a living just from the tundra. I think it's inspiring, really. The things humans are capable of—we live down here in such a soft environment and you know, no one here really knows what it is like to struggle. I'll bet you, or your people anyway, do. Winter ten months a year, raw seal and caribou—heavens. Maybe to you it just seems normal, like how everyone lives. You know what? It isn't. You people are so strong. We southerners couldn't last an hour and a half up there. Though I suppose there might be some ways about living down here that strike you as difficult, or crazy anyway.

"Have you ever been to Winnipeg before? It must seem so busy and crowded to you. You get used to it pretty quickly, though. There's great shopping over at Portage Place. I'll bet someone here would take you when you're feeling better.

"You just don't feel much like talking, do you? That's okay, I'll come back later."

At shift change for the nurses, Marie waited for the din rising from the staff room to peak. Then she got out of bed and walked to the elevators beside the nursing station. There was a worried-looking parent couple just stepping off, and she swung in behind them into the elevator car. When the door closed she pulled the tube out of her stomach, gagging and choking as she did so. She rode the elevator down to the main floor and walked quickly out into the lobby. She looked around the empty building until she found the reception desk.

"Where is the lost and found, please?"

The man sitting there, pushing eighty and wearing a bright red button that said VOLUNTEERS MAKE THE WORLD GO 'ROUND, stood up slowly and pulled out a box the size of a tabletop and heaved it onto the desk.

"Great, there's my sweater, and pants and jacket," Marie said for the benefit of the smiling man. "How did I lose those?" He nodded, and she walked into the women's washroom off the atrium.

In Kat's room later that night, Amanda, Beth, Lewis, and Kat all tried to sleep in a space that seemed scarcely large enough to stand in. They had come here to blow a spliff and eat the pizza they had stolen from an inattentive Domino's driver, who had left a car window ajar while making an apartment delivery. They were all nodding off halfway through the pepperoni and double-cheese thick crust.

Amanda had never seen where Kat lived, and was curious. His room was the size of the largest of her parents' washrooms, and in it was a bed and a hot plate and almost nothing else. A green plastic garbage bag of dirty T-shirts and jeans, another of clean. On the wall were drawings he had made of Japanese swords and symbols he had been moved by. Also, a few efforts at anime drawings, and the sentiment of these surprised her. These were children, however armored and sexualized, and he had drawn them with innocence apparent upon their faces. Of all of them it was Kat she worried most about—he seemed to her more lost and troubled than the others, or herself. Her parents would have been puzzled by this distinction she drew. He displayed no outward evidence of distress, and never complained or even revealed much about where he was from, or where his family was, but the extent that he had drawn into himself, reaching backward in time to Saturday-morning cartoons and Teenage Mutant Ninja Turtles, moved her. *He sees his own future,* she thought, *and pushes it out of his mind.*

Kat and Beth lay down on his bed, and Lewis and Amanda curled up on the floor beside them. They wrapped a thin and spotted blanket Kat had offered them around themselves and used their jackets as pillows. The floor was hard, but the day had induced in them a tolerance for discomfort.

When Kat and Beth began fucking, Lewis had been snoring for most of an hour. Amanda heard him wake at Beth's soft cries, and stir, rolling toward her. She was aroused as well and she turned and pressed herself into him. The single window emitted a pale green streetlight glow that lit up Beth's bony frame and the muscles of Kat's narrow back. Kindly, the light pressed less insistently on Amanda and Lewis. As he rolled onto her and entered her, she gasped, and saw Beth turn her head to see where the sound had come from. After a moment of the faint sliding, sucking sound of their passion, Beth turned away again and looked at her own lover. It had not been clear to Amanda that Beth and Kat had been seeing each other except within their group, but from the way they moved together, from the ratio of hunger to tentativeness and fear, it was clear that they had. She wondered why this would have been kept a secret and she wondered which of them had wanted it to be.

Marie walked south down Sherbrooke Avenue and studied the rows of fifty-foot-high elms arching over that street. The sidewalk was busy and the traffic hurtled past her six feet away and it seemed to her incomprehensible that the people sharing the sidewalk with her were not more frightened than they seemed.

When she came to the bridge over the Assiniboine River, she studied the water flowing under it and felt for the first time that urge to leap that city dwellers became accustomed to. She had seen bridges before, but she had not walked over one of them, these enormous arching concrete ribbons; neither had she understood how real the rivers they crossed were, or how comparable the Red and Assiniboine rivers were to the great rivers of the tundra, the Kazan, the Thelon, the Back. Somehow she had imagined that a river that brooked bridging so easily could not itself be of any substance. There were no bridges where she lived, and none within five hundred miles, though there was a frigid river emptying into Hudson Bay every ten miles along the coast, all flowing east. What a person, or a caribou, has to do when confronted with one of these is walk across, or swim. In spring and early summer, the current is formidable and the caribou calves die in raven-glutting numbers whenever a herd resolves to cross deep water. Children died too often in water like this; every family had a list of names of wee daughters and grinning boys who fled this world in a swirling eddy of seabound river water.

Marie levitated above the Assiniboine on the Maryland Street Bridge, walking effortlessly over the thick green water from the north bank to the south and then onto Wellington Crescent. She passed houses the size of Rankin Inlet airport hangars, lawns like rolls of green velveteen laid upon their yards with nails and a spirit level. On one such lawn, after looking around to see if anyone was watching, she lay down on her back, stretching her arms widely and studying the sky. The clouds rolled over her, the heat rising up off the grass. Perspiration rolled down her face as the sun found purchase and really began to light into her. The sun looked exactly the same as it did in the north, but she could never remember feeling heat like this. It was like looking closely into a fire. Even with her eyes shut she could see it. How did people bear to work outside? She opened her eyes, squinting, and looked at the trees towering over her. The mosquitoes had found her. She reached between her shoulders and swatted one. Then she noticed someone observing her through a curtained window. She rose, not looking, and walked over to the sidewalk and continued east, the houses growing grander as she went.

She crossed back to the north bank of the Assiniboine over the Osborne Street Bridge. She was not certain where she was, relative to the hospital. She did not know where she was going, had no real idea where she would spend the night. She was lonely, as she had been for years, and she wanted both to get as far away as she could from Rankin Inlet, which had become a torment for her, and to run into the arms of her mother, her sister, her family, crawl into her room, put Joy Division on her Walkman and not emerge, and not be bothered. As they had not bothered, or been bothered about her, for years.

She asked a woman where Portage Place was and she was directed to the mall abutting the downtown length of Portage Avenue, just a few blocks from the Osborne Street Bridge. When she spotted the glass arcades of the building she gasped; it was more beautiful than she had imagined. She could not have guessed that a building in the city could seem so light; there were real live trees growing inside, and sparrows flying among them.

She found the HMV quickly and lost herself among the CDs: here was music she had read of but never heard, and there were headphones with which to listen to sample CDs, as long as you wanted, no charge. She had never heard XTC before, or the Beastie Boys, Tone Loc, or Public Enemy. She listened to *Appetite for Destruction* in one stretch, glancing away every time the cashier looked at her. She gathered together a mound of disks she longed to own: R.E.M.'s *Eponymous,* the Monks' *Bad Habits,* Marianne Faithfull's *Broken English,* and then she set them down in front of the skeptical-looking cashier. She began ringing them in and then Marie pretended to have misplaced her wallet. "I'll be right back," she assured the girl and left, aching to hear that music.

In the courtyard she sat at one of the little tables and smiled at the knots of boys and girls sitting all around her. One clique dressed entirely in black, the boys in eye shadow, the girls like princesses of the undead: Marie assumed they were in a band and was certain she would like their music. She was too shy to approach them; instead she concentrated on willing them to acknowledge her, yearning for one of them to catch her eye. She could not have known how she looked to them, like just another Indian kid tossed out of home and destined for trouble. She could not have anticipated how far short of her own hopes she was falling, falling, falling, as she sat there and felt sadness lapping over her like water, green and pungent in the middle of an unseasonable spring.

In the diner around the corner from Kat's room they sat together and blinked. They had slept twelve hours and were still exhausted— from the dope trip, and the sex, and the hot restless sleep that supervened for irregular stretches through the night, never more than a couple of hours at a time before one of them was rolling over and sighing. Now they were waiting for their eggs, the moment almost familial in its intimacy. What each of them wanted now was to be among people who knew him or her well and approved of him or her. They settled for this.

When the food came, they tucked into it without comment. The toast and the sausages slid over their tongues with textures of unanticipated complexity and nuance. The orange juice and the coffee were perfect complements, and the sound of the foil covers being peeled from the wee marmalade packages tasted itself like orange peel. In the light of this early-afternoon moment, it was dazzling.

When the ambulance pulled into the Children's Hospital emergency room, it was dawn and the sky was glowing purple, radiant streaks of prairie sky shooting out from the east. She had been spotted by an early-morning jogger, facedown among the reeds along the river, motionless and pallid, her preposterous-looking and stolen clothing hanging over her like drapery. She was already cold, her sodden lungs full within minutes of striking the water. Even if she had been able to swim, it would not have mattered; she had knocked her head on an edge of the bridge as she fell and she had known nothing more.

Ten seconds before the last of her thoughts, she had not contemplated ending them. She had been standing on the bridge, stung by the unfriendliness of the mall, and by her unprecedented anonymity. The water looked just like it does in the north, except greener maybe, more algae. She could not buy the music she wanted, she could not make her way in this place, the only alternative to Rankin Inlet, not without help. There was no help. Her father had gone from her, despite all his promises. He was the only one who ever looked out for her, really. She could not picture an end to this that would be bearable. Locked in the hospital room. Locked in Rankin Inlet. Alone and fighting tears in the Portage Place food court, with nothing to eat and no money to buy anything.

She had wanted to read a comic book, and had stopped at a newsstand, but hadn't the nerve to flip through one under the dour gaze of the man behind the till. Some Cree boys saw her there, members of Indian Posse, with emblazoned jean jackets, and invited her to go to a party with them. She walked quickly away and they had followed her for a short while, hooting derisively. They had frightened her.

She wanted company and she wanted to be safe. She wanted to be sitting at the supper table, her dad and her mom passing around the food. That was gone from her. This is what it would be from here on: just her, in the world. The wind picked up. It was getting darker. She didn't have enough clothes on. She swung one leg over the side of the bridge. Then, the other, and she was sitting on the edge. Cars drove past. One honked its horn. It was dark enough that she couldn't see the people inside, only the headlights. There were lights everywhere in the city. Apartment high-rises lit up like monuments. As she fell, they streaked out into serpentine blurs against the night sky.

When Balthazar got to his office the phone was ringing. He set down his jacket as he reached for the handset. It was Sara Miller, the head of pediatric psychiatry. She outlined the events of the evening before and that morning, and as she did, Balthazar's throat tightened to the point where he wondered if he was having his first episode of angina. It let up a bit as he sat down. "Of course, there will be an inquest into this, into how she got out of hospital, how thoroughly her suicidality had been assessed, what could have been done differently, better," Miller said.

"This is just awful" was all he could croak.

"I agree. On behalf of my department, I apologize to you. I've already spoken with Mrs. Robertson and conveyed the same sentiment."

He detected her indignation in that statement and heard a flash of the conversation that had erupted in her office over Marie's death. His every instinct was to calm her, to settle things down, to assure her that she ought not to feel too bad, that suicidal ideation is hard to assess, especially among Aboriginal teens, the most suicidal demographic ever studied.

Miller listened and felt disdain for the man, for the ease with which he accepted this travesty that had led to the death of his patient. She formed an opinion in that moment about his dedication, and the quality of his work. The sureness of her instinct was largely responsible for her professional success, and she was not wrong, in this instance—or at least, her opinion was broadly shared. As her respect for him declined, she felt her own sense of embarrassment and failure fade. "Well, part of what caught everyone flat-footed was the unusual nature of the case— it's the first instance of a serious eating disorder diagnosed in an Inuit child that I've ever heard of. As a patient population, these young women are prone to self-injury, of course, and in the context of an Aboriginal patient, in the future such patients will have to be considered at maximally high risk for self-injury."

And as they retreated from the fact of the dead girl to the big picture, these dry words settled their grief a little. "I suppose we're just going to see more and more of it over time," Balthazar replied.

"Maybe the case report should be published," she said. "I'll have to review the literature."

"It might be quite interesting," Balthazar agreed, and inanely thanked her for the phone call. "It isn't often that I get feedback from the teaching hospitals," he said. As she hung up the phone, Miller did not wonder why.

Balthazar walked out of his office, pulling on his jacket, and left the hospital. He saw Victoria's house down the road and he walked toward it. This was the day she was to have flown to Winnipeg to be with Marie. It was after nine, and Justine would be in school, he thought. Had Victoria been alone when she received Miller's call? He hoped not, and, despite himself, and to his great shame, he hoped she had been, as well.

When he knocked on the door, he heard steps approaching it and thought they were too heavy to be hers. Simionie opened the door and when the two men recognized each other, a flash of sympathy wrapped around a core of suspicion flew between them. This was a complex emotion to be communicated in the cast of an eye, but one second after the door opened, Victoria realized who was there and flew at him, her streaked and anguished face swollen and contorted. She pushed Simionie aside and struck Balthazar square in the face with a closed fist. Him: falling back down the steps onto the gravel; her: following him and kneeling upon the much larger man, hitting him again and again as she gasped and sobbed. "You killed my baby!" she shrieked at him over and over as he pulled his arms over his head and tried to ward off her blows.

Simionie approached her from behind and tried to pull her off, but she flung her elbow back into his face and he let go of her. Every conscious pair of eyes in the hamlet watched this scenario play out—Simionie, clutching his broken nose, Victoria's elbow crimson with his blood, and Balthazar, wailing like a child, "I'm so, so, sooooorrrrrrry." He lay on his belly, his huge chest shaking, his arms over his face, his head, sobbing.

"You . . . you . . . you . . . yooooooooooo," she cried again and again, the strength of her blows weakening now, her hair wet from her tears and hanging against her face and over her eyes, her chest shaking, her baby cold and dead, and motionless, not eating, not breathing, not opening his wee eyes, his little purple lips puckered like a flower's bud, no matter how closely she held him, the child did not move, did not reach for his mother, just lay there, dead, not suckling, his mother's aching breast running in a steady stream, milk flowing over the dead child's chest, to no avail.

chapter twenty-three

■

They lit their bong and dropped a little coke on some pot Kat had left over. Lewis took pride of place, and was soon leaning back and grinning. The girls followed and then Kat too drew deeply on the bong, and for a long moment they thought Lewis had been duped, that they had just inhaled vaporized bath crystals.

They were suburban kids, each of them, well acquainted with weed and with E. But cocaine, down, and crystal meth were not as well known to them. These carried the cachet of genuine menace, and so long as the kids were possessed of their suburban timidity, they had not spent their money on such drugs. They were less timid now, roaming between their various sleeping spots—Kat's room, Lewis's apartment, and the couches available to them—and they imagined themselves to be up for the challenge. The girls suspected in one small and distant part of their beings that they were underestimating the capacity of the world to crush them, but they pushed such thoughts away and threw themselves into entirely new sensation.

And so, as their jaws began to tingle, they did not recognize the first rush of nearly pure cocaine, sweeping through their lungs and toward their brains. As it passed into them, they reeled. The intensity of the euphoric pleasure that struck them that first time was beyond anything they had experienced; these were years full of new feelings for them, but nothing, not sex, not pot, not new freedom, had disoriented them as pleasurably as this.

After that initial numbing wave of sensation, they were silent for many uncountable minutes, and then slowly they began talking and, in throwing out words to one another through that void, they realized that each was not alone there and that they should put out the pipe and not smoke anymore.

The girls spoke to each other in low, melodic tones, full of long pauses and gropings for the appropriate adjective, about what they were feeling and how good it was. The boys leaned back and laughed, raw and rippling in their teenaged power and grace. Everyone was too hot, sweating sheets of salt water, as they became aware of their own pulses throbbing flutteringly at the base of their throats.

Kat asked Lewis what he was thinking about; Lewis replied that he was realizing for the first time how fucked up everything was—how he had always thought that, mostly, he was fucked up. But everyone thought they were fucked up, right? And if everyone thought that, then maybe none of them was—maybe it was the world.

Kat said, "I know exactly what you mean."

Beth asked Amanda if she knew she was loved. Amanda paused for a long minute, forgetting what the question was as she looked at the smallest cobweb imaginable in one corner of Kat's room, between the ceiling and the wall, wondering whether spiders would ever use old cobwebs built by other spiders that had moved on, or died, recycling them. She suspected not, because if it wasn't being used then presumably this was for a reason—it had not kept its builder well enough fed. Which was a shame when you really thought hard about it. Love. Oh, yes. Yes, who loved her? Well, her parents in their fashion, she supposed. And her uncle Keith, and . . . Lewis? She studied him. No, Lewis did not love her, she saw now, but would hold on as tightly as he needed, say what he needed, to stay afloat.

Beth whispered, "I know what you mean," and Amanda wondered how her thoughts had been audible. "Shhhhhh," Beth added. "We have to make our own way. The boys are lost in this world. They're beautiful to watch, but they're lost."

■   ■   ■

Lewis was talking about guns. "They are the most perfect thing humanity has made, a peak technology. They haven't changed fundamentally now in eighty years. The new ones have plastic grips, maybe, and the machine tools that make them are computer-controlled rather than manual, but the workings, the design, is almost unchanged."

"Like a bicycle, maybe."

"Yeah. Like a fucking bicycle."

"It's weird, that this would be the thing we perfect before all others," Kat said.

"Maybe not. Does anything else give you the thrill the way a gun does, when you hold it?"

"No."

"Wanna see mine?"

"What?"

"C'mon."

Amanda said, "Did you ever think you were pregnant?"

Beth said, "Yeah. I had an abortion last year. I guess I never told you about it."

"No, you didn't. Was it okay?"

"It was awful. Some guy I met at a party was the father. I never even knew his name."

"Are you sorry?"

"Sorry I didn't use protection. I go back and forth about the abortion." She began rocking her arms in front of her, as if cradling a neonate, and tears ran from her eyes. "I'm sorry, little baby . . ." She looked up at Amanda. "I still have dreams I'm talking to her."

"Would you do it again if you got pregnant again?"

Beth looked down at her arms and smiled, then leaned to kiss an imaginary forehead. She looked up at Amanda. "And kill this beautiful baby?"

"But," Amanda quavered, "it's not actually a baby yet."

"I know," Beth said, smiling at her imagined baby, cooing into her sixteen-year-old's arms, stick-thin and laced with blue veins.

Lewis led Kat into the hallway and down to the basement of the squalid apartment building. There was a storeroom there, which had been left unoccupied, forgotten by the building super, whose capacity for remembering was limited. Lewis had put a lock on the door and it had not been noticed—or anyway sawn off. After a month, he had begun to use the room as his own.

There was a mattress inside, and some clothes and cigarettes. He lifted up the mattress to show Kat his bolt-action .22 rifle.

Kat inhaled sharply.

"It was my dad's from when he was a kid on the farm. I found it in the garage years ago and hid it in the rafters. He never mentioned it. I think he figures it was accidentally thrown out or something." He slid the bolt back and aimed at the dimly lit opposite wall. *Click.*

"Wow." Kat's eyes were gleaming. "Have you ever fired it?"

"No."

"Do you have any ammunition for it?"

"My dad had a box of shells I found with it. Here." Lewis held up a faded cardboard box of .22 long rifle shells.

"No way."

"I'm gonna take it down to a firing range one of these days and see what it can do." He aimed at the wall and drew back and then seated the bolt. *Click.*

"It's beautiful."

Lewis nodded. He took the magazine out of the rifle and opened the box of shells. He watched the shells spill into his hand, little cylinders of brass and lead and rattly gunpowder within. He pressed the shells into the magazine one by one with deft, oft-practiced movements. Then he put the magazine back into the rifle. He aimed it at the wall and worked the bolt, seating a round in the chamber. He pulled the bolt back again and the unfired cartridge flew across the room and bounced onto the concrete floor. He worked the bolt again and again until all ten rounds had been ejected onto the floor. He looked over at Kat.

"I wish we lived in the country and could just go get lost in the woods. Could shoot some squirrels, tin cans, whatever."

"Can I hold it?"

"You gotta be careful."

"I know."

"Amanda, what's the story with your 'rents?"

"Why?" she heard herself answer as she studied her own reflection in the night-shiny window, rain running slowly over the glass in a confluent sheet, dispersing the blue glow of the streetlight. What she saw in the window was a girl, seventeen years old, and not, as she usually imagined, older-looking, or much younger-looking, but seventeen, and tired and high, her eyes blinking slowly with the concentration of being that high, her hair long and thick and a bit dirty, her complexion flushed, her cheeks full. She was not as full-faced as she had been a few months earlier, when she lived with her parents, and the dye job had grown out enough that her sandy blond roots showed through in a manner that satisfied her. She saw anxiety in the girl's expression, and she saw too that she was, after all, a little beautiful.

"Well, maybe you shouldn't just break things off with them, if they were never actually awful, only stupid—well, maybe they'll come around."

"They are only interested in their-fucking-selves, Beth."

"Who isn't?"

"You, for one."

"I love you, Amanda."

Amanda pulled her eyes from the window (they stretched out like taut rubber bands, resisting the turning movement of the head they were attached to, before finally breaking loose and slapping back into their sockets) and settled them on her friend. They were both so high, they had the sense of speaking to each other inside a large and echoing room, their words flowing out of their mouths and swirling around like currents of pigment in a watery centrifuge, finding their target only after long and circuitous trajectories. And when they arrived, it seemed their words and sentences were disordered, their meanings concealed, but anyway, who knew what they really meant? Certainly not the speaker.

"Wow, you're really high, huh?" Beth said, touching Amanda's shoulder.

"Did you ever want to do just one thing that everyone would always remember and know afterward who you were, and what you thought about all this shit?"

"Yeah, all the time. Like Spider-Man, a normal guy, right, just swept up in the world and its problems, and then he has his chance to do something great, even if no one else knows about it," Kat said.

"That's a fucking comic book, man."

"And an animated television show."

"Are you fucking kidding me?"

"Maybe I am."

"I envy the guys that got to go to Nam or to fight the Japs, or whoever. That's what's normal for guys like us to do, to go out there someplace where it's hard. Fucking get your ass kicked a little." Lewis aimed the rifle around the room. "Kick some ass yourself," he added. He aimed into the corner and squeezed the trigger. As the diminutive click sounded, he made a wet rushing sound in his cheeks, intended to evoke the movie sound of a rifle firing, full of rumbling, thunderous portent. At that moment, he looked and sounded and thought exactly like one million other comic book readers, envisioning heroic action sets, himself the archetype, more muscular and silent than he actually was, with a lethal aim and a convulsive temper as well. He looked above the sights back at Kat and added, "Come back a man."

■   ■   ■

Beth and Amanda lay down together in that dim room. They had forgotten about the boys, did not even wonder where they had gone to. Neither was tired, the drug still arcing through them in a succession of small sparks. Even when they closed their eyes, their lids shone with bright, spiraling lights. It was gripping, but it was ceasing to be entertaining to them—it had been going on for hours now, and was not letting up. Like LSD that way, but happier, more euphoric. Which itself became dull with time, as it must for all but the most thoroughly unhappy. And this response—their boredom—for the first time in their lives became a beneficial thing.

Kat, like almost every other boy he knew, had been raised by his mother, and there had never been any hunting or fishing trips in his urban boyhood. To him, rifles were devices from movies with mythic more than practical purposes. He held Lewis's .22 to his shoulder just as Lewis had, and aimed at the wall. He looked along the crude open sight and squeezed the trigger. *Click.* He tried to pull the bolt back but it was locked. He fumbled with the action before figuring out that he had to rotate the bolt up to unlock it, and then he pulled it back, feeling the firing pin spring resisting him, and then he slid it forward and locked the bolt. *Click.*

He laid the rifle across his knees and admired the dull brown wood. He pulled the magazine from it and examined it. He spilled cartridges into his hand from the decades-old box of shells. He could barely make out the word Remington, it was so faded. He put a shell in the magazine. And then another. After ten were in, he couldn't fit any more. He inserted the magazine into the rifle. He worked the bolt again, and once more shells flew across the room. Lewis watched him, leaning back against the wall of the little storage cupboard. Kat lifted the rifle and pointed it at Lewis. Lewis grinned. "Careful, buddy," he said. They were both very high but in that moment a kind of clarity settled over them, a sense of the triviality of their own disordered lives, made so evident by this device and its power and the way it urged a person to use it. And then Kat's finger tightened on the trigger.

Two floors above, Beth and Amanda sat up abruptly. Kat said nothing, letting the rifle settle back to the floor, its animated insistence fading now. Then he looked at Lewis, who was looking at his shirt, which was slowly starting to turn red. "Jesus Christ," Lewis said. Kat did not move. Lewis coughed. He opened his shirt and the two boys looked at the small hole in the center of his chest. Bright arterial blood pumped out of it, unrestrained now by his clothing.

"Look at that," Lewis said. And then he slipped to the floor and closed his eyes. Kat sat there.

■

chapter twenty-four

Simon Alvah had detected signs of imminent breakup for fully two
weeks but the ice had not begun to move. It was July already, and the
sky hung warm and heavy. The floe edge was so close to shore, it looked
as if he could hit it with a well-thrown rock. But the ice, right up until
the moment it fractured, was resolute and monolithic. There were
pools of meltwater collected upon it, and teals and pintails swam in
them, pausing in the journey to their high Arctic nesting grounds. All
around him, Alvah saw resurgent signs of summer, but still his steel sailboat was stuck fast.

He had read of whaling crews who had frozen in, as he had, for the
winter, and had remained stuck the following unusually cool and brief
summer. For long anxious moments he wondered if the same thing
could happen to him. Admittedly, the consequences would be less absolute—he would walk to town and buy a snowmobile to haul in more
food and fuel for his boat. The whalers had had to cut up their boots to
make stew, and burn the furniture to heat the vessel. Flying home, however, would have been no more an option for him than it was for them.
The boat had not failed him and he could not abandon it.

During those two weeks in which he expected daily to see the ice
break apart and fall away, he rose every morning to study the appearance of the sky, search the air longingly for a suggestion of southerly
winds. One of these mornings on which he stood there, smelling the air
and squinting into the west, he discerned a figure moving slowly across

the rotten sea ice, wending in great arcs to avoid the huge pools of melt-water. Alvah watched the figure for three hours before it got close enough to the boat that he could make out the wild beard and oily parka. The dogs were thin and few, and evidently tired of running through the thick wet snow. The walking man stopped often to let them rest before urging them forward.

When finally he stood beside the boat, Alvah had grown nervous enough that he had unpacked his rifle and laid it beneath a sheet of canvas in the cockpit. "Hello," he said when they had taken each other in.

"Hello," Pauloosie said.

"How may I help you?" He knew it was the boy.

"When the ice melts, are you leaving here?"

"Yes."

"Can I come with you?"

"Would you be prepared to wash?"

Balthazar knocked on the priest's door. He listened closely but there was no sound inside. The idea of leaving without saying goodbye to Father Bernard, at least, saddened him. He turned from the door and walked to the stairs, half carrying, half dragging his heavy bags. He had clunked down a couple of steps when the priest opened his door. "Ah, it's you," the priest said.

"I'm leaving. I want to say thank you."

"Yes, I heard about Marie. I assumed you would do something like this."

It was the first time the priest had rebuked Balthazar. He needed no more rebukes, and he turned away. "Wait. Come in for a moment. Have a cup of tea," the priest added.

Balthazar set down his bags. He looked at his feet. He left his bags on the stairs and turned around and walked back to the priest's apartment. Father Bernard smiled faintly. He waited for Balthazar to enter and then he closed the door behind them and walked to his kitchen. Balthazar stood in the living room. Twenty years of friendship and all he wanted was to get out of there. The priest watched him as he put the teakettle on to boil. "Where are you going?" he asked.

"To New York."

"Will you come back?"

"No."

"Will you work down there?"

"I don't think so."

"So this is it, the end of your career."

"It appears so."

"I'm sorry it is under such circumstances."

"Well. Me too."

"You could write to me."

"Thank you. I'll send you records."

"I'd like that."

"How much longer will you stay here?"

"I don't know. I'm tired too."

"They will miss you when you go."

"Some of the old ones, maybe. I will miss you."

"I'll miss you too, Bernard."

"Victoria needs to grieve. When she has finished, she will see more clearly."

"She sees clearly now."

"You act as if you've never had an unfortunate outcome before."

"No. I'm not inexperienced in losing patients. Especially Victoria's family members. I don't know what's got into me."

The priest smiled ruefully. "If you had faith, I could prescribe a penance."

"You make it sound tempting, somehow."

The priest looked at the kettle. "It is a kind of egotism, self-flagellation such as this. The time for fervor is in the approach to God, not in response to his reversals."

Balthazar didn't wait for his tea, walked out of the apartment and to the stairs, where he picked up his bags.

▪   ▪   ▪

When the west wind rose, at last, and the ice fractured, the sea cleared in an afternoon.

The next morning Pauloosie heaved the last of his dogs out of Alvah's skiff and onto the beach north of Rankin Inlet. They weren't quite as skinny as they had been—Alvah had been generous with his tinned meat, and then they had shot a seal that had climbed up onto the ice surrounding the boat. But the dogs remained malnourished, diminished creatures. Pauloosie stepped out of the skiff too and knelt. These were not pets, and were not used to being stroked. They stood around him, uncomfortable with his display of weakness. They stepped back, and then they stepped forward. They sensed he was about to leave and this distressed them. What they had just done, they had done together; they believed that as much as he did. One of them broke down and whined, and then the others joined in. They did not approach any closer. When he stood, they backed farther away. He turned and pushed the skiff off the beach. The dogs looked toward town and began walking as Pauloosie started the outboard motor.

The next day, Simon Alvah and Pauloosie pulled up the anchor and motored out of the Marble Island lagoon. Alvah turned the boat into the wind and, for the first time in a year, he hoisted the mainsail. As it rose, flies that had taken shelter in the folds of Dacron fell out onto the deck and wiggled their little legs in surprise. Alvah tightened the mainsheet and turned the boat to starboard, north. The boat heeled over and began making headway slowly. He unrolled the genoa and tightened the jib sheet. *Umingmak* picked up speed and the starboard rail hung lower, almost touching the water. The water behind the stern began to roil. Pauloosie held on to the boat, now at an alarming angle, and opened his eyes wide with fear. Would it roll right over? Alvah assured him they were okay. Pauloosie said, "I know." And gripped the windward rail tighter.

All that day they charged north, the west coast of Hudson Bay just visible to port, hanging on the horizon like a smudge of brown limning the water. When twilight came, just before midnight, Alvah told Pauloosie he should get some sleep. Pauloosie nodded and went below. He crawled into the sleeping bag Alvah had given him and listened to the water rushing by.

He woke a few hours later and already it was dawn. He stumbled up to the cockpit and saw Alvah sitting there, watching the sun rise. "What time is it?" Pauloosie asked.

"Almost three."

"Are you tired?"

"Not in the least."

Pauloosie sat down in the cockpit alongside Alvah. The boat was well balanced and steered herself. "How far have we gone?"

"A hundred miles."

"Just being blown by the wind."

"Yes."

"Do you know how much work it is to dogsled a hundred miles?"

Alvah reflected on the question for a moment. "No," he said.

"A lot more than this."

"You can run a dog team all winter, though. Do you have any idea what it was like, spending the winter cooped up in this thing?"

"Yes."

"Well, I suppose you would, wouldn't you?"

"Look," Pauloosie said, pointing ahead of the boat. "Belugas."

Alvah watched them stream alongside, glowing white in the dim light. "Gorgeous."

"Tasty."

They both laughed.

Alvah made breakfast as Pauloosie kept an eye out up top. The smell of pancakes rose from the galley. Then there was coffee. Pauloosie's hunger had been established over months on the land and had not begun to abate even after two weeks of reliable food on board. (After the first meal they ate together, Alvah had revised his estimation of the stores they would need by a factor of four and had made another trip into town for food.)

With the scent of the ice-strewn sea sharp in the air, and in the knowledge that every minute put Rankin Inlet farther behind him, this food smelled better to Pauloosie than anything he could remember. The pleasures of raw seal steak notwithstanding.

chapter twenty-five

When Pauloosie's dogs walked into town, for a while they were not recognized. Finally one of the old men, Panigoniak, came back from walrus hunting and saw them. He walked over to Tagak's house and asked Winnie if he could speak with Emo. Emo came to the door, and did not know him, a man he had hunted with hundreds of times in the previous eighty years. So Panigoniak asked if Tagak was home, and Winnie said no. Then he told her that her grandson's dogs were on the bay ice, with the other dogs. He had fed them, he said, but they didn't look healthy. Winnie nodded, and the old man left.

Victoria picked up the telephone and listened to her mother's news, then laid her head down on the kitchen table and shut her eyes. Simionie, with whom she had been playing cribbage, understood this to be a tragedy that could not be shared with him. So he found his jacket and went outside. As he closed the door behind him, he could hear her beginning to sob. He checked his watch. It was four in the afternoon. Justine would be home from school soon. He sat down on the porch steps and waited. When he spotted her dark blue parka round the corner as she trundled home, he stood and walked away. He had been listening to Victoria's crying for an hour and had carved a groove into the wooden step he had been sitting on with his fingernails.

In bed that night, one in the morning and the sky scarcely dimmed, Johanna and Doug lay alongside each other and tried to summon sleepiness. They were as enlivened by the all-day-and-night sun as the tundra mammals were and felt, just as keenly, the unceasing desire to move, eat, and have sex. They had done all these things, and still they were restless. In moods like this, it becomes easy to speak of things prematurely.

"Are you sure?"

"No. I tried to see Dr. Balthazar today, but he's not around for some reason. I'll see one of the nurses tomorrow. The only reason I haven't said anything before now is, I wanted to know first. I shouldn't have said anything."

"So what makes you think you are?"

"Might be. My breasts ache. I'm late."

"Holy mackerel."

"Holy mackerel."

"Ha."

"What do you mean, 'ha'?"

Doug started laughing, his joy filling him, leaking out of his eyes and his mouth and his nose like a soda swallowed hastily, mucus running everywhere, and Johanna rose up on one elbow to look at him quizzically, wondering if this was some stress-response variant she hadn't seen before. Then she saw his eyes shining in the twilight, and tears running down his face, and he could not have been more transparently happy, and she breathed out for a long, long time, and rolled over on her back, smiling.

When they rounded the Bering Strait it was October already and they were very late, moving south not much faster than the edge of the pack ice did. The equinoctial gales had come upon them when they were off Point Barrow, and they had nearly been driven ashore in that shallow, icy water, the lee shore at all times threatening, the smooth, featureless coast offering up only the breaking combers exploding in geysers of white water. The onshore wind had driven them so close one night, they were certain they would die. The next morning the wind was fractionally lighter, though still slashing with icy ire, and they turned into it as closely as they could and motor-sailed away from the shore. When the sun had risen, they had been five hundred yards from the surf. They did not mention it.

They made Dutch Harbor in late October. The crab fishery was in full operation; the docks were crowded with exhausted and excited young men and pickup trucks. The bars were full, and raucous. Alvah's advice was to stay away from them. Pauloosie was taken for an Aleut, but that language was not really comprehensible to him. He picked up cognates, as an Italian listening to Catalan might, but he could not converse except in the expletive-laden English he heard shouted from every corner those busy weeks. The Aleut thought he was one of them, until he opened his mouth. Pauloosie realized how far from home he was, with surprise; he wanted only to keep going.

They bought better foul-weather gear, and sunscreen and boxes of tinned food and coffee and bags of rice and noodles. Alvah produced rolls of greasy American dollars from somewhere inside the boat and together they hauled crates of gear and provisions to the dock where *Umingmak* lay tied. The boat was uninjured by its time in the Arctic Ocean, but the stores were depleted. All this replenishment was carried out by the two men without any discussion of where it was they were bound. But they were in the Bering Sea, and winter was coming. So the boat was going somewhere.

When the storage lockers of *Umingmak* were all full, the water and fuel tanks brimming, every locker packed with rope and fishing lures and Chef Boyardee, they sat there one night and drank whiskey together and did not speak. Finally, Alvah asked Pauloosie what it was he was thinking about doing next.

"Staying on the boat, if there is a place for me," he said.

"There is. Where would you want to head?"

"South," he said.

"Everywhere is south of here," Alvah said.

"Which makes me easy to please," Pauloosie said.

They left the next day, due south, driven by a Bering Sea low out of the northwest, which threatened to dismast them from the moment battle was joined. The Bering Sea in winter is the worst open water in the world, and late October is pretty close to winter. The sea rose behind them in huge moving moraines of water. Until this point, Pauloosie had considered travel by these means to be a softer, duller proposition than by dog team. However, in a storm on the tundra, one builds an iglu and waits. It remains possible to die, but chiefly from starvation, a much slower proposition than the intense imminent peril represented by breaking seas the height of jack pines curling up astern.

Alvah was inspiring to watch, Pauloosie thought, as they tied down every movable object and doused sail until the boat was flying the equivalent of a small tablecloth from its headstay. Still they flew along at six knots, sliding down waves as if they were snow-covered hills. Over and over again, Pauloosie vomited over the rail, wet black hair streaming into the sea as he gasped.

After her high school graduation ceremony, Justine had told her mother that she would not be staying in Rankin Inlet, but Victoria hadn't believed her. She could no more imagine her daughter living anywhere else than she could herself. Justine could only imagine living anywhere other than Rankin Inlet. She had thought Winnipeg, for a while. But after Marie's trip down there, she changed her mind to Toronto.

There was less drama involved in her leaving than either of them had expected. Victoria gave Justine money, and Justine bought a plane ticket and packed a suitcase. When it became clear that she really was going, Victoria gave her more money. She and Simionie drove Justine to the airport on the day of the flight, and before she boarded, her mother gave her even more. Justine was embarrassed. Victoria didn't know what else to do. "I feel like your father, suddenly," she whispered to Justine as they hugged. Justine nodded, not trusting herself to speak. "But he'd have more advice for you than I do."

"I'll be fine," Justine said throatily.

Victoria nodded. She started crying. Justine turned and walked to the plane. Simionie waited in the truck in the airport parking lot. Victoria collected herself and then went back to the truck. Simionie drove her home to her empty house.

By the time they were off the coast of Washington the weather was easing noticeably. The effluvia of the Columbia River and the Strait of Juan de Fuca colored the sea a dull brown hundreds of miles offshore, and everywhere there were floating trees. Pauloosie was over his seasickness now and understood the boat well. Simon Alvah slept soundly at night and no longer listened intently to the sound the sea made against the hull. Above, Pauloosie stretched out in the warming night air and studied the stars, as clear as on the tundra, a place he suspected he was not going back to. He watched as the bear slipped slowly closer to the horizon. One night, after he had caught an odor rising from his sea bag, he had fished out all his caribou clothing, his kamiks and his parka and his mittens, and tossed them into the sea. The moon was bright that night and he watched them floating as the boat reached southward, until they were gone.

■

chapter twenty-six

Off the coast of California, thirty-four degrees north, they picked up the trades, which Alvah had been speaking of for weeks. A week later Pauloosie was still marveling at the warmth and steadiness of these winds out of the northeast. Where he had lived, the weather always came out of the setting sun. He had assumed that it was so everywhere—if something as fundamental as that was changeable, what wasn't?

And as they moved south, all the constants fell away. In this world, the sea stretched without confinement, either by ice or by landmasses. Waves, Alvah told him, born a thousand miles away in the winter storms they had fled, shuddered south and were appreciable as long, slow ripples under the boat, even now. South of the equator, the waves from the storms of the Southern Ocean, fiercer even than what they had left behind, rippled northward. Before there were compasses in this part of the world, when it was overcast sailors had navigated by such signs. Here were fish that flew like dragonflies, skimming the water for hundreds of yards, arching and wheeling upon it with perfect control and grace before slipping below the surface again. Tuna swam at sixty miles an hour and possessed meat as dark and rich as that of a seal; seabirds soared on wings ten feet long. There were albatrosses that flew out here for the first seven years of their lives, never alighting on land, before finally returning to one of the rocky islets, to mate. All these creatures he could not have imagined on the ocean he was from. If the differences in the water and the air weren't enough, the differences in the animals that dwelt there made the point clear.

By the time they crossed the equator, the unchanging stars them-selves had changed entirely. The Southern Cross rose up before them, and the Milky Way, brighter and more viscous, stretched across the sky, looking exactly like the ribbon of glowing water they trailed behind them in their wake—another unfamiliar phenomenon, sprung from the vital-ity and unexpected warmth of the sea. And the big bear slipped entirely below the horizon. The first night Pauloosie looked up and could not see it or the North Star, he felt vertiginous. The southern constellations rose from the horizon in front of them as the bear settled astern, and Pauloosie marveled at an entirely different set of patterns in the night sky than what he had known, all those months of night, out on the tundra.

Both men, after their lonely winters, were finished with the idea of that sort of solitude. Still, they did not speak easily with each other. "In December," Alvah finally told Pauloosie, "the RCMP visited me, on Marble Island. They wanted to know if I had seen either you or this schoolteacher who was missing."

Pauloosie looked up from the starlit water, toward him. It was too dim to see his expression.

"What did you tell them?"

"That I hadn't."

Pauloosie looked back at the water.

Alvah continued, "Did you?" Pauloosie kept looking at the water. After an hour, Alvah went below and fell asleep.

When the trades failed, they did so in an instant. A thunder squall moved through, just like a dozen others had that week, and then when it pushed on an hour later, it left them behind in motionless water. The two men and the boat sat together for the following week, bobbing slowly in the swell, water as glistening as spilled mercury, until finally a breath of wind appeared and the boat eased over to one side and began nosing its way south. The southwest trades built slowly over the next few days and soon the men and the boat were shuddering their way south.

When Hiva Oa, the easternmost port of entry in French Polynesia, finally showed itself above the horizon, it appeared like a brown arrow-head poking through something elastic. After two months at sea, the idea of land seemed hardly credible. It seemed much more likely that this was water jutting up into the sky, a stationary wave of some kind.

As they approached, Ua Huka bulged up over the horizon as well, and then the smaller rocks of Moane and Maeretiva, all flat brown and arid-looking, the islands clustering together in the otherwise millions of square miles of empty ocean like herding land mammals seeking solace. When they rounded the eastern tip of Hiva Oa, on the windward side, the island abruptly took on a verdant aspect that astonished Pauloosie. Even in the brief vigorous flowerings of the tundra, lushness like this was never seen. Then the smell of the island struck them both and they were intoxicated. Wood fires, orchids, and the sap of a million trees and vines: all these gave off scent like nothing previously.

By the time they approached the mountain, it was dusk and they could see the lights of the village, the occasional headlights of trucks and cars and scooters winking their way along. *Umingmak* bucked sharply in the short, steep waves bouncing off the island, and Alvah and Pauloosie stumbled in this unfamiliar rhythm. It was too dim to make the entrance to the harbor and so they anchored in the wide and exposed Atuona Bay. In the morning they set their dinghy in the water and rowed ashore and walked to the gendarmerie. Pauloosie had not known trees like this before. He stared at the thousand-meter volcanic spire rising, jungle-clad, into the clouds. The Marquesans chattered to one another as they passed. "That's what Inuktitut sounds like to me," Alvah said.

"That sounds nothing like Inuktitut," Pauloosie said, laughing.

They were so far away from the place they had left.

devotion (ii)
to oneself

I met my brother on an island near Seattle. He went there after his marriage dissolved, in order to heal himself, he said. "You mean, put it all behind you?" I said. He thought I was oversimplifying things.

He was staying on a farm that seemed to be maintained for precisely this purpose. When I got off the little float plane that deposited me on the dock, he met me with a taller bearded man who wore what looked for all the world like a Nehru jacket. My brother shook my hand and introduced his companion as Yogi something. "You're kidding," I said. They both smiled at me.

Over tofu and wheatgrass that night, we talked about our recent difficulties. His daughter had taken the departure of her father badly, had gotten involved with boys who came to a bad end. In the wake of all that, I flew to the city where she lived and the two of us lived together. She was pregnant, we subsequently learned, with twins, and she delivered her babies and I helped her with the diapers and the feeding and all that. It was a difficult few years, and for a long time I felt like I was much too old to be doing infant care. But it was necessary. And later, only the shortest time later, Amanda and her daughters became most of what I woke up in the morning to see.

Matthew asked me about his daughter. It was a delicate point. Amanda remained angry with him for having been so weak—the drinking, the being subsumed by her mother. He and Amanda haven't been close. It has felt as if he has become her uncle, and I something rather more involved than that.

When the meal was finished, we both helped gather the dishes and then wash them. I made a joke about not having been able to pay the check, but nobody laughed. They all smiled, of course. They hardly ever stopped smiling, I noticed. My brother did, when I told him how angry his daughter was with him. But otherwise he was implacable. It was smile-o-rama, there among the tofu. None of them could have made, or recognized, an actual joke to save his life. But they all remained determined to smile.

chapter twenty-seven

When he disembarked *Avaruilta's* in Taiohae Bay, on Nuku Hiva, Balthazar veered drunkenly along the jetty abutting the sea. He had not eaten anything solid in the week he had been on board, and his clothes hung loosely off him for the first time since he had finished his residency. He saw the priest standing at the front of the jetty from a hundred yards away and took time to compose himself before he approached the old man. They were both old men now. When they had met he had thought of the priest as belonging to the generation before his, but now, he realized, he had become the older of the two. He had caught up with and passed Father Bernard like a bicycle racer.

He watched the priest looking out at the horizon, likening this harbor to Rankin Inlet, the same comparison that presented itself to him. They were both at that moment recalling the handful of late-July days that had been as warm as this in Rankin Inlet; they both remembered how the children had squealed as they ran into the river water, still cuttingly cold. They watched these children in this place, who seemed like the younger brothers and sisters of those in their memories, leap into the sea off the jetty, noses plugged, legs bicycling, and water erupting in great geysers over their friends.

He was almost upon Father Bernard, and thinking the old man had gone blind, or addled, when he asked without turning his head if the *docteur* had had a good trip. Balthazar replied that he had.

"*C'est magnifique, hein?*"

"It is," Balthazar replied, staring out. "It really is. So much larger than the Arctic Ocean."

"All those islands, hemming it in."

"The trip here, from Papeete, was like nothing I've ever done."

"I thought you would enjoy it. That's one of the last of the copra schooners in this part of the ocean. You met the captain, Armande?"

"He introduced himself the first night out, as a friend of yours. I was sleeping on deck and he came looking for me."

"I travel with him to the smaller islands when he goes there—the Australs, the Gambiers. He has been very kind to me since I arrived."

"He asked me if I knew your friend, *l'esquimau*."

"It is a small place, and newcomers are uncommon. Everyone has heard of him."

"Has he done well?"

"He has married a woman here, a Marquesienne, and he is thought to treat her well. He is liked."

"How does he spend his time?"

"He is a fisherman. He harpoons mahimahi."

"Whales?"

"Fish. Dolphin-fish. You likely ate it en route."

"The white fish."

"Yes. It might have been his. Armande buys whatever Pauloosie has to sell, when he is in port. He approves of adventurers."

"What happened to *Umingmak*?"

"Alvah moved on. He was headed for the Cook Islands, but who knows where he ended up. He was not as well liked. They considered him deranged here. Always alone."

"How long has Pauloosie been here?"

"Two years."

"Looking to becoming a permanent situation."

"It appears so."

"Does he talk about the north?"

"Not to me."

"How did you find him?"

"I wasn't looking for him. I decided it was time to leave Rankin Inlet a few months after you did—I missed your jazz, I missed what the
people there had been—and I told my bishop I wanted to retire. He
told me to come here—it was the same, he said, but different."

"Yes," Balthazar said, looking around.

"When people learned where I had come from they immediately
began repeating stories they had heard about this man who looked Polynesian but could not speak their language, who had come ashore on
Hiva Oa, with an unusual technique for fishing for mahimahi. People
had supposed he was *esquimau,* but he didn't speak of his origins. I
thought he was likely Melanesian, and fleeing trouble, and didn't think
very hard about the story. Then a baptismal certificate crossed my desk,
from Hiva Oa. A little girl had been named Iguptak."

"Bumblebee."

"Yes."

"How extraordinary."

"We will go visit him."

"I'd like that."

That night Balthazar sat on his hard bed in the rectory of the church
and marveled at the scent of the air. The northeast winds sliding over
the mountain carried with them the aromas of drying vanilla beans and
rotten papayas and mango blossoms and ripening guavas—vitality sub-
limating off the volcanic rocks themselves and into the air.

He had not heard from Victoria since he had left Rankin Inlet. He
had written her a few times, hoping to rekindle something of their
friendship, but she had not replied. He had not really expected her to.
But he would have liked to have known whether she read his letters,
whether she knew that he had bought a house for him and his niece to
live in, how he helped her raise her twin daughters, watching them
while Amanda worked as a dental hygienist down the street. It was

closer than he'd ever imagined he would come to being a father. But there he was, at fifty-five, changing the little girls' diapers and preparing meals for the four of them and feeling as much of an imposter as he had felt himself to be when he had worked in Rankin Inlet. He still worked on his journals, and his reading: stacks of the *New England Journal,* and *JAMA,* and the British *Lancet* crowded his rooms just as they had in Rankin Inlet. Though without any possible application to a sick person, this knowledge was less electric, stimulating him now only as an abstraction. When he had received Father Bernard's letter inviting him to visit, and alluding to Pauloosie's presence in the Marquesas, he had leapt at the chance.

And now he was here, and it appeared it wasn't all an elaborate joke. And even as he contemplated meeting the boy, no longer a boy at all, he thought about the words he would choose in writing to Victoria, to tell her where Pauloosie had ended up. Father Bernard hadn't written her himself, he said. He thought it might be better to come from Balthazar and did not elaborate on what he meant by that. Balthazar took him to mean that it would be better for everyone concerned if the forgiveness was across the board. The priest seemed to think that the way things had been left was a lingering calamity for all of them. The priest was right. It was all he ever thought about, and had been for three years. Who could have guessed that there would be a chance at reconciliation?

October 10, 1995

Dear Victoria:

I am in Hiva Oa, in the Marquesas, French Polynesia. Father Bernard came here to work after he left Rankin Inlet. He wrote to me a month ago and asked me to visit. He wanted me to visit Pauloosie with him, he said. I was as surprised as I imagine you are, reading this. It seems that your son hitched a ride with Simon Alvah when he left Rankin Inlet. They sailed around to Alaska and made their way here. It all sounds improbable, I know. And Bernard coming to this part of the world seems equally improbable, but improbabilities surround us, of course. One need only consider the fact of diamonds under the tundra.

Pauloosie is well. He is married to a woman here named Riri and the marriage seems happy. They have an infant daughter, named Iguptak. I'm telling you all this because I think it might persuade you to come here. You should do that. Bernard is here, I am here, Pauloosie, your granddaughter, and your daughter-in-law are all here. We all want to see you. You should come meet these people. You mustn't wait for Pauloosie to invite you himself. He is as proud as your father is, and, he points out, it was you who threw his clothing into the snow. The point is, you must reconcile. Your granddaughter needs to know who you are. You need to know her. And you need to know your son again. Pauloosie gave me his permission to write to you, telling you all this. I know he wants to see you.

I realize that it will not be your inclination to take advice from me anymore. I understand that. Again, I am sorry for the death of Marie. I didn't predict what happened there, and am still astonished by it. But on the subject of your son and your granddaughter, I think you will conclude as I have, that you must know each other.

To come here you will need a passport. You can get an application for one from the post office. Someone will have to be your guarantor—the new doctor can do this, or whoever is the mayor these days. It will take a few weeks, so you should start this soon. You will need photographs taken. The flights are easier than you'd think. You'll need to fly to Winnipeg, and then down to Los Angeles, where you can get an Air Tahiti flight to Papeete. From Papeete you can get another flight here to Hiva

Oa through an airline called Tahiti Nui. The travel agent will be able to help you with all this.

If you have more questions you could write to me at Poste Restante, Hiva Oa. Or to Bernard, at the church. Or to your son. The address is his name, and the island, Hiva Oa. It is not a big place. Everyone knows him. He is well liked. You should see him, harpooning the mahimahi. No one's seen anything like it before.

"He can be a little humorless."

"Oh my God, yes," Pauloosie said, shaking his head. "Humorless Kablunauks. It kills them to laugh, sometimes."

"Why did he come here?" Riri asked.

Bernard and Pauloosie looked at each other. Pauloosie answered. "To bring my mother to me."

"It would resolve something that has been left suspended," the old priest said.

"I don't care one way or the other, if she wants to come, she can come. If she doesn't—I've been happy until now, I'll stay happy," Pauloosie said, rising to pour more wine into Bernard's cup. The baby was asleep long ago and Riri's fish stew had each of them sated and at ease.

"How much longer will Balthazar stay?"

"I'm not sure. It has been what, a month now?"

"Six weeks."

"I suppose he's waiting to hear from your mother."

"It seems like she isn't interested in what he has to say. He could take a hint."

Bernard shrugged. "He goes fishing with the men in the morning, and walks back into the mountains in the afternoons. He looks like he has more peace of mind than I've known him to have in thirty years. He's getting so thin."

"Well, it isn't like he causes trouble," Pauloosie said.

"And he always brings presents for Iguptak when he comes to supper," Riri added. "You Americans. If I were as far from home as you are and someone I had known well showed up to visit, I wouldn't be pushing for his departure. He is very kind, which is the other thing that neither of you is saying."

Balthazar's letter had ridden the boat back to Papeete and then had flown to Paris, where its semi-legible address had caused a series of Gallic snorts, and then it was finally sent to Canada, where it made its way up to the Arctic after a series of layovers—and all the while Balthazar was sleeping, eating, swimming, and fishing six thousand miles away and wondering why she hadn't answered even this news. But she hadn't known the news, had only continued her life in Rankin Inlet, and gone to the meetings of the Ikhirahlo Group and listened to the plans that Okpatayauk (who had been paroled and was now back in the community) and Tagak proposed. She knew better than to cede her control of the company to her brother or anyone else, but neither was she interested in the details of the bookkeeping. What she thought about instead was Justine, who lived in Toronto, a production assistant at MuchMusic television. She spoke to her daughter on the telephone every day. And she thought about her father, now lost in his own memories, and her mother, dying slowly of lung cancer.

When she saw Balthazar's name on the envelope she almost threw it out, assuming it would be another apology or, worse, one of his periodic attempts at self-justification. She did not have the strength to address either. This is why she looked around for the garbage can as she removed the envelope from her box in the post office. Then she noticed the unfamiliar stamps, and the return address: Poste Restante, Hiva Oa, and these intrigued her and so she opened it. And as she read his words, in that crowded, bustling little post office, it was as if she had inhaled a breath mint once again and she felt as if she could not breathe.

She ran home, almost blind with emotion, and found the doorknob to her house and turned it and stumbled to the kitchen table, and pulled a roll of paper towels off its dispenser and blotted her eyes dry and read the letter again. She had a granddaughter. Iguptak. A little bumblebee.

As if he had any right to lecture her on maintaining her family—which had been cared for by him until half of them were dead. But what he said about Pauloosie was probably right. He was alive and it had been years since she had spoken with him, years more since she had held him. What had happened between him and his father was not knowable, she thought, and anyway what had been knowable was not understandable. Least of all, she suspected, by those two.

Simionie knocked on the kitchen door then and came in. He nodded at Victoria sitting at the kitchen table. He sat down across from her and removed a whetstone from his pocket and then he took out his fish knife. He dropped a long glob of saliva on the whetstone and began running the knife over it in a blurred figure eight until the steel blade sang; he looked up then, at Victoria. "What's up?"

"Balthazar has written again."

"You should write him back, Victoria."

"Don't tell me what to do."

"What does he say?"

"He found Pauloosie."

"Where?"

"French Polynesia."

"Where is that?"

"I'm not sure. He wants me to come see him."

"What do you think?"

"It's way farther away than Winnipeg."

"What are you going to do?"

"What do you think I should do?"

"You're asking me?"

"Yes."

He raised his eyebrows and looked back at his knife, swirling across

the whetstone in his hand. "You have to go. I'd come with you, if you
wanted."

"I don't want you to come."

"Okay."

"I don't know if Pauloosie wants to see me."

"One way to find out."

"Hi, Mom."

"How did you know it was me?"

"I got call display."

"What's that?"

"My phone knows that it's you calling and tells me."

"You'll have to explain to me sometime how that works."

"I'm not sure I could."

"Balthazar wrote me a letter saying he found Pauloosie."

". . ."

"Did you hear me?"

"What are you going to do?"

"Go there."

"Where?"

"French Polynesia."

"Tahiti."

"Near there, I guess."

"I was there last winter."

"What?"

"One of the producers took me, for a week."

"Did you see him?"

"We never left the hotel pool. It was a music industry bash. And
anyway, there are a lot of islands there, Mom. Like, thousands."

"This one's called Hiva Oa."

"Never heard of it."

"I'm going to get a passport."

"Mom, I would have told you if I had seen Pauloosie, for Pete's sake."

"I know."

"Are you going to be okay with the long flight?"

"That will be hard."

"Do you want me to come with you?"

"No. Simionie offered to too."

"Why?"

"We're good friends."

"To say the least."

"Never mind."

"You're so restrained."

"So you wanna tell me about your producer boyfriend?"

"I get your point."

"Okay, then."

"Well, you tell me when you're back, okay?"

"I will."

"And give my love to my brother."

"Yes."

Victoria got on a hired truck at the airport, the landing strip of which comprised a ledge of barely level earth dug out of the top of a mountain ridge overlooking the island like a hunting knife stood on edge. It had been twenty-two hours of flying and hotel rooms in Winnipeg and Tahiti, but she was there. She knew how to ask directions. When she was disoriented in Faaa, in Tahiti, she wished Père Raymond were accompanying her on this trip, with his effortless French and imperturbable demeanor. She tried to remember that language, stumbled, and was steered back into English by an officious gendarme, and was eventually led onto her airplane, a lumbering propeller-driven cargo craft that could have as easily been bound for the gravel runway beside Repulse Bay.

The islands swept past her: the myriad Tuamotos, rings in the sea, low atolls around turquoise lagoons, and then Nuku Hiva, the first of the Marquesas, and finally Hiva Oa. She stood the moment the airplane stopped moving, to the hissing of the attendant, and walked stiffly off the airplane with more relief than she had felt since disembarking from the government ship in Montreal.

The truck took her into town. The driver asked her where she was staying, and she asked him if he knew Pauloosie Robertson. *L'esquimau?* the man asked and she said yes.

She stepped down from the truck and the driver handed her her enormous suitcase. She dragged it over the dirt path that led into the low concrete structure that was the home of her son. Chickens scratched in the dirt and mangoes and papayas lay split on the ground, fallen from the trees overhead. Fragments of coral lay scattered all around. She knocked on the door. Riri opened it. There was a long moment of assessment and then Victoria introduced herself.

The two women sat down. Riri was carrying Iguptak and she handed her daughter to Victoria. Victoria hadn't held such a small babe in her arms since her second son. At gatherings, when the children were passed around, she had long ago gotten into the habit of excusing herself. She lived in a sufficiently small settlement that everyone understood—better, arguably, than did Victoria herself, who had simply concluded that she had never been comfortable with babies. But there was no gracious way to decline her granddaughter, and as the child turned to her breast she caught herself even starting to offer what she could not provide, and she smiled at herself and lifted her to her face, and smelled the top of her scalp and then sat back, smiling, looking at her son's daughter.

"My parents live just a few houses down from here—my father helped Pauloosie build this house—and this is their first grandchild too," Riri said.

"I would like to meet them."

"So you've come to make up with Pauloosie?"

Which is not how Victoria would have put it at all, but, without a concise alternative explanation, she found herself nodding.

When Balthazar knocked on the door, it was to drop off a tuna he had been given that morning. Behind Riri, holding the little girl, was an older woman who looked as if she might have been from one of the out-islands. He smiled at her and handed Riri the fish and started to turn away, and then it was as if his muscles recognized her better than his eyes had. His neck cranked around and his eyes fixed on her and there she was. There.

"Victoria."

"Keith. I got your letter. Thank you."

"I'm glad you came," he managed. Then, looking wide-eyed at Riri, "Is Pauloosie around?"

"He went out fishing early this morning. He doesn't know she's here."

"Oh, my."

"Come in." She pulled him through the door and directed him toward a chair at the kitchen table opposite Victoria's.

"Victoria," he said again.

"Yes," she said, softening a little, amused by him.

"This is Riri," he said, gesturing, "I mean, you say 'Lilly' but write it Riri, which doesn't make a lot of sense, if you ask me, the letters all being imported anyway—they might as well reflect the local pronunciation. But they don't. Anyway. This is Pauloosie's . . ."

"Yes, I know. And this is little Iguptak," she said, holding her granddaughter in front of her and displaying her to Balthazar, as if he, in turn, had not already met the infant.

"Riri, may I use your phone to call the priest? I told him I would, if Victoria came."

"Sure."

"Is that Father Bernard you're talking about?"

"Yes."

"Your letter said he was here."

"He is."

"Invite him for supper," Riri said.

"Okay," Balthazar said, inserting his thick fingers into the rotary dial, misdialing, starting over again, and misdialing once more.

They ate late into the night, fresh tuna steaks, and taro and rice, bottles of Burgundy brought by the priest. Pauloosie and his mother did not embrace, but sat across the table, looking often at each other, and nodding. Victoria said Iguptak was the most beautiful baby she had ever seen, and Pauloosie accepted the statement as it was intended, and acknowledged the layers of meaning within it.

Bernard said, "When I saw the name Iguptak cross my desk, I tell you, it was like a hallucination: I tasted raw seal in my mouth, and felt wind on my face. I was so happy. I telephoned the *curé* here five minutes later, and he told me what he knew of you. I caught the next boat here. I was so happy, meeting a friend in a faraway place. As we all are tonight."

"Father, I think you're feeling the wine," Victoria said.

"I am. And it is a pleasure to drink wine like this with friends of mine from my young days."

"You are still young, Father."

"And you are kind." Then he said, "What a relief it is on my heart to see you three eating together again."

There was a long silence and the fish was chewed carefully, though it held no bones. Riri said, "My daughter needs to know her ancestors."

"I want her to too," said Victoria.

And Pauloosie: "Yes."

With that Father Bernard sat back in his chair, grinning widely. It was very late, and, old man that he was now, like Balthazar, he was tired. His lids sagged and he rose with effort. "We should go, Keith, let these young people say the things that need to be said."

"Yes," Balthazar said, though he wanted only to watch Victoria late into the night, listen to her voice, observe her black eyes flashing liquidly. "In the morning I will be buying my ticket home," he said, and all present nodded at this. Everyone at the table rose to say goodbye to the two gray men. They were led to the door, and Bernard was kissed in succession. Then Balthazar's hand was gripped by Riri, and then Pauloosie, and finally Victoria. He reached to embrace her.

"Keep in touch," he said thickly as she stiffened.

She pulled him closer and whispered in his ear: "I don't want to stay in touch with you."

And then she looked at him and he could not meet her eyes and she turned away from him toward her son and her granddaughter.

The two old men walked silently down the unlit dirt road on Hiva Oa, making for the rectory where both were staying. Bernard's heart sang, as he studied the brilliant southern hemisphere stars overhead. Balthazar did not speak.

big blues

Anomie. Ennui. *The French have the best names for it, but it was the Americans who invented teenagers and adolescence and it is among the Americans that the phenomenon is the most impressive. People say that change is hardest for the old, but this is unlikely, because the old have the simple expedient available to them of just refusing to. New forms of music—swing, rock, hip-hop—are not embraced by anyone over forty, except poseurs. New languages are all but unavailable to anyone over thirty. Revolutions in thought are launched by mathematicians before thirty, and physicists before they are thirty-five. Poets: twenty-five. Change is not so difficult for adults because, for the most part, they just don't.*

Deep fundamental change breaks like surf upon children. And it is change that injures us when we become wealthy, not some Calvinist idea that riches corrupt the flesh and soul. Poverty remains the most potent toxin for humans, but the next most potent poison is confusion. When we are confused about what and how much we should eat, about how much assistance to receive from our machines, about how much attention to pay to our parents and our aunts and uncles, and, God help us, our children, we become ill, we sicken ourselves. We stop moving and we stop attending to the necessary rituals. We become fat and hubristic, and we lose confidence in our own capacity.

And as we deracinate ourselves, sadness settles over us. We lose the nourishment that roots provide us. We replace that nourishment with other satisfactions: mobility and movement, anonymity and freedom. These are all very satisfying things, which is why people pay a steep price to obtain them. But roots remain necessary— no matter how thin and chemically enriched the substrate of one's growth.

I traveled to the Pacific Islands at the end of my career in Rankin Inlet, to visit friends I had known in the Arctic. The account of their migration is an interesting one, but not my subject here—I will confine myself to the following: they both sought escape from what had become too familiar.

One of them was the priest I lived alongside, if not precisely with, all those years on the tundra. The other was a young man whom I delivered in the Arctic; he sailed south from Rankin Inlet on a sailboat that had overwintered on Marble Island, off the coast near there. They arrived on Hiva Oa independently, and when the priest learned of the other's existence, he sought the younger man out and visited him, then wrote me a letter telling me this news. Though the two were never close when they lived beside Hudson Bay, on this warmer ocean, the priest eats supper with the young man and his wife every other Saturday night.

When I went to dinner at the young man's house, the local doctor was also a guest, a Parisian woman who told me about the way diabetes was sweeping the islands, diabetes and gout and vascular disease and crises cardiaques *(a phrase that captures the urgency of the moment nicely), and how none of these had existed twenty years earlier. She could not have been more than thirty, and spoke with the sort of fervor I was capable of at that age. The wind off the sea moved through the little house and my friend's baby cried briefly in her crib, settling when her mother tucked a sheet over her. It seemed both utterly dissimilar to and exactly like the Arctic.*

My young friend told me that he would remain in this place, that here he was able to accept change, because he was less a part of it. He had given up on the traditions of the Inuit, and although doing so had wounded him, he could bear the loss if he was not constantly confronted with it. Here he dealt with the place as it was—he did not agonize over what it had been. The priest, also at supper that night, listened and did not comment. The man's wife had heard this from him already—I could tell from the way her nodding anticipated his words—and when he was done, she told us stories of the islands, of the way her people had died when the French came. The Marquesans, the most dominant of all the Polynesian cultures, had wilted like cut stems at contact. The Marquesans were one hundred thousand when European boats first visited them. Now, with half a century of healthcare and subsidized food, they are ten thousand.

These were melancholy tales, and when the priest and I walked back to the rectory to sleep, we did not speak.

What I thought about was whether anyone knows with any certainty whether people in other times were sadder or happier than they are now. I think that this much is true: when they were sad, they were sad about things— the relentless death of their children, the failure of the crops and the hunt, the appearance of blood in the sputum of their wife. These were the daily facts of their lives. My experience is that all parents, no matter how inured, are eviscerated by the passing of a child, so the people of earlier times were likely very sad—and often. But I think they were less likely to be sad about nothing, in the way we are. Which is the state that words like anomie try to describe, which psychiatrists endeavor to treat with their serotonin-receptor antagonists. It is the state that poisons us and our ambitions, leading us to immobility.

And then I was at the door of the guesthouse I had been lent. I said good night to my friend the priest and I watched him amble his way down the moonlit path to the main residence. I thought how odd it was, that the process that leads us to static motionlessness begins as a response to too rapid change. In the palm trees all around, the wind roared.

part three

eskimo poetry

Hard times, dearth times
Plague us every one,
Stomachs are shrunken,
Dishes are empty . . .
Mark you there yonder?
There come the men
Dragging beautiful seals
To our homes.
Now is the abundance
With us once more
Days of feasting
To hold us together.
Know you the smell
Of pots on the boil?
And lumps of blubber
Slapped down by the side bench?
Joyfully
Greet we those
Who brought us plenty!

Recorded and translated from the Inuktitut by Knud
Rasmussen, *Report of the Fifth Thule Expedition, 1921–24*

chapter twenty-eight

It was a gorgeous early-summer morning. Balthazar stood by the window of the apartment at the top of his house. He could hear Amanda and the girls downstairs, finishing breakfast, chattering and dropping dishes into the sink. He had been writing all night and felt disembodied from sleepiness and fading concentration. John Coltrane was playing "My Little Brown Book," one of Bernard's favorite recordings. On the coffee table was a letter he had gotten from Nuku Hiva the week before. Iguptak was nine now, and was taking her catechism with Bernard. Pauloosie and Riri were well. Bernard sent his regards to Amanda and the twins. He had included a letter from Iguptak in imperfect English to Lola; they had been corresponding for the last year.

Balthazar straightened his desk and picked up the dishes left over from the night before. The wooden floors glowed in the morning sun. He walked softly to the kitchen, his sock feet slipping quietly along the wood, and placed his dishes in the kitchen sink. He rinsed them and squirted some dish soap over them, wiped them down, dried them, and put them away in the cupboard of his tiny kitchen. He walked back into his living room and sat down on the couch. He opened Bernard's letter and reread his gossipy account of the island, and paused on the priest's enjoinder to come visit him again.

Maybe. Maybe. It would have to be soon, though.

In the envelope were photographs Bernard had passed along from Pauloosie, of Iguptak and her mother. Bernard had also included another photograph, of Victoria and Justine, who was in Rankin Inlet on a visit. Victoria's bright eyes shone with pleasure as Justine's long lanky arms draped around her neck. More lines in both of their faces now, of course. Justine's beauty evoked only one memory for Balthazar. He shut his eyes and leaned his head back on the couch. He and Victoria were sitting down by the bay. Before she had met Robertson. She was lonely and eager to talk about the world. He was from New York. The ice was just going out. He didn't know how long he would work there. The summer, anyway. He had applied for an ophthalmology residency and was hoping to hear back soon. She said she was disappointed to hear that. He smiled when she said that, and felt the world shift a little.

He lay down on the couch, stretching out his shrinking body. He breathed deeply and, on the rock beside the ice, he told Victoria that he had never met anyone like her. She smiled and touched his arm. He leaned his head forward and so did she. Their foreheads touched, and from that point on, it was clear, everything would be different.

He felt the hand on his shoulder and resisted it, longing to remain where he was. Victoria grew indistinct and he strained to keep her with him.

"Keith. Keith."

It was Amanda.

"Hi."

Her anxious face slackened. "I thought you had started using again."

"No. You know I don't do that anymore."

"I know, but are you feeling okay?"

"Just enjoying the morning sun."

"Can you watch the girls?"

"Of course." And he sat up, slipped back down, and then with a heave sat up again.

"Are you having any pain?"

"No."

"Because I have that prescription if you are."

"I'm fine, Amanda."

"Girls, you take it easy on your uncle, okay?"

Lola and Claire stood in the doorway, smiling at him. "Of course, Mom," Lola answered.

"I'll be back before supper. There's food in the fridge, okay Keith?"

"Sure."

"I'll pick something up for you if you want me to."

"I'm fine, dear."

At the 2002 MTV video awards, Justine sat back in her seat and tried to contain herself. She was a little high, but that was the least of it: the rumor was that Axl Rose, and a reconstructed version of Guns N' Roses, would be playing that night. And then Jimmy Fallon was smirking onstage and everyone in the audience bit their lip. Axl had been gone ten years, sequestered in his Malibu compound, doing a Brian Wilson, and pining, it was said, for Stephanie Seymour, spending thirteen million on an album no one thought he would ever finish, *Chinese Democracy*. Nine producers, eighty different session musicians, each fired more quickly than the last, and yet nothing released to the public from the man who had eviscerated the bloated, bleached-hair metal music that prevailed when *Appetite for Destruction* had seared its way across the world.

Then there he was, Jimmy Fallon introducing him. The curtain rose and it was not the old band of course, far too much bitterness among them for that, but it was Axl, at least, and the power chords, and the voice, rising with the lights. He was not what he had been, but which of us is? He had been so lithe, and supple, and look at him. Thickened, coarse—missing the King's girdle, but at least Elvis kept his voice. That soaring, wailing voice could only ever have belonged to a young man, which was part of why it had been stirring. And he had been gaunt because of his excesses. Eventually, as he put it, the choice becomes whether to consume oneself along with everything else.

He had still consumed rather a lot: his friends, Slash and Izzy and Duff, his women, none of whom were in contact with him anymore, and a trail of empties that stretched behind him, even as he walked across the stage, stiffly attempting the old postures, the old venom. And the room took all this in at a glance, and, in the way of such rooms, the interest wandered. But for those who had been fourteen in 1988, the moment was piercingly sad, and they bit their lip as they mourned their own youths too, and their own increasingly evident obsolescence.

Justine shut her eyes and wished she were less high. She liked her job, and she was good at it. The people who worked for her liked her. She was twenty-eight. She didn't need to be doing this anymore.

The hunter ran in the snow, barefoot and faster than he could believe. His feet slid through the coarse frozen snow with each step only until they caught purchase, and then his body was flung up and forward again, and what was chasing him fell farther behind but did not tire either, and they ran like this into the night and under the moon's glistening cool light. When he had awoken he was in a strange place with cloth on the ground and pointed corners that leapt out at him as he moved in the darkness. He picked up his panna, which had been sitting miraculously beside the door, and ran into the night. He recognized the stars but nothing else. There were no iglus in this strange place. He could see the sea ice shining under the moon, but there were no sleds there either.

On the horizon, the mine complex glowed electrically. The cavernous metal building that housed the processing facility approached completion now, and the lights that lit it bounced off the low clouds and lit them, as a city does on the prairie. It was only through this, the nighttime glow on the horizon, that the mine was visible from the town. The hunters avoided it, superstitiously abhorring that light, and the noise, and the tailings deposited around it. The miners themselves mostly remained on site until it was time for them to fly home. But for a few men, Tagak and a hundred others, it was the link that allowed them access to the world beyond caribou hunting and searing cold, the thing that gave them credibility, in their middle age and diminishing eyesight. Emo glanced at that glow and did not understand it, was not able to account for it, and so felt frightened.

He heard breathing and growling behind him. He began loping forward, pausing often to listen for footfalls. There were more than one of them, but he stayed quiet and ran as fast as he could and they dispersed behind him, roaring incoherently in the rising wind as he pulled away.

Once, he remembered as he ran, a bear had surprised him and his dogs as he lay camped out on the tundra. He awoke to the sight of three of his dogs swinging from their teeth as they clung to its shoulders, two others flying off into the snow, swatted lethally by one of those enormous paws. He had flung himself forward with his long knife in front of him and buried it to its hilt in the bear's chest. It had coughed then, and sat down suddenly, alternately hiccupping and coughing blood into the snow. He had been nineteen years old.

Another time, long after this, he had been attacked in the night by a spirit, had swung his panna at its throat; he remembered being very frightened then and running away. He remembered now, with a clarity that had not been available to him subsequently, how the creature had turned into a man as he had grasped his throat and then fallen into the snow, bleeding. His daughter's husband, a shaman, it turned out, for who else could change his form so quickly? It answered many questions about the disarray he had brought into their life, but he died sure enough, with his throat split open, which was surprising, for he had been a man with many powers. Afterward Emo had wondered why he hadn't healed himself. It had suited his purposes, evidently, to die like that. The disarray he brought multiplied after his death. He had felt the wicked man's spirit hanging over them at his granddaughter's funeral, and a hundred other times.

On those two occasions at least, when he had been frightened, he had stood his ground. He stopped then and looked behind him. He heard no sound. He held his panna at his side. If anything came at him he would be ready. He had not realized how short of breath he was. What was this cloth on his back and over his legs? He cut it away and then, exhausted with the exertion, he sat down. The snow was very cold on his ass. It didn't matter. He was used to cold.

At the moment Emo sat down in the snow, two miles away, his daughter stood in her kitchen. She had been playing cribbage with Simionie. It was late and Simionie stood to put on his parka. Victoria surprised herself and reached for his hand. Taking him in tow, she walked to her bedroom. Simionie followed.

And as her father's breaths grew shallower, and his recollections of his youth more vivid and precise, she made love to Simionie slowly and with great seriousness. Neither of them spoke. Their familiar skin slid along each other's like warm, slick ice sliding up on the bay, and they gasped into each other's ears, and she bit his shoulder as she came and wrapped her legs around him and pulled him deep inside her. And he squeezed his eyes shut and thanked whichever of the gods it was who had finally interceded on his behalf.

The striking thing about the coastal Inuit communities of Hudson Bay is their size—these are tiny places. Repulse Bay has five hundred people. Rankin Inlet, the regional megalopolis, twenty-four hundred, Baker Lake, eighteen hundred. Anonymity is inconceivable here, and the notion that it could be something sought, incomprehensible.

I first came to Repulse Bay about thirty years ago. In Inuktitut, the name is Naujjut, "the place where the seagulls lay their eggs." The town clings to the sea, in a shallow rind around the bay. The nurse there knows every single person in town. When she goes walking in the evening, if she spots an unfamiliar face among the children playing by the sea, she approaches him and establishes whose cousin he is, from which of the nearby communities he comes. The children crowd around her, grinning.

Nearby is a relative term. The closest town is Pelly Bay, a hundred and fifty miles to the north. Coral Harbour is the next, on Southampton Island two hundred miles to the east. Baker Lake, to the south, is three hundred miles. In the spring, which is glorious here, the people travel on snowmobiles between these communities, for days out on the tundra, just to visit with one another for a few days before heading back. The distances involved and the spareness of the land seem not to make community more tenuous here, but rather more necessary and altogether more potent.

This story is the best way I can think of to illustrate what I mean:

Once, a woman suffered a ruptured ectopic pregnancy in Repulse Bay. She was brought to the nursing station and my friend the nurse started IVs on her. She called the doctors in Churchill, hundreds of miles to the south, and they flew north immediately, but between the weather and refueling stops it was six hours before they would get there. She ran fluid into the woman through IVs that lined her arms from her fingers to her shoulders, but her blood pressure fell steadily. I was in Rankin Inlet at the time. As soon as any of us heard what was happening in Repulse Bay, we all thought the same thing: Oh no.

There happened to be a schoolteacher in Repulse Bay with hemochromatosis—a blood disease that was treated by regular phlebotomy, bleedings, essentially. My friend had a stack of blood bags in the supply room to do this with. As we flew north, she got these bags out and had the janitor sort through the records of every woman who had given birth within the last year or two—all of whom would have been tested for hepatitis and HIV, and whose blood type she would know. She had the janitor get on the CB radio and call them in to donate blood. The town fanned out across itself to bring these people to the nursing station. They lay down, one after the other, and my friend started draining their blood into the phlebotomy bags. As soon as the bags were full she hung them above the sick woman and ran them into her.

When I arrived the whole town was standing around the nursing station, looking terrified, many of them weeping. The whole town, as in everyone over the age of twelve. They all had their sleeves rolled up. The janitor was arguing with an especially determined knot of people who were insisting that their blood be collected too.

This time of year, in the late summer, the tundra's beauty is easy to appreciate. The cinnamon brown low hills that ripple across Kivalliq catch the sun and shine like old rope. The narwhals surface in the bay, waving their tusks in the air; only a few miles out of town, the last of North America's great herding land mammals, the tuktu, caribou, paw the grass and the moss by the many thousands and shiver collectively when they smell predators approaching. Contained within this beauty, and perhaps its necessary consequence, are the people here—who huddle similarly close and watch for one another's peril.

October 15, 2004

Dear Father Bernard,

Keith passed away last week, quietly, at home. You knew that he had colon cancer, I hope. He was sixty-six. He was comfortable and lucid until the end. He asked me to make sure you knew, and asked if I would write to you to ask you to pass on this news to whichever of his friends you are in contact with.

I've been cleaning out his apartment and I found a notebook in his desk that he had apparently been writing in for some time. Most of the entries seem to be about the time he spent practicing in the north and I thought you might be interested in it.

Keith spoke often of you, Father, and regarded you as his best friend. I know it's been years since you've seen each other, but you should know that his admiration for you remained very strong.

Yours truly,
Amanda Balthazar

acknowledgments

My thanks to Anne Collins, who watched over and guided *Consumption* as it made the transition from a collection of essays about cultural change and epidemiology to a novel, over the course of four years and many, many meticulous line edits. I could not be more grateful; nothing like this book would have been possible without her insight and patience. My thanks also to Nan Talese, who was similarly patient. My agent, Anne McDermid, and her assistant, Jane Warren, have given helpful advice throughout this adventure as well.

The people of Kivalliq—with and for whom I have worked over the course of the last ten years—told me the stories that inspired this novel, and helped me with the Inuktitut. On the language front, Andrea Sateanna White and Sam Aliyak have been especially helpful. The doctors and nurses I have met and have learned from while working in the north are too numerous to list, but I must mention my friend and mentor, Dr. Bruce Martin, the director of the University of Manitoba J. A. Hildes Northern Medical Unit, who has been a tremendous support. Sue Lightford, Scott Bell, Doug Manuel, Nikki Stilwell, Pam Orr, Maria Fraser, my brother Michael Patterson, Martha Keeley, Mark Viljoen, and Megan Saunders have taught and inspired me. If there are clinicians reading this who have any interest in working in the most beautiful place in the world, among the finest people, please call Dr. Martin at the University of Manitoba at (204) 789-3711. He will take care of you in every way imaginable.

Thank you to Ellen Reid for twenty years of unflagging friendship, advice, and hospitality.

And finally, thank you to the lovely and patient Shauna Klem, and to Molly Patterson for her shining smile and steady stream of crayon drawings.

Kevin Patterson grew up in Manitoba, Canada, and put himself through medical school by enlisting in the Canadian Army. When his service was up, he worked as a doctor in the Arctic and on the coast of British Columbia while studying for his M.F.A. He is the author of the memoir *The Water in Between*, which was a *New York Times* Notable Book. *Country of Cold*, his short fiction collection, won the Rogers Writers' Trust Fiction Prize, as well as the inaugural City of Victoria Butler Book Prize. He lives and practices critical care and general internal medicine on Saltspring Island, Canada.

a note about the type

The text of this book is set in Perpetua, a typeface designed
by Eric Gill and released by the Monotype Corporation between 1925 and 1932. This typeface has a clean look with
beautiful classical capitals, making it an excellent choice for
both text and display settings. Perpetua was named for the
book in which it made its first appearance: *The Passion of
Perpetua and Felicity.*